The Farmers' Daughters

Jack O'Connell
Seattle
12 January 1983

By William Carlos Williams

The Autobiography
The Build-Up
Collected Earlier Poems
Collected Later Poems
The Embodiment of Knowledge
The Farmers' Daughters
I Wanted to Write a Poem
Imaginations
In the American Grain
In the Money
Interviews with William Carlos Williams
Kora in Hell: Improvisations†
Many Loves and Other Plays
Paterson, Books 1-5
Pictures from Brueghel and Other Poems
A Recognizable Image
The Selected Essays
Selected Poems
A Voyage to Pagany
White Mule
The William Carlos Williams Reader

† *City Lights Books*

THE FARMERS' DAUGHTERS

THE COLLECTED STORIES OF
WILLIAM CARLOS WILLIAMS

Introduction by Van Wyck Brooks

A NEW DIRECTIONS BOOK

To our Pets, Grandchildren and Pals!

Contents

Introduction

Although I have met him only once or twice, I feel that
I am a friend of William Carlos Williams. This is nothing
for him to acknowledge or reject—it is simply because
he is so human. I was always attracted by the legend of
the small-town doctor who was yet, intellectually, a man
of the world and who avoided a "money practice" with
the instinct of an artist for whom the unsuccessful were
the most rewarding. He had none of the "complacency
that comes to so many men following the successful scamper for cash," a phrase of his own in "Old Doc Rivers."
He has never wanted to save a person because he was "a
good and useful member of society. Death had no respect
for him for that reason, neither has the artist." So Dr. Williams says somewhere. But "the actual calling on people,
at all times and under all conditions . . . when they were
being born, when they were dying, watching them die
. . . has always absorbed me. I lost myself in the very
properties of their minds." Not all his stories, by any
means, deal with a doctor's patients; but many of them
are concerned with the "Wops of Guinea Hill," with the
Italians and Polacks who were factory workers, or old
German harness makers; and his compassionate absorption in them is reflected with masterful art in these candid
stories or, more often, sketches.

Dr. Williams has the advantage, rare in these provisional
times, of what Henry James called "saturation," the result
of a lifelong immersion in the life of a single neighborhood, the New Jersey towns of Rutherford, Paterson and
Passaic. He has never moved away from "Nine Ridge
Road," a landmark for his visitors and correspondents, and
this gives him the authenticity of Sherwood Anderson, in

whose stories one feels the man who has "been there."
Of Paterson, the scene of Williams's long continued poem,
he says, "I had taken part in some of the incidents that
made the place. . . . I had in my hospital experiences
got to know many of the women; I had tramped Garret
Mountain as a youngster, swum in its ponds, appeared in
court there, looked at its charred ruins, its flooded streets,
read of its past in Nelson's history of Paterson, read of
the Dutch who settled it. I took the city as my 'case' to
work up." Meanwhile, he had practised in the Passaic
Hospital and he actually lived in Rutherford. He has said,
"I give my life willingly to experience and to prove that
Keyserling was right in saying, localism alone can lead
to culture." But he undoubtedly owed to his travels some
of the sense of proportion with which he viewed the local
scene. His English father and his mother were born in
the West Indies, he heard French and Spanish spoken
when he was a boy, and he had gone to school for a year
in Paris, where some of his relatives were living. He had
known, at the University of Pennsylvania, H. D. and Ezra
Pound, who remained through his life a somewhat difficult
friend; and later, ."with antennae fully extended," as he
said in *In the American Grain*, he fell in with Joyce, Ger-
trude Stein, Picasso and Brancusi. Then Ezra Pound took
him to talk with Léger. But "nothing came of it," he
remarked, "save an awkward realization . . . of that resistant core of nature upon which I had so long been driven
for support. I felt myself with ardours not released but
beaten back in this centre of old-world culture where
everyone was tearing his own meat, warily conscious of
a newcomer but wholly without inquisitiveness." However, drawn back inevitably to the world of his childhood,
he saw this now in the scale of mankind.

In New York, meanwhile, as an interne at the French
Hospital, where he went in for obstetrics and the diseases
of children, he saw the Armory Show and encountered
Stieglitz with Marsden Hartley and John Marin. He had

known Charles Demuth in Philadelphia and he met Paul Rosenfeld, "with his half-embarrassed rotundities," who became a good friend. New York was seething with interest in the arts; he saw something of Greenwich Village and he even painted a little himself. But, committed to the practice of pediatrics, he found that "the city of the hospital," in his native region, was his "final home," and he began to live a furiously crowded life there, called out at all hours of the night, delivering babies in back streets, attracted to the little houses of the very poor. They were perhaps "behind the shoe shop between Fourth and Fifth," with roofs out of line,

> the yard cluttered
> with old chicken wire, ashes,
> furniture gone wrong,

as he wrote in "Pastoral," one of his early poems. "I got to love these people, they were all right." He gave birth, as one woman phrased it, to nearly every baby born on the streets above the old copper mines, and he never knew, he said, better people, although, sleeping across three chairs, waiting for the parturition, he was unwilling to lie on the beds. Home at 3 A.M., he would stand in the bathtub in his overcoat, undressing by stages, dropping each garment on the floor outside the tub and invariably finding three or four bedbugs. He faced every complication that could be thought of, and he fell in with every sort of individual one could imagine in some phase of his development. "Let the successful," he says, "carry off their blue ribbons; I have known the unsuccessful, far better persons than their more lucky brothers." He talked with taxi drivers, porters on trains who had been his patients, colored men and women whom he intimately knew and a furnace man, a character, who lived in a shack four feet high that was like an animal's burrow in a swamp. But this man lived uncomplaining, alone, self-respecting, his life had "achieved the dignity of the human spirit, so that the dirt and debasement" did not matter. The doctor would leave his office in the evening feeling that he could not keep his eyes open; then he would sit in his car in front of some house waiting to get the courage to climb the steps. But once he saw the patient all that would disappear. In a flash the details of the case would begin to formulate themselves and the hunt was on. I am quoting from the autobiography of William Carlos Williams.

All this time he was writing the poems that made him famous. He was also writing the stories of *Life Along the Passaic River* and one or two other collections. He had seen thousands of patients over a forty-year period, and people asked him, How do you do it? You must have at the very least the energy of two men. But, as he saw it, one occupation complemented the other; they were two parts of a whole; one rested the man when the other fatigued him; and, as far as the writing was concerned, it took next to no time at all. "When by chance we penetrate to some moving detail of a life, there's always time to bang out a few pages. The thing isn't to find the time for it—the difficulty is to catch the evasive life of the thing." Five or ten minutes could always be found. He had his typewriter in his office desk. If a patient came in when he was in the middle of a sentence, down would go the machine, and, when the patient left, up the machine would come again. Moreover, after a complete absorption with either a poem or the delivery of a child, he came away, not fatigued, but rested. A peace of mind resulted from adopting as one's own the patient's condition, to be struggled with toward a solution. He went into his office harassed by personal perplexities, and, after two hours of intense application to the work, he came out at the finish completely rested, ready to smile and to laugh as if the day were just starting. So he never felt that the practice of medicine was anything but his food and drink, the thing that made it possible for him to write.

Comparing himself with Ezra Pound, Dr. Williams said his own upbringing assumed rather the humility and caution of the scientist. He could not tolerate in his old friend the "side" that went with all his posturings as a poet. He felt that it behooved him to be at his own superlative best, to live inconspicuously and work single-mindedly, and he considered himself a man in the front line, in the trenches, the only way he could respect himself and go on treating what came to him, men, women and children. Henri Fabre was one of his gods. "His example has always stood beside me as a measure and a rule. It has made me quiet and induced in me a patient industry and, in spite of my insufficiencies, a long-range contentment"; and seeing people for him was a trivial business unless one added zest to the picture. That is how he came to find writing a necessity. He did not treat a man as something to which surgery and drugs applied—"to treat him as material for a work of art made him somehow come alive to me."

That explains in part the vitality of these tales, many of which are about Dr. Williams's patients, seen, heard and felt with an actuality that is unmistakable and that recalls the typewriter in the doctor's office. Sometimes they are sketches of travel that involve meetings of doctors in Switzerland, Italy or wherever, and there is the story "The Farmers' Daughters," a tale of two Southern girls who told the doctor much about their lives. One of the best is "Old Doc Rivers," a character study of a surgeon who had practiced once in Rutherford when Williams was a young man, a brilliant eccentric with an uncanny feeling for diagnosis who had somehow gone wrong in his development. He would hit the dope and spend months in the insane asylum, yet people sought him out and sometimes waited months for him while he hopped himself up right before the patient. Insatiably interested in human nature, Dr. Williams talked with garage mechanics, with boys on the road from Canada who

had nothing in their pockets, or he heard stories of homo-
sexuality told him by women or men involved in them,
to which the doctor listened with the back of his ears.
The important thing was to have an outstanding character
whose history becomes gradually known as the story pro-
gresses. There are tales of a school friend on a revenue
cutter in the Pacific and one called "Ancient Gentility"
about a courteous old Italian who handed the doctor a
snuffbox for his pleasure. Where had the refinement origi-
nated, the gentleness that revealed itself beside the crimi-
nality one found on Guinea Hill? Then there is the story
"Pink and Blue," laid on the farm which the doctor visited
among the primitive people in the foothills of the Catskills,
the story of "Belle," who appeared in pink before the
husband who advertised for her and was buried in a blue
dress after surprising developments. "Jean Beicke," Dr.
Williams says, was "the best short story I ever wrote,"
the tale of a scrawny, misshapen, worthless piece of
humanity whom all the nurses and doctors loved as
she lay in her crib week after week. It was the story
that perhaps showed best the doctor's tender sympathetic
feeling.

Dr. Williams's father and mother had grown up with
the colored people in their West Indian islands, and he
himself had, ingrained in his very bones, a love of the
Negroes, "furnaces of emotional power." A Negro soldier,
whom he was doctoring for a venereal disease, gave him
the courage to persist in the use of his native language—
it was "always a treat to hear him"; and this new language,
live and immediate, accounts very largely for the spell of
these crisp fresh sketches and stories. There is not a word
too much in any of them and their vivacity and natural-
ness reflect what Dr. Williams calls "the great sights that
I see every day." They are great sights in fiction as well as
in fact.

VAN WYCK BROOKS

The Knife of the Times

The Wind of the Time

The Knife of the Times

As THE YEARS passed the girls who had been such intimates as children still remained true to one another.

Ethel by now had married. Maura had married; the one having removed to Harrisburg, the other to New York City. And both began to bring up families. Ethel especially went in for children. Within a very brief period, comparatively speaking, she had three of them, then four, then five and finally six. And through it all, she kept in constant touch with her girlhood friend, dark-eyed Maura, by writing long intimate letters.

At first these had been newsy chit chat, ending always however in continued protestations of that love which the women had enjoyed during their childhood. Maura showed them to her husband and both enjoyed their full newsy quality dealing as they did with people and scenes with which both were familiar.

But after several years, as these letters continued to flow, there came a change in them. First the personal note grew more confidential. Ethel told about her children, how she had had one after the other—to divert her mind, to distract her thoughts from their constant brooding. Each child would raise her hopes of relief, each anticipated delivery brought only renewed disappointment. She confided more and more in Maura. She loved her husband; it was not that. In fact, she didn't know what it was save that she, Ethel, could never get her old friend Maura out of her mind.

Until at last the secret was out. It is you, Maura, that I want. Nothing but you. Nobody but you can appease my grief. Forgive me if I distress you with this confession. It is the last thing in this world that I desire. But I cannot contain myself longer.

Thicker and faster came the letters. Full love missives they were now without the least restraint.

Ethel wrote letters now such as Maura wished she might at some time in her life have received from a man. She was told that all these years she had been dreamed of, passionately, without rival, without relief. Now, surely, Maura did not dare show the letters to her husband. He would not understand.

They affected her strangely, they frightened her, but they caused a shrewd look to come into her dark eyes and she packed them carefully away where none should ever come upon them. She herself was occupied otherwise but she felt tenderly toward Ethel, loved her in an old remembered manner—but that was all. She was disturbed by the turn Ethel's mind had taken and thanked providence her friend and she lived far enough apart to keep them from embarrassing encounters.

But, in spite of the lack of adequate response to her advances, Ethel never wavered, never altered in her passionate appeals. She begged her friend to visit her, to come to her, to live with her. She spoke of her longings, to touch the velvet flesh of her darling's breasts, her thighs. She longed to kiss her to sleep, to hold her in her arms. Franker and franker became her outspoken lusts. For which she begged indulgence.

Once she implored Maura to wear a silk chemise which she was sending, to wear it for a week and to return it to her, to Ethel, unwashed, that she might wear it in her turn constantly upon her.

Then, after twenty years, one day Maura received a letter from Ethel asking her to meet her—and her mother, in New York. They were expecting a sister back from Europe on the *Mauretania* and they wanted Maura to be there—for old times' sake.

Maura consented. With strange feelings of curiosity and not a little fear, she stood at the gate of the Pennsylvania station waiting for her friend to come out at the wicket on the arrival of the Harrisburg express. Would she be alone? Would her mother be with her really? Was it a hoax? Was the woman crazy, after all? And, finally, would she recognize her?

There she was and her mother along with her. After the first stare, the greetings on all sides were quiet, courteous and friendly. The mother dominated the moment. Her keen eyes looked Maura up and down once, then she asked the time, when would the steamer dock, how far was the pier and had they time for lunch first?

There was plenty of time. Yes, let's lunch. But first Ethel had a small need to satisfy and asked Maura if she would show her the way. Maura led her friend to the Pay Toilets and there, after inserting the coin, Ethel opened the door and, before Maura could find the voice to protest, drew her in with herself and closed the door after her.

What a meeting! What a release! Ethel took her friend into her arms and between tears and kisses, tried in some way, as best she could, to tell her of her happiness. She fondled her old playmate, hugged her, lifted her off her feet in the eager impressment of her desire, whispering into her ear, stroking her hair, her face, touching her lips, her eyes; holding her, holding her about as if she could never again release her.

No one could remain cold to such an appeal, as pathetic to Maura as it was understandable and sincere, she tried her best to modify its fury, to abate it, to control. But, failing that, she did what she could to appease her old friend. She loved Ethel, truly, but all this show was beyond her. She did not understand it, she did not know how to return it. But she was not angry, she found herself in fact in tears, her heart touched, her lips willing.

Time was slipping by and they had to go.

At lunch Ethel kept her foot upon the toe of Maura's slipper. It was a delirious meal for Maura with thinking of old times, watching the heroic beauty of the old lady and, while keeping up a chatter of small conversation, intermixed with recollections, to respond secretly as best she could to Ethel's insistent pressures.

At the pier there was a long line waiting to be admitted to the enclosure. It was no use—Ethel from behind constantly pressed her body against her embarrassed friend, embarrassed not from lack of understanding or sympathy, but for fear lest one of the officers and Customs inspectors who were constantly watching them should detect something out of the ordinary.

But the steamer was met, the sister saluted; the day came to an end and the hour of parting found Ethel still keeping close, close to the object of her lifelong adoration.

What shall I do? thought Maura afterward on her way home, on the train alone. Ethel had begged her to visit her, to go to her, to spend a week at least with her, to sleep with her. Why not?

A Visit to the Fair

IT WAS a picturesque old place on a back road at the bottom of a narrow valley. The roof was sound, though, so they could move in without great cost.

Bess took it fine. She brushed all her old life aside—all but her attachment to her children and friends—and buckled down to the job.

But Fred didn't improve and while the chicken business kept them from starving outright it did that and that was about all. They lived, they even got along pretty well, but they were on their uppers and what was going to happen next?

Then, one spring when the hens were going badly Fred had a hunch he wouldn't last through the year and refused to blow in his last few dollars on new birds. Bess pleaded with him, did everything she knew how to do to move him; turned right and left for aid, then gave up.

Now surely the poorhouse or worse seemed staring them in the face.

But the summer passed and in the fall—they still had the old Stutz—Bess started up a little apple business. It paid rather well.

One afternoon in the latter part of September, she set out for town a little earlier than usual and at the top of the back road stopped to leave some egg crates at one of the farms.

Mr. Tibbet walked back to the gate with her.

It's a shame for a woman like you to be living down there, he was saying when they came up to the car.

Oh, no, said Bess in her hearty voice, I like it.

There's something I'd like to ask you, Mrs. Rand, he continued.

Go ahead, said Bess, suspecting nothing at all.

Well, he said, I'm a little backward about coming out with it.

Say it, said she, wanting to get going and feeling quite unconcerned.

Well, how would you like to go to the fair in Danbury with me today?

Bess was taken aback. You can't imagine how I felt when he said that, she confessed later, I just can't tell you how it affected me.

Oh, she spoke up, I couldn't do that. It's three now and I'm going to meet my daughter at the station.

Well, he said again, that's all right, how about tomorrow? You see, he continued without waiting for her reply, Mrs. Tibbet and I used to go every year; we've taken in that fair every year for the past fifty years or more, I guess, and since she's gone, I want to but I just haven't the heart to go alone. I thought you being lonesome down the hill there might like to go with me.

Bess was staggered. Well, she began, I'll speak to Mr. Rand when I get back tonight and, if I can arrange it for someone to stay with him and take care of the work—I'll let you know.

All right, he said, and with that she drove off.

When she got home from the village that night, she asked her husband what she should do.

You'd be a darned fool if you didn't take him up, said he. Go on.

So she called up the man and said she'd go with him.

I'll call for you about ten o'clock, he answered. But Bess wouldn't have that. No, she replied, I'll drive up there. You wait for me. No, sir, said she afterward, I didn't want all these—you know the kind of people they are down here—I just didn't want them to know anything about it. It would be all over town in no time. Not that there was anything wrong in it, but you know how I felt.

The next morning she drove up to Mr. Tibbet's place, put her car in his barn and closed the door.

He had his own Buick sport roadster ready; he asked her if she wanted to drive, she refused, so he took the wheel and they were off.

He was a big, fine-looking man—born shortly after the Civil War as he told Bess. Yes, about the same time as my mother, she had replied. But he had fixed himself up in a well-fitting suit for the day, was obviously delighted to have her beside him. He was out for a good time. So was she.

When they came to the Fair Grounds, it was close to noon.

What shall we do? he said.

I don't know, what do you mean?

Well, what do you want to do? Shall we have dinner first and go over to the grounds later? Say the word.

She told him she didn't know. She had been to the same fair once as a girl but that was long ago and she really didn't know what to expect.

Well then, he said, let's eat first. I don't know what they'll have in the tent, but I know of a place near here where we can go and we'll feel more like looking at the exhibits later.

So he took her to a good restaurant where he proceeded to order dinner. He went at it whole hog. Nothing was too good for her. In fact, she had to be careful not to express a casual wish lest he press to grant it until finally she had to remind him they'd better be getting on.

In the Fair Grounds they took in everything. As she said, it was a pity they didn't have any fur coats for sale for then she would have been all fixed up for the winter. He was in a mood to buy her anything.

She regretted the dinner too before long, so constantly did he ply her with candy, ice cream, fruit, peanuts—everything which he could see to buy that she would accept—for nothing that she looked at did he wish to deny her.

She, of course, kept him well in hand. He was a great companion but she kept well on her guard. They laughed, talked and then took in the races. That was the best. They were great races, in fact. During the afternoon a world's record for two-year-olds in harness on a mile track was established so that Bess felt it had been a great day.

The afternoon slipped by, it was time to remind Mr. Tibbet that they had better be starting for home. But when she did so, saying that she would have to be there by half-past five, he wouldn't hear of it.

Oh, no, he said, Why, we always stay for the fireworks.

For the what? said Bess.

Why, for the fireworks, said Mr. Tibbet. Call your house on the phone and see how things are. We'll take in the barbecue, see the fireworks and I'll have you back before midnight.

No use protesting. Bess found a phone booth, called up the farm and Fred told her to go to it.

Tibbet was delighted.

The barbecue was wonderful. Whole pigs and lambs were being turned on spits, halves of beeves and everything to go with it. The food was superbly cooked—no doubt a century-old technique; they sat down at the long tables and once more contented themselves to the full.

Between the exhibits of the fireworks, they had vaudeville acts, everything suitable to be shown out of doors including the great diving horse Fire Bell who, with a woman on her back, plunged from a platform thirty feet into a tank of water.

It was novel and exciting. But in the midst of it, Bess caught sight of one of her neighbors, who, as she laugh-

ingly told of it later, hardly saw an act or a rocket from
that time on for watching her and Mr. Tibbet.

This tickled Bess. Mildly exasperating to her, it only
enhanced her hardly suppressed excitement the more. She
could not believe it that she, Bess Rand, was here in the
midst of these strange sights, doing things she had not
imagined possible for her to do, enjoying as she had not
imagined she could enjoy such things—only two days, a
day and a half ago.

Then it was all over. In the crowd they wandered over
to the parking space where Tibbet asked her once more if
she did not want to drive.

No, said Mrs. Rand.

So he drove her home, to his house where she had left
her car in his barn and they talked and talked. In fact, he
didn't seem as if he wanted to stop. He got her car out
for her and, though it was midnight or near, he stood there
with his foot on the running board after she had taken her
seat at the wheel and would not let her go.

It isn't right, he said again and again, for a woman like
you to be living down there. Why don't you come up here
and live on the hill?

She just laughed.

It's only ten minutes from town here.

It's only twelve minutes from where I live, said she.

You're some driver then, he continued, but that's no
place for you down there just the same.

I wanted my son to build up here, he added. But he
wouldn't do it. He's building a house down in the town
now. Bought a miserly little plot for five hundred dollars.
I offered him any plot on the farm he would pick out. Do
you think he'd do it? No, sir. I begged him, I'm telling you,
with tears in my eyes. Wouldn't do it. What am I going
to do?

Bess released the emergency brake, but he didn't take the
hint so she pulled it up again and sat back once more.

Why don't you move up here?

How can I, she said, with all my family?

That's nothing, he rejoined, bring them along. Bring 'em all. There are twenty-eight rooms in the house. I guess that will hold you. Bring your furniture. Bring everything.

But, she said, I've got a hired man there, I like him and he sort of depends on us.

Bring him along, we can find work for him to do.

But I've got my business. We've got to work to live— the cow, the chickens, why, we've got two thousand chickens there.

What, he says, there's loads of room here for a few chickens and a cow. Why, we've got everything here, just crying for someone to make use of them. And Bess knew that was right, the house would have been a delight to her. Electricity, two kitchens, one for summer and a small one for winter with an electric stove, running water, bathrooms, showers, old furniture. And she could see that he meant what he said.

But she only laughed and shook her head.

He said nothing then for a minute but he was more than a little taken aback, she could see that, so she added:

Well, there's one thing I'll say: for the past year we've been pretty much thinking we were bound for the poor-house. But I can see now that we don't have to go there. And she laughed.

I should say not, he beamed again. You'll never have to go to the poorhouse in these parts. Any time you change your mind and want to come up here, you say the word and we'll move you in.

At that, since it must be well after midnight, Bess thought she really should be going, so, by way of parting, she said what she had said several times before, that she had had a wonderful time that day.

It was wonderful of you, Mr. Tibbet, to take me to the Fair. I don't know how to thank you for all your kindness.

You've been wonderful to me and I've had a really great day.

Well, he said, Mrs. Rand, I'm glad you did, I'm very glad you did. I wanted to treat you right because, well, he said, I wanted you to have a good time because I thought if you did, maybe sometime you'd go out with me again.

Hands Across the Sea

Aᴛᴇʀ ᴛʜᴇ ᴡᴀʀ there were even more unreasoning racial hatreds than formerly, but they were changed. There was a letdown here as in everything else. In a Hotel like the Christian Hospice at Geneva all races mixed, especially around the time of the fall meeting of the League; they looked at each other and talked and it was a new world.

Mrs. Andrews, German in spirit like her father, but an American, found the British she met as objectionable as ever but they piqued her curiosity more than those of most other nationalities.

Dr. McFarland particularly attracted her. He was a fine-looking man, good brown hair and a ruddy complexion, a Scotchman really and not English at all. But to her he was English; she bristled at this—and it was not too unpleasant a sensation.

Her husband, whom she loved dearly, had returned to America leaving her in charge of their two half-grown boys in school several miles up the lake. Mrs. Andrews had decided to remain at the hotel; she was taking a few French lessons, walking a good deal, writing letters and trying to keep from feeling too lonesome until after Christmas, at least, when she planned to run up to Paris for a little gaiety.

Perhaps it was that McFarland was a physician that first attracted her to him, for her husband was the same, and also half-English, one of those American hybrids of whom so much is expected.

What is one to do in a hotel like that? It resembles a ship. Either one becomes acquainted with those seen every

14

day or talks to nobody. Mrs. Andrews and the Englishman singled each other out for attention rather early by looks, by speech, at first casual, and finally by intimate association.

He was certainly the most interesting person in the place, among the men at least, and it was obvious that he cared little for anyone else there besides Mrs. Andrews— rather an attractive trait from a woman's viewpoint. In fact, the older women, some of whom Mrs. Andrews greatly admired, resented McFarland and his cocksure ways quite openly.

Regular Cockney English, said one American lady, I dislike him heartily. Just the type.

But Mrs. Andrews didn't think so.

She soon found him to be a great talker, full of information which attracted her and she listened avidly. It was something she could follow, through familiarity with her husband's daily routine but at the same time it was new, new and serious, serious and full of worth as she gauged the world.

His distinguished, un-American accent, his hard, fit body, his direct absorbed look, and his manner of the scientific man liking his job, held her attention. And he was deferential as a listener—she could talk and he would give heed. She liked that, for she wanted to talk, she wanted someone to talk to especially about the things which he was so apt in. His conversation seemed made providentially perfect for her ears.

He had been a soldier in Mesopotamia from 1914 to the end. As a physician, he had encountered all sorts of conditions there crying for sanitary skill of the highest order. It had been on a grand scale and he had ended by becoming an expert in the organization of sanitary and hygienic programs for the care of whole regions, whole countries, cleaning up whatever it might be from the plague to infestations by the tse tse fly.

He told his story well and she learned it all. How, after

the war he had returned to England to have a go at general practice. But it had been quite impossible. Had one money, he might sit down and wait for a practice but, being poor, he would jolly well starve for all any one ever did to give him a chance. This didn't suit McFarland. Mobilizing his war skill, he had the good fortune to land a berth with the Sanitary Committee of the League of Nations by which he was now employed as a sort of field executive with head-quarters in Geneva. From there he sallied out to whatever part of the world to which he might be sent on deeds of mercy.

Now it might be malaria on the Campagna south of Rome. Now it might be some cattle pest in Yugoslavia, now a sanitary encounter of whatever sort in Greece, now yellow fever in Brazil, and so it would go. And back to Geneva he would come at the end of each campaign, full of new stories and the Christian Hospice would be his resting place.

It was great stuff. Mrs. Andrews and the doctor went over it all many times, discussing the international aspects of it, the scientific as well as the humane, the incredible stupidities of peoples, their antagonisms, until they got to know each other pretty well.

They would sit in the little second-floor lobby of the hotel until long after the usual retiring hour; the old ladies would look at them. And later on, they got to taking walks along the lake, crossing the bridge to the Promenade des Anglais and even, occasionally, of an afternoon, sipping a bock on the terrace of the Café Mont Blanc. But their favorite ramble, or rather Mrs. Andrews' favorite one, where she had walked with her husband just before he left for the States, was in the Jardin des Plantes, the neat little lawns among the smooth-leaved holly trees.

Strange, it seemed, that here was a man whom she liked, a doctor too, leading a fascinating life, the very thing Bob, her husband, longed for, a single fellow free to go, to be his own master. And what did he really desire? Naturally what else but to have a wife, a home, a place he could call his own, where he could settle down with children and quit his wandering. Or if not quit it, at least have a retreat waiting for him at the end. He wanted a woman, serious, attractive of course, but intelligent, who would follow him with love and interest. Without that, what is a man's life worth?

Mrs. Andrews would smile to herself thinking of the very opposite expressions she had heard all too often from Bob's almost foaming mouth, when he would want to be quiet, want to relax, and had to go on without respite. To hell with his home, his kids, herself, everything, she had often thought he felt, if he could only get out and away—anywhere.

McFarland sought Mrs. Andrews out more and more. He would be gone a week, a month, sometimes, and not a little to her surprise she found herself waiting quite eagerly for him to return—much as she waited on the proper days for her weekly letter from Bob—which, if it didn't come, as once in a while it would happen—she cried herself to sleep in her solitary room upstairs.

She knew by now that Dr. McFarland was interested in a girl in England whom he seriously considered marrying. For at length, having told her of his work till both he and Mrs. Andrews were well acquainted with all its phases, this girl became more and more often the burden of talk between them.

About this time, it being near Christmas, the doctor informed Mrs. Andrews that he expected his mother from England the following week for the holidays. Mrs. Andrews said she would be very glad to see her.

The two ladies got along beautifully together. Mrs. McFarland turned out to be a simple, motherly person, not at all English, as Mrs. Andrews said later, she was so considerate and gentle. While the old lady in her turn was amazed at what she found in Mrs. Andrews.

Why, she exclaimed, almost at the first, why you are not an American, are you? I can't believe it. Americans are so overbearing, so offensive, really. But you, why I liked you at once. When my son wrote to me about you in his letters, I tried my best, but I couldn't really believe it. Now I see it is quite so, you are really charming.

Mrs. Andrews told her that no doubt there were many Americans who were most disagreeable, to say the least, that she herself often blushed for the crude things they did and said but that people at home were really not like that—most of them.

There was a particularly objectionable party of our countrymen in the dining room those days and both ladies were more than a little conscious of them.

No, really, you must not believe we are all like that, said Mrs. Andrews.

McFarland dearly loved his mother and with good reason. It was she, a widow, who had put him and his brother through school and this was the first time she had ever left England for a vacation.

Don't you think it is a horrid life for him though? asked the older lady. I do wish I could induce him to come home and take up a practice there. But he will not. I worry for him very often. He is sent only where there is illness, and of the most dangerous kind. If only he would come home. I have been expecting that he would marry. He has told you about Miriam. But I don't know, they don't seem to hit it off. I can't tell why. Young people are not as they were. He admires you so much. I can easily understand it. I am sure your husband is most fortunate.

But, if Mrs. McFarland was puzzled as to why her son didn't settle down, Mrs. Andrews was not.

Many a time in recent weeks, they had discussed Miriam

and McFarland had asked his American companion her opinion as to what he should do.

She is a lovely girl, he said, I have known her for years. She lost her husband at the front; scarcely married, she found herself a widow like any number of others. I suppose we're engaged, he added, but I can't quite see it.

Oh, said Mrs. Andrews, you're rather selfish perhaps and don't want to give up your freedom.

No, no, no, no, said the doctor. Really you mustn't say that. But she does want to have it too much her own way. And I just wonder if she will be willing to buckle down. What I want is a wife whom I can rely on, someone who will be there when I am away and I shall know what she is about. I can't say that I like a woman to be too independent.

Ha, ha, thought Mrs. Andrews to herself, the British will out at last.

And she told him so. Oh, yes, she chided him, you want a nice mouse who never thinks a thing but what you tell her to think who . . .

Now, now, said he, laughing. I'm not as bad as that, am I?

Quite, said Mrs. Andrews, imitating a favorite expression of his, unless you have some woman to put you in your place.

In the American fashion?

Not at all. We are not like that at all, said Mrs. Andrews.

Ho, ho, said he, quite, I'm afraid.

We do want to share alike with them, continued the lady, but we don't at all expect to rule them any more than we expect them to rule us. But the British husband doesn't even wish his wife to have a will of her own. I'm glad for her sake that your young lady is giving you food for thought before she consents to be your slave. I rather admire her. Take my advice and grab her before it is too late.

Do you mean that?

Of course I mean it.

Well, perhaps you are right, perhaps you are right.

McFarland was good company, full of fun often in a crowd and two or three times when the Andrews boys were in at the hotel for a week end he had them up to his room to see his bagpipes, which he played rather well. But they looked at him as children will at a man who is friendly with their mother when their father is away—and weren't very crazy about him. But he was all right.

Then it got to be toward the end of the year and Mrs. Andrews was preparing with the greatest interest and excitement to return home. The steamship bookings were made, the trunks were being packed, the last instructions given at the school. But one thing stuck in her mind. She wondered if Dr. McFarland would get back from Egypt in time to bid her good-bye.

He had been away for a month organizing the work of ditching and draining in an effort to control a serious out-break of malaria in the region of the great dam. He had said he would come back before she left but here it was two days more and . . . Well, she smiled at herself looking in the glass over her chiffonier, if he comes, he comes, if not, so much the better. Quite.

But she felt curiously relieved when she saw him come striding into the dining room that evening where she was sitting with the other ladies eating her last supper at the hotel.

The Sailor's Son

As THE FERRY CAME into the slip, there was a pause, then a young fellow on a motorcycle shot out of the exit, looked right and left, sighted the hill, opened her up and took the grade at top speed. Behind him an older guy sitting firm and with a face on him like a piece of wood ripped by without a quiver.

That day Manuel waited in vain for his friend to visit him on the farm where he had taken a job for the summer. It came on to rain about eleven in the morning. The cows had been put to pasture, the chickens fed, the eggs collected. It was Sunday. He had been down for the papers and had taken them up to the big house. What the hell? He might as well go up to his room and write to Margy.

Lousy weather, he said to himself cutting across the lawn uphill through the slippery, wet grass. I suppose he guessed it and didn't want to risk the bad roads. But that boy is there, all right, he certainly is there.

In his room, on the third floor of the dignified country house where he was employed that year, he got out the ruled pad and a pencil and proceeded to write.

Dear Marge: Where have you been keeping yourself? I'm starting on the third month up here and you haven't been up to see me in six weeks. Why don't you come up some week end sometime?

Then he stopped and thought a minute during which he tapped the butt of the long pencil against his closed lips, tap, tap, tap, tap, thinking; going on after a moment:

Drop me a line when to expect you. There's not much

news except I'm pretty much alone here. I don't mind it though as long as I can earn something—until I can get a job in the city. Not much chance for that now, I guess. I often think how good you are to me, giving me money and keeping me this spring while I was hunting for work. I'll never forget it. As soon as I can get back to New York and make what I ought to be getting, we can make our dream come true. I can just see a little apartment all neat and pretty. At first, I suppose, we'd both better work so we can save up a few dollars, but after a year I like to think you'll quit that office for good. Christian didn't show up today. I suppose it's the rain. If you run into him, tell him I wanted to know why he didn't show up. I hope you can get up here sometime. I'm crazy to see you. This is a good place though, good food and all that but I've got to see my friends. So long, dearie, Yours, Manuel.

He put the letter in an envelope, addressed it and stuck it into his coat pocket. He took out his pipe and started to smoke. The rain beat down on the roof over his head with a drumming as of fingers tapping with their soft pads. He felt nervous and oppressed. He put his pipe aside; it didn't have the taste he expected of it and lay down on the bed wondering. What the hell? He felt lonesome and neglected.

But downstairs Mrs. Cuthbertson felt relieved. She liked Manuel, his work was satisfactory, he drove the car excellently and was docile and obedient. He was a real good boy. But she didn't have much use for the bozo who drove up from the city each week end on a motorcycle for a visit to stay over till Sunday.

It's an old friend, Manuel explained to her, I've known him from the other side. I don't mind paying for his m ls if that's what you mean, Mrs. Cuthbertson. Or he c ide down to the town for them.

Now, I've told you, Manuel, said Mrs. C., that I like you and I want you to stay here and help me. You are not so strong, you look twice as well as when you came up here this spring. But I don't think that young man is a good influence on you. I can't find you anywhere when he is here. I'd tell him not to come up so often. Once a month is all right but not every week end. That is not what we hired you for. I don't like his looks. He has a fresh look in his eyes. You are not the same nice boy when he is here.

It was Mrs. Cuthbertson's habit to talk this way to the young men she hired to do the work for her in summer. She picked out boys that she liked and then looked after them. She talked their talk and most of them liked her. But this time she had not been quite frank with Manuel. She did not tell him that what she really objected to was his friend's air of proprietorship over Manuel, and the whole farm for that matter, when he was there. He drove up on his motor-cycle; put the machine anywhere at all in the garage and proceeded to eat fruit, wander about the lawns and enjoy himself as if he owned the place. Manuel shared his meals with him and at night his bed. This was the point on which Mrs. C. stuck. Yet she didn't quite feel that she wanted to come out with it—just yet.

Mrs. Cuthbertson knew that Manuel was engaged to be married. Why didn't his girl come up to visit him more often if he was lonely? It would have been much better. But this young man was a nuisance. Manuel was a different person when he was there, silly, excited and worth nothing. At first she thought it would only last a few times, but every Saturday it had been the same. Mrs. C. was determined it should not continue longer.

But the following Saturday being fine, sure enough about four in the afternoon you could hear the chug chug of the motor as it took the steep hill, up the dirt road leading to the farm entrance. And there was the boy himself, the same cocky youngster who had shot out of the ferry entrance the week before. He honked his horn.

As Mrs. C. heard this, she called to Manuel to warn him. But he was already out the back door. She called to him from the kitchen window but though he must have heard her, he kept right on going at a run to meet his friend.

Hello, kid, geez' I'm glad to see you. I almost passed out last week. Why didn't you come up? Did the rain keep you?

Sure, what the hell, he lied, don't you think I'd a been here if I could a made it? How are you, Baby? Feelin' your oats?

You said it.

And with that, Manuel swung open the garage doors and The Kid rolled his cycle into the space, standing it over against the wall, on one side.

Mrs. Cuthbertson was watching from the kitchen window, her jaw set and a determined look in her eyes. Pretty soon she saw the men come out of the garage and after hanging around the corner of the building, talking a minute, she saw Manuel cast a quick look up at the house, then the two disappeared behind the stonework.

Mrs. C. waited a few minutes and went out. The hay barn lay directly behind the big stone garage building, its entrance concealed from view as far as the house on the hill was concerned. Mrs. Cuthbertson walked slowly along on the grass avoiding the cinder roadway and approached the barn. She saw no one about so she went further and listened. She thought she heard voices in the barn but listen as she would, she could not make out what they were saying.

With that she boldly walked up to the big doors and, being a powerful woman, she swung one of them open and walked in. The men were lying in the hay. She looked, felt her stomach rise into her throat, then she let her tongue go. The visitor she ordered off the farm at once. He laughed and walked past her out of the door without a quiver. But with Manuel it was different.

After rearranging his clothes, he sat down in the hay where he was and cried like a child. Then he got up and came to her begging her not to send him away. She felt sorry for the boy and after a few strong words ordered him up to his room to pack.

But there she was. The work had to be done. She had no one to take his place. So after an hour, she called the fellow down again and told him exactly what was on her mind. You may stay this week out, she said, until I get someone to take your place, but then you go.

He begged, he pleaded, in vain. Then he went upstairs, wrote another letter to his girl and the following morning when he had gone down with the milk he mailed it.

The next Sunday the girl, or woman rather, appeared. Why had Manuel been fired? Was he not good enough for the job? Mrs. Cuthbertson told the woman as much as she had the words for—but, to her surprise, it made no great impression.

The boy is lonesome up here, said the woman. Why do you keep his friends away? I am engaged to marry him, I don't care what he does. Why should you worry? Well, that was a hot one. Manuel begged to be kept on. He had nowhere else to go. He could not get a recommendation. What should he do? Tears came to his eyes. Finally the fiancée grew abusive and Mrs. Cuthbertson losing her temper very nearly struck her. It was a wild moment. But in the end Manuel was fired. And the woman took him back to the city with her where she told him she would pay for a room until she could find work for him elsewhere.

An Old Time Raid

WE WERE HAVING an absinthe party over at the Franklin House. It was a regular thing with us in those days. We'd drink absinthe and shoot pool, then drift out around midnight wherever else we were going. Sometimes up to Paterson. You know.

That night I was going home.

As I started across the tracks an eastbound freight train was coming head on into the station. I hadn't seen it at all. I just got over in time—as it went through. "Dago" and Charlie Hanson had been right behind me. I knew tiat. I looked back and—they weren't there!

Well, I stood there and waited. Let me tell you it seemed a year. You know how long those trains are; I waited until the whole thing had gone by. And I couldn't see them anywhere. I didn't know what to do. I thought maybe they'd pick them up down the line next morning—I didn't know what to think.

So I went home.

I can remember keeping my eye on the middle crack in the sidewalk and finding myself in the gutter every once in a while, then getting back and looking around for the crack again.

I never opened my mouth.

A couple of days later old man Schultz came up to me on the morning train and wanted to know what had happened to Dago. I told him I didn't know a thing about it. And I didn't. Then next day old man Hanson came up to me on the station platform and asked me the same thing about Charlie.

Well, they kept pestering me like that for a couple weeks. They knew I had been with the boys over at the Franklin House—and that's all I could tell them. I'll give them credit though, they never came to our house or spoke to my old man. They were square all right. Well, I guess they're all dead now there's no reason why I shouldn't talk.

I didn't hear a word, didn't know a thing about them for a couple of months. I didn't know any more than anyone else.

Until one day, two months later—it was about eleven o'clock in the morning and I was sitting at my desk down on Broom Street looking over my samples. I was an outside salesman for Grossbeck and Co.—suit goods and that sort of thing. They had our desks facing the window, a whole row of them—right on the street you might say.

I looked up and there was "Dago" Schultz outside grinning and looking in at me.

I beckoned for him to come in.

He came around and plunked himself down in my desk chair and put his feet up on the desk. He had half a bun on. Said he had been down in Philadelphia with Charlie, they were running elevators. Charlie had stayed on.

I asked him what I could do for him.

He said he was hungry.

I could see he was half lit and wasn't going to hang around there much longer with his feet on my desk if I knew what was good for me. So I told him I'd take him out to a restaurant up on 59th Street where we could get some beer. I got him out, checked my samples in a cigar store and took him up to a place, Gruber's, you know, one of those good old German places. I used to go there quite often and they knew me. That was some time after 11 A.M.

and there was no one in there at that time. I ordered something for Dago and some beer for myself.

Well, he got it into his head he wanted to practice throwing the plate of food up in the air. You know. He'd chuck it up so that the food went up and the plate after it, then he'd catch the plate and the food on it without dropping a thing.

But he wasn't so good just then, the trick went wrong, he spilt the whole mess and broke the plate.

By that time the waiter came over to me. You see he knew me, I was a regular customer of the place—and told me we'd have to cut it out. I told him it was all right, that we'd pay for anything that was broken so he left us alone for awhile.

But as it got to be around twelve o'clock the regular customers started to come in for lunch, you know how it is in those places and he tipped me off we'd have to beat it.

After that we got down around 14th Street Dago was still feeling pretty good with the jag he'd had to begin with and the beer we'd had at lunch.

I don't know how it is now around there but in those days there were a lot of pushcarts along the curb at that time of day selling fruit. Dago went up to one of these carts and I stood back against the wall of the houses waiting for him. Well, before I knew it I was catching apples, bananas, oranges that he was picking up out of the cart and flinging at me wham, wham, wham as hard and as fast as he could handle them—and me catching them and putting them down on the ground at my feet.

As I remember it that little side show cost me about two dollars before I could get him away.

At that time the old Dewey Theatre was just across the street from where Tammany Hall used to be and when we got opposite it Dago made up his mind that that was the one place he wanted to go in this world. And I was to get tickets—though the show didn't start for two hours or more.

You know how those places were in those days. There was a fellow in a uniform out in front and the minute he saw us he yells out "schicker." Now I was working for a kike firm and I knew what that meant. He'd probably seen the banana-throwing stunt up the street—and anyway "schicker" meant drunk. He was passing the word on to the window that Dago was drunk and not to sell us tickets.

That got me sore. I was stone sober, you see, and I wasn't gonna let them get away with that. So I walks up to the window and puts up an argument. The outcome of which was that they gave me two tickets in the back row of the balcony, the worst seats in the house.

You know how these old places were. There was the lobby but the balcony entrance was outside, from the street. You went up one flight of stairs, then there was a platform, then you went up again to the top of the balcony and so down to your seat.

Well, it was still around noon and the show didn't start for another hour and a half anyway so we started wandering down the street.

I don't know exactly what we did then but I remember we crossed over 14th Street just opposite Tammany Hall and started sauntering back on the other side. We hadn't gone far when we came to one of those brownstone residences that had gone over to business. You know a flight of stairs going up from the sidewalk, then the entrance. They had a sign in one of the windows "Stenographer and Typist Wanted."

That was nuts for Dago. He wanted to go in and apply for the job. I tried to steer him off but nothing doing, so in we goes.

Remember now, this is a true story and I'm telling you this just the way it happened.

When we got in they had a machine there on a regular

stand but they said they wanted a girl and the job wasn't open to men. But Dago started to talk, told them he wanted the job and if they'd give him a chance to show what he could do, and all that sort of thing.

They told him all right to go ahead—probably just to get rid of him—so with that he sits down, lifts his feet and starts to bang his heels up and down on the keyboard as hard as he could go.

Why all this? I dunno. Anyhow—they started to yell for the police and out we went and up the street. Having the tickets we thought the best place for us to duck for was the theatre—and get out of the way. It was still early—much too early for the show. But anyway up we went into the balcony and the minute Dago saw where the seats were he started to show 'em what he thought of 'em. The place was filling up by that time.

You weren't allowed to smoke. They had big cards hanging down from the ceiling on strings—or wires—I dunno. No smoking. There was one right in front of us. This probably gave Dago the idea. He got out a cigar and started to light up.

He had no more than got started when an usher came up to him and pointed to the sign. You know. Dago took a good puff and blew the smoke out and said, "I'm not smoking." That's all that was said, *that time*. Pretty soon another usher came around and the same thing happened. Mind you the show hadn't started yet, we were just sitting there waiting. I never did see the show.

You know in those days they were used to that sort of thing, and that didn't faze 'em much. They were in the habit of handling rough customers. So after a while as Dago was sitting there smoking, the official bouncer came up to us, a big guy, in a uniform. You know the face.

I was sitting on the aisle and Dago was next to me on the inside.

This guy leaned over and told Dago to cut out the cigar.

The same thing took place. Dago took a good puff and told the guy, "I ain't smoking." With that this fellow reaches in across me and grabs Dago. With one hand. Out he yanks him, I suppose, right across my lap—with one jerk. Drags him to the top of the stairs and throws him clean down to the first landing.

I don't know exactly what happened then, whether this big guy was off his balance or I got more nerve than I thought I had or what but I gave the guy a shove and down he went after Dago.

By this time Dago was up and shoved the guy the rest of the way down and he after him.

Well, you can imagine something was happening by that time. The crowd outside had got word of it and there was a mob around the door in no time. And a young cop came up and started to grab Dago. Geesus! I've often felt sorry for that guy.

Dago got him up against the wall and pounded him so hard that he actually dropped his club. And you can tell how the crowd was in those days. When Dago beat it they opened up for him—I saw it with my own eyes—and closed after him so that when the cop started after him he couldn't get anywhere.

Geesus! and I had the hardest job convincing them that I was his friend and that I was with him. I walked up and down 14th Street for half an hour and I couldn't get anyone to come across. That's the way they felt. They thought I was a plainclothes man, I suppose.

Finally I located him in the basement of a saloon where they'd hidden him until the fuss cooled down.

And then the son of a gun started to think—started to remember we had tickets for the show and that we hadn't seen it and he was going back to get our money back.

I quit there. I told him he was a damned fool but—nothing doing he was going back and cash in on his tickets. And I after him.

That was when I saw him come flying out of that lobby in the air! Bodily. He landed right at my feet and we started down the street on the run.

There was a window cleaner up on a ladder with his pail and stuff and as he went by Dago kicked this guy's ladder out from under him and down he came.

At the corner of Broadway there was a cop waiting and he clipped Dago over the head with his club. And that ended that. He split his scalp open for six inches and they had an ambulance and carted him off to the hospital. And I didn't see him again for a month.

He was a good-hearted guy. If you lent Dago five dollars he'd pay it back to you. He wouldn't come around whining a month later and tell you a hard-luck story and end up by handing you three dollars—he'd pay up—if he had it—whatever he had borrowed.

It must have been two or three years after that, we were standing on the corner—you know, by the station around midnight and the last train was just pulling out as we were trying to make up our minds whether to go to Paterson or not.

A couple of the boys started after the train and Dago behind them. I didn't go so I saw the whole thing.

Dago was an expert train hopper—you gotta know that. He'd use one hand only, grab the bar and swing far out, then let the motion of the train swing him back halfway up the steps.

Well, whether he was drunk or not or just didn't see, as he swung out after getting a grip on the rail, a freight coming from nowhere in the opposite direction just clipped him . . .

What would he have become if he had lived? He's a whole lot now that he's dead. Makes me think of an old man I knew, when they'd ask him how far back he could remember he'd say, I can remember back to when the U. S. was a republic. That's where Dago Schultz belongs. You know.

The Buffalos

ONCE I HAD a beautiful friend whom I loved and who loved me. It was not easy for us to see each other, every moment that we could spend together having to be stolen. So that it was only at great cost of trouble and invention that we succeeded in our small enterprises. Even then, it was sometimes months together before we could meet at all.

Thus our moments were very precious and for a long time we enjoyed them to the full. What did we do? Is it necessary to say, for who would believe it, either way? We were happy together and we were young enough to have illusions so that the time passes pleasantly uphill and downhill as it does under such circumstances.

But the lady, whom I shall call Francie, had one defect—or habit, rather, which at first amused me. She was a great talker for woman's rights.

All this happened in those days when Mrs. Pankhurst in England and the others here would be parading the streets with banners demanding equal rights with men. Votes for Women was their slogan which they put forward on every occasion.

This might be well enough for the run of those who with seamed faces and angry looks talked from platforms and even upon street corners but it was nothing for the lovely woman with whom I rushed so eagerly to spend my hardly won minutes.

Often such matters did not come into our talk but we would sway as one person in thought and word during an entire afternoon.

33

But at other times, whether it was the moon or what we had eaten that day or how we had slept the night before or what, things would at once on my arrival start to run away. And the invariable twist which the conversation would take would be toward politics and woman's rights.

I objected. It wasted our time. But this only inflamed the spirit of the lady to such a point that I found I was getting nowhere. Of course it was important, she objected, for women to have the vote. What did I mean?

I meant, I tried to explain, that the important thing for us to do when we were together was to enjoy each other and not to run off on something which concerned us not at all.

No, she almost snorted, it does not concern us. It does not concern you, you mean. You have the vote, what do you care? But we who are the mothers of the nation are not supposed to have the brains for it. No, we haven't the brains of a street cleaner.

But that isn't it, I tried to say. I acknowledge that you women are perhaps far more suited to rule than we men are but why bother about such a trifle. I would gladly give you my vote, I said, if I could. But you, my dear, are beautiful, do you not understand?

Rot, she retorted. You are trying to treat me like a child. If you haven't the manhood to treasure the vote, your prerogative as a citizen of the United States, I must say I thought more of you. President Roosevelt . . .

Oh, my God, I couldn't help crying.

Yes, Roosevelt, she repeated. And I must explain that the lady always pronounced the former president's name as though it had an a in the middle. Roosavelt is for us and with his help, I tell you, it will go through. But you are a Democrat, she ended haughtily.

Don't imagine that she was fooling when she said these things. Not on your life. And that is what gave me my first idea. I could have pretended to be won over or I might perhaps have diverted the flood of conversation with a gift or a loving gesture of some startling sort. But one day when Francie was in the middle of one of her suffragist tirades I noted how beautiful she was in the heat of her excitement and I resolved then and there that I was luckier than I thought.

I took it as my pleasure from that time forward for almost a month to be greatly interested in what she had to say, raising objection after objection to torment her. Meanwhile I drank in the fiery looks of her scornful eyes, the lovely curl of her lips. I watched the glow mount in her cheeks. All her features would brighten, take a form and a fire that was delectable to me. I had found a way to enjoy this bad habit from which I could not break her.

Occasionally at the very height of her railing at me I would quietly take her in my arms. And if she did not grow at once furiously angry she would say no more and the time for my departure would rush upon us like a storm.

But the woman was really obsessed with this idea. I grew tired of my pastime of inciting her to display her plumage, so to speak. It really was too much. What in the world could she mean? Was it a form of shyness, of dull wit? an attempt to upset my too tranquil pleasure in her till it became something more biting? Was she not really trying to defend herself, to break down my guard—to have me take her—more seriously than I desired? I thought of all the reasons but decided finally that I didn't give a damn for them anyway. Beautiful as she was—and often a passionate mistress—I was growing bored.

So one day when she had started again on her favorite theme I halted her rather abruptly. Let me tell you a story, I said.

She made no reply but sat up a little straighter, her full lips pressed firmly together, and looked me square in the eye.

I have been down in the meadows on an inspection trip today, I told her, and while I was there one of the foremen of our ditching gang pointed out a hut to me. It is his own but he has rented it to three men who live there the year round, except in the cold of winter, when they board in Jersey City, he told me.

There are three of them, young fellows who earn their living there in that desolate spot, can you imagine how? In the late fall they begin to gather the down from the dry cattails which they pack into bags and sell as stuffing for cheap furniture. Later they trap muskrats. There are many of these rodents still in the swamps, and do you know what a muskrat skin brings? A dollar and a half for a good one sometimes. And in the spring and summer they pick blueberries.

But what has this to do with me? Francie asked.

Do you not see? answered I. The men earn their living that way, they are independent, self-supporting. The three work together; when two are out the third prepares the meals. They even have a few dollars over sometimes for small pleasures. Then the three go off together, to Jersey City, to Hoboken or wherever it might be.

Yes, I suppose they go to a saloon and get drunk.

Oh, I suppose so, but at least they manage it very well together and have done so for several years.

Now this gave me an idea, I continued. What is it that causes all the trouble in this world? Property, of course. It is what we own, the thing that gives us our importance—as it seems—the thing that has been largely the monopoly of the male down through the centuries, the thing finally that has governed the vote. And the thing for which we go to war, the thing for which we fight, even to quarrels between lovers.

And my idea is this. Let the men get rid of their property. If the women want the vote, give it to them, give them all the votes there are to be had, give them the votes the men have had also. And at the same time give them all the property of the world. They are the ones who biologically need it most, they are the ones economically, reasonably who should have it. You have convinced me by your suffragist arguments that you are right.

Francie looked at me hard but said nothing, perhaps she already sensed my waning affections.

And then, I said, we should have a society something like this: The women, possessing all the land, all the means for acquiring industrial wealth, would live in cities scattered over the country, walled cities defended by whatever weapons or armaments happened to be the fashion and from which all men should be excluded.

Meanwhile the men would gather in herds about the woods and plains, like the buffalo who used to be seen from the train windows on the great plains in the middle of the last century. Divided into tribes the men would spend their time hunting, fishing and fighting as men used to do—with fists, with stones, clubs as they may desire—and no doubt they would be far happier than now.

Then once a year, at the proper times certain women of the cities would send out chosen emissaries, eunuchs perhaps, to treat with the tribes—then in the pink of condition, trained, hardened by their rigorous life out of doors—and those most able, most vigorous, most desirable would be admitted for the breeding.

At this Francie jumped to her feet, fire in her eyes and turning her back on me left the room. I quietly took up my hat, took out a cigarette and lit it and jumping into my roadster before the door turned quietly down the driveway and went my way. Perhaps as I went I saw a curtain slightly rustled in a window of the second floor, perhaps it was only my vanity that made me believe this.

Mind and Body

FOR OURSELVES are we not each of us the center of the universe? It must be so, it is so for me, she said. It has always been so. I am the only one in my family who has had the courage to live for himself. Naturally, she added, we know that the rest of the world exists, but what has that to do with ourselves? Because someone says Sigrid Undset is a great writer, what of it? I don't think so. I will not read her books. To me they are dull. I am not a musician but writing must have some music in it to be readable and she has no music. I hate her. That is what I think and that is what I say.

I know people think I am a nut. I was an epileptic as a child. I know I am a manic depressive. But doctors are mostly fools. I have been very sick. They say it is my imagination. What is that? I know when I am sick and I have seen them. I saw a woman the same type as myself. The day before she died she was excited, as I am now, she would talk with you, argue as well as I am doing now. And the next day she was dead.

I have pains here, in my stomach. It has been terrible. For nine days I have been stopped. I feel it in my heart, like a cramp. It must be something. How can they say it is my imagination? They don't know. They're fools. Last night I got desperate and I cured myself with some soapy water. But I was worried. Can you blame me? So my husband says, Go on out and see an honest man. I have only ten dollars in my pocket, but I would pay fifty, if I had it, to find out. What is the matter with me?

They always get mad at me because I manage to find out what they are thinking. I got hold of the chart and I saw that it said "Neo-plasm." I knew from my Greek what that meant, new growth. That means a tumor. But I don't think the Doc himself knew when he read the report.

He examined me a dozen times and his theory was (I could overhear him talking to his assistant): I try this and then if it doesn't work I try that, then I try something else. When something works that is the way I find out what is the matter with the patient. I knew from his questions that he wanted to give me the filthiest diseases. He put everything on me. I could taste the carbolic in my mouth, and the mercury. I know that he painted me with silver nitrate because I heard the assistant say, "My God what has she been doing to herself?" But it was he who did it. I got sick of him finally and went home.

And what do you think he said to me? He said that what I needed was a man. What do you think of that? I told him I had a man at home, and a very good one. What do you think I have, a cancer? I bleed every once in a while. Tell me what you think. I don't care if I die. Nothing frightens me. But I am tired of dealing with fools.

I ventured to ask her if she had tried Atropin and Luminal for her colitis. They're no good for me, she said. Everything works the opposite from what it does in anyone else. I take Atropin for a few days then it dries my mouth, makes me worse than I was before. Luminal does not quiet me, it keeps me awake. No, there is nothing in that, nothing in that.

Tell me more of the history, I said. You have been operated on?

Yes, eighteen years ago, they took out the appendix, they said it was all tied up with the right ovary. A doctor had examined me and said there was something wrong on the left side. When I was opened up they found nothing there at all. Perhaps it is that, perhaps it is the adhesions, bands that pull sometimes. Anyhow it is not imagination.

I knew the story of her past. Her father had been a Norwegian sea captain, one of the better known of the old sailing families, powerful physique, a man who would be away for months, seldom at home. Her mother, also a Norse woman, had been frail, dying when Ingrid and her sister and two brothers were still children. On the father's side there had been several who had spent their last days in an asylum.

I am compensating for my childhood now, she continued. I do not believe in being repressed. I am the only one of my family that lets go. If I tire you, you must forgive me. When I have talked it out I feel better. I have to spit it out on someone. I do not believe in being good, in holding back. You're not too good, are you? People like that make me tired. Martyrs too, they're perverted, I detest them. I tell them they're the most selfish people on earth. Nobody wants them to be martyrs but themselves. They do it because it gives them pleasure. I say to them, all right, you are good. What does that mean? It means that goodness is its own reward. Don't expect to get paid for it. You have chosen that selfishly, just the same as I choose to do as I please. They are hypocrites if they want more. Everyone must choose for himself. Is it not so? I do not expect people to thank me if I do what I please.

She turned and said to my wife Emily who was sitting near her, your hair would look better if you took more care of it. You should do it. Look at my hair. Her hair was bobbed rather long and was of a reddish chestnut, a great flamelike mane which stood up almost flickeringly above her right ear. I think the hair can reflect the way we are. I can will my hair to be glossy and a better color. Of course you must brush it. But even if I am sick I can make it look well. I remember once I saw your mother, she turned again to Emily, and I saw she was not careful with herself, so I told her: You should take more care of your hair. You look like a servant girl.

People should speak out what is in their minds. Don't you think so? We should believe in ourselves. When I was confirmed in the Lutheran Church . . . How do you think I look?

Marvelous, I said, I never saw you looking better.

She laughed. It is because I do not worry. I am nervous, yes, but I do not worry. I simply want to know what is the matter with me. I have no inhibitions. That is why my face is smooth. In the hospital they were kidding me. They said, What is that girl doing here? They said I looked nineteen years old. And I do, sometimes.

It was true. I knew she was in her forties, but she looked clear-eyed, her complexion was ruddy, her skin smooth. Her bearing was alert, her movements perhaps too quick but not pathological.

People should speak out what is in their minds. Don't you think so? We should believe in ourselves. It took me a long time to learn that. It first came to me in college. My mother always wanted us to learn, to get up in the world.

She had won a scholarship from a Brooklyn high school to Cornell where she had majored in Latin, Greek and Logic, and again won a fellowship in Logic. The instructors retreated in disorder before her attacks till she quit the game and, needing money, went to teach Latin in a high school from which, after a month, she ran away. The slowness of the pupils drove her mad. From there she went to a New York business school, graduated in no time and became private secretary to one of New York's leading merchants—managing his affairs single handed when he was absent, a huge organization, a lieutenant in whom he had implicit confidence till he died.

What is book learning? she went on. Nothing at all. College ruins everything that is original in the young. It comes just in their formative years and if they have anything original in them by teaching them to copy, copy, copy, we ruin it all.

It may be true for some, I broke in, but to me it is the attitude which is taken toward it that counts. To me, what I intend for my boys, if they wish to go, is that it is a ticket. If they go in there, without reverence for the knowledge of their instructors but take it all just as a means for something which they need, I don't think it will hurt them.

Maybe you are right, she agreed, it is the attitude—if they can take it properly—which counts. But I ate it up out of books. Finally it turned me cold. Those men know nothing at all. It is life, what we see and decide for ourselves, that counts.

When I was confirmed in the Lutheran Church—to please my mother—when I was learning the catechism, I asked the preacher if I had to believe everything he said was true. And if I didn't believe it would I go to Hell? And if all the others in the other churches would go to Hell because they didn't believe it? For that was something that I didn't believe at all. All the others say the same thing to their people. How ridiculous that is? I told him.

He was shocked, she went on, and told me it was wicked for me to talk that way. So I perjured myself and joined the church to please my mother.

It is all fear. When we were children my mother would lie on the bed and pray to God to spare us from the lightning. I thought that was ridiculous. I said to her, How foolish. If God wants to strike me down, is it for me to ask him to spare me? I never felt afraid. If I am hit, what of it?

But Yates is afraid. Yates is her husband. He does not like lightning.

That's odd, I commented. For I knew him to be a steady Catholic.

Yes, he is afraid of it.

Did you not become a Catholic when you married him? asked Emily.

Yes, I did, said she. Why not? This is the way I felt.
Yates was brought up by the Jesuits. His old father and
mother are still in Ireland. He offered to join my church but
I knew what that would mean. They might even say we
were not married at all, and I knew how that would hurt
his family.

Yates, she had met, incredibly, in an asylum where she
had been confined after her breakdown. She had gone there
of her own will to be cured and there she had decided to
remain, to become a nurse to attend the insane. She thought
that her life work at the time. And there she had encountered little, lame Yates, the gentle-voiced and kindly nurse
—employed in the care of male patients, as she was in the
care of females. It had been a most happy marriage, she
with her erratic voluble disposition, he with his placid mind.

What should I do? she continued. I saw that he was not
the kind to question himself intimately.

How is he? asked Emily who greatly admired the little
Irishman. Why didn't you bring him out with you today?

Oh, I told him I didn't need him, said she. After last
night when I thought I was going to die I felt so much
better today that I told him I wanted to come alone. He's
working and I didn't want to take him away from his work.
What was I saying, oh yes, she continued, you remember
what Caesar says in his Commentaries about the barbarians.
It is better for them to have their barbaric worship than no
religion at all. Let them cling to it.

Yes, what was the use of my asking him to give up his
religion? He believes in his dogma and it is a comfort to
him. He feels a part of it. That is what makes the Irish
whole as a nation, their religion. They feel something solid
under their feet and so they have courage to go ahead.

Like the Jews, I said.

Yes, exactly. It is their religion. So I said to myself, to
keep that for him I won't ask him to join my church but
I will join his. He has that and his nursing and it makes him

happy. If I take that away what could I give him in return? He would be lost. When I was talking to the Jesuit, who came to teach me what the church meant, I told him I could not believe that. He said, I should. I asked him, Do you? But he did not answer me.

And I'm a little superstitious too, she went on. When I was in the hospital I stopped breathing. I said to myself, Why go on any more? Next time my breath stops I will not breathe again and then it will be done. I didn't care. They asked me where I wanted to be sent. At first I didn't know what they meant. Then I caught it. They meant after I was dead. So I gave them all the details.

But Yates got nervous, so without telling me anything about it he had the priest come up to me to give me the sacrament. I was surprised but, I tell you something came over me and I felt happy. I felt that I wanted to live. I do not believe all the stuff they tell you. But I must say that I was glad.

Yes, I agree with you, it is a comfort, no doubt. But what about Socrates? He took the cup quietly—without religion.

Oh, you have read that too, she said and seemed pleased.

Yes, I went on. It is good to feel a solidarity with a group but do not forget that that kindly old priest by telling you that there is just one way to be saved, by excluding all the other people of the earth represents a cruelty of the most inhuman sort. For myself, I went on, if I were dying in Africa and the chief of the tribe who was my friend asked the chief medicine man to do a ceremonial dance for me, with beating of tom toms to conduct me into the other world, I should feel a real comfort which I believe would be a greater solace to me than the formula of some kindly priest.

I suppose so, she added, but it is the same: Someone to tell our troubles to is what we need. I suppose I bore you with all I am saying today but I must talk. You must think

I'm crazy. When I go away for two or three days Nuffie stays in my chair till I come back.

What is that? I said.

She laughed. Nuffie is my little dog. It is a Spaniel. She stays in my chair till I come home. Would you believe it, when I have bronchitis or anything she will come up to me and smell around my chest until she finds the place where I have a pain. Then she will lick that place and the pain goes right away.

I laughed.

You don't believe it, but it is true.

You mean she can smell a pain?

Well, I don't know. Dogs have a special sense. I think they know more than we do at times. Anyhow it is so. Perhaps she hears the little râles, with her sharp ears. You do not believe me, do you?

How can I doubt you? I said.

I believe in such things as second sight, said she. Sometimes I quarrel with my sister. And the dog does not like that. She goes away. We both have hard heads. We take opposite sides and neither one wants to give in. But this time Nuffie went to my sister and consoled her first. I was furious. So I stopped talking. I thought if Nuffie did that she was right. And then she came over to console me. But she went to my sister first. I said no more.

Yes, I believe in second sight. You know how I am. I say what is in my mind and people don't like that. So I had a quarrel with my brother-in-law. We didn't speak to each other for a year. Then one day I saw a tall fellow carrying two cans of paint on the street and I knew it was he. I went past him and we did not say anything to each other. But when I got past I turned around and so did he. We each did that three times. But we did not speak. It scared me. I said to myself, he is going to die and he is calling me to go with him. Would you believe that?

He was perfectly well, mind you, but that is what I

thought. Then within a month he caught pneumonia and he sent for me. I was so glad to have a chance to talk to him and to comfort him. I saw at once that he was a dead man but my sister could not see it. She cannot see those things in people's faces. She thought he was going to get well. He asked me what I thought about it, and I could see that it exhausted him even to talk that much. But I said of course he would recover; to rest and it would be all right. I had to say that and I could see that he was easier. But he died next day. I was frightened then, perhaps that is what is the matter with me now. My parents died at forty-five and fifty-two. Add them together and divide by two and you will get the age at which you yourself will die. That is this year. Don't you think you'd better go upstairs and get your clothes off if you want me to examine you? I asked her.

Yes, she said, it's getting late. I know I'm an awful nuisance. Where shall I go? In the office? Upstairs. All right. You won't see anything much, she added, with a wry face. I am nothing at all now. Just like a man. My legs are hairy like my husband's. I have often wondered what sex I am, she laughed. I used to wonder as a child with my flat chest and my narrow hips if I was not more a man than a woman. I am sure I am more a man than Yates is, she commented.

Yes, I put in, aren't we all more or less that way— fortunately.

Certainly it is so.

Perhaps your trouble is that you need some woman to love.

I have always loved women more than men, she agreed. Always. It amuses me. In the hospital the nurses used to kid me. They used to say, Look out for her, she's that way. I enjoyed it.

When she was lying on the bed half-bared she spoke again of her physique:

I have no lung trouble, of that I am sure for I have a

good chest like my father. But I have nothing else to show you to thrill you. When I was being examined the old fool of a doctor—it is always an old man who thinks you are trying to flirt with him—the young ones know better. The old fool tried to tickle me. I felt nothing at all. I asked him what he was trying to do, so he stopped.

I carefully palpated her abdomen but could find nothing at all. Truly she was built like a man, narrow hips, broad deep chest and barely any breasts to speak of. Her heart action was even and regular. Only flushed cheeks, the suggestively maniacal eyes, the quiver of the small muscles of the face, her trembling fingers told her stress. She awaited my verdict with silence at last. I could find nothing.

Yes, she said, only two men have found the exact spot. And she pointed to a place in her right iliac quadrant. One was a young doctor at the Post Graduate Hospital who has become famous since then, and another was the surgeon who operated on me the first time. The rest just feel around the abdomen as you have done.

But do not forget, I said in my own defense, that there is a place in the abdomen in major hysteria which if it is pressed upon will definitely bring on a convulsive attack.

She looked at me with interest.

Yes, the Greeks connected it with those organs. That is its name. Perhaps I should have everything cut out.

Not on your life, I told her.

No, I believe that too. I don't want any more operations. So you do not think I have a cancer.

Not from the evidence I have found so far. If I could see the X-rays I might have a different opinion, but I do not think so. From what you say and the length of time that the symptoms have been going on, the fact that you have not lost weight, that you are ruddy and well—I believe that you are suffering merely—but that is quite enough—from what Llwelyn C. Barker calls—I have forgotten the term—what we used to call mucous colitis. It is a spasm of the large intestine which simulates all sorts of illnesses for which people are frequently operated on.

I left the room while she dressed. While I was away she told my wife: I want to live because I have found my place in life. I am a housekeeper. I have my husband and my work to do and that is my world. I have found, she added, that we must live for others, that we are not alone in the world and we cannot live alone.

To me she said when I had taken her to the bus and we were waiting: Well, you haven't told me what is the matter with me. What is it? Don't tell me I am nervous.

There has never been an anatomic basis discovered for an opinion in cases like yours, I said, until recently. Apparently the cause was laid down in the germ plasm when you were created.

Yes, my family history is bad, she agreed. They were an old family, run down. Yes, I come from an old family. I should have married a robust type. But my inferiority complex would not let me. I did not take up when I had the chance. I didn't have the nerve. Instead I looked for someone that I could mother, someone to take care of. That is how I took to Yates, he needed me so much. I wonder what was the matter with him. He didn't walk till he was twelve with his big head and little legs.

The anatomic basis for your condition, I continued, seems to have been detected in a new study called capillaroscopy, a study of the microscopic terminal blood vessels. In people of your type these terminal loops between the arteries and the veins are long and gracile. They are frail, expand and contract easily, it is the cause of all the unstable nervous phenomena which you see.

Yes, I can feel it often, she agreed. The blood goes into my face or into my brain. I often want to run or scream out, it is so hard for me to stand it.

Others have short more or less inert loops. Those are the lethargic types, the stable, even dispositions.

Here's the bus, she cried out. Good-bye. And she grasped the tips of my fingers in her hurry to be gone.

Good-bye, I called after her. Bring Yates with you next time. Remember me to him. Good-bye, good-bye.

The Colored Girls of Passenack—Old and New

GEORGIE ANDERSON came to our house in 1895 or there-abouts when my brother and I were from ten to twelve years of age. She cannot have been more than eighteen her-self, a strong, slim girl for whom both of us had the greatest admiration. She was full of fun, loved rough-house games and told stories to us of her life down south before she came up to work in the vicinity of New York City.

Left-handed, she could stand in our back yard and peg a stone into the top of a big chestnut tree two houses below us along the street. We ourselves could just about reach its middle.

Georgie was black. Sometimes they'd send her up a mess of chincopins, which she said grew on bushes down in Carolina. We were much impressed.

I can still remember how in the evenings we'd rush to get through supper and pile into the kitchen where she and Adolph, her attentive admirer, would be sitting. We couldn't get there fast enough for the talk and the fun.

My father's half-brother, Godwin, enjoyed Georgie also—but he was more bent on teasing her than anything else. He was a little queer in the head so the spooks of which he was continuously talking became very real to him and to us all finally. But Georgie professed not to believe in such trifles. Godwin however enjoyed his game and kept at it for weeks, giving many accounts of his prowess in the spirit world.

There was an alarm clock among other things on a little shelf over the range in our kitchen. Godwin, once after supper when we were all sitting there, told Georgie he felt a spirit very strongly within him that night. He'd shake his head and make a growling sound in his throat telling us all that it was the spook trying to get hold of him. Georgie kept saying, Aw gwan, as usual, but we were all intently watching my uncle. The gas flare was as bright as always when suddenly my uncle looked fixedly at the clock on the shelf. Do you see that clock? he said to Georgie. Yes, she answered, I sees it. Well, if I tell that clock to jump off the shelf, said my uncle, it will do so. Gwan, said Georgie, let's see you do it. Do you want me to make the clock jump off the shelf? said my uncle. Yes, that's jus' what I want, said Georgie. At that my uncle made a few passes with his hand and talked to the clock while all our eyes were fastened on it with vivid fascination. He kept talking slowly then at the end loudly and firmly he said to the clock, Jump! And as he raised his hands the clock leaped into the air and landed with a crash at our feet. Georgie let out a wild yell and fled through the back door into the dark. My brother and I, though mystified were not quite convinced but struggled heroically between laughter and amazement. My father came into the room at the crash and gave Godwin a disgusted call-down after telling him he would have to pay for the clock. He had had a black thread tied from one of its feet around his right wrist.

Georgie was wild as a cat. More than once she would return at dawn from a night out and climb the grape arbor onto the rear roof so as to gain access through the bathroom window to the attic stairs and her room.

She liked my father, who knew colored people from his West Indian days, but she had a holy respect for him. He didn't say much to her but when he did you could see she felt it. One day when she was late with breakfast as usual, as she came into the room he turned to her and said, Come on, you Virginia Creeper, get a move on you. That mortally offended Georgie. No sir, she didn't mind being cussed but no man was going to call her no Virginia Creeper. What associations the term had in her mind I could never imagine.

Girls were paid twelve dollars a month in those days. God knows they didn't deserve more. Georgie was a vile cook and a sloppy washwoman but I imagine even my parents rather forgave her her worthlessness for the sheer vitality and animal attractiveness there was in her. She had a queer trick too which my father caught her at one day. She seems to have belonged to a religious group known as "Clay Eaters" back home. He went down in the cellar and found her eating a little heap of earth which she had gathered for herself. He asked her what she was doing. She told him quite simply that she was eating dirt, that the Bible said we all had to eat a peck of dirt in our day and that she was eating hers little by little now.

Naturally she was to us boys like the rest of femininity, a source of sexual curiosity. For myself I know I desired nothing on this earth as I did a sight, a mere sight of a naked female. I even prayed at night for knowledge of the sort. I begged it of God, I pleaded, I promised all sorts of virtuous abstinences if only I could clap my eyes upon a girl naked before me. My wish went no further at that time, save perhaps that I might talk to her, stroke her, and so make her understand my desire.

Some of the boys at school were more daring, however. One day we had two of that sort in the attic. It was a rainy day, we had been playing tops, slamming them down hard on the attic floor.

I remember the names of the two ring leaders: Willie Harris and Joe Hedges. No doubt we had been swapping smutty cracks of one sort or another when we heard Georgie come up and go into her room. This room was made of heavy canvas only which my father had calsomined on the inside. It was our servant girl's room. Here was our chance!

As it happened Georgie had come up to give herself a bath. She knew we were there, she even spoke to us while we were up to our smart trick. I think she surely saw each eye clapped to the hole in turn but she went on with what she was doing just the same. I remember my own turn at the peep hole as if it were this morning. I suppose Georgie was the first woman I ever saw naked—the first young woman anyway. She had nothing but a china basin to wash herself in. This she had placed on the floor. She was standing in it, facing me fully naked washing herself down with a sponge. My view was not too good, I was half lying on the floor with the others pulling at me to take their turn also but it was a thrilling picture.

I remember one other colored woman, many years later, who had come to my office for a pretended examination, stripped herself naked before me. She was built in the style of Goya's *Maja Desnuda*, but her laughter and gestures were pure Africa. Mable Watts, her name was. She cared little for her own race due to the great success she had had with white men about town. She liked me and I liked and admired her, having cared for her many years through the greatest misfortunes. She would tell me "everything," always coming to me for advice and assistance when she was in trouble. She must have had a magnificent constitution, for in spite of the most harrowing experiences she never seemed to grow older or to lose her flashing smile and good nature. My wife too admired her for her intelligence and ability as a maid. Her service at table was a delight, her washing which she did like lightning, was perfect in every way. But she knew too much—and, well, she just wasn't wanted around too long where men were likely to be.

But she wasn't fresh. She offered and when refused laughed it off without a word. Why don't you go on the stage, Mable? I said to her. No, I don't want to end up in a ditch with a knife in my back, was her reply, and anyhow it's too much work.

I delivered her of her two children, a boy and a girl. She lived in a little clean house down near the railroad. Her husband left her after that and she took in a boarder who gave her a venereal disease. I had her operated on for that and after she was well she took another boarder who, I am certain, strangled and killed her small daughter—who, he said, had had a convulsion while he was alone with her.

Mable quit her place then and took a job in the house of a friend of mine, sending her boy to charity school in the southern part of the state. She paid for his keep there, sent him presents and visited him occasionally, especially when he would be ill. Meanwhile when my friend's wife went west with her own two children Mable kept house for him. He didn't want her to leave when the wife came back but Mable thought it better that she go—I agreed with her and it was so ordered.

It took her a long time to get her divorce from the man who had run away but finally she succeeded in paying a lawyer the two hundred necessary. She worked hard all the time and kept herself immaculate on the street, her aprons were like snow, her dresses, usually black, were well cut. While on her hair, which she dressed not as they do today, all slicked down, but up, in some peculiar high and convoluted fashion, she would place a maid's cap, pure white and crisply starched.

Everybody knew her and liked her. She was always independent, always smiling, an individual by herself never in the least embarrassed or subservient in her manner. Yet never pushing or insolent. She'd stop the policemen and talk with them but when passing older and more decorous citizens whom she knew, she was serious and respectful.

She told me many times of being picked up by fellows in cars or on motorcycles and taken for a ride but she always had the fear of being stuck in the back with a knife or landing in a ditch, so this game didn't attract her overly.

She married a colored minister at least ten years older than herself finally, but I don't think she has stuck it out with him. She doesn't seem to have grown a day older

during the past eighteen years—though she is a bit heavier—
as she told me recently.

The colored girls of today have learned the trick of dress
very ably. It's curious that in one generation they changed
so much, but their very bodies don't seem what they were
when I was a child. Perhaps it's the way they dress but I
don't think so. Many of them have exceptionally fine
features. And the vivacity, the awareness in their manner
is like nothing the white can offer. The American white
girl today is shopworn compared to the Negress—at her
liveliest. All the simplicity of mind which "virtue" should
imply lies with the Negress. It is not easy to give accurate
values to what I am attempting.

Put it this way: about New York City the old-fashioned
Negress is gone—or almost gone. In her place we have the
wives and children of employed men who own their own
houses, often keenly intelligent individuals who live entirely
apart from the rest of us. The release which the taboo
against the race induces comes out sometimes in the faces of
the young girls as a princely and delicate beauty—which
with the manner of their walk, the muscular quality of their
contours, the firmness—makes most white girls clumsy,
awkward, cheap beside them. There is nothing much in the
depths of most white girls' eyes. Colored girls—a few of
them—seem a racial confessional of beauty lost today elsewhere.

I've seen tremendous furnaces of emotional power in certain colored women, unmatched in any white—outside,
perhaps, the devotional females who make up "society," and
whose decadent fervors are so little understood. There, in
the heat of "entertainments," of pleasure perhaps, the
Negress can be matched. Perhaps the fervent type is more
accessible in the colored race because it is not removed to
socially restricted areas. I don't know. But I do know that
I have had my breath taken away by sights of colored
women that no white woman has equalled for me.

Once I went to call on a patient in a nearby suburb. As the door opened to my ring a magnificent bronze figure stood before me. She said not a word but stood there till I told her who I was, then she let me in, turned her back and walked into the kitchen. But the force of her—something; her mental alertness coupled with her erectness, muscular power, youth, seriousness—her actuality—made me want to create a new race on the spot. I had never seen anything like it. I asked the lady of the house some time later what had become of the girl. Oh, she said, she was a married woman. Her husband was a smart caterer. They got mixed up with the law somehow, bootlegging, I suppose, and had to beat it. I once caught her with her hand right in my purse. When I spoke to her she merely closed the purse and handed it to me as if nothing had happened. There was nothing more said about it.

A wide-eyed, alert girl who worked for us a short time this year—another magnificent physical specimen, had recently obtained a divorce from her husband. Oh, there are too many girls after him, she told my wife. He don't have to work. She had a baby which she was boarding with a neighbor when she went out in the morning.

She told of having worked in a Chinese laundry during the past year. The Chinese had several of these girls ironing in the front of the shop behind the window facing the street. All they did was iron the shirt fronts and sleeves, the Chinese themselves did the cuffs and collars.

But this man began to make advances to her—so that she had to leave the shop one day and send her husband to collect her back pay, which he did. She said one of her friends who had worked in the same shop had been taken ill once and that the Chinese had taken her in a cab to New York to the hospital—and that was the last they ever saw of her.

One of my patients told me that her laundress—herself a young colored woman—told her that if any colored girl in

Passenack sixteen years of age or over said she was a virgin you could put her down for a liar. One day this same colored laundress told my friend in the middle of the morning that she had to go home. But you can't do that, Julia, said my friend to her. Why, the work isn't finished. I'm sorry, Mrs. R., but I gotta go, replied the laundress, I just had a hunch that my husband ain't alone in bed the way I left him this morning.

So the woman went away—nothing could stop her—and in a couple of hours she returned. Well, said my friend, did your hunch work out the way you thought it would? Yes, just the way I thought, said the laundress. I knew he was lying to me. What happened? asked my friend. Oh, nothin' special. When I got there he was sitting on the edge of the bed with one of those girls down there I was tellin' you about. He said they weren't doing nothing but I know better.

And what did the girl do when you arrived? asked my friend.

She? She didn't do nothing, said the laundress. She just set there. I told her to git on out of my house but she just laughed at me.

What? and is she still there?

Yes, ma'am. You don't know them young colored women. They're all banded together. What they likes best is the married men, the young married men mostly and they all sticks together and if we married women gets in their way they don't stop at nothing. That's what ruins husbands, when a lot a young girls just keep 'em for their pleasure.

A Descendant of Kings

His MOTHER died following his birth and he was reared—
or yanked up, as they say—by his paternal grandmother, a
big-boned Englishwoman with a violent hatred for money
and its effects, though she held onto it fast enough when she
got it. And the old girl needed money badly for the ideas
she had in the back of her head. Her offspring were "gentlemen."

The boy Stuart's father was a real gentleman right
enough and of the old school, charming but useless. If his
wife had lived, things might have been different for Stewie,
for she was Scotch and able. Anyhow she endowed the boy
with the frame of a bull and that was all she had time to do
for him.

They lived in an eastern city. But that was just the
going-to-school-place where Mr. Worthen, the father, had
his job of the moment in charge of the export department
of a wholesale drug house—since he did know Spanish and
had a nice way—*simpatico*—about him in dealing with
Spanish-speaking peoples.

But the real home of the boy was "the shore," a one-room
summer shack where the old lady used to take him in summer for the outdoor season, which was her own very life.
This "shore" was her veritable kingdom which she ruled
by every wile of which an aging person is capable. Here
she had her way, though God knows she had it almost
everywhere as far as her limited means would permit.

In this place though, means meant little and this she understood by instinct and fought to maintain. Here she was free,

free of neighbors, free of too great exertion from stairs. Life was cheap, so in a way she was free that way also. She had a garden, she herself tended it at first. There was no water: she got barrels (as they do in South America) and caught rain water in them for her purposes and God help anybody who said it was unfit to drink, full of mosquito larvae though it was from lack of proper cover.

But most of all, she had the sea, or really Long Island Sound—always before her, not twenty feet from her front door. This was the very breath of life to her. The sea! Already in April she would begin to grow restless in her city flat. She could not breathe. Her eyes would torment her. She would be lame. Then would come a clear, hot day and overnight she would be gone—to the shore to be cured till autumn came again—but at some cost to the boy.

They arrived at the shore. The place would be full of mice nests in all the chiffoniers and bureau drawers. Leaks would have the beds ruined. The rain barrels would be gone, smashed, the grass rank, the garden overgrown. But now she would begin to live. She could breathe again, as she would say. She was her own mistress. And with her would come the small boy Stewie. Every year this would happen, it was his life, too. It was the life of an animal, or a gypsy following the seasons.

But there was one serious drawback against which the rest of the family fought in vain. When the old lady would leave the city at the break of spring, as the boy grew older, he would have to be taken out of school, before the term had been completed, and in the fall he would come in again a month or two later than the rest. As he was not a brilliant scholar this was fatal to his chances for advancement.

No use arguing though, no use complaining or sending notes, the old lady would not be swayed from her habit and purposes. Let the teachers rave as they might she was back at them with an obdurate, cold fury that almost knocked them backwards out the door. They were no match for her and she would win, every time, as far as she personally was concerned. What good was school anyway? Outdoors was best. The boy was young and the air would do him more good than all the teaching in the world.

And she was right, too, in a way. But the school had to have its revenge. This consisted in making the boy take his work over again each fall. First it would be a half year. Then a year until he dropped hopelessly behind and finally when he was sixteen he stopped entirely without completing the eighth grade. But he got to know the water like a seal. He could dive and swim, sail a boat or take a canoe out into the waves in the manner of a veteran.

But what is he going to do with himself? People asked the old lady. To this, as to everything else which she didn't want to talk about, she answered by changing the subject. Once she had tried it in winter—stuffing the cracks with newspapers and sending the boy to school there, but it had been cold. She almost died of pneumonia.

All right, so be it: The boy continued to grow, and having slipped back so far in school—finding himself supported in reasonable comfort by the fates and his uncle, he devoted himself to what was at hand without worry.

He was just seventeen when the United States entered the war, but he jumped into the Navy for all that, by the aid of a few judicious lies, and was sent out to the Great Lakes Training Station. There he dug trenches for sewer pipes and washed corpses in the morgue during the influenza epidemic. A hot job for a gob and that was all he got out of it. Except he fell off a bridge into a small stream once and the truck landed on top of him, more or less, so that only his nose stuck above water. It took them half an hour to get him out. Not so bad for a young fella', what? is all that cost him.

And also he met a girl. It was a romantic affair. His first real passion. God, how he loved that girl! She was of a good

Chicago family and Stewie's mind for the first time perhaps took an inward turn.

Up to that moment, he had gone on like a straw on the stream of the old lady's will, but this was different. In his nobby sailor's outfit, with the thrill the girls got out of that sort of thing during the war anyway, things were going fine. She met him at canteen dances, she even invited him out to her house—and a swell house at that. Boy, he thought he was made.

By this time, Stewie was fully grown, and physically a splendid specimen. He was a gay kid, too, could dance like a breeze, the music just played around his strong legs like summer lightning. His eyes were blue, his cheeks ruddy, he was always singing, laughing—a regular careless kid. He had found a girl and the iron had been plunged in.

But when the war was over, so was that. The girl gave him her picture and told him to come out to see her some-time. And he came back home and began to think it over. It didn't take much thinking to realize what had taken place. When he looked at the old lady fussing over the oil heater in the tiny kitchen, frying this, messing with that; when he even looked at his own clothes, his shoes, his shorts—and realized that he hadn't a nickel to his name and no way to earn it, it came over him with compelling force why the girl had turned him down. That wasn't the worst. What the hell did he know? He knew nothing at all.

The worst was that he felt humiliated. Who the hell was he? Just a nut. Couldn't do anything, didn't know anything, had nothing. He had no background, no place even to live in that you could call a home. That's why she had dished him. And how he had counted on her. How he had counted on her! For a while he had thought he was made. Ha, ha.

Maybe some fellows would have busted out and taken a job anywhere, anyhow. Not he. He stripped off his clothes, hopped into a pair of trunks and went for a swim. The salt water was good, the sun was better. He had a body, nobody could deny that. He had a body.

It was building up quite a bit along the shore in those days. Little places, for the summer, were coming closer and closer. The city was extending the gas mains down along Ocean Avenue to the old lady's original shack. Water was on the way and as a consequence there were more people around those parts than formerly.

In the old days Stewie and his older cousins, when they would be there in the summer, would jump out of bed in the morning, run across the grass to the shore, and hop into the water naked, for that sort of swim only possible when the bare body seems to hang in icy space relieved of its weight, caressed, floating . . .

But now it was different. Especially was it different with respect to girls. The shore was full of them, of all ages, girls and women, unattached, married and unmarried. The old lady at first fought them off. For she had a tongue that could cut with a knife's edge. As a consequence they still remained fairly much alone.

Stewie, however, had kept on growing and pretty soon the "pots" began to get past the old lady's guard. One especially, with her gentle voice and helpful winning ways, succeeded more than the rest in penetrating into this lioness' den. She was older than Stewie, had rather a hard, good-looking face and still boasted of a lean straight figure which had won her a position as a model to several commercial artists in New York City. This and her frizzly blonde hair which she wore about her head as a halo made her something to look at.

And she was gently sophisticated.

Stewie fell for her like a meteor. She had everything. She soothed him too and she knew the world. She understood his needs and she had courage, the bodily courage lacking too often in women. He admired her and finally he loved her.

It was at this time that Stewie came to realize that women were his all in life. He knew it was an old story but for him, sunk as he felt himself, with only the blue sky and the blue sea as his own, he knew that only from a woman could he get the courage to pick himself up and go on.

And Muriel was the girl of girls.

For the moment he gave himself up to unadulterated joy.

In the fall he planned to get work, at anything he could find, to make good. But for the present, yum, yum. He was with Muriel morning, noon and night. Days and long ecstatic nights with her, the two of them, lying in a hammock, on a porch bench, on the sand, anywhere at all; Muriel was game for everything and Stewie satisfied her to the full, repeatedly, continually. That and the ocean were his bread and wine—filled his mind and his days. It was an idyllic—or bestial—existence as one may choose to consider it.

Stewie worked that winter, and the next summer things continued as before, a round of unabated pleasure, the boy's mind was heated to a rosy glow which he veritably saw, day and night as he plugged hard at what work there was for him—though there was damn little for him to do, really.

Then, one day he caught Muriel with another man whom he knew. She just laughed.

Stewie was knocked out. Absolutely. It went down through him as though it had been a long bayonet extinguishing every living spark in his whole body. He just stood and looked. Then he turned, walked off and went for a swim.

But in the night it started to get him really. He saw it as clearly, as distinctly as through his open doors he saw the stars measuring his fate in the fleckless sky. He knew the boy she had fallen for, he was a Yale grad, an engineer. Give the girl credit. But he was sinking, sinking into fathomless space with wide open eyes. She had hit him hard where he was weakest. Motherless, in woman his world all lay, and woman had cut the world from under him, he was sinking into the night. It was awful.

He brooded and began to lose weight. When it was time to return to the city for the winter, he refused to go. Plead with him as she might, this time the old lady was beaten, she had to go and leave him. What was he going to do? How did he know? Where was he going to stay when it got cold? Who the hell's business was that? What would he eat? Beans and bananas, chewing gum, caviar and roast duck. With that she left him. And later on it grew cold.

Stewie stuck it out. He did odd jobs around the more permanent places at the shore, where people stayed into the cold weather, and got enough for the eats that way for awhile. Then when these people left—well, he just didn't know how he got grub enough. He would live on a can of cold beans for two or three days sometimes. Then someone would invite him up to the house here and there as they heard about him and so it went on till after Christmas.

Meanwhile, he had somehow got hold of a ukelele which one of the summer people had given him when they returned to the city. He had long, powerful fingers and a great sense of rhythm, so for lack of anything else to do all the autumn days and evenings he strummed the uke. He'd strum by the hour there at the deserted shore all by himself in that cold room; he'd read cheap magazines, eat once or twice a day, strum some more, sleep in his clothes till noon, get up, strum some more, and when it grew very cold, never open the door of the shack for days at a time.

How he kept from going batty is ascribable to nothing but his youth and natural vigor. How much of the old lady was in him and stood by him now it cannot be stated but he stayed on just the same. What else was there to do?

But as the temperature got down to zero, real suffering began. Now he was in danger. The wind howled about his ears, the little summer shack seemed about to leave its moorings to be blown finally into the sea and be lost forever. He wished it would. He stuffed newspapers in all the cracks, the place seemed little else than cracks after the first bitter gale. Now he did not get out of bed at all but, using a folded newspaper, he would gather it together when necessity compelled and opening the door a moment, fling the wad of it as far as he could out into the snow.

He knew only one thing, there was no reason for moving, he saw nothing at all, he had no desires, no aims—he stood still not even waiting, he merely stood still.

Then a Jew lawyer he had known, living about half a mile back along the road, came down to the shack one day and took the boy up to his house with him. The man couldn't believe that the boy was still actually there when someone had mentioned it. But being convinced of the truth of the thing, he came and acted. Stewie was, for the moment, saved. Mr. Stone gave him a room, food and a job taking care of his furnace. So there Stewie remained for February and part of March—and still he strummed his uke.

But with the advent of good weather he was off once more to the shore.

To sum it up, he had come through. And he had come through with the mastery of the ukelele to his credit. And now he made it pay.

The first effect was upon the girls and women. By now Stewie was a husky young man and he had not been embittered by his privations of the winter just gone, the effect of those hard times being only to make him lustier and more heart free than ever—or so it seemed. He played his uke, he grabbed off a guitar for himself somewhere, he soon had a second-hand banjo to his credit, and in no time he had them all rippling under his fingers, like leaves on a sunny day.

Boy, how the girls flocked round now for this third act. Stewie got a job in a hotel orchestra nearby. Now you couldn't hold him. Let the old lady call him as much as she pleased. He was gone. Work! No, suh! Not Stewie. Not from that time on. He couldn't soil his hands, he had a career before him and try and stop him.

The girls almost pulled him apart. He had a room of his own back of the main shack now and his door was open day and night, figuratively and literally. He'd been hurt, but the sex was paying back its injuries as warm rain heals the injuries of the snow. I don't think it would be possible to exaggerate the number of girls of all ages that prostrated themselves before, about and beside Stewie in those years. He had them all. And also he still had everything. A magnificent physique, skill to dance, swim, sing and nothing in the world to worry about. Let them come. And they came, a hundred or more as time went by.

Virgins from the age of nine up to women with families whose husbands were away at the office—he knew them all. One girl in particular he admired and wanted to marry. She was a teacher in a public school in Boston who was summering there. They went everywhere together, did everything together. They spent hours swimming and wandering in the woods together where he made a number of nude photographic studies of her in all positions. He admired this sort of thing expertly.

Then she, too, double-crossed him. And this time something went wrong with Stewie. The women pursued him as always, one chased him with a lighted cigarette to enliven him, both running naked into the dark with yells and shrieks half of terror and laughter. But it was no go. He was of no use to them further. Or only occasionally with long intervals of rest between.

He went to leading specialists. They said he was all right—that it was quite usual for big husky guys, Australians many of them for some reason, to get that way. He did what they told him. It did no good.

Again there came a girl. He told her how it was. She was game and they went out into the woods together for a long walk. Failure.

On the way back they were passing down a lane which was full of cows returning from pasture. In the midst of them Stewie knew there was a bull, but he thought the beast would be quiet so he told the girl to keep ahead of him and to run for the fence lower down in the enclosure if anything should begin to happen.

After they had gone a short distance toward this objective the bull lifted his head and looked at them. Stewie was watching him and told the girl to go on faster, he would stand where he was awhile. The girl started to move and at the same time the bull came forward a few paces. He was dehorned and had a ring in his nose but he looked ugly.

Hurry, said Stewie to the girl. With that, she began to run, got safely to the fence and began to climb over. Stewie turned from the bull to look. At that moment, the animal struck.

With the first impact he knocked the man down and dislocated his right shoulder. As Stewie lay on the ground with the bull standing over him, his knee apparently on the man's chest and his wild eye not a foot away, slowly, with his left hand, Stewie tried to get a finger into the nosering. But the bull wrenched his head aside and as Stewie stood up, the animal caught him once more and threw him into the air eight feet onto a stone pile.

Again the animal closed and began to maul and worry the man, half tossing him, pounding him with his head, rolling and roughing him about generally. Stewie was sore and bleeding. He was hurt seriously but at last with greatest difficulty he got his fingers finally into the loose ring and with a wrench had the animal at his mercy. Slowly he got to his feet.

How, he doesn't know, but in the end Stewie took up a rock and drove the beast off, joined the girl and together they went to a nearby hospital where he was put on the operating table and his shoulder re-set.

A month later he could walk on his hands again as usual and got his job back in the theatre orchestra.

An ad in some Western health journal did him more good than anything else as far as his original infirmity was concerned. For he did get over it fairly well in the end though he was never again as able as he had been as a kid—naturally.

Pink and Blue

THE BANDLERS had had a good many men at Fernycrest since they bought the place ten years back. Most interesting specimens, some of them—if one may speak so of any human being—whose list would be a story in itself. They'd stay a month or two, sometimes perhaps six months, then quit or get themselves fired for one reason or another. George was the current incumbent of the job, George Tompkins, not a bad sort—in his way.

A splendid voice, good looking and a fine worker; the only thing was he liked the hard cider. That's the first thing he spoke of when he came there. He was willing to stay the winter but the cider barrel he wanted full up.

He was lonesome too after a while, lacking a woman. The story was that he'd been married several years before, lost his wife at the time of childbirth. But, in general, he was a good man and things were going along pretty well under his care.

Then one day after he had been on the place a month or so, he showed Mrs. Bandler the photograph of a woman— the smooth, round smiling face of a woman near thirty years of age as far as could be made out from the portrait.

What do you think of her?

Good looking, who is she?

I guess I'm going to marry her, said George.

What! said Mrs. B., and looked again at the picture which she held in her hand. It was an interesting, simple face with a direct noncommittal glance to it that was neither coquettish nor serious, a face—like the countryside, a country

69

woman dressed up to be photographed; that vague, place-
less look of our rural anonymities.

Well, George, she looks all right. Where did you get
her?

I haven't got her yet. That's just her photograph, said
George.

Lonesome, and with nothing else to do of an evening, he
had stumbled across one of those odd features sometimes
found in country newspapers, a "Cupid's Club," where those
inclined to matrimony might find their mates. He read there
an appeal, had answered it, and here he was with the
woman's photograph in his hand ready for the next step.
He liked the picture.

Mrs. Bandler thought quickly and decided to encourage
him. It might work out well.

A week later during a small afternoon bridge which she
was giving for several friends from the city, came a knock
at the house door. It was George. Looking past him, there,
standing in the middle of the front lawn, Mrs. Bandler saw
a figure. She gasped as George, with mingled pride and
embarrassment, told her who it was.

Yes, Ma'am, there she is.

Belle came forward, quite unabashed, a plump attractive
thing dressed all in pink from head to foot, hat, dress,
stockings, shoes, even her complexion touched up to match.
She was really a picture—a veritable azalea bush in blossom
though not quite so young as the photo might give one to
think. Yet she was attractive.

George, of course, was beside himself with the excitement
of pleasure anticipated. He waited upon Mrs. B's approval,
then seeing that she—tremendously amused, really—was not
antagonistic, he said: She just came down from Clinton
Springs so I could look her over. What do you think of her
now? he added in a lower voice.

Fine, said Mrs. Bandler.

That was enough for George. Belle and he made up their

minds on the spot to be married as soon as she could go back home, get her things together and come down again. And within a week, true to her promise, Belle was there, her few belongings at her side.

Mrs. B. who was fully alert to the dramatic possibilities of the situation had gone out of her way to heighten the effect. It was October by that time so she and her little colored maid decorated the parlor of the old farm with autumn leaves and wild flowers.

We had it real pretty, she told me afterward. Bessie was to be bridesmaid and Pa and I were to give the bride away. George had spoken to the minister and everything was arranged for that night.

So there they sat. Supper had been over for some time and George and Belle were all dressed up, waiting, the others along with them, the three witnesses.

The minister didn't come.

It got to be around ten o'clock. Finally George, who had been hitting the hard cider pretty freely during the afternoon, began to get mad and God damn the minister up and down. He got madder and madder but it did no good. After a while Mrs. Bandler suggested that something must have gone wrong and that they'd better wait till morning.

No Siree! not Belle. She had made up her mind to be married that night and that night she was going to be married.

So George and Pa got into the buggy and went down for the minister. He had missed the road earlier in the evening and failing to find the house had turned around and gone home to await developments, which was, after all, the sensible thing to do.

And George and Belle were married after all. That was that.

But the very day following the ceremony things began to happen. Belle's tall, lanky son along with her father, a decrepit old man, arrived and installed themselves on the newly wedded couple. Belle hadn't said a word of this to George; that was probably the reason she had been in such a sweat to get it over with the night before, knowing that they were on the way. But George was crazy about her by this time and took it all good-naturedly after the profanity of his first surprise.

Well, there they were.

The arrangement had its disturbing aspects, but Mrs. Bandler, looking forward to the winter, thought it at least tolerable. George, however, soon found things not so fully to his satisfaction. Belle, in the high dignity of her new position, set rapidly to work. She first laid in a complete stock of aluminum ware—on the installment plan—bought dishes, bedding, supplies of all sorts right and left far beyond George's ability to pay for them and finally, to cap the climax, had visiting cards printed for herself: Mrs. George Tompkins, At Home Wednesdays.

Well, when Mrs. Bandler saw that, she pursed her lips, nodded her head and said that that was fine. Belle was extremely proud of them.

So things went along; George stopped some of the credit at the stores; the lanky boy did a little work here and there and the old man just sat around.

As the weeks advanced, however, George began to grow suspicious of Belle. She was always writing letters—in a good hand, be it said, and on the neatest paper. But there was too often a little flurry when he entered the sitting room from outdoors, a feeling as of something having been hidden—or so George thought—and he didn't like it.

Who are you writing to? he had asked her several times.

Oh, people back home, was all she told him. But he grew more and more uneasy. Until finally one day when she had given several letters to her boy to take to the town and mail, George waylaid the kid and took them away from him to find out for himself what was going on.

And he got an eyeful. With the open letters in his hand,

he started for home muttering and cursing. Two of them had been of trifling interest but the third was something else again. It had been addressed to a man in the next village, a newcomer as George discovered later, who was certainly on terms of the greatest intimacy with his wife.

George was wild. He accused Belle of everything in the world, reasonable and unreasonable, beat her, threatened to throw her out of the place and then, crazy about her really, quieted down and took her to himself once more.

It seems that Belle had had a little house up in Clinton Springs, still had one, in fact, where she had lived for many years with her old father and the boy. It was from this place, following George's answer to her advertisement in the Cupid's Club, that she had written him. But the house was not her own; she had been a kept woman.

The lover, an oldish man, could not or would not marry her; whence, apparently, Belle's longing to have a proper "Mrs." applied to her name.

But this fellow, Favier, was not content to give the woman up so easily. When she had married George, he had moved down to the neighboring village to be near her, to protect her and perhaps—who knows?—to win her back again. It was to him the letter had been directed.

Winter came on and the Bandlers leaving their summer home and the new worries it entailed, moved back to the city, not however, before George had become fully aware of the situation as it concerned Belle and Mr. Favier. To hell with him, was George's final comment and with that Mrs. Bandler made up her mind everything would go along well enough for the next few months, at least.

But earlier in the season she had one day, very much to her surprise, received a call from this same curious Mr. Favier. He actually came up to the big house one day to find out about Belle, to ask if she were really married, to see if she were getting along all right. A quiet, middle-aged man, respectable and patient, an extraordinary love for and devotion to Belle stood out from every motion that he made, every word that he uttered. It was a queer case.

And so the winter set in.

About the middle of January, however, came a letter which made Mrs. Bandler hop post haste into a train and head off again into the now deserted countryside, in the dead of winter surely by every sign from the car windows on that two-hour ride into the snowy, frozen hills. Belle had written that George was going to kill her, had already tried it and that she was in direst need.

Once before, about the first of December, Mrs. B. had had to go back to the farm to settle a fight, once when George had beaten Belle and driven her and her tribe out into the deep snow—through which they had to walk to town and find a place for themselves that night as best they could. But the very next morning, George had gone down with the milk as usual and seeing Belle standing in the cold at the corner of the street by the Inn, it had been too much for him. He had taken her up, gathered her family along with her and installed them down in the cottage once more. Mrs. B. didn't know whether to laugh or to weep.

But this time it was different. Arriving at the wintry station, Mrs. B. decided not to go directly out to the farm. Though she wasn't of a timid nature, she felt it would be wiser to be a little on her guard against getting mixed up alone with a drunken maniac. She put up at the Inn after arranging with the village cop—whom she knew well—to watch for George in the morning and to arrest him.

This was done as planned. Tompkins was taken before the local Justice of the Peace; Mrs. B. told her story and paid the fellow off; he was put on the next train by the police and told never to show his face in the county again. Goodbye, George Tompkins.

Then Mrs. B. went out to the farm and told Belle what had happened.

Who arrested him? asked she.

Ed Harris.

Yes, I know him, he's a fine-looking fellow, was all Belle had to say in reply.

And so, after a good talk, it was arranged for her to stay on, for the present at least, to keep the place going while a local farmer was engaged to come up every day for the milking, hauling and other work.

But to make certain that things were not to run down too fast, Mrs. B. thought it best to remain there herself, for a week or more. And Belle took charge and told again the whole story, about Mr. Favier, about herself, about George.

Then, after a few days, she turned once more to her writing, the neat, firm hand, the spotless notepaper. Mrs. Bandler watched the woman for awhile, then broke in upon her occupation.

What in the world are you writing all those letters for, Belle, she said at last.

Oh, I'm writing to the Cupid's Club, Belle replied.

The woman was incorrigible.

This is from a fellow who wants to marry me, she added, smiling and showing a letter. But I don't think I'll take him.

Mrs. Bandler shook her head and laughed outright, thinking to herself, well, yes, she's what they call a bitch all right, a regular bitch. Just a la-la. She must have driven poor George crazy, she and the hard cider.

Years later, when Belle had passed finally from those parts, one day there came a visitor to the farm. Mrs. Bandler was confined to her bed with a sore throat, but the maid said it was an old man and that he wanted to see her very particularly; could he come up?

All right, let him come.

It was Mr. Favier, looking serious and humbled. Mrs. B. was shocked at the change in his appearance, she felt sorry for the man, whatever it might be that was the matter with him, and invited him to sit down.

It's about poor Belle, he began. I thought you'd like to know. She's gone.

He was brokenhearted, sat there and cried his eyes out. Then he went on to tell the story. After she had left the Bandler farm, so many years now past, Belle had returned to her home in Clinton Springs. And there she remained, writing her letters as usual under the patronage of Mr. Favier, until one day he noticed when he dropped in to see her in passing that she was no longer well. He tried to make her go to bed, but she refused. No, she said, not now. I'm going to die. He tried to reassure her as best he could but to no avail.

Yes, Belle went on calmly, I'm going to die. And I've got something I want to ask you.

It was no use trying to stop her, she forced the old man into a chair by the sheer certainty of her manner and compelled him to listen:

I'm going to die, she repeated, and I want you to do something for me after I'm gone. Promise me now that you'll do it.

Mr. Favier had no heart for further argument; he promised.

All right then, said Belle, this is what I want. I want you to lay me out in a blue dress, with blue stockings and blue shoes just the way I'm telling you; and I want you to give me a funeral with flowers.

The man could neither speak nor move. Then I want you to bury me by my Ma, she continued; and I want a tombstone and I want my name carved on it: Belle Tompkins.

These wishes Mr. Favier faithfully carried out and, passing through the village on his way back from the funeral, he had come to Mrs. Bandler to tell her this last news of his dearly beloved friend.

Old Doc Rivers

Horses. These definitely should be taken into consideration in estimating Rivers position, along with the bad roads, the difficult means of communication of those times.

For a physician everything depended on horses. They were a factor determining his life.

Rivers prided himself on his teams. It was something to look at when he came down the street in the rubber-tired sulky with the red wheels. He'd sit there peering out under the brim of his hat with that smile of his always on his face, confident, a little disdainful, but not unfriendly.

He knew them all. . . .

Hello, Frank, how's the wife?

Not so good, Doc.

The old trouble, eh? Tell you what I'll do. I'll drive around and take ner up to the hospital this afternoon.

Can't get her to do it, Doc.

Scared?

Guess you hit it.

All right, you old rascal; have a cigar. And he'd turn away, with the horses pawing and shaking their heads right and left, ready to go.

A young man and a bachelor, this was the happiest period of his life, when he was exhilarated by an occupation, the sun, the cold, the motion of the horses, their haunches working muscularly before him as he sat and smoked. Maybe it was that and a mad rush to get from place to place; it came and went in a moment. He saw it, realized it, there was nothing else and—he had the rest of his life to live.

This is how he practiced. . . .

Come in, Jerry—making a pass at him with his open hand
—How's the old soak?

Fer Christ's sake, Doc, lay off me. I'm sick.

Who's sick? Have a drap of the auld Crater. He nearly
always had a jug of it just behind his desk. Did a dog bite
you?

Look a' this damned neck of mine. Jesus, what the hell's
the matter with you? Easy, I says.

Shut up! You white-livered Hibernian.

Aw, Doc, fer Christ's sake, gimme a break.

What's the matter, did I do anything to you?

Listen, Doc, ain't ya gonna put something on it?

On what? Keep those pants buttoned. Sit down. Grab
onto these arms. And don't let go until I'm through or I'm
likely to slit you in half.

Yeow! Jesus, Mary and Joseph! Whadje do to me, Doc?

I think your throat's cut, Jerry. Here, drink this. Go lie
down over there a minute. I didn't think you were so
yellow.

What! Lie down? What for? Whadda you think I am,
a woman? Wow! Have you got any more of that liquor?
Say, you're some man, Doc. You're some man. What do
you get?

That's all right, Jerry, bring it around next week.

That's some relief.

The phone rang. It was one of the first in the region.
Wanted at the hospital.

Hey, Maggie!—to the dour old Irish woman who sullenly
cared for his world: Tell John to drive around to the side
door.

Wait a minute now, wait a minute. There's a woman out
there has been wantin' to see you for three days. She looks
real sick. She's been here all morning waitin' for you.

Get her in.

Doctor . . .

Yes, I know—he could see that her color was bad. Where is it? In your belly?

Yes, Doctor.

He made a quick examination, slipping on a rubber glove without removing his coat, washing his hands after at the basin in the corner of the room. The whole thing hadn't taken six minutes.

Leaning over his desk he scribbled two notes.

Take thirty drops of it tonight, in a little water. And here, here's a note to Sister Rose. Get up to the hospital in the morning. Don't eat any breakfast.

But, Doctor, what's the matter with me?

Now, now. Tomorrow morning. Don't worry, Mother. It'll be all right. Good-bye, and he pushed her out of the door.

John's waiting for you, said big Margaret as he was struggling with his coat, his hat, a cigar, stopping in the corner of the porch to light it. A few moments later he was into the carriage and off.

He leaned back, seeing nothing. The horses trotted up the Plank Road. Past the railroad cut. It was a dark spring night. The cherry blossoms were out on the McGee property. Past the nurseries. Down the steep hill by the swamp. The turn. By the Cadmus farm. The County Bridge; clattering over the boards. Over the creek. The creek was flowing swiftly, an outgoing tide, a few lights streaking it, a few sounds rising, a faint ripple and a cool air.

Naturally, he must have given value for value, good services for money received. He had a record of thirty years behind him, finally, for getting there (provided you could find him) anywhere, anytime, for anybody—no distinctions; and for doing something, mostly the right thing, without delay and of his own initiative, once he was there.

He was ready, energetic and courageous. The people were convinced that he knew his stuff—if anyone knew it.

And they would pay him well for his services—if they paid him at all.

But what could he do? What did he do? What kind of a doctor was he, really?

Thinking it over, it occurred to me to drop in at the hospital in the small nearby city where he took many of his operative cases to see for myself exactly what he had been about all these years. To satisfy myself, then, as to the man's scope I went to the St. Michael's Hospital of which I am speaking and induced the librarian to get out the older record books for me to look at.

As usual in such cases, something other than the thing desired first catches the eye.

These were heavy ledgers, serious and interesting in appearance with their worn leather covers and gold lettering across the front: Registry of Cases treated at St. Michael's Hospital, etc., etc. There were a dozen of them in all from the year 1898 on. I felt a catch at the throat before the summary of so much human misery.

Opening at random, there it lay, the whole story of the hospital, what had been done and the result, along with the doctors' names and other like information, listed in tall columns. These were carefully written in through the months and years in longhand of many characters, minute and tall, precise and free, in blue, in green, black, purple and even red; with stub pens, sharp pens and even pencil, across two full pages with two narrower fly leaves between.

I chose the years 1905 and 1908 and began to thumb over the leaves looking for Rivers' name. But my eye fell instead upon the list of patients' occupations. Such a short time ago and yet some of these entries struck me as odd: Liveryman, coachman, bartender! Nothing in years has so impressed me with the swiftness of time's flight.

In the doctors' column, there was Rivers, dead surely of the effects of his addiction, but here another who had shot himself in despair at the outcome, it is said, of an affair with the wife of another physician on the same page, his friend. While this one had divorced his wife and married once again—a younger woman. Another at sixty had quietly laid himself down upon his office couch and said good-bye and died. This one had left town hurriedly taking himself to the coast, possibly to escape jail—leaving a wife and child behind him. Some had grown old in the profession and been forgotten though they were still alive. One of these, ninety and more, totally deaf, still morosely wandered the streets and scarcely anyone remembered that he had been a doctor. Queer, all that since 1908.

What had Rivers really accomplished?

Surgically, there were, to be sure, more than enough of the usual scrapings, and appendicitis was common. But here is a list of some of his undertakings; I copy from the records: endometritis, salpingitis, contracture of the hand, ruptured spleen, hernia, lacerations (some accident, no doubt). There were malignancies of the bowel, excisions of the thyroid, breast amputations; here an ununited fracture of the humerus involving the insertion of a plate and marked "Cured" in the final column. There were normal maternity cases, Caesarean sections, ruptured ectopic pregnancies. He treated fistulas, empyema, hydrocele. He performed hysterectomies, gastro-enterostomies, gall bladder resections. He even tackled a deviated nasal septum. There were fractures of all the bones of the body, nearly, and many of those of the head, simple and compound.

And at the far edge of the right-hand page, you would see the brief legend "Cured" as often following his name as that of any other doctor.

On the medical side, the old familiar "neurasthenia" which meant that they never did discover what was the matter with the patient; but also nephritis, pneumonia, endocarditis, rheumatism, malaria and typhoid fever. Most left the hospital cured.

And who were they? Plumber, nurseryman, farmer,

saloonkeeper (with hob-nail liver), painter, printer, house-wife, that's the way it would go. It was a long and interesting list of the occupations of the region from tea merchant to no occupation at all.

Acute alcoholism and D.T. were frequent entries.

It was not money. It came of his sensitivity, his civility; it was that that made him do it, I'm sure; the antithesis rather of that hog-like complacency that comes to so many men following the successful scamper for cash. Nervous, he accepted his life at its own terms and never let it beat him—to no matter what extremity he was driven.

But sometimes I know he had to quit an operation half way through and have another finish it for him. Or perhaps he would retire for a moment (we all knew why), return, change his gloves, and continue. The transformation in him would be striking. From a haggard old man he would be changed "like that" into a resourceful and alert operator.

Going further, I asked several men who had been in the habit of standing opposite him across the operating table their opinion of him as a surgeon—what had been the secret of his success.

Again, I began to pick up odd pieces of news. Dr. Jamison, who had been an intern in the hospital during several of Rivers' most active years, recalled how he would awaken sometimes in his room on the first floor at night to find Rivers asleep outside the covers on his bed beside him snoring like a good fellow. And once on a trip to the state hospital for mental diseases at Nashawan, one of the attendants of the place had come up to the group to ask them if the person he had found in a semi-conscious condition leaning against the wall down the corridor was one of their party. It was Rivers; something had gone wrong with his usual arrangements and he was coked to the eyes.

In sum, his ability lay first in an uncanny sense for diagnosis. Then, he didn't flounder. He made up his mind and went to it. Furthermore, he was not, as might be supposed, radical and eccentric in his surgical technique but conservative and thoroughgoing throughout. He was not nervous but cool and painstaking—so long as he had the drug in him. His principles were sound, nor was he exhibitionistic in any sense of the word.

And what a psychologist he was. There was a boy down in Kingsland who had had diarrhoea for about a week. Several doctors had seen him and prescribed medicine but the child had been eating almost anything he wanted. Finally they called in Rivers. He pulled down the kid's pants, took one look and said, Hell, what he needs is a circumcision. And he did it, there and then, kept food away from him a day or two (because of the operation) and of course the kid got well. That's how smart he was.

Only twice did I personally assist him at operations.

The first case was that of a man called Milliken, an enormous, hulking fellow in his late thirties, swarthy, hairy-chested and with arms and legs on him fit for the strong man in the circus. He ran a milk route at one end of the town. It was acute appendicitis.

When we got to the little house where he lived, a double house I recall, the only room big enough to handle him in was the parlor. We rigged up a table in the usual way. Rivers said we were ready and told the big boy to climb on up. Which he did.

I forgot to mention that Milliken was a great drinker. He also forgot to mention it to me at the time.

Go ahead with the ether, said Rivers.

Well, it didn't take me long—not more than twenty minutes—to find out that ether wouldn't touch this fellow anyway you gave it—unless it might be by a tube. There are individuals like that, powerfully muscled men and alcoholics.

By this time Rivers and his assistant were ready

Wait a minute, Doc, managed to mumble the patient.

For, strange to say, the man had been docile up to that point so that we thought he was under. But it was not so.

I could see that Rivers was losing patience but I was already pouring a stream of ether upon the mask. They were ready for the incision, scrubbed up, the sheet in place, just waiting.

Rivers was fidgeting and I wasn't in a particularly pleasant mood myself. Finally he spoke sharply to me asking if I didn't know how to give an anesthetic. I could feel my face flush but I didn't say anything. Instead I took out the chloroform and began to give that, carefully. Rivers looked approval but said nothing. We all waited a moment or two for this to take effect. By this time, we were all sweating and mad—at the patient, each other, and ourselves.

The outcome was that, after three attempts at an incision —at which time an earthquake occurred under our grips, Rivers gave it up and turned to me.

Here, he said, Gimme that mask. Come up here and assist Willie. I'll show you how to get this man under.

I wanted to scrub. He said, No, put on the gloves. I obeyed. There was nothing else to do. Asepsis had gone to the winds long since in our efforts to keep the man from walking out of the room.

Rivers just took the chloroform bottle and poured the stuff into that Bohunk. I expected to see him turn black and pass out.

But he didn't.

After a few minutes, we were told by Rivers to go ahead.

His assistant just touched the skin with his knife and up flew the man's knees. I was tickled to death.

Go ahead, go ahead, cried Rivers excitedly, hold him down and go to it.

That's what we did. One man held the head and arms. I finally quit entirely as an assistant, lay on my stomach across the man's thighs and grasped the legs of the table on the other side. One man, alone, did the actual work. It is to his credit that he did it well.

It must have been a month after that I saw the patient, one day, standing in front of the fire house. Curious, I went up to him to find out if he had felt anything while the operation had been going on.

At first he didn't know me, but when I told him who I was, expecting to get a crack in the eye maybe for my trouble, he came up with a start:

Did I feel anything? said he. My God, every bit of it, every bit of it. But he was a well man by that time.

It was the case though of an old German harness maker of East Hazleton, Frankel by name, which first raised doubts in my mind as to Rivers' actual condition. I received the call one day and went to the address given, where I knew the old man and his wife lived above the store.

They had the kitchen already rigged up as an operating room, a plain deal table with a smaller one at the foot of it with blankets and a sheet over them for the old man to lie on. There were sterile dressings, the instruments were boiling on the gas stove and everything was in good order as far as I could make out.

As soon as I had entered, Rivers called into the hall for the old fellow to come on along, we were ready for him. He had been in bed in the front of the house and I shall never forget my surprise and the shock to my sense of propriety when I saw Frankel, whom I knew, coming down the narrow, dark corridor of the apartment in his bare feet and an old-fashioned nightgown that reached just to his knees. He was holding his painful belly with both hands while his scared wife accompanied him solicitously on one side.

The old fellow was too sick for that sort of thing but Rivers just motioned him without a word uttered to climb up on the table where they put another sheet over him and

I was told to start the anesthetic. I did so, silent, and not too well pleased with the way things were going.

Rivers asked the wife if she had any more of that good whisky about the place. She brought it out. He poured himself nearly a tumblerful, filled the glass with water at the sink and, while he was drinking, held up the flask with the other hand toward his confrere and to me, gesturing. We refused. With that he finished his glass, plugged the cork in the bottle and dropped it into the side pocket of his coat which hung nearby on a chair.

He was in his undershirt and suspenders, sleeves rolled up. From this time forward, things went ahead normally and properly, more or less, according to the usual operating-room technique of the time.

Rivers made the incision. He took one look and shrugged his shoulders. It was a ruptured appendix with advanced general peritonitis. He shoved in a drain and let it go at that, the right thing to do. But the patient died next day.

I tell you there was a howl about the town: another decent citizen done to death by that dope fiend Rivers. Several of my friends cautioned me to watch my step. You may be sure, in any case, that I thought carefully over what had occurred but I did not come to any immediate conclusion.

And yet the man could be—often was—kindly, alert, courteous. Most interesting it is to hear that he played the violin excellently and would often spend an evening, in the early days, playing duets with the one musician of any note that could be encountered in the neighborhood—the organist at the nearby cathedral.

When little Virginia Shippen, aged five, had a kidney complication following scarlet fever, Rivers came in day and night, did—as he thought—everything that could be done to save her. Still she remained unconscious, dropsical; the kidneys had ceased to function. One evening Rivers told them that he was through—that she would be dead by morning.

At this point, the mother asked if he would object if she made a suggestion. She wanted to try flaxseed poultices over the kidney regions. Go ahead, said Rivers.

The next day the child's kidneys had started slowly to function, sanguineous, muddy stuff, but she was conscious and her fever had dropped. Rivers was delighted, praised the mother and told her that she had taught him something. The child grew up and lived thirty years thereafter.

He was short with women:

Well, Mary, what is it?

I have a pain in my side, doctor.

How long have you had it, Mary?

Today, doctor. It's the first time.

Just today.

Yes, doctor.

Climb up on the table. Pull up your dress. Throw that sheet over you. Come on, come on. Up with you. Come on now, Mary. Pull up your knees.

Ooh!

He could be cruel and crude. And like all who are so, he could be sentimentally tender also, and painstaking without measure.

A young woman, one of my early friends and patients, spoke to me of his kindness to her. Her foster parents—for she was an adopted child—would never have anyone else. For months she went to him, two and three times a week, while he with the greatest gentleness and patience treated her. It was a nasopharyngeal condition of some sort, difficult to manage. Little by little, he brought her along till she was well, charging them next to nothing for his services.

Money was never an end with him.

The end was, he made this girl, who was frail and gentle, one of his lifelong admirers.

But on another occasion in the drug store one day a boy

about ten came up to him with a sizable abscess on his neck. They had not been able to find the doctor in his office so the boy had followed him there.

Come here, said Rivers, Let's see. And with that he took a scalpel out of his vest pocket, and made a swipe at the thing.

But the boy was too quick. He jerked back and the knife caught him low. He turned and ran, bleeding and yelling, out of the door. Rivers chuckled and paid no further attention to the incident.

Naturally there were certain favorite places which he'd visit more often than others. First of all was the Jeannette Mansion in Crestboro, two miles above Hazleton north along the ridge, where a number of French families had settled sixty or eighty years previously.

They were rather a different class, these French, from some of the other inhabitants of the region and showed it by keeping a great deal to themselves in their large manor houses surrounded by the billowy luxuriance of tall trees.

A fence, the beginning of all culture, invariably surrounded the property as a frame, giving a sense of propriety and measure. Ease and retirement seemed to blossom here, though naturally this was often an appearance only.

Not, I think, that these things meant anything consciously to Rivers, but they were there and he passed among them. In that way they must have influenced him more than a little. For he liked it all, obviously. Though, of course, it was the people really who attracted him.

He was a Frenchman, an Alsatian—I can't think of his name, said my informer, old Dr. Trowbridge. When you get older, your memory is not so good. Wait a minute. No, well, anyway, he went back to France. So and so lives in the house now. He had several daughters—they were a very gay family.

I had been asking the old doctor how it was that Rivers began to take the dope. Oh, he must have been taking something before he came here. I don't know how else to explain his eccentricity. Anyway, when he went to Europe, to Freiburg to study with Seibert, the pathologist (I don't think he studied very much), this man, oh, what is his name? he had gone back to France—had to give Rivers the money to return to America.

Jeannette, that's it—he was a high liver. He built himself a greenhouse in the back and put all kinds of plants in it. He must have spent hundreds and hundreds of dollars on it. He would sit out there and play cards with his friends. Not difficult surely to understand the attraction this had for the tormented doctor. For, if Jeannette was a voluptuary, his friend Rivers was no laggard before any lead which he could find it in his conscience to propose.

To play cards, to laugh, talk and partake with the Frenchman of his imported wines and liquors was good. After a snowstorm, of a Sunday morning, to sit there at ease—out of reach of patients—in a tropical environment and talk, sip wines and enjoy a good cigar—that was something. It was a quaint situation, too, in that crude environment of those days, so altogether foreign, incongruous and delightfully aloof.

It would take a continental understanding—reinforced as it is by centuries of culture—to comprehend and to accept the complexities and contradictions of a nature such as Rivers'. Not in the provincial bottom of the New Jersey of that time had the doctor found such another release.

The man was now at the height of his popularity and power.

Intelligence he had and force—but he also had nerves, a refinement of the sensibilities that made him, though able, the victim of the very things he best served. This was the man himself whom the drug retrieved.

He was far and away by natural endowment the ablest individual of our environment, a serious indictment against all the evangelism of American life which I most hated—at the same time a man trying to fill his place among those lacking the power to grasp his innate capabilities.

I don't believe Jeannette doped. It cannot have been other than as to a last hope, a veritable island of safety, that Rivers went to the mansion. The only influence that might possibly have saved him, as they say, had it but been known. In any case, they were gay and the time passed; at the mansion he was free, enlivened—then when that was finished, he was again beaten.

The mansion was relaxation to him, but he couldn't live there and his restlessness would in the end pass beyond it.

No doubt, there would be periods when he didn't hit the dope for months at a time. Then he'd get taking it again. Finally he'd feel himself slipping and he'd head off—overnight sometimes—leaving his practice as it might lie—for the woods.

This flight to the woods or something like it, is a thing we most of us have yearned for at one time or another, particularly those of us who live in the big cities. As Rivers did. For in their jumble we have lost touch with ourselves, have become indeed not authentic persons, but fantastic shapes in some gigantic fever dream. He, at least, had the courage to break with it and to go.

With this pressure upon us, we eventually do what all herded things do; we begin to hurry to escape it, then we break into a trot, finally into a mad run (watches in our hands), having no idea where we are going and having no time to find out.

He wanted to plunge into something bigger than himself. Primitive, physically sapping. Maine gave it. To hunt the deer. He'd bring them home and give cuts of venison around to all his friends.

But that, too, ended pretty badly. After his eyes had been affected, by abuse and illness, he one day by accident shot his best friend in the woods, a guide he always followed, shot him through the temples as dead as a door nail.

Characteristic of the man is it that he made amends to the unfortunate's family faithfully as best he could, everything that was asked of him, to the last penny. And then, when the last payment had been made, he invited a young doctor of his acquaintance to dinner with him in New York —for a rousing celebration.

Rivers made a hobby one time of catching rattlesnakes, which abound in the mountains of North Jersey. He enjoyed the sport and the danger, apparently, while there was a scientific twist to it in that the venom they collected was to be used for laboratory work in New York.

A patient of mine gave me an impression of his office as it looked in those days:

There were six of us kids, brothers and sisters. I myself must have been about ten years old. We used to go up and sit there Sunday mornings. We'd be crazy for it. We used to like to look at his trophies. He had 'em too, moose and deer heads up on the wall and fish of all kinds.

He was a great hunter. I remember one time he was telling my father how he was bitten by a rattler, on the arm. Being a doctor, he knew what he was up against. He asked his guide to take his knife and cut the place out. But the guide didn't have the nerve. So the Doc took his own hunting knife in the other hand and sliced it wide open and sucked the blood out of it. I suppose he took a shot of dope first to steady himself. We were in the office with my father and he rolled up his sleeve and showed us the cut—right down the middle of his arm.

It was about this time too that he once had Charlie Hensel in to see him, one evening when there were quite a few others besides, out in the waiting room. Put on the gloves, Charlie, he said—he always had a couple of pairs of them lying around the place somewhere—and let's see what you can do.

But Charlie was good in those days and he knew the Doc

was in no shape for him to be roughing it up with. He shook his head and said, No, not tonight, Doc.

That nettled Rivers. Scared? he said. What's the matter, a young fella like you? Come on, put'em on.

All right, said Charlie in his sweet, easy voice. Just as you say. He told me the story shortly after it happened.

So they started in to spar after pushing back the desk and clearing a little space for themselves.

Charlie tapped the old boy lightly on the face a couple of times keeping away from the body. At this the Doc let go a hot one for Charlie's middle.

Come on, come on, he kept saying.

But Charlie could see that the Doc was getting winded so he tapped him again and was going to say he guessed that would be enough for tonight when the Doc drove in a swift one which caught Charlie on the temple just as he was going to drop his hands. Come on, come on, he said once more, a young fella like you.

So Charlie, wanting to end the business, feinted, just easy and then lifted the Doc one under the chin that sent him staggering backward to the wall. There he sat down unexpectedly in the consultation chair they had placed back out of the way. It shook the building.

The trouble with you, Charlie—the trouble with hitting you, Charlie, said the Doc slowly after a while, is that you ain't got any belly at all. Which was true enough. Charlie was very narrow across the middle then—like a sailor.

He'd have spells when his brother even could do nothing with him. He would go completely mad. He put in several sessions at the State Insane Asylum—six months or more—on at least two occasions.

When he'd been there a month or so, he'd begin to ask the Superintendent, who was a friend of his, whether he didn't think he could go out to work again. You're as good a doctor as I am, old man, would say this one finally. If you think you can make it, go ahead. And back he'd turn again to the old grind.

Then one winter he got so low with typhoid fever that it looked as if this time the game was up. They wanted a nurse; he refused to have one. And nobody wanted him as a patient either. He was completely gone with dope and the disease. Finally he himself asked for a girl he had known some years before at Blockley Hospital, a nurse he had once seen there and admired.

She took on the case.

He married her when he was able to be up and about again, and they went to Europe on a honeymoon. No doubt, she loved him.

Yes, I can remember his wife, said a lady to me. When she first came out she was a pretty little thing, just like anybody else. But I can still see her one day when she came into the store knocking against the counters, first on one side then on the other; she was covered with diamonds, her hands and her neck—she didn't seem to know where she was going. Her face didn't seem to be bigger than the palm of my hand.

A great many of his more respectable friends left him now. They'd still call him—if he was right—but he was too greatly distrusted.

You know how it used to be, said one of my best friends to me one day much to my surprise. You'd get some doctor and fool around with him for a while and get another and they'd all say something different and you wouldn't know where the hell you were. And this is the story he told me:

Well, this happened many years ago. I was sick and my old man was worried. Finally the druggist tipped us off. Get Rivers, he said. He's a dope but when he's right you can't beat him. And I tell you what I'll do—because he knew the old man well and he himself had been something of a rounder in his day—I'll call up Rivers and get him down here at the store. And, if he's right, I'll send him up.

So he did.

Later in the day when the Doc came into the room he took one look at me. This boy's got typhoid fever, he said. Just like that—that's how he did it. And I'll tell you what I'll do. To prove it, I'll take his blood now and send it in to my brother—he was doing nothing but blood work at that time—and I'll let you know in a few days.

Sure enough, he was right. He had the jump on the thing. The result was I had a light case and we had Rivers for years after that as our family physician.

He'd sit at the table writing a prescription and you could see his head fall down lower and lower—he'd go to sleep right there, right in front of your eyes. My old man would shake him every once in a while and finally he'd get up and go out.

When he started to hit the dope, his brother did his best to get him into some hospital in the city. He knew he was good and, if he could get him in there in a proper atmosphere, he thought he could save him. But the old boy was too foxy. He liked it out here, his friends, the life or whatever it was and they couldn't move him.

The thing, one of the main things, that got the other doctors down on him was his habit of going off—just disappearing sometimes. He liked to go fishing, and he was a crack shot. He'd have important cases, or anything. But that didn't make any difference. You'd call him up to find out why he hadn't been there and they'd say, He's gone away for a few days, we don't know where.

All you could do was get another doctor.

A couple of years after that, one summer when my old man had gone off on a trip somewhere, he sent me down to the only boarding house in town—you know where I mean. He'd left me in the house alone the year before and he wasn't any too satisfied with some of the things we pulled off while he was away. Well, this time Rivers heard of it and wanted me to come over and live with him.

I don't know how he got me out of there, but he did. The old gal who ran the place didn't want to let me go, knowing my father and all that. But Rivers persuaded her that I was sick, I guess, and needed treatment and that the best way for me was to live at his house where he could keep his eye on me. So I got my things together in two minutes, you can bet, and into his buggy I hopped and over we went.

My old man hasn't forgiven him for that to this day.

Sunday mornings were the times. It was a regular show. Because most of his patients were poor people and they could come only on Sunday. I'm telling you you never saw an office like it. He had the right idea, he was for humanity —put it any way you like. They'd be sitting all over the place, out in the hall, up the stairs, on the porch, anywhere they could park themselves.

When it was somebody that didn't know me, he'd say I was a young doctor. I was just seventeen then. He'd give me a white coat and tell me to come on. Jesus! Naturally I thought he was great. And I'll tell you in all those four months I never used to see any of those butcheries they'd talk about. Everything he did was O.K. I suppose I'd think different now, but then I thought he was a wonder.

I do remember one woman, though. God, it was a crime. You can imagine what I mean. Here I was, a kid never knowing anything at all. I was having the time of my life. Yes, everything, you're right. I held her while he did the job. I often think of it.

That was the romantic period of my life, those four months I lived with him.

He never kept any track of money. There wasn't a book around the place. Any money he got he shoved it in his pocket. But he never paid for anything, either.

Clever? That boy was there! He'd go over to his desk

and you'd see him fumbling around with some instruments. And right in front of you he'd give himself a shot and, unless you were wise, you wouldn't see him do it.

He was foxy too. He'd stall for a few minutes to give it time to act. That was when he had anything important to do. He'd wait a few minutes, then he'd come out steely-eyed and as quiet and steady as the best of them.

That was the difference between him and her. It made her crazy. She didn't know how to control it, but it steadied him down.

Many's the time he'd wake me up in the middle of the night to go out with him. Down at Johnny Kessler's was one of his hangouts where he'd go for soft-shell crabs and clam chowder.

Once he gave me some tickets for a show in New York. Some dirty racket, I've forgotten. He told me to get some of my friends and go in and have a good time. He gave us the tickets and started us off on his own liquor. It was the first show of that kind I'd ever taken in.

When I came home next morning, he himself took care of me, undressed me and put me to bed.

I can remember one night while I was living there, he waked me up at two o'clock in the morning. It was in summer, one of those hot, muggy nights. I'd been operated on too, the day before, he'd taken out my tonsils or something and I was feeling rotten. But that didn't make any difference, I had to go out with him just the same.

We got the old buggy and started out. We went down in the meadows, at two A.M. mind you, down to Mooney's saloon, the old halfway house, you know where it is. He went in and left me there. The mosquitos nearly ate me alive. He had a case in there or something, maybe he took a few drinks. I don't know what.

Anyway, I sat there slapping mosquitos. The old man came out after a while and told me the Doc was asleep and that they didn't want to wake him. So I, kid like, not wanting to make a fuss or anything, I said all right and just sat there. He left me there in that buggy till five A.M. Jesus!

Then he came out and we went home. When we got there, he said, Let's have some lamb chops! So out we went again, to the butcher's. He went to the door and of course it was closed. So he went up on the porch around at the side and stamped and banged until that fellow had to get up and come down and get him his chops out of the ice box.

Then we went home and he cooked them in the kitchen. And, say, he could cook. He was a wonderful cook. He could make a piece of meat taste like nothing in the world.

We ate the chops and then I went to bed.

When Doc wasn't in his office, he wasn't home, that's all.

When practice was light in summer and there'd be nothing else to do, as it happens sometimes to us all, he'd call his coachman and say, Hitch 'em up, Johnny—or Jake, or whoever it might be that was driving for him at the time—and start out, nobody at first knew whither.

Where are we headin', Doc?

He nodded to the left, down the hill.

It was a clear June day—the kids were still in school—about two in the afternoon. John let the horses jog lazily down the macadam.

Someone hailed him: Well, Doc, where you sneakin' off to? Swimmin'? The Doc gave the man a broad wink as much as to say: Go to hell.

Down near the track there was a bunch of willows by the ice house where the road turns before straightening out to go through the cat-tails. Maybe he saw them, maybe he didn't, you never knew.

Hello, Doc. Where ye goin'?

He just nodded his head. They just smiled and nodded in reply.

Killy-fish rippled the road ditch, a diminutive tempest, as the carriage and the hoof beats of the horses slightly shook the ground in passing.

Without further sign from the Doc, John turned to the left at Mooney's halfway house and continued up the road. Along this road, so I have been told—and the house is still there—lived a woman who kept a regular hangout for Rivers. It might have been a common joint, I don't know, but that isn't the way I heard it.

Certainly it was in an unusually isolated location, one of the old places, like the mansions on the hill only smaller, more suitable to farming. She was a descendant of the original builders.

Hello, Jimmie, how are you? Come in, bring your cigar with you.

That's the way it began. That's the way it always began. He would be just starting a stogie.

Hello, Doc, how's the boy? would say her brother. He ran the farm for her since her husband walked out.

I hope he's sunk in the mud, was all she'd say when that subject came up for comment.

By this time John would have turned the horses around and be on his way home.

The house is still there in much the same condition as formerly, quite close to the road with the farm buildings piled up in the rear, mostly given over to pigeons now. Rivers was known to about live there at one time.

Anyhow, you could see the chickens walking around in the yard all day. They had a colored man who had grown up on the place to take care of the few remnants of the garden that still remained; he went by the windows toward the middle of the afternoon and you could hear him call the chickens and see them run.

What could the attraction have been? Just one thing. Someone else, something else, to take him out of it. She was a good drinker. She gave him a rest.

But certainly she had, and I guess he knew it pretty well too, quite a bit put away. You know how these old farmers sometimes are. The increase in land valuations grow to be enormous; they have no need to move to become wealthy selling off sections of the original farm to the Polacks and promoters. She was one of those, hearing of cities and seeing trains crawling right before their eyes night and day, who remain isolated—peculiarly childish. Hot and eccentric.

Rivers would find an abandoned corner like that to wander into.

The drink alone would have been enough in itself to attract him. But she was a woman. The loafers around the bar at Donnelley's were all right. She was a woman. Maybe he never thought much of that but she *was* just the same.

Plenty of woman.

His sensitiveness, his refinement, his delicacy—found perhaps a release in this backhanded fashion. Can you believe it?

Jesus, she could put up a fight if she wanted to.

She didn't give a good God damn for the whole blankin' world—if you could believe her when she was drunk. And she said it—many times—to her brother and the Doc who put her to bed before he went home.

Then he'd have to come back next day and get her out of it—if they could find him. That's how they came to call him the first time.

Come on, Jimmie, let's get married, she would say.

Sure, where's the priest? and you could tell by his voice that you wouldn't ask him that many times before you wouldn't see him again ever.

Then he quit her. They'd drunk up all her booze, or her brother put a stop to the affair but, anyway, he quit.

I saw her just once many years later when she was completely abandoned.

It was the night we had her up at the Police Station for running through the gates at the railroad crossing. There were five in the car. It was a marvel the train didn't crash them. I was police physician at that time. They wanted me to pass on her, whether or not she was drunk.

She shoved her face close up against mine and yelled at me: Have you a sister, have you a brother? Then tell me I'm drunk. Her breath reeked half across the room. Look at me! Then she went off into an unrepeatable string of filth and profanity. And that's what I think of youse. I said it. You heard me.

It was the first and only time I saw her—if indeed she was the one of whom I had heard spoken. She must, at least, have been a good bit more attractive formerly.

As far as I know, he took all the ordinary hypnotics— morphine, heroin and cocaine also. What dose he ever got up to, it's hard to say. I've seen three grains of morphine do no more than make a woman—lying in a maternity ward—normally quiet.

Of course, it got him finally; he began to slip badly in the latter years, made pitiful blunders. But this final phase was marked by that curious idolatry that sometimes attracts people to a man by the very danger of his name. It lived again in the way many people, not all, still clung to Rivers the more he went down and down.

They seemed to recreate him in their minds, the beloved scapegoat of their own aberrant desires—and believed that he alone could cure them.

He became a legend and indulged himself the more.

But he did do awful things. It is said that he had made the remark that all a woman needed was half her organs— the others were just a surgeon's opportunity. Half the girls of Creston were without the half of theirs, through his offices, if you could believe his story.

It amused me to hear Jack Hardt describe how old Rivers would drop in at their tiny farm out in the reeds along the turnpike by the cedar swamp; a very small place, just a few feet of ground rescued from the bog with room only for a chicken coop, a doghouse, a barn and a hay rick. The old man used to make a fairly decent living off it, though, formerly, selling salt hay. I remember Jack's telling me how the hired men would sleep on the hay in winter with the snow seeping through on them between the boards and the one in the middle sweating from the body heat of his companions.

Rivers was a frequent caller at that place and always welcome there. The boy knew him well. The Doc would go out into the old privy they had at the back of the yard and stay there for an hour or more sometimes. The kids would go out and peep at him asleep on the seat.

He'd do the same anywhere. One woman up on the hill who did not know him well had him in to see her. He asked if she had a spare room with a bed in it. She said, Yes, not thinking what was in his mind. He went in and stayed. She was frightened to death. She frantically called up several friends but she could interest no one. Rivers had lain down on the bed and there he slept until nearly five in the afternoon, when his man called to fetch him.

The man knew to a dot when to come. In the morning after Rivers failed to show up, he had simply driven off. When the drug had worn itself out, he was there.

Rivers just got up, said nothing, and went home.

Sometimes, though, it was not so harmless.

How did he get away with it?

It is a little inherent in medicine itself—mystery, necromancy, cures—charms of all sorts, and he knew and practiced this black art. Toward the last of his life he had a crooked eye and was thought to be somewhat touched.

An impressionable lady once caused him an unpleasant half hour because of these things. It appears that he had for some reason taken a flier with her in hypnotism and unexpectedly succeeded in putting her under. But he could not rouse her to normal consciousness again when he was through with the experiment and finally becoming himself frightened, called frantically for his friend Willie to come down and help him get her out of the office. The two men, no doubt as mystified as the patient herself at the turn of affairs, were thoroughly scared before—after great efforts —they succeeded in bringing the lady to herself once more.

My wife remembers him staring in at our front door through the screen. He had come to ask if I had any death certificates. She couldn't tell which eye was looking at her. But she noted the wistfulness of his stoop, his eager smile, his voice, his gestures. She felt sorry for him.

But most feared him—in short, dared not attack him even when they knew he had really killed someone.

A cure for disease? He knew what that amounted to. For of what shall one be cured? Work, in this case, through sheer intuitive ability flooded him under. Drugs righted him.

Frightened, under stress, the heart beats faster, the blood is driven to the extremities of the nerves, floods the centers of action and a man feels in a flame. That's what Rivers wanted, must have wanted. The reaction from such a state required its tonics also.

That awful fever of overwork which we feel especially in the United States—he had it. A trembling in the arms and thighs, a tightness of the neck and in the head above the eyes—fast breath, vague pains in the muscles and in the feet. Followed by an orgasm, crashing the job through, putting it over in a fever heat. Then the feeling of looseness afterward. Not pleasant. But there it is. Then cigarettes, a shot of gin. And that's all there is to it. Women the same, more and more.

He had no time, had to be fast, he had to improvise and did—to a marvel.

When a street laborer was clipped once by a trolley car, his arm almost severed near the shoulder, Rivers was the first to get there. Such cases were always his particular delight. With one look he took in the situation as usual, made up his mind, and remarking that the arm could be of no possible further use to the man, amputated it there and then—with a pair of bandage scissors.

Such deeds took the popular fancy and the rumor of them spread like magic.

It's funny too, the answer of the Sisters in the hospital when some of the doctors wanted to prevent him from operating there—principally because he would pass out, finally, in the middle of a case and someone else would have to go in and clean it up for him. The Sisters would say in reply to such complainers: What do you wish us to do? So long as people go to the man, we will keep a bed free for them here. Do you want us to go back on them?

It was an unanswerable argument.

He was one of the few that ever in these parts knew the meaning of all, to give himself completely. He never asked why, never gave a damn, never thought there was anything else. He was like that, things had an absolute value for him.

But one of the younger doctors, a first-rate physician who began practicing in the town a month or two prior to my own arrival, had it in for Rivers. My wife would sometimes say to me, If you know he is killing people, why do you doctors not get together and have his license taken away from him?

I would answer that I didn't know. I doubted that we could prove anything. No one wanted to try.

Dr. Grimley, though, did want to do something that day.

He had had a Hungarian girl, who was scared as hell of the knife, under his care with a strangulated hernia. Grimley tried his best to reduce it but without success. He knew the danger and urged her by every means at his command to go to the hospital and have the operation. She refused.

He very properly told her that, unless she did as he told her, he would no longer handle the case and that she would die.

The next day she called him again. As soon as he entered the room, he could see that it was all over. She had called in Rivers. He had told her that he could cure her. God knows what condition he was in at the time. He pressed upon the sac until it burst. The next day she died.

Grimley was wild. I met him at the corner by the drug store. Though a very quiet man he was fairly foaming at the mouth. He wanted to have Rivers arrested, he wanted to have him prosecuted for malpractice and to put him out of the way once and for all—said he'd do it.

He never did.

In reality, it was a population in despair, out of hand, out of discipline, driven about by each other blindly, believing in the miraculous, the drunken, as it may be. Here was, to many, though they are diminishing fast, something before which they could worship, a local shrine, all there was left, a measure of the poverty which surrounded them. They believed in him: Rivers, drunk or sober. It is a plaintive, failing story.

Typical of their behavior is the tale of a very sober and canny butcher whom I know well who had a small daughter that had what seemed to me to be typical epileptic fits. They called me in and I told the parents there was little I could do for them.

Later I saw them again and they confessed to me frankly that they had taken the child to Dr. Rivers. I wished them luck.

A year later, I had occasion to talk to them again of the child. She had not had a convulsion for several months. Rivers had cured her. How, I do not know.

Yes, the father said, it took us quite a while to get him working but once he really got his mind down on the case, it didn't take him long till he had her where he wanted her. They believed it and it was so.

People sought him out, they'd wait months for him finally —though he did, of his own volition, give up maternity cases toward the end. When everyone else failed, they believed he'd see them through: a powerful fetish. He would save them.

The end was recounted to me by a young patient of mine, a teller in the bank. His father had always had Rivers. So when the old man fell and broke his arm, they called up the Doc who came and deliberately hopped himself up right before the patient—undisguisedly, so indifferent had he become.

That finished it. It was the look in his eyes. He's crazy, said the patient. Take him away. I don't want him fooling around me. I'll get another doctor.

But it would not be just to say that this was really the end, for that gives a wrong impression. Rivers was through, yes, in some ways, but he did not quit by any means. The truth is that during his last years he bought a good-sized lot on the square before the Municipal Building in the center of town. Here he built a fine house, had a large garden, lawns and a double garage, where he kept two cars always ready for service.

Here he continued to practice for several years while his wife bred small dogs—Blue Poms, I think, for her amusement and for sale, one or more of which Rivers would often take out in the car with him on his calls, holding them on his lap, for in those days he himself never sat at the wheel.

Life Along the Passaic River

Life Along the Passaic River

About noon of a muggy July day, a spot of a canoe filled by the small boy who no doubt made it, lies west of the new 3rd St. Bridge between Passaic and Wallington, midstream opposite the Manhattan Rubber Co.'s red brick and concrete power plant. There's a sound of work going on there, and a jet of water spouts from a pipe at the foundation level below the factory onto the river's narrow mud bank which it has channeled making a way for itself into the brown water of the two hundred foot wide stream. The boy is drifting with the current but paddling a little also toward a couple of kids in bathing suits and a young man in his shirt sleeves, lying on what looks to be grass but is probably weeds across the river at the edge of an empty lot where they dumped ashes some years ago, watching him. These youngsters who make boats out of barrel hoops and a piece of old duck, wherever they find it, live by the river these hot summer days. It's a god-send to them.

They're all over the city as soon as they can walk and say, Paper! even when perhaps it's the only thing they can say. Pre-kindergarten stuff, watching the next corner below their brother's where he can keep an eye on them and at the same time cover twice the ground, coming tearing uphill encumbered by the news under the left arm to get change for a quarter. Or along the canal where they back the freights in, by the cobbled street in front of the wholesalers, sorting over half-rotten oranges and fennel and stuffing the outer leaves of lettuce heads into a burlap bag. Struggling home with firewood on a misassorted set of four wheels. Or clown-grey with ashes from the dumps and another wagon of the sort woggling under a sack of reclaimed coals, a morning's work. Blind, crippled, orphaned. Classroom perverts driving the teacher mad. Vaccinating herself with a piece of sharp tin to obey the order, remain in line, and circumvent the sloth of her parents. Objecting to being called out of their names: Don't call me Dick Baker. Here they are, on the steps of the Y.M., about a hundred of them from black Wops right on through to white-haired Polacks, a regular zoo, lined up before the main entrance having their pictures taken. Restless. With the sun in their faces making them blink. Just sitting there waiting.

Most of the younger men who have jobs wear blue shirts and sit on the pavement along the wall outside the factory smoking during the noon hour. But this one was standing on a corner on the way north out of town. Not bad looking. The kind you don't mind picking up, just about of age, in an unpressed suit and a soft hat. No violent jerking with the thumb and hand. Just the eyes. Thanks. He gets in. Cigarette? I don't mind. How far you going? Westover. Where's that? Not far, just up here a way. I'll tell you when we come to it. Takes a light. Looking for work? Just came off the road. Selling? No, just dropped off the freights for a while, leaving again tomorrow morning. This your home town? Yes. How far'd you get? The coast. You don't say. How are things out there? Worse than here. No work? Shakes his head. I was up and down the whole coast and back again through the country. Have you a trade? Yes, baker's apprentice. But I don't like the ovens and the hours. Not for me. Tell me something: How does a fellow eat when he's travelling that way? Back doors. Hm. Can you always get something? Most always, I didn't eat so bad. But there must be times—Sure. Once in a while. I went forty-eight hours twice without eating. How was it? Not bad. I always take good care of myself. Lots of them gets sick; the hospitals are full of them all over the country. Not me. I never been sick a

day. The next corner. Here? That's it. You mean here? Sure.
There's a good swimming hole back in the woods there. Just
the day for a swim too, I envy you. Why don't you join us?
—Courteous, with every air of travel and experience—I
haven't a suit. You don't need any.

All the streets of the Dundee section of Passaic have men
idling in them this summer. Polacks mostly, walking around
—collars open, skinny, pot-bellied—or sitting on the steps
and porches of the old-time wooden houses, looking out of
place, fathers of families with their women folk around
them. You see a few niggers, but they're smiling. Jews, of
course, trying to undersell somebody else or each other and
so out of the picture. But the Polacks look stunned, mixed
up, don't know what it's all about. Not even enough coin to
get drunk on. They'll do for the whole bunch. The kid in
the boat is probably a Polack. Anyhow, it doesn't make any
difference, the Polacks will do.

I'll bet the boat isn't four feet long, doesn't look as if it
would hold even a child. It's almost up to the gunwales as it
is in the small waves of the river. It's only been a few years
since the river water was so full of sewage and dye-waste
from the mills that you didn't want to go near it, much less
swim in it as they do now—or boat on it. It was a good job
to build the Passaic Valley Sewer and clean up that stink
hole. And in a way, although they need the money, it's a
good job to get the Polacks out of the factories even if it is
because there's no work for them. And it's a good job to
have the kid paddling that way on the river and the other
kids off to camp. It's what they need. You can see it by the
looks on their faces. They've needed it a long time. You can
see that too on their faces.

They're a husky bunch, mostly. Take for instance the one
in the derby hat who was coming up the street just now—a
six-footer, looking like the usual bum in the vaudeville shows
you'd think might be leaning down any minute to get his
hooks onto a cigar stub. No hurry. And as he gets near

the 1927 open car parked at the curb with the two wooden-faced guys sitting in the front seat staring off into space, loafing, suddenly he gives a hoarse yell at them as much as to say, To hell with you! without looking up, and goes on slowly by, a kind of threatening, cursing growl with plenty of lung power behind it as if he might be chasing kids he'd caught stealing peanuts from a stand. The two hardly noticed him, didn't even move. And he didn't even raise his face either but went on by as if he'd never said a word. Looked drunk. What are you going to do with a guy like that. Or why want to do anything with him. Except not miss him.

Yeah, I know. The kid in the boat is only a kid and don't know a thing more than he's doing. You can't expect a big Polack in a derby to go paddling a canoe on the river just for the hell of it. He's up against it; he's got to be what he is. O.K. Let him stay lit then. Something like that. Maybe it'll slow things up and let them sink in a little after a while. Take that other thickhead they made a place for down at the finishing mill, in Joe Hick's department; they do everything for him and he turns on them and abuses them. Fine! That'll make 'em think. But some of the younger guys, a few girls and kids of all ages from around four to ten, go down and fish for crabs all day long where the old docks are mostly rotted away and the reconditioned excursion boat Mary Ann is tied up. They've started running it to Coney Island every Sunday, a dollar the round trip, the first time such a thing has been tried around here for the past quarter of a century. Not a bad racket at that and a good trip, well worth the dollar—if you've got it.

It's all right in the sun, but the sun can't do everything. It can't make up for what's past. Even the kid in the boat, when he comes in, take a look at him. He's sun-burned all right; but the shape of his head is funny, his chest's too high, and he's got that old look to his face you see sometimes. The same goes for the young guys in the street passing the ball, waiting for Sunday so they can get out on the lot and show their stuff. It's the way they live, from the start up. Two rooms. Three kids in one bed. And all that. Take the girls for instance, take a good look. Not so bad, some of them. But they try to get their big feet into shoes three sizes too small for them and think they're making a hit. Anybody that knows anything spots them the minute they make the first move. It's written all over them. No use trying to kid yourself about things like that. If your shoes fit you and they're made of good leather, if you know what good leather is, and you have straight heels on them, you're getting somewhere. What did you say? The girls' feet look like flat tires in most of the things they don't know enough not to buy and to wear. Try and stop them doing it.

Look at this one lying on the autopsy slab at the hospital; you can see the whole thing. Twins. About five months on the way. Just a kid she was, nineteen, with a lot of soft yellow hair piled up in shiny coils, and her mottled face half leaning toward it. Good legs. A fine pair of breasts. Well-shaped arms. She's dead all right, and if you get what I mean, that's not such a bad thing either. But good God, what for? And the way she did it! all burned down her neck that way. Some guy got to her—someone that couldn't marry her maybe. Her mother gave it to us straight when she says the kid never stepped out nights like some of the other girls. Maybe that's why it happened. She was always home, the only one the old woman could count on to do anything around there. But anyway somebody has her. She's caught. So what? You can imagine, a religious girl like that. Who's going to give her fifty dollars for a doctor even if she knows enough to find one and go to him? She knows it won't make any difference anyway. She's sunk. So she drinks the stuff while her family's left her to attend a funeral. If you can make sense out of that, go to it.

It's all right to be wise, but you got to watch that too. There's no way to learn it easy. And it brings plenty trouble.

All you gotta do is rake in the old coin. Is that so? Last week two of those kids were out in a boat on the river a mile below the city when the oar of one of them struck something half sunk in the water. The body of a man. They pushed it in to shore and quickly called up the police. The head and arms had been cut off and the feet too when they came to look—though that didn't make him any deader. A few hours later they found another body stuck somewhere further up stream. Nobody knows who they were. Dumb all right. But there's no kidding even about a couple of dead punks when you can't find out who did it—so's to send their kids to college. Sure. What are they gonna do? Somebody's got to put up a fight and break into the rich racket. It can't always be the same guys. Somebody's got to get the good screws. They ain't nobody's suckers. All they say is: There it is. Somebody's gonna get it. Why not me? They're not taking it from nobody. If their kids wanna go to college, they can send 'em. And they'll have the best there is there. Sure. Just a lot of gorillas, a lot of mugs. Who says so? That don't bother them none. And if that's all the kids is gonna learn, phooie for them. And if they don't learn nothing else it's because they ain't never gonna know nothin'. And there ain't nobody can't teach 'em.

When they had the big strike at the textile mills, and that bright boy from Boston came down and went shooting off his mouth around in the streets here telling us what to do: Who paid for having their kids and women beat up by the police? Did that guy take a room down on Monroe St. and offer his services for the next ten years at fifty cents a throw to help straighten out the messes he helped get us into? He did not. The Polacks paid for it all. Sure. And raised up sons to be cops too. I don't blame them. Somebody's got to take the jobs. Why get excited? But they ain't moved away none; that's what I'm saying. They're still here. Still as dumb as ever. But it's more than that guy ever give up or could think to do to help them.

Just the same old crap. What are you gonna do with more money when you get it? Take a trip to the old country? You'll come back. It's no different there from here, except worse because it's lasted longer. Then what are you gonna do? Nobody's gonna teach it to you; you got to learn it yourself. Maybe though the kids'll get wise quicker and do something—if they get the breaks with the factories still more interested in dumping sewage cheap than keeping the river clean, and fighting it through the courts every time the Commission tries to finish the job right and puts the screws to them. That kind of thing.

Farther downstream at the County Bridge where they are replacing the rotten piling and timber-work of the bridge apron, twenty or more men lean every day on the iron guard rail and beside them small boys and little girls in beach pyjamas soiled across the behind, looking through the latticed grill work, watching the work going on below. The telephone cable got fouled in some way, and they had to send a diver down to free it for repairs. He worked from a scow tied under the middle span. You can see the diver now, in his undershirt, bareheaded and beginning to be bald, kneeling on the scow deck with his deflated suit laid out before him, the helmet—toward the bridge—and the clumsy bootlike feet being the only parts of it to keep their shape. Sailor fashion he's sewing up a tear in the fabric of one leg while the line on the bridge, Polacks mostly, lean their bellies against the hot iron-work looking down at him, learning something. A whole lot of things. Teaching them too, maybe.

It's an eye opener what you have time for these days. Somebody with nothing else to do but take a walk for himself found a coin, said to be gold! along the riverbank above the bridge this week. So it's been a regular mob of them walking up and down there ever since, thinking where there's been one piece maybe you'll find another, if you look long enough. And someone did find another coin, copper! today, with the date 1864 on it. But where there used to be a tree, a big tree, some years ago there's the remains of it now, a stump lying on its side with roots sticking up into the air ten feet or more above the riverbank. Tired of walking in the mud and finding nothing, a Polack, another one in his shirt sleeves, a man of about thirty I imagine, has climbed up among these roots to sit, holding on among them as in a saddle, where he can look down and watch the others prowling around with crooked sticks in their hands poking up the mud.

Not many gets away with the big stuff, straight, if you can call it straight, or crooked. The young men, in their twenties or early thirties, when they have a hard job on their hands often use shirts with the sleeves ripped out at the shoulders to give themselves more arm room. Swell looking muscles. What for? What good are they to a man when someone lands a slug of lead between his ribs? And you don't get to be a Delegate lifting quarter-ton bales onto a truck all day long either. You might as well take and trim the rim off an old soft hat the way they do sometimes, to keep their hair slicked down while working, that is, if you don't travel. Then you can run a scollop around the edge and cut the top full of airholes, stars, circles, and all that. And good luck to you. You got to say, sometimes, the older men, out of work and sitting around with their families, may be getting the breaks after all, as far as that goes. The kids will run out like the four orphans from the asylum—in the dark and storm—when they saw the railroad tracks undermined. They flagged the train with their coats, standing between the rails, determined not to give ground at any cost. And as a reward asked to be taken to see The Babe knock it, just once, out of the lot. Cuckoo! Cuckoo as a funny strip. But at that it's not so funny.

The Girl with a Pimply Face

ONE OF THE LOCAL DRUGGISTS sent in the call: 50 Summer St., second floor, the door to the left. It's a baby they've just brought from the hospital. Pretty bad condition I should imagine. Do you want to make it? I think they've had somebody else but don't like him, he added as an afterthought.

It was half past twelve. I was just sitting down to lunch. Can't they wait till after office hours?

Oh I guess so. But they're foreigners and you know how they are. Make it as soon as you can. I guess the baby's pretty bad.

It was two-thirty when I got to the place, over a shop in the business part of town. One of those street doors between plate glass show windows. A narrow entry with smashed mail boxes on one side and a dark stair leading straight up. I'd been to the address a number of times during the past years to see various people who had lived there.

Going up I found no bell so I rapped vigorously on the wavy-glass door-panel to the left. I knew it to be the door to the kitchen, which occupied the rear of that apartment.

Come in, said a loud childish voice.

I opened the door and saw a lank haired girl of about fifteen standing chewing gum and eyeing me curiously from beside the kitchen table. The hair was coal black and one of her eyelids drooped a little as she spoke. Well, what do you want? she said. Boy, she was tough and no kidding but I fell for her immediately. There was that hard, straight thing about her that in itself gives an impression of excellence.

I'm the doctor, I said.

Oh, you're the doctor. The baby's inside. She looked at me. Want to see her?

Sure, that's what I came for. Where's your mother?

She's out. I don't know when she's coming back. But you can take a look at the baby if you want to.

All right. Let's see her.

She led the way into the bedroom, toward the front of the flat, one of the unlit rooms, the only windows being those in the kitchen and along the facade of the building.

There she is.

I looked on the bed and saw a small face, emaciated but quiet, unnaturally quiet, sticking out of the upper end of a tightly rolled bundle made by the rest of the baby encircled in a blue cotton blanket. The whole wasn't much larger than a good sized loaf of rye bread. Hands and everything were rolled up. Just the yellowish face showed, tightly hatted and framed around by a corner of the blanket.

What's the matter with her, I asked.

I dunno, said the girl as fresh as paint and seeming about as indifferent as though it had been no relative of hers instead of her sister. I looked at my informer very much amused and she looked back at me, chewing her gum vigorously, standing there her feet well apart. She cocked her head to one side and gave it to me straight in the eye, as much as to say, Well? I looked back at her. She had one of those small, squeezed up faces, snub nose, overhanging eyebrows, low brow and a terrible complexion, pimply and coarse.

When's your mother coming back do you *think*, I asked again.

Maybe in an hour. But maybe you'd better come some time when my father's here. He talks English. He ought to come in around five I guess.

But can't you tell me something about the baby? I hear it's been sick. Does it have a fever?

I dunno.

But has it diarrhoea, are its movements green?

Sure, she said, I guess so. It's been in the hospital but it got worse so my father brought it home today.

What are they feeding it?

A bottle. You can see that yourself. There it is.

There was a cold bottle of half finished milk lying on the coverlet the nipple end of it fallen behind the baby's head.

How old is she? It's a girl, did you say?

Yeah, it's a girl.

Your sister?

Sure. Want to examine it?

No thanks, I said. For the moment at least I had lost all interest in the baby. This young kid in charge of the house did something to me that I liked. She was just a child but nobody was putting anything over on her if she knew it, yet the real thing about her was the complete lack of the rotten smell of a liar. She wasn't in the least presumptive. Just straight.

But after all she wasn't such a child. She had breasts you knew would be like small stones to the hand, good muscular arms and fine hard legs. Her bare feet were stuck into broken down leather sandals such as you see worn by children at the beach in summer. She was heavily tanned too, wherever her skin showed. Just one of the kids you'll find loafing around the pools they have outside towns and cities everywhere these days. A tough little nut finding her own way in the world.

What's the matter with your legs? I asked. They were bare and covered with scabby sores.

Poison ivy, she answered, pulling up her skirts to show me.

Gee, but you ought to seen it two days ago. This ain't nothing. You're a doctor. What can I do for it?

Let's see, I said.

She put her leg up on a chair. It had been badly bitten by mosquitoes, as I saw the thing, but she insisted on poison ivy. She had torn at the affected places with her finger nails and that's what made it look worse.

Oh that's not so bad, I said, if you'll only leave it alone and stop scratching it.

Yeah, I know that but I can't. Scratching's the only thing makes it feel better.

What's that on your foot.

Where? looking.

That big brown spot there on the back of your foot.

Dirt I guess. Her gum chewing never stopped and her fixed defensive non-expression never changed.

Why don't you wash it?

I do. Say, what could I do for my face?

I looked at it closely. You have what they call acne, I told her. All those blackheads and pimples you see there, well, let's see, the first thing you ought to do, I suppose is to get some good soap.

What kind of soap? Lifebuoy?

No. I'd suggest one of those cakes of Lux. Not the flakes but the cake.

Yeah, I know, she said. Three for seventeen.

Use it. Use it every morning. Bathe your face in very hot water. You know, until the skin is red from it. That's to bring the blood up to the skin. Then take a piece of ice. You have ice, haven't you?

Sure, we have ice.

Hold it in a face cloth—or whatever you have—and rub that all over your face. Do that right after you've washed it in the very hot water—before it has cooled. Rub the ice all over. And do it every day—for a month. Your skin will improve. If you like, you can take some cold cream once in a while, not much, just a little and rub that in last of all, if your face feels too dry.

Will that help me?

If you stick to it, it'll help you.

All right.

There's a lotion I could give you to use along with that. Remind me of it when I come back later. Why aren't you in school?

Agh, I'm not going any more. They can't make me. Can they?

They can try.

How can they? I know a girl thirteen that don't go and they can't make her either.

Don't you want to learn things?

I know enough already.

Going to get a job?

I got a job. Here. I been helping the Jews across the hall. They give me three fifty a week—all summer.

Good for you, I said. Think your father'll be here around five?

Guess so. He ought to be.

I'll come back then. Make it all the same call.

All right, she said, looking straight at me and chewing her gum as vigorously as ever.

Just then a little blond haired thing of about seven came in through the kitchen and walked to me looking curiously at my satchel and then at the baby.

What are you, a doctor?

See you later, I said to the older girl and went out.

At five-thirty I once more climbed the wooden stairs after passing two women at the street entrance who looked me up and down from where they were leaning on the brick wall of the building talking.

This time a woman's voice said, Come in, when I knocked on the kitchen door.

It was the mother. She was impressive, a bulky woman, growing toward fifty, in a black dress, with lank graying hair and a long seamed face. She stood by the enameled kitchen table. A younger, plumpish woman with blond hair, well cared for and in a neat house dress—as if she had dolled herself up for the occasion—was standing beside her.

The small blank child was there too and the older girl, behind the others, overshadowed by her mother, the two older women at least a head taller than she. No one spoke.

Hello, I said to the girl I had been talking to earlier. She didn't answer me.

Doctor, began the mother, save my baby. She very sick. The woman spoke with a thick, heavy voice and seemed overcome with grief and apprehension. Doctor! Doctor! she all but wept.

All right, I said to cut the woman short, let's take a look at her first.

So everybody headed toward the front of the house, the mother in the lead. As they went I lagged behind to speak to the second woman, the interpreter. What happened?

The baby was not doing so well. So they took it to the hospital to see if the doctors there could help it. But it got worse. So her husband took it out this morning. It looks bad to me.

Yes, said the mother who had overheard us. Me got seven children. One daughter married. This my baby, pointing to the child on the bed. And she wiped her face with the back of her hand. This baby no do good. Me almost crazy. Don't know who can help. What doctor, I don't know. Somebody tell me take to hospital. I think maybe do some good. Five days she there. Cost me two dollar every day. Ten dollar. I no got money. And when I see my baby, she worse. She look dead. I can't leave she there. No. No. I say to everybody, no. I take she home. Doctor, you save my baby. I pay you. I pay you everything—

Wait a minute, wait a minute, I said. Then I turned to the other woman. What happened?

The baby got like a diarrhoea in the hospital. And she was all dirty when they went to see her. They got all excited—

All sore behind, broke in the mother—

The younger woman said a few words to her in some language that sounded like Russian but it didn't stop her—

No. No. I send she to hospital. And when I see my baby like that I can't leave she there. My babies no that way. Never, she emphasized. Never! I take she home.

Take your time, I said. Take off her clothes. Everything off. This is a regular party. It's warm enough in here. Does she vomit?

She no eat. How she can vomit? said the mother.

But the other woman contradicted her. Yes, she was vomiting in the hospital, the nurse said.

It happens that this September we had been having a lot of such cases in my hospital also, an infectious diarrhoea which practically all the children got when they came in from any cause. I supposed that this was what happened to this child. No doubt it had been in a bad way before that, improper feeding, etc., etc. And then when they took it in there, for whatever had been the matter with it, the diarrhoea had developed. These things sometimes don't turn out so well. Lucky, no doubt, that they had brought it home when they did. I told them so, explaining at the same time: One nurse for ten or twenty babies, they do all they can but you can't run and change the whole ward every five minutes. But the infant looked too lifeless for that only to be the matter with it.

You want all clothes off, asked the mother again, hesitating and trying to keep the baby covered with the cotton blanket while undressing it.

Everything off, I said.

There it lay, just skin and bones with a round fleshless head at the top and the usual pot belly you find in such cases.

Look, said the mother, tilting the infant over on its right side with her big hands so that I might see the reddened buttocks. What kind of nurse that. My babies never that way.

Take your time, take your time, I told her. That's not bad. And it wasn't either. Any child with loose movements might have had the same half an hour after being cared for. Come on. Move away, I said and give me a chance. She kept hovering over the baby as if afraid I might expose it.

It had no temperature. There was no rash. The mouth was in reasonably good shape. Eyes, ears negative. The moment I put my stethescope to the little boney chest, however, the whole thing became clear. The infant had a severe congenital heart defect, a roar when you listened over the heart that meant, to put it crudely, that she was no good, never would be.

The mother was watching me. I straightened up and looking at her told her plainly: She's got a bad heart.

That was the sign for tears. The big woman cried while she spoke. Doctor, she pleaded in blubbering anguish, save my baby.

I'll help her, I said, but she's got a bad heart. That will never be any better. But I knew perfectly well she wouldn't pay the least attention to what I was saying.

I give you anything, she went on. I pay you. I pay you twenty dollar. Doctor, you fix my baby. You good doctor. You fix.

All right, all right, I said. What are you feeding it?

They told me and it was a ridiculous formula, unboiled besides. I regulated it properly for them and told them how to proceed to make it up. Have you got enough bottles, I asked the young girl.

Sure, we got bottles, she told me.

O.K., then go ahead.

You think you cure she? The mother with her long, tearful face was at me again, so different from her tough female fifteen-year-old.

You do what I tell you for three days, I said, and I'll come back and see how you're getting on.

Tank you, doctor, so much. I pay you. I got today no

money. I pay ten dollar to hospital. They cheat me. I got no more money. I pay you Friday when my husband get pay. You save my baby.

Boy! what a woman. I couldn't get away.

She my baby, doctor. I no want to lose. Me got seven children—

Yes, you told me.

But this my baby. You understand. She very sick. You good doctor—

Oh my God! To get away from her I turned again to the kid. You better get going after more bottles before the stores close. I'll come back Friday morning.

How about that stuff for my face you were gonna give me.

That's right. Wait a minute. And I sat down on the edge of the bed to write out a prescription for some lotio alba comp. such as we use in acne. The two older women looked at me in astonishment—wondering, I suppose, how I knew the girl. I finished writing the thing and handed it to her. Sop it on your face at bedtime, I said, and let it dry on. Don't get it into your eyes.

No, I won't.

I'll see you in a couple of days, I said to them all.

Doctor! the old woman was still after me. You come back. I pay you. But all a time short. Always tomorrow come milk man. Must pay rent, must pay coal. And no got money. Too much work. Too much wash. Too much cook. Nobody help. I don't know what's a matter. This door, doctor, this door. This house make sick. Make sick.

Do the best I can, I said as I was leaving.

The girl followed on the stairs. How much is this going to cost, she asked shrewdly holding the prescription.

Not much, I said, and then started to think. Tell them you only got half a dollar. Tell them I said that's all it's worth.

Is that right, she said.

Absolutely. Don't pay a cent more for it.

Say, you're all right, she looked at me appreciatively.

Have you got half a dollar.

Sure. Why not.

What's it all about, my wife asked me in the evening. She had heard about the case. Gee! I sure met a wonderful girl, I told her.

What! another?

Some tough baby. I'm crazy about her. Talk about straight stuff . . . And I recounted to her the sort of case it was and what I had done. The mother's an odd one too. I don't quite make her out.

Did they pay you?

No. I don't suppose they have any cash.

Going back?

Sure. Have to.

Well, I don't see why you have to do all this charity work. Now that's a case you should report to the Emergency Relief. You'll get at least two dollars a call from them.

But the father has a job, I understand. That counts me out.

What sort of a job?

I dunno. Forgot to ask.

What's the baby's name so I can put it in the book?

Damn it. I never thought to ask them that either. I think they must have told me but I can't remember it. Some kind of a Russian name—

You're the limit. Dumbbell, she laughed. Honestly—Who are they anyhow.

You know, I think it must be that family Kate was telling us about. Don't you remember. The time the little kid was playing there one afternoon after school, fell down the front steps and knocked herself senseless.

I don't recall.

Sure you do. That's the family. I get it now. Kate took the brat down there in a taxi and went up with her to see that everything was all right. Yop, that's it. The old woman took the older kid by the hair, because she hadn't watched her sister. And what a beating she gave her. Don't you remember Kate telling us afterward. She thought the old woman was going to murder the child she screamed and threw her around so. Some old gal. You can see they're all afraid of her. What a world. I suppose the damned brat drives her cuckoo. But boy, how she clings to that baby.

The last hope, I suppose, said my wife.

Yeah, and the worst bet in the lot. There's a break for you.

She'll love it just the same.

More, usually.

Three days later I called at the flat again. Come in. This time a resonant male voice. I entered, keenly interested.

By the same kitchen table stood a short, thickset man in baggy working pants and a heavy cotton undershirt. He seemed to have the stability of a cube placed on one of its facets, a smooth, highly colored Slavic face, long black moustaches and widely separated, perfectly candid blue eyes. His black hair, glossy and profuse stood out carelessly all over his large round head. By his look he reminded me at once of his blond haired daughter, absolutely unruffled. The shoulders of an ox. You the doctor, he said. Come in.

The girl and the small child were beside him, the mother was in the bedroom.

The baby no better. Won't eat, said the man in answer to my first question.

How are its bowels?

Not so bad.

Does it vomit?

No.

Then it is better, I objected. But by this time the mother had heard us talking and came in. She seemed worse than the last time. Absolutely inconsolable. Doctor! Doctor! she came up to me.

Somewhat irritated I put her aside and went in to the baby. Of course it was better, much better. So I told them. But the heart, naturally was the same.

How she heart? the mother pressed me eagerly. Today little better?

I started to explain things to the man who was standing back giving his wife precedence but as soon as she got the drift of what I was saying she was all over me again and the tears began to pour. There was no use my talking. Doctor, you good doctor. You do something fix my baby. And before I could move she took my left hand in both hers and kissed it through her tears. As she did so I realized finally that she had been drinking.

I turned toward the man, looking a good bit like the sun at noonday and as indifferent, then back to the woman and I felt deeply sorry for her.

Then, not knowing why I said it nor of whom, precisely I was speaking, I felt myself choking inwardly with the words: Hell! God damn it. The sons of bitches. Why do these things have to be?

The next morning as I came into the coat room at the hospital there were several of the visiting staff standing there with their cigarettes, talking. It was about a hunting dog belonging to one of the doctors. It had come down with distemper and seemed likely to die.

I called up half a dozen vets around here, one of them was saying. I even called up the one in your town, he added turning to me as I came in. And do you know how much they wanted to charge me for giving the serum to that animal?

Nobody answered.

They had the nerve to want to charge me five dollars a shot for it. Can you beat that? Five dollars a shot.

Did you give them the job, someone spoke up facetiously.

Did I? I should say I did not, the first answered. But can

you beat that. Why we're nothing but a lot of slop-heels compared to those guys. We deserve to starve.

Get it out of them, someone rasped, kidding. That's the stuff.

Then the original speaker went on, buttonholing me as some of the others faded from the room. Did you ever see practice so rotten. By the way, I was called over to your town about a week ago to see a kid I delivered up here during the summer. Do you know anything about the case?

I probably got them on my list, I said. Russians?

Yeah, I thought as much. Has a job as a road worker or something. Said they couldn't pay me. Well, I took the trouble of going up to your court house and finding out what he was getting. Eighteen dollars a week. Just the type. And they had the nerve to tell me they couldn't pay me.

She told me ten.

She's a liar.

Natural maternal instinct, I guess.

Whisky appetite, if you should ask me.

Same thing.

O.K. buddy. Only I'm telling you. And did I tell *them*. They'll never call me down there again, believe me. I had that much satisfaction out of them anyway. You make 'em pay you. Don't you do anything for them unless they do. He's paid by the county. I tell you if I had taxes to pay down there I'd go and take it out of his salary.

You and how many others?

Say, they're bad actors, that crew. Do you know what they really do with their money? Whisky. Now I'm telling you. That old woman is the slickest customer you ever saw. She's drunk all the time. Didn't you notice it?

Not while I was there.

Don't you let them put any of that sympathy game over on you. Why they tell me she leaves that baby lying on the bed all day long screaming its lungs out until the neighbors complain to the police about it. I'm not lying to you.

Yeah, the old skate's got nerves, you can see that. I can imagine she's a bugger when she gets going.

But what about the young girl, I asked weakly. She seems like a pretty straight kid.

My confrere let out a wild howl. That thing! You mean that pimply faced little bitch. Say, if I had my way I'd run her out of the town tomorrow morning. There's about a dozen wise guys on her trail every night in the week. Ask the cops. Just ask them. They know. Only nobody wants to bring in a complaint. They say you'll stumble over her on the roof, behind the stairs anytime at all. Boy, they sure took you in.

Yes, I suppose they did, I said.

But the old woman's the ringleader. She's got the brains. Take my advice and make them pay.

The last time I went I heard the, Come in! from the front of the house. The fifteen-year-old was in there at the window in a rocking chair with the tightly wrapped baby in her arms. She got up. Her legs were bare to the hips. A powerful little animal.

What are you doing? Going swimming? I asked.

Naw, that's my gym suit. What the kids wear for Physical Training in school.

How's the baby?

She's all right.

Do you mean it?

Sure, she eats fine now.

Tell your mother to bring it to the office some day so I can weigh it. The food'll need increasing in another week or two anyway.

I'll tell her.

How's your face?

Gettin' better.

My God, it *is*, I said. And it was much better. Going back to school now?

Yeah, I had tuh.

The Use of Force

THEY WERE new patients to me, all I had was the name, Olson. Please come down as soon as you can, my daughter is very sick.

When I arrived I was met by the mother, a big startled looking woman, very clean and apologetic who merely said, Is this the doctor? and let me in. In the back, she added. You must excuse us, doctor, we have her in the kitchen where it is warm. It is very damp here sometimes.

The child was fully dressed and sitting on her father's lap near the kitchen table. He tried to get up, but I motioned for him not to bother, took off my overcoat and started to look things over. I could see that they were all very nervous, eyeing me up and down distrustfully. As often, in such cases, they weren't telling me more than they had to, it was up to me to tell them; that's why they were spending three dollars on me.

The child was fairly eating me up with her cold, steady eyes, and no expression to her face whatever. She did not move and seemed, inwardly, quiet; an unusually attractive little thing, and as strong as a heifer in appearance. But her face was flushed, she was breathing rapidly, and I realized that she had a high fever. She had magnificent blonde hair, in profusion. One of those picture children often reproduced in advertising leaflets and the photogravure sections of the Sunday papers.

She's had a fever for three days, began the father and we don't know what it comes from. My wife has given her things, you know, like people do, but it don't do no good.

131

And there's been a lot of sickness around. So we tho't you'd better look her over and tell us what is the matter.

As doctors often do I took a trial shot at it as a point of departure. Has she had a sore throat?

Both parents answered me together, No . . . No, she says her throat don't hurt her.

Does your throat hurt you? added the mother to the child. But the little girl's expression didn't change nor did she move her eyes from my face.

Have you looked?

I tried to, said the mother, but I couldn't see.

As it happens we had been having a number of cases of diphtheria in the school to which this child went during that month and we were all, quite apparently, thinking of that, though no one had as yet spoken of the thing.

Well, I said, suppose we take a look at the throat first. I smiled in my best professional manner and asking for the child's first name I said, come on, Mathilda, open your mouth and let's take a look at your throat.

Nothing doing.

Aw, come on, I coaxed, just open your mouth wide and let me take a look. Look, I said opening both hands wide, I haven't anything in my hands. Just open up and let me see.

Such a nice man, put in the mother. Look how kind he is to you. Come on, do what he tells you to. He won't hurt you.

At that I ground my teeth in disgust. If only they wouldn't use the word "hurt" I might be able to get somewhere. But I did not allow myself to be hurried or disturbed but speaking quietly and slowly I approached the child again.

As I moved my chair a little nearer suddenly with one cat-like movement both her hands clawed instinctively for my eyes and she almost reached them too. In fact she knocked my glasses flying and they fell, though unbroken, several feet away from me on the kitchen floor.

Both the mother and father almost turned themselves

inside out in embarrassment and apology. You bad girl, said the mother, taking her and shaking her by one arm. Look what you've done. The nice man . . .

For heaven's sake, I broke in. Don't call me a nice man to her. I'm here to look at her throat on the chance that she might have diphtheria and possibly die of it. But that's nothing to her. Look here, I said to the child, we're going to look at your throat. You're old enough to understand what I'm saying. Will you open it now by yourself or shall we have to open it for you?

Not a move. Even her expression hadn't changed. Her breaths however were coming faster and faster. Then the battle began. I had to do it. I had to have a throat culture for her own protection. But first I told the parents that it was entirely up to them. I explained the danger but said that I would not insist on a throat examination so long as they would take the responsibility.

If you don't do what the doctor says you'll have to go to the hospital, the mother admonished her severely.

Oh yeah? I had to smile to myself. After all, I had already fallen in love with the savage brat, the parents were contemptible to me. In the ensuing struggle they grew more and more abject, crushed, exhausted while she surely rose to magnificent heights of insane fury of effort bred of her terror of me.

The father tried his best, and he was a big man but the fact that she was his daughter, his shame at her behavior and his dread of hurting her made him release her just at the critical moment several times when I had almost achieved success, till I wanted to kill him. But his dread also that she might have diphtheria made him tell me to go on, go on though he himself was almost fainting, while the mother moved back and forth behind us raising and lowering her hands in an agony of apprehension.

Put her in front of you on your lap, I ordered, and hold both her wrists.

But as soon as he did the child let out a scream. Don't, you're hurting me. Let go of my hands. Let them go I tell you. Then she shrieked terrifyingly, hysterically. Stop it! Stop it! You're killing me!

Do you think she can stand it, doctor! said the mother.

You get out, said the husband to his wife. Do you want her to die of diphtheria?

Come on now, hold her, I said.

Then I grasped the child's head with my left hand and tried to get the wooden tongue depressor between her teeth. She fought, with clenched teeth, desperately! But now I also had grown furious—at a child. I tried to hold myself down but I couldn't. I know how to expose a throat for inspection. And I did my best. When finally I got the wooden spatula behind the last teeth and just the point of it into the mouth cavity, she opened up for an instant but before I could see anything she came down again and gripping the wooden blade between her molars she reduced it to splinters before I could get it out again.

Aren't you ashamed, the mother yelled at her. Aren't you ashamed to act like that in front of the doctor?

Get me a smooth-handled spoon of some sort, I told the mother. We're going through with this. The child's mouth was already bleeding. Her tongue was cut and she was screaming in wild hysterical shrieks. Perhaps I should have desisted and come back in an hour or more. No doubt it would have been better. But I have seen at least two children lying dead in bed of neglect in such cases, and feeling that I must get a diagnosis now or never I went at it again. But the worst of it was that I too had got beyond reason. I could have torn the child apart in my own fury and enjoyed it. It was a pleasure to attack her. My face was burning with it.

The damned little brat must be protected against her own idiocy, one says to one's self at such times. Others must be protected against her. It is social necessity. And all these things are true. But a blind fury, a feeling of adult shame, bred of a longing for muscular release are the operatives. One goes on to the end.

In a final unreasoning assault I overpowered the child's neck and jaws. I forced the heavy silver spoon back of her teeth and down her throat till she gagged. And there it was —both tonsils covered with membrane. She had fought valiantly to keep me from knowing her secret. She had been hiding that sore throat for three days at least and lying to her parents in order to escape just such an outcome as this.

Now truly she *was* furious. She had been on the defensive before but now she attacked. Tried to get off her father's lap and fly at me while tears of defeat blinded her eyes.

A Night in June

I was a young man then—full of information and tenderness. It was her first baby. She lived just around the corner from her present abode, one room over a small general store kept by an old man.

It was a difficult forceps delivery and I lost the child, to my disgust; though without nurse, anesthetist, or even enough hot water in the place, I shouldn't have been overmuch blamed. I must have been fairly able not to have done worse. But I won a friend and I found another—to admire, a sort of love for the woman.

She was slightly older than her husband, a heavy-looking Italian boy. Both were short. A peasant woman who could scarcely talk a word of English, being recently come from the other side, a woman of great simplicity of character—docility, patience, with a fine direct look in her grey eyes. And courageous. Devoted to her instincts and convictions and to me.

Sometimes she'd cry out at her husband, as I got to know her later, with some high pitched animalistic sound when he would say something to her in Italian that I couldn't understand and I knew that she was holding out for me.

Usually though, she said very little, looking me straight in the eye with a smile, her voice pleasant and candid though I could scarcely understand her few broken words. Her sentences were seldom more than three or four words long. She always acted as though I must naturally know what was in her mind and her smile with a shrug always won me.

Apart from the second child, born a year after the first,

during the absence of the family from town for a short time, I had delivered Angelina of all her children. This one would make my eighth attendance on her, her ninth labor.

Three A.M., June the 10th, I noticed the calendar as I flashed on the light in my office to pick up my satchel, the same, by the way, my uncle had given me when I graduated from Medical School. One gets not to deliver women at home nowadays. The hospital is the place for it. The equipment is far better.

Smiling, I picked up the relic from where I had tossed it two or three years before under a table in my small laboratory hoping never to have to use it again. In it I found a brand new hypodermic syringe with the manufacturer's name still shiny with black enamel on the barrel. Also a pair of curved scissors I had been looking for for the last three years, thinking someone had stolen them.

I dusted off the top of the Lysol bottle when I took it from the shelf and quickly checking on the rest of my necessities, I went off, without a coat or necktie, wearing the same shirt I had had on during the day preceding, soiled but—better so.

It was a beautiful June night. The lighted clock in the tower over the factory said 3:20. The clock in the facade of the Trust Company across the track said it also. Paralleling the railroad I recognized the squat figure of the husband returning home ahead of me—whistling as he walked. I put my hand out of the car in sign of recognition and kept on, rounding the final triangular block a little way ahead to bring my car in to the right in front of the woman's house for parking.

The husband came up as I was trying to decide which of the two steep cobbled entry-ways to take. Got you up early, he said.

Where ya been? his sister said to him when we had got into the house from the rear.

I went down to the police to telephone, he said, that's the surest way.

I told you to go next door, you dope. What did you go away down there for? Leaving me here alone.

Aw, I didn't want to wake nobody up.

I got two calls, I broke in.

Yes, he went away and left me alone. I got scared so I waked him up anyway to call you.

The kitchen where we stood was lighted by a somewhat damaged Welsbach mantel gaslight. Everything was quiet. The husband took off his cap and sat along the wall. I put my satchel on the tubs and began to take things out.

There was just one sterile umbilical tie left, two, really, in the same envelope, as always, for possible twins, but that detail aside, everything was ample and in order. I complimented myself. Even the Argyrol was there, in tablet form, insuring the full potency of a fresh solution. Nothing so satisfying as a kit of any sort prepared and in order even when picked up in an emergency after an interval of years.

I selected out two artery clamps and two scissors. One thing, there'd be no need of sutures afterward in this case.

You want hot water?

Not yet, I said. Might as well take my shirt off, though. Which I did, throwing it on a kitchen chair and donning the usual light rubber apron.

I'm sorry we ain't got no light in there. The electricity is turned off. Do you think you can see with a candle?

Sure. Why not? But it was very dark in the room where the woman lay on a low double bed. A three-year-old boy was asleep on the sheet beside her. She wore an abbreviated nightgown, to her hips. Her short thick legs had, as I knew, bunches of large varicose veins about them like vines. Everything was clean and in order. The sister-in-law held the candle. Few words were spoken.

I made the examination and found the head high but the cervix fully dilated. Oh yeah. It often happens in women who have had many children; pendulous abdomen, lack of muscular power resulting in a slight misdirection of the forces of labor and the thing may go on for days.

When I finished, Angelina got up and sat on the edge of the bed. I went back to the kitchen, the candle following me, leaving the room dark again.

Do you need it any more? the sister-in-law said, I'll put it out.

Then the husband spoke up, Ain't you got but that one candle?

No, said the sister.

Why didn't you get some at the store when you woke him up; use your head.

The woman had the candle in a holder on the cold coal range. She leaned over to blow it out but misdirecting her aim, she had to blow three times to do it. Three or four times.

What's the matter? said her brother, getting weak? Old age counts, eh Doc? he said and got up finally to go out.

We could hear an engineer signaling outside in the still night—with short quick blasts of his whistle—very staccato —not, I suppose, to make any greater disturbance than necessary with people sleeping all about.

Later on the freights began to roar past shaking the whole house.

She doesn't seem to be having many strong pains, I said to my companion in the kitchen, for there wasn't a sound from the labor room and hadn't been for the past half hour.

She don't want to make no noise and wake the kids.

How old is the oldest now? I asked.

He's sixteen. The girl would have been eighteen this year. You know the first one you took from her.

Where are they all?

In there, with a nod of the head toward the other room of the apartment, such as it was, the first floor of an old two-story house, the whole thing perhaps twenty-five feet each way.

I sat in a straight chair by the kitchen table, my right arm, bare to the shoulder, resting on the worn oil cloth.

She says she wants an enema, said the woman. O.K. But I don't know how to give it to her. She ain't got a bed-pan or nothing. I don't want to get the bed all wet.

Has she had a movement today?

Yeah, but she thinks an enema will help her.

Well, have you got a bag?

Yeah, she says there's one here somewhere.

Get it. She's got a chamber pot here, hasn't she?

Sure.

So the woman got the equipment, a blue rubber douche bag, the rubber of it feeling rather stiff to the touch. She laid it on the stove in its open box and looked at it holding her hands out helplessly. I'm afraid, she said.

All right, you hold the candle. Mix up a little warm soapy water. We'll need some vaseline.

The woman called out to us where to find it, having over-heard our conversation.

Lift up, till I put these newspapers under you, said my assistant. I don't want to wet the bed.

That's nothing, Angelina answered smiling. But she raised her buttocks high so we could fix her.

Returning ten minutes later to my chair, I saw the woman taking the pot out through the kitchen and upstairs to empty it. I crossed my legs, crossed my bare arms in my lap also and let my head fall forward. I must have slept, for when I opened my eyes again, both my legs and my arms were somewhat numb. I felt deliciously relaxed though somewhat bewildered. I must have snored, waking myself with a start. Everything was quiet as before. The peace of the room was unchanged. Delicious.

I heard the woman and her attendant making some slight sounds in the next room and went in to her.

Examining her, I found things unchanged. It was about half past four. What to do? Do you mind if I give you the needle? I asked her gently. We'd been through this many times before. She shrugged her shoulders as much as to say, It's up to you. So I gave her a few minims of pituitrin to intensify the strength of the pains. I was cautious since the practice is not without danger. It is possible to get a ruptured uterus where the muscle has been stretched by many pregnancies if one does not know what one is doing. Then I returned to the kitchen to wait once more.

This time I took out the obstetric gown I had brought with me, it was in a roll as it had come from the satchel, and covering it with my shirt to make a better surface and a little more bulk, I placed it at the edge of the table and leaning forward, laid my face sidewise upon it, my arms resting on the table before me, my nose and mouth at the table edge between my arms. I could breathe freely. It was a pleasant position and as I lay there content, I thought as I often do of what painting it was in which I had seen men sleeping that way.

Then I fell asleep and, in my half sleep began to argue with myself—or some imaginary power—of science and humanity. Our exaggerated ways will have to pull in their horns, I said. We've learned from one teacher and neglected another. Now that I'm older, I'm finding the older school.

The pituitary extract and other simple devices represent science. Science, I dreamed, has crowded the stage more than is necessary. The process of selection will simplify the application. It touches us too crudely now, all newness is over-complex. I couldn't tell whether I was asleep or awake.

But without science, without pituitrin, I'd be here till noon or maybe—what? Some others wouldn't wait so long but rush her now. A carefully guarded shot of pituitrin— ought to save her at least much exhaustion—if not more. But I don't want to have anything happen to her.

Now when I lifted my head, there was beginning to be a

little light outside. The woman was quiet. No progress. This time I increased the dose of pituitrin. She had stronger pains but without effect.

Maybe I'd better give you a still larger dose, I said. She made no demur. Well, let me see if I can help you first. I sat on the edge of the bed while the sister-in-law held the candle again glancing at the window where the daylight was growing. With my left hand steering the child's head, I used my ungloved right hand outside on her bare abdomen to press upon the fundus. The woman and I then got to work. Her two hands grabbed me at first a little timidly about the right wrist and forearm. Go ahead, I said. Pull hard. I welcomed the feel of her hands and the strong pull. It quieted me in the way the whole house had quieted me all night.

This woman in her present condition would have seemed repulsive to me ten years ago—now, poor soul, I see her to be as clean as a cow that calves. The flesh of my arm lay against the flesh of her knee gratefully. It was I who was being comforted and soothed.

Finally the head began to move. I wasn't sorry, thinking perhaps I'd have to do something radical before long. We kept at it till the head was born and I could leave her for a moment to put on my other glove. It was almost light now. What time is it? I asked the other woman. Six o'clock, she said.

Just after I had tied the cord, cut it and lifted the baby, a girl, to hand it to the woman, I saw the mother clutch herself suddenly between her thighs and give a cry. I was startled.

The other woman turned with a flash and shouted, Get out of here, you damned kids! I'll slap your damned face for you. And the door through which a head had peered was pulled closed. The three-year-old on the bed beside the mother stirred when the baby cried at first shrilly but had not wakened.

Oh yes, the drops in the baby's eyes. No need. She's as clean as a beast. How do I know? Medical discipline says every case must have drops in the eyes. No chance of gonorrhoea though here—but—Do it.

I heard her husband come into the kitchen now so we gave him the afterbirth in a newspaper to bury. Keep them damned kids out of here, his sister told him. Lock that door. Of course, there was no lock on it.

How do you feel now? I asked the mother after everything had been cleaned up. All right, she said with the peculiar turn of her head and smile by which I knew her.

How many is that? I asked the other woman. Five boys and three girls, she said. I've forgotten how to fix a baby, she went on. What shall I do? Put a little boric acid powder on the belly button to help dry it up?

The Dawn of Another Day

THERE WERE a coupla guys prowling around here this morning but when they seen me they beat it.

Thanks.

Any luck?

No. Not with these hands.

What are you gonna do, hang around this tub all winter? And say, where the hell do you keep the key to that booze, anyway? I bet it's around your neck. Scotch.

You said it, with a tank like you on board. Did Pauline come with the laundry?

Yeah, she brought it.

Did she take the dirty stuff?

No. She wouldn't come aboard when she found out you weren't here. Said she'd come back later.

The men looked at each other and the owner of the boat smiled broadly. The other, in an old slouch hat and a seared, sour face under it, didn't change his expression.

Why don't you stick to booze and leave the girls alone?

Any objections if I don't?

These coons are loaded up with gonorrhoea and everything else, you damn fool. Go on home and get to bed or the misses'll think you fell in the river or something.

To hell with her. Are you holding out on me with that liquor? What you doing, saving it to celebrate the end of Prohibition? Get it out.

The main motor highway ran along the opposite side of the river toward the city, three miles farther down. As it had already begun to grow dark you could see the first lights of the cars going back and forth intermittently beyond the two or three broken down houses on that shore, old houses occupied by negroes, in whose windows also dim lights appeared.

The younger man had gone forward into the store room of his craft where you could hear him unlock a door. After a moment he came back into the small saloon and put an un-opened bottle of bourbon whisky on the table. His companion had already got out glasses and a cork screw.

Will you take it straight or shall I pour it down your neck, you old sweetheart?

You act as if you was lending your wife to your best friend. How much more you got of it in there?

None of your damned business.

Is that so? Well, suppose I don't accept your offer and don't accept—

Go on, your tongue's sticking to the roof of your mouth already so you can't talk straight. Do you want it or shall I chuck it into the river?

No! for Christ's sake, Ed, don't do a thing like that, said the older man turning pale and getting up suddenly.

The other let out a roar of laughter so that his friend sank down again sourly and rested his arms on the little table. You'd leave me here by myself to die of cold and starvation gladly if I ever did run out of it, said Ed pretending serious-ness.

Pour it out before you drop it. The men each had three fingers of it. The older man reached for the bottle at once and wanted to fill his friend's glass again.

No thanks, not tonight.

What's the matter? Thinking of your Mama and Papa in Miami?

Maybe.

Does that mean I gotta quit too?

The other didn't answer so Ed took the bottle and filled up once more.

Watch it, kid.

Listen here, Ed. What the hell's the matter with you? Sore at somebody or something? Why don't you take this lousy yacht of yours down to the yard and let them drag it out?

I'm broke, you nut. Broke. Can you understand that. No money, Get it? I'm tied up here for the winter, free. Get it? Free. So drink up and get the hell home out of here so you can come back some time when I need you.

If *you're* broke, so's the King of England. Sell the rotten tub . . .

Did you ever try to sell a yacht second hand these days? The trouble with you, Fred, is you've never seen fifty dollars all at once in your life so you still think the stork brings it.

Oh yeah? Well, boy, I made more money and lost it before you was born than you'll ever see.

Cheating at cards?

Maybe it was, maybe it wasn't. What's that to you? I ain't got it now. If I had I wouldn't be taking guff from a spoiled baby like you pouting and sulking because Papa won't buy him another nice new seat on the Exchange so he can skin hell out of another bunch of suckers. Listen baby, close this dump up and go south to your family.

You don't get it, Fred. Listen. Get all your brains together. Now, try hard and let it sink through that thick skull of yours: I'm broke. Broke. No money. You know, money. What you use to buy things with. And my old man's going to commit suicide tomorrow. The whole family's broke. Stoney. Flat. The servants are keeping them, bringing in food.

Maybe you're right, kid. Maybe you're right. Doing your laundry free, eh! Just 'cause they like you. Some guy. A liar like you never should go wanting in this little world.

O.K., boy. Have it your way.

I bet she'll be back inside an hour. Mind if I stay?

Stay all night if you like, kid. I'm going to get supper.

The place was heated by an ordinary coal range which had been rigged up with an iron pipe through the temporary woodwork of old lumber enclosing the original cabin. Ed took the pan from inside the oven door, lifted the stove lid, put the pan on and dropped a lump of butter into it. The butter began at once to melt and run down to the edge of the pan. Ed poked it thoughtfully with a fork and watched it melt.

Did you ever read Das Kapital, Ed? asked the man who was still drinking at the table.

What! Say that again.

You heard me the first time. Did you ever read it? You think I'm a drunken bum, don't you. Just because of the face I got on me—

You're drunk.

Smart guy. You know everything, don't you? Well, if you should ever grow up and be old enough to let your own pants down without askin' your mother to do it for you you'll find out I ain't drunk. And that you ain't half as smart as you think you are.

You got me wrong, Fred. I don't think I'm smart. But I'm smart enough to pull out of this hole on my own. You wait and see if I don't.

Don't need nobody, huh? Just a chance to use your brains. Big business, huh? Self reliant, rugged Americanism . . .

And I'm lucky too. Lucky to have a place I can bunk in without rent. And lucky I got you to keep me from drinking myself to death on expensive booze. It didn't take you long, Senator, to smell it out after I tied up here. How do you want your eggs?

Turn 'em over. You know I was a great reader at one time.

How long were you up for?

—and I'll tell you one thing: I'm a Communist. I tell you I'm a Communist and I'm gonna take that black baby of yours right out from under your runny nose. You're too God damned thick to know your—

Come on, come on. Pick the threads off your vest, Rosenblatt. Pull up the table and tell us how to run the world to hell and gone into the slime—

Now listen to me, young fellah, said the one called Fred getting upon his dignity and eyeing his friend with a glassy look. My father was an Irishman and my mother was German and I'm telling you they're the two finest races on earth. But I'm a Democrat—Now wait a minute. Wait a minute. You'll not be taking me for a fool. I been to college too. Maybe you wouldn't think it but it's true. I played on the ball team. I'm a Democrat and I'm a Communist. You didn't know I could talk and read German. I was over there when I was twenty and read that book. And I'm telling you everything that God damned Kike said in it is coming true. I took my knocks and I've lived rough but I never been a four flusher like the kind of people you come from.

Do you mean that?

Christ no, I don't mean it. What would I do without you, Ed? But by Christ I do mean it! in one way.

Eat your eggs and lay off that booze; you'll be in a hell of a fine condition to take Pauline when she gets here, you old cripple.

Will you let me try it?

What do you want me to do, jump overboard? Be yourself. Why she could tie you into knots, you poor simp. Did you ever look at her arms?

Did you ever look at her legs, my boy, you know—from behind? And what a behind! while we're speaking of it, Eddie, I don't understand this generation. You're all shot with the tea and ginger ale sloshing around in your guts.

So you're a Communist.

I believe in the Revolution. It's here. It's got to be here. I read that whole God damned book three times, in German. Would you believe that?

No.

I read that lousy book till I damned near knew it by heart.

And the old bugger is right. To hell with the Capitalists that enslave the resources of the nation. You know yourself 5% of the people of the United States own 95% of the money. And 95% of the people own only 5% of the money. Now that's not right. We got to have a revolution and take it away from them.

You don't need any fancy theory of a revolution by the proletariat to do that. Be yourself, Fred. We're not back in the last century. Russia was. More power to her then. I'm for Russia. We'd be rotten sports if we didn't help their game. Let 'em work it out. But they're nothing but a lot of monkeys, a lot of thick heads. That sort of thing can never happen in America. We're not that thick. You don't need anything but brains. Looka here. You want to break up the game of the Capitalists? You want to know how to do it?

Sure, Bright Eyes, tell us.

Just stop inheritances. Redistribute everything a man has accumulated at the end of his life.

Yeah? And how you gonna do it? You'll have to start by castrating every guy that passes his bar examination seven days after they admit him. If you think that's bright it's no wonder you're living on a discarded yacht for the winter—if you can stand it. Better go back to your wife and kids and graft on your wealthy Ma-in-law. She still has it. Am I right?

Yes, you're right.

And you're broke. Ain't you?

You said it. But I'm not going to stay broke. Take that from me.

Oh you're not aren't you. The resources of the country are limitless! You're going to rise from your ashes like the Phoenix on the revenue stamps and make another fortune by skinning the life out of suckers like me.

No. But if you're an American and keep your nerve you don't need Capitalism—I don't care what you call it. Communism. Your damned Revolution—

Go on. Go on. Did you ever read the book?

I thought you were drunk?

That's what you thought. Did you ever read the book? Answer me that. Well, if you haven't, get it and read it. And don't read just Chapter 14 like the rest of the soap-box orators shootin' their mouths off nowadays. Read the whole thing. And you won't talk like such a damned fool. Why that's a masterpiece of calculation. How in hell are you gonna take inheritances away? Christ man, they'll have the army and the navy and every God damned cop in the country chasin' you for a public enemy and shooting you so full of holes that—Come here with that bottle. What is this, a cheap joint? Put up your glass if you don't want me to finish it alone. Come on now. Be a man.

O.K. Pour me another—to keep you from having it run over into your lungs and drowning you to death.

I can take it. Yes sir, began Fred again—

Aw shut up. I'm going up on deck for a smoke. It's too stinking hot in here, he continued, banking the stove, with all you lousy Communists sweating and farting around the place. Here, have a cigar. I still got a few left. And don't get the wrong end in your mouth. Here, pull! he said holding a match. Then taking the cigar out of his friend's mouth again, he added, You damn fool, do I even have to bite the end of it off for you too.

Ed opened the cabin door letting in a cool blast of air from the outside and went on deck. It was a cloudy November night. The man pulled his coat tightly around him and it being high tide hopped over the boat-side two feet down to the edge of the old wharf where the yacht was made fast.

He turned and looked down between the boat and the old planks of the wharf wondering how she'd take it if they had much ice that winter.

It being coolish he walked toward the road puffing at his cigar and thinking. He stopped, thinking he saw someone turn back from the entrance to the littered area between the river bank and the roadway.

Is that you, Pauline?

Who's that? came back the woman's voice.

It's all right, called back the man knowing she'd recognize his voice. You can come ahead.

He watched her coming stepping carefully along the indistinct path toward the water. She was no girl but a rather short well built woman of about thirty.

Gee, I'm glad to see you. I pretty near lost my nerve. Is that guy still here?

Yes, he's inside. Thanks, Pauline, for bringing my laundry this afternoon. I forgot to tell you I'd be away.

The only reason I come tonight is I'm washing tomorrow early and say why do you have a guy like that hanging around you here. You ain't used to that.

He's a great convenience to me. You know, Pauline, it's damned nice of you to take this interest in me.

Say, you need some new shirts. I darned your socks but I can't fix those cuffs any more, you'll have to do something about it. Go on, get that dirty wash, I got to get home to my husband.

Wish you could have picked it up this afternoon. You would have saved yourself a trip.

Not with him there.

He's not such a bad egg. Wait a minute, I'll get that stuff.

The last streak of orange light had faded out of the west beyond the bare trees as the man and woman stood talking at the edge of the bulwark of the moored yacht. Ed stepped up onto the boat again and opening the cabin door went inside. He left the door open as he did so, deliberately. The young colored woman went curiously up to the wharf edge and tried to peer inside. In the intense stillness of this isolated spot, above the faint lapping of the water somewhere down under her feet, she could hear the slow, heavy breathing of a man drunk and asleep. As Ed came up again with the small parcel of wash tied about with the arms of the shirt which acted as the container, she was laughing softly.

Let me look down in there.

Sure. Go ahead.

Ain't that a pretty sight! The big souse. Why don't he go home and take care of his family, at his age. I don't see how you let a man like that hang around you. All he wants is the whisky you got stowed away down there somewhere. The face on him's enough. I know him, don't worry. And he's ugly. And I mean ugly. Ugh! And she pulled back shivering.

You got him wrong, Pauline. You'd be surprised. He's an educated man.

He don't look it.

No, he doesn't look it. That's right.

How are you making out? It's getting pretty cold these nights. Do you think you're going to be able to stick it?

Hope so.

What's the idea of you hanging around here for anyway? There must be some places you can go. It just don't seem good sense to me. I don't know what you're going to do when it gets real winter.

To tell you the truth, Pauline, neither do I. Forget it. I'm pretty low tonight, just don't like to talk about it.

I wish there was some way I could take care of you.

You wouldn't be any use to me, Pauline with the mugs there are hanging around here.

But you ain't used to this. You're used to having women round you, looking after you. You're going to get sick.

Well thanks, Pauline, for coming for the wash at this late hour and everything else. I'll walk out to the road with you.

It's nice out tonight, isn't it, said the woman walking at his side. When they got to the roadway they stood a moment awkwardly, she swinging the laundry back and forth like a child and he just standing there.

Well, I gotta go, she said finally. Take care of yourself.

Wait a minute.

What you want.

Just hate to see you go somehow. Stick around a little while and talk to me.

What are we going to talk about?

I'm pretty low tonight, Pauline. Pretty low. I just feel like starting out straight from here and running all night, straight ahead and never coming back.

You can't do that. You got too many good things back there.

I feel pretty cowardly tonight. I'd like a good comfortable chair, a warm room, light, a good book to read—

I don't blame you.

And a nice warm, comfortable bed.

The woman giggled to herself. Well, I gotta get going, she said after a moment.

Stick around a while longer. You don't have to go yet.

Say listen boy. When you begin to talk about nice, comfortable warm beds, you give me the shivers. And it don't come from no cold weather neither. I gotta go.

What do you mean?

You know what I mean. I gotta get going.

Wait a minute. Wait a minute. You're miles ahead of me. Listen, Pauline . . .

No sir. I'm not listening to nobody. Not even you. I gotta go.

Come on back on board with me.

With that man sleeping down there? Not me.

He won't wake up. Why he's got almost a quart of whisky into him. He won't wake up till noon tomorrow. You couldn't wake him with a gun. Come on.

Wait a minute, boy. You're going awful fast.

O.K., said the man letting go of her, maybe you're right, maybe I am getting a little ahead of myself. I'm sorry Pauline. No disrespect intended.

I suppose you got the idea I'm all burned up to go back there with you, said the woman watching him.

Never gave it a thought, he answered her. Just needing company. Real company. And hating to be alone tonight.

Neither spoke for several moments. You don't want me, she said finally.

Plenty, was all he answered her this time.

She grinned. That sounds good to me.

Good girl. Come on. And he turned abruptly toward the boat.

Hey, what about that guy?

We'll get by him. They started again toward the boat walking far apart and he a little ahead of her. No further word was spoken till they got to the wharf edge.

Wait here a minute, he cautioned her.

No, I want to see too.

Ed stepped up to the boat's deck and gave his hand to Pauline who took a big step up after him. She had a small powerful hand and gave a little puff and smothered grunt as she came up to the deck. He opened the cabin door and looked in while she behind him put one hand on his shoulder and stared down curiously also.

Fred was sprawled out on the cushion seat along the side wall opposite. Ed went in and shook him, taking a chance. Hey, wake up you bum!

Not a stir.

So he disappeared forward and after a moment came back with a blanket and a pillow. Straightening his friend out he shoved the pillow under his head, covered him with the blanket and then, turning, came over and reached up his hand to the woman to help her down the two steps into the boat's small saloon.

Ed led her around the center table to the door opening forward to the staterooms. Pauline was biting her lower lip and stepping carefully. He closed the door behind them then led her another step or two in the dark to another door through which they passed and which he closed also. There was no light except that from the night outside coming in at the porthole which opened off shore. Across the river were the same glares of passing autos and the duller lights in the windows of the old houses backed down toward the water. It was chilly and damp in the room.

Not much room in here, is there? whispered the woman.

More than we'll need. Listen, Pauline, before we go any further with this, are you all right? You know what I mean.

You got nothing to worry about.

She stripped and Ed put a blanket around her. She was a tight, muscular woman with fine arms and the velvety skin of her race. Hurry up, hurry up, she said, don't keep me waiting here in this cold place.

Why didn't you ever go on the stage with such a body as you have woman. You'd have made a hit.

Not for me. Not that kind of life. I don't want to end up in a ditch with a knife sticking in my back. They never leave you alone. Come on, boy. Love me! She coaxed, urging him to hurry.

There wasn't much room but they made themselves comfortable finally as best they could. Then, after a while, Ed fell into a gentle sleep. When he wakened Pauline was holding him in her arms. He did not move.

Do you know, Pauline, he began quietly, it takes emotion, and deep emotion, to change the thoughts and habits of a lifetime. And danger—the way I've been feeling recently.

Hey, shut up! Not so loud.

He won't hear us. You've done something to me tonight —right out of nothing. Something I never could have believed possible. You're marvelous.

You're not so bad yourself, boy.

Do you know where I feel it most? Ed went on slowly. In the head. She chuckled and moved against him. Something just went that way, deep down inside me: pow!

Say what kind of crazy talk is this?

Class consciousness. Something I've been fooling around with for a long time not knowing what it was all about.

Come on, love me.

Now listen, lay off a minute. I got to tell this to somebody and you've got to listen to me.

Say, listen yourself, I got to be getting home to my old man or he'll kill me. Come on.

When they had dressed and were on their way out Pauline was all curiosity to look once more at Fred lying in drunken sleep where his friend had stretched him. I don't see how you can stand him, said the woman. Then, turning, she caught sight of a small clock set into the saloon wall. Is that right? she turned to Ed. Eleven o'clock?

Yes, I try to keep it fairly accurate.

You mean that short little while we were back there is almost two hours! Oh boy!

Is it all right?

Oh he won't know where I been. Good night! I'm going. What a bum! she turned again to the man still breathing heavily asleep on the wall seat.

I'll walk down to the bridge with you, Ed said to her when they were again on the wharf in the darkness.

Will you?

Certainly.

The sky had become entirely clear and you could see the Pleiades over in the east. They walked out to the road in silence and turned left on the deserted, unlit roadway to the bridge, its scattered red lights ahead of them. Why don't you kick that dirty bum out, she asked Ed finally.

Can't do it, Pauline.

He isn't in your class. They kept on walking side by side in the darkness toward the bridge.

Pauline, there are some things you don't know a thing about. That's the funny part of it . . .

All I know is, that guy makes me sick. He don't belong

to you. I can't stand him. How old is he, anyhow? He ought to know better.

Forget it, woman. That man means a lot to me. And he never meant more to me than right now. For a little while before I saw you tonight I was about ready to be an awful backslider. But you did something to me tonight I'll never forget, Sister. I never quite got what it was all about till what you did for me tonight.

Did you like it?

Maybe you don't get me, Pauline. I liked it fine. I can't tell you how much I did like it. But . . .

Well, what?

You got me all turned over inside. Something kind of snapped inside my head. Come here a minute. I want to kiss you.

Say, are you crazy for sure? Somebody's likely to see you —out here near these lights.

Come here. And he kissed her lovingly on the mouth.

Are you gonna quit and run like you said you were this evening?

Wait and see.

But I can't come back there and see you if that guy's hanging around there all day and night. Can't you drive him out?

Listen, sister. I'm not getting rid of that guy. That's final. So long.

O.K., brother. She went toward the bridge while he turned back through the starry night toward the boat.

Jean Beicke

DURING A TIME like this, they kid a lot among the doctors and nurses on the obstetrical floor because of the rushing business in new babies that's pretty nearly always going on up there. It's the Depression, they say, nobody has any money so they stay home nights. But one bad result of this is that in the children's ward, another floor up, you see a lot of unwanted children.

The parents get them into the place under all sorts of pretexts. For instance, we have two premature brats, Navarro and Cryschka, one a boy and one a girl; the mother died when Cryschka was born, I think. We got them within a few days of each other, one weighing four pounds and one a few ounces more. They dropped down below four pounds before we got them going but there they are; we had a lot of fun betting on their daily gains in weight but we still have them. They're in pretty good shape though now. Most of the kids that are left that way get along swell. The nurses grow attached to them and get a real thrill when they begin to pick up. It's great to see. And the parents sometimes don't even come to visit them, afraid we'll grab them and make them take the kids out, I suppose.

A funny one is a little Hungarian Gypsy girl that's been up there for the past month. She was about eight weeks old maybe when they brought her in with something on her lower lip that looked like a chancre. Everyone was interested but the Wassermann was negative. It turned out finally to be nothing but a peculiarly situated birthmark. But that kid is still there too. Nobody can find the parents. Maybe they'll turn up some day.

Even when we do get rid of them, they often come back in a week or so—sometimes in terrible condition, full of impetigo, down in weight—everything we'd done for them to do over again. I think it's deliberate neglect in most cases. That's what happened to this little Gypsy. The nurse was funny after the mother had left the second time. I couldn't speak to her, she said. I just couldn't say a word I was so mad. I wanted to slap her.

We had a couple of Irish girls a while back named Cowley. One was a red head with beautiful wavy hair and the other a straight haired blonde. They really were good looking and not infants at all. I should say they must have been two and three years old approximately. I can't imagine how the parents could have abandoned them. But they did. I think they were habitual drunkards and may have had to beat it besides on short notice. No fault of theirs maybe.

But all these are, after all, not the kind of kids I have in mind. The ones I mean are those they bring in stinking dirty, and I mean stinking. The poor brats are almost dead sometimes, just living skeletons, almost, wrapped in rags, their heads caked with dirt, their eyes stuck together with pus and their legs all excoriated from the dirty diapers no one has had the interest to take off them regularly. One poor little pot we have now with a thin purplish skin and big veins standing out all over its head had a big sore place in the fold of its neck under the chin. The nurse told me that when she started to undress it it had on a shirt with a neckband that rubbed right into that place. Just dirt. The mother gave a story of having had it in some sort of home in Paterson. We couldn't get it straight. We never try. What the hell? We take 'em and try to make something out of them.

Sometimes, you'd be surprised, some doctor has given the parents a ride before they bring the child to the clinic. You wouldn't believe it. They clean 'em out, maybe for twenty-five dollars—they maybe had to borrow—and then tell 'em to move on. It happens. Men we all know too. Pretty bad. But what can you do?

And sometimes the kids are not only dirty and neglected but sick, ready to die. You ought to see those nurses work. You'd think it was the brat of their best friend. They handle those kids as if they were worth a million dollars. Not that some nurses aren't better than others but in general they break their hearts over those kids, many times, when I, for one, wish they'd never get well.

I often kid the girls. Why not? I look at some miserable specimens they've dolled up for me when I make the rounds in the morning and I tell them: Give it an enema, maybe it will get well and grow up into a cheap prostitute or something. The country needs you, brat. I once proposed that we have a mock wedding between a born garbage hustler we'd saved and a little female with a fresh mug on her that would make anybody smile.

Poor kids! You really wonder sometimes if medicine isn't all wrong to try to do anything for them at all. You actually want to see them pass out, especially when they're deformed or—they're awful sometimes. Every one has rickets in an advanced form, scurvy too, flat chests, spindly arms and legs. They come in with pneumonia, a temperature of a hundred and six, maybe, and before you can do a thing, they're dead.

This little Jean Beicke was like that. She was about the worst you'd expect to find anywhere. Eleven months old. Lying on the examining table with a blanket half way up her body, stripped, lying there, you'd think it a five months baby, just about that long. But when the nurse took the blanket away, her legs kept on going for a good eight inches longer. I couldn't get used to it. I covered her up and asked two of the men to guess how long she was. Both guessed at least half a foot too short. One thing that helped the illusion besides her small face was her arms. They came about to her hips. I don't know what made that. They should come down to her thighs, you know.

She was just skin and bones but her eyes were good and she looked straight at you. Only if you touched her any-where, she started to whine and then cry with a shrieking, distressing sort of cry that no one wanted to hear. We handled her as gently as we knew how but she had to cry just the same.

She was one of the damnedest looking kids I've ever seen. Her head was all up in front and flat behind, I suppose from lying on the back of her head so long the weight of it and the softness of the bones from the rickets had just flattened it out and pushed it up forward. And her legs and arms seemed loose on her like the arms and legs of some cheap dolls. You could bend her feet up on her shins absolutely flat—but there was no real deformity, just all loosened up. Nobody was with her when I saw her though her mother had brought her in.

It was about ten in the evening, the interne had asked me to see her because she had a stiff neck, and how! and there was some thought of meningitis—perhaps infantile paralysis. Anyhow, they didn't want her to go through the night with-out at least a lumbar puncture if she needed it. She had a fierce cough and a fairly high fever. I made it out to be a case of broncho-pneumonia with meningismus but no true involvement of the central nervous system. Besides she had inflamed ear drums.

I wanted to incise the drums, especially the left, and would have done it only the night superintendent came along just then and made me call the ear man on service. You know. She also looked to see if we had an operative release from the parents. There was. So I went home, the ear man came in a while later and opened the ears—a little bloody serum from both sides and that was that.

Next day we did a lumbar puncture, tapped the spine

that is, and found clear fluid with a few lymphocytes in it, nothing diagnostic. The X-ray of the chest clinched the diagnosis of broncho-pneumonia, there was an extensive involvement. She was pretty sick. We all expected her to die from exhaustion before she'd gone very far.

I had to laugh every time I looked at the brat after that, she was such a funny looking one but one thing that kept her from being a total loss was that she did eat. Boy! how that kid could eat! As sick as she was she took her grub right on time every three hours, a big eight ounce bottle of whole milk and digested it perfectly. In this depression you got to be such a hungry baby, I heard the nurse say to her once. It's a sign of intelligence, I told her. But anyway, we all got to be crazy about Jean. She'd just lie there and eat and sleep. Or she'd lie and look straight in front of her by the hour. Her eyes were blue, a pale sort of blue. But if you went to touch her, she'd begin to scream. We just didn't, that's all, unless we absolutely had to. And she began to gain in weight. Can you imagine that? I suppose she had been so terribly run down that food, real food, was an entirely new experience to her. Anyway she took her food and gained on it though her temperature continued to run steadily around between a hundred and three and a hundred and four for the first eight or ten days. We were surprised.

When we were expecting her to begin to show improvement, however, she didn't. We did another lumbar puncture and found fewer cells. That was fine and the second X-ray of the chest showed it somewhat improved also. That wasn't so good though, because the temperature still kept up and we had no way to account for it. I looked at the ears again and thought they ought to be opened once more. The ear man disagreed but I kept after him and next day he did it to please me. He didn't get anything but a drop of serum on either side.

Well, Jean didn't get well. We did everything we knew how to do except the right thing. She carried on for another two—no I think it was three—weeks longer. A couple of times her temperature shot up to a hundred and eight. Of course we knew then it was the end. We went over her six or eight times, three or four of us, one after the other, and nobody thought to take an X-ray of the mastoid regions. It was dumb, if you want to say it, but there wasn't a sign of anything but the history of the case to point to it. The ears had been opened early, they had been watched carefully, there was no discharge to speak of at any time and from the external examination, the mastoid processes showed no change from the normal. But that's what she died of, acute purulent mastoiditis of the left side, going on to involvement of the left lateral sinus and finally the meninges. We might, however, have taken a culture of the pus when the ear was first opened and I shall always, after this, in suspicious cases. I have been told since that if you get a virulent bug like the streptococcus mucosus capsulatus it's wise at least to go in behind the ear for drainage if the temperature keeps up. Anyhow she died.

I went in when she was just lying there gasping. Somehow or other, I hated to see that kid go. Everybody felt rotten. She was such a scrawny, misshapen, worthless piece of humanity that I had said many times that somebody ought to chuck her in the garbage chute—but after a month watching her suck up her milk and thrive on it—and to see those alert blue eyes in that face—well, it wasn't pleasant. Her mother was sitting by the bed crying quietly when I came in, the morning of the last day. She was a young woman, didn't look more than a girl, she just sat there looking at the child and crying without a sound.

I expected her to begin to ask me questions with that look on her face all doctors hate—but she didn't. I put my hand on her shoulder and told her we had done everything we knew how to do for Jean but that we really didn't know what, finally, was killing her. The woman didn't make any sign of hearing me. Just sat there looking in between the bars of the crib. So after a moment watching the poor kid beside her, I turned to the infant in the next crib to go on with my rounds. There was an older woman there looking in at that baby also—no better off than Jean, surely. I spoke to her, thinking she was the mother of this one, but she wasn't.

Before I could say anything, she told me she was the older sister of Jean's mother and that she knew that Jean was dying and that it was a good thing. That gave me an idea—I hated to talk to Jean's mother herself—so I beckoned the woman to come out into the hall with me.

I'm glad she's going to die, she said. She's got two others home, older, and her husband has run off with another woman. It's better off dead—never was any good anyway. You know her husband came down from Canada about a year and a half ago. She seen him and asked him to come back and live with her and the children. He come back just long enough to get her pregnant with this one then he left her again and went back to the other woman. And I suppose knowing she was pregnant, and suffering, and having no money and nowhere to get it, she was worrying and this one never was formed right. I seen it as soon as it was born. I guess the condition she was in was the cause. She's got enough to worry about now without this one. The husband's gone to Canada again and we can't get a thing out of him. I been keeping them, but we can't do much more. She'd work if she could find anything but what can you do with three kids in times like this? She's got a boy nine years old but her mother-in-law sneaked it away from her and now he's with his father in Canada. She worries about him too, but that don't do no good.

Listen, I said, I want to ask you something. Do you think she'd let us do an autopsy on Jean if she dies? I hate to speak to her of such a thing now but to tell you the truth, we've worked hard on that poor child and we don't exactly know what is the trouble. We know that she's had pneumonia but that's been getting well. Would you take it up with her for me, if—of course—she dies.

Oh, she's gonna die all right, said the woman. Sure, I will. If you can learn anything, it's only right. I'll see that you get the chance. She won't make any kick, I'll tell her.

Thanks, I said.

The infant died about five in the afternoon. The pathologist was dog-tired from a lot of extra work he'd had to do due to the absence of his assistant on her vacation so he put off the autopsy till next morning. They packed the body in ice in one of the service hoppers. It worked perfectly.

Next morning they did the postmortem. I couldn't get the nurse to go down to it. I may be a sap, she said, but I can't do it, that's all. I can't. Not when I've taken care of them. I feel as if they're my own.

I was amazed to see how completely the lungs had cleared up. They were almost normal except for a very small patch of residual pneumonia here and there which really amounted to nothing. Chest and abdomen were in excellent shape, otherwise, throughout—not a thing aside from the negligible pneumonia. Then he opened the head.

It seemed to me the poor kid's convolutions were unusually well developed. I kept thinking it's incredible that that complicated mechanism of the brain has come into being just for this. I never can quite get used to an autopsy.

The first evidence of the real trouble—for there had been no gross evidence of meningitis—was when the pathologist took the brain in his hand and made the long steady cut which opened up the left lateral ventricle. There was just a faint color of pus on the bulb of the choroid plexus there. Then the diagnosis all cleared up quickly. The left lateral sinus was completely thrombosed and on going into the left temporal bone from the inside the mastoid process was all broken down.

I called up the ear man and he came down at once. A clear miss, he said. I think if we'd gone in there earlier, we'd have saved her.

For what? said I. Vote the straight Communist ticket. Would it make us any dumber? said the ear man.

A Face of Stone

He was one of these fresh Jewish types you want to kill at sight, the presuming poor whose looks change the minute cash is mentioned. But they're insistent, trying to force attention, taking advantage of good nature at the first crack. You come when I call you, that type. He got me into a bad mood before he opened his mouth just by the half smiling, half insolent look in his eyes, a small, stoutish individual in a greasy black suit, a man in his middle twenties I should imagine.

She, on the other hand looked Italian, a goaty slant to her eyes, a face often seen among Italian immigrants. She had a small baby tight in her arms. She stood beside her smiling husband and looked at me with no expression at all on her pointed face, unless no expression is an expression. A face of stone. It was an animal distrust, not shyness. She wasn't shy but seemed as if sensing danger, as though she were on her guard against it. She looked dirty. So did he. Her hands were definitely grimy, with black nails. And she smelled, that usual smell of sweat and dirt you find among any people who habitually do not wash or bathe.

The infant was asleep when they came into the office, a child of about five months perhaps, not more.

People like that belong in clinics, I thought to myself. I wasn't putting myself out for them, not that day anyhow. Just dumb oxen. Why the hell do they let them into the country. Half idiots at best. Look at them.

My brother told us to bring the baby here, the man said. We've had a doctor but he's no good.

167

How do you know he's no good. You probably never gave him a chance. Did you pay him?

Sure we paid him.

Well what do you want me to do? To hell with you, I thought to myself. Get sore and get the hell out of here. I got to go home to lunch.

I want you to fix up the baby, Doc. My brother says you're the best baby doctor around here. And this kid's sick.

Well, put it up there on the table and take its clothes off then. Why didn't you come earlier instead of waiting here till the end of the hour. I got to live too.

The man turned to his wife. Gimme the baby, he said.

No. She wouldn't. Her face just took on an even stupider expression of obstinacy but she clung to the child.

Come on, come on, I said. I can't wait here all day.

Give him to me, he said to her again. He only wants to examine it.

I hold her, the woman said keeping the child firmly in her arms.

Listen here, I spoke to her. Do you want me to examine the child or don't you. If you don't, then take it somewhere.

Wait a minute, wait a minute, Doc, the man said smiling ingratiatingly.

You look at throat, the mother suggested.

You put the baby up there on the table and take its clothes off, I told her. The woman shook her head. But as she did so she gradually relented, looking furtively at me with distrustful glances her nostrils moving slightly.

Now what is it.

She's getting thin, Doc 'think somethink's the matter with her.

What do you mean, thin?

I asked her age, the kind of labor she had had. How they were feeding the baby. Vomiting, sleeping, hunger. It was the first child and the mother was new at nursing it. It was four and a half months old and weighed thirteen and a half pounds. Not bad.

I think my milk no good, said the woman, still clinging to the baby whose clothes she had only begun to open.

As I approached them the infant took one look at me and let out a wild scream. In alarm the mother clutched it to her breast and started for the door.

I burst out laughing. The husband got red in the face but forced a smile. Don't be so scared, he said to his wife. He, nodding toward me, ain't gonna hurt you. You know she hasn't been in this country long, Doc. She's scared you're gonna hurt the baby. Bring it over here, he said to her and take off his clothes. Here, give 'im to me. And he took the infant into his own hands, screaming lustily, and carried it to the table to undress it. The mother, in an agony of apprehension kept interfering from behind at every move.

What a time! I couldn't find much the matter and told them so. Just the results of irregular, foolish routine and probably insufficient breast milk. I gave them a complemental formula. He chiseled a dollar off the fee and—just as he was going out—said, Doc, if we need you any time I want you to come out to the house to see it. You gotta watch this kid.

Where do you live, I asked.

He told me where it was, way out near the dumps. I'll come if you give me a decent warning, I told him. If you want me call me in the morning. Now get that. You can't expect me to go running out there for nothing every time the kid gets a belly ache. Or just because she thinks it's dying. If you call me around supper time or in the middle of a snow storm or at two o'clock in the morning maybe I won't do it. I'm telling you now so you'll know. I got too much to do already.

O.K., Doc, he said smiling. But you come.

I'll come on those conditions.

O.K., Doc.

And sure enough, on a Sunday night, about nine o'clock, with the thermometer at six below and the roads like a skating rink, they would call me.

Nothing doing, I said.

But Doc, you said you'd come.

I'm not going there tonight, I insisted. I won't do it. I'll ask my associate to make the call or some good younger man that lives in that neighborhood but I won't go over there tonight.

But we need you Doc, the baby's very sick.

Can't help it. I tell you I'm not going. And I slammed up the receiver.

Who in the world are you talking to like that, said my wife who had put down her book as my voice rose higher. You mustn't do that.

Leave me alone, I know what I'm doing.

But my dear!

Four months later, after three months of miserable practice, the first warm day in April, about twenty women with babies came to my office. I started at one P.M. and by three I was still going strong. I hadn't loafed. Anybody left out there? I asked the last woman, as I thought, who had been waiting for me. Oh yes, there's a couple with a baby. Oh Lord, I groaned. It was half past three by then and a number of calls still to be made about the town.

There they were. The same fresh mug and the same face of stone, still holding the baby which had grown, however, to twice its former size.

Hello Doc, said the man smiling.

For a moment I couldn't place them. Hello, I said. Then I remembered. What can I do for you—at this time of day. Make it snappy cause I've got to get out.

Just want you to look the baby over, Doc.

Oh yeah.

Listen Doc, we've been waiting out there two hours.

Good night! That finishes me for the afternoon, I said to

myself. All right, put it up on the table. As I said this, feeling at the same time a sense of helpless irritation and anger, I noticed a cluster of red pimples in the region of the man's right eyebrow and reaching to the bridge of his nose. Like bed-bug bites I thought to myself. He'll want me to do something for them too before I get through I suppose. Well, what's the matter now? I asked them.

It's the baby again, Doc, the man said.

What's the matter with the baby. It looks all right to me. And it did. A child of about ten months, I estimated, with a perfectly happy, round face.

Yes, but his body isn't so good.

I want you should examine him all over, said the mother.

You would, I said. Do you realize what time it is?

Shall she take his clothes off? the man broke in.

Suit yourself, I answered, hoping she wouldn't do it. But she put the infant on the table and began carefully to undress it.

No use. I sat down and took out a card for the usual notes. How old is it?

How old is it? he asked his wife.

Ten months. Next Tuesday ten months, she said with the same face on her as always.

Are you still nursing it.

Sure, she said. Him won't take bottle.

Do you mean to say that after what I told you last time, you haven't weaned the baby?

What can she do, Doc. She tried to but he won't let go of the breast. You can't make him take a bottle.

Does he eat?

Yeah, he eats a little, but he won't take much.

Cod liver oil?

He takes it all right but spits it up half an hour later. She stopped giving it to him.

Orange juice.

Sure. Most of the time.

So, as a matter of fact, she's been nursing him and giving him a little cereal and that's all.

Sure, that's about right.

How often does she nurse him?

Whenever he wants it, the man grinned. Sometimes every two hours. Sometimes he sleeps. Like that.

But didn't I tell you, didn't I tell her to feed it regularly.

She can't do that, Doc. The baby cries and she gives it to him.

Why don't you put it in a crib?

She won't give it up. You know, that's the way she is, Doc. You can't make her do different. She wants the baby next to her so she can feel it.

Have you got it undressed? I turned to the mother who was standing with her back to me.

You want shoe off? she answered me.

Getting up I went to the infant and pulled the shoes and stockings off together, picked the thing up by its feet and the back of the neck and carried it to the scales. She was right after me, her arms half extended watching the child at every movement I made. Fortunately the child grinned and sagged back unresisting in my grasp. I looked at it more carefully then, a smart looking little thing and a perfectly happy, fresh mug on him that amused me in spite of myself.

Twenty pounds and four ounces, I said. What do you want for a ten month old baby? There's nothing the matter with him. Get his clothes on.

I want you should examine him first, said the mother.

The blood went to my face in anger but she paid no attention to me. He too thin, she said. Look him body.

To quiet my nerves I took my stethoscope and went rapidly over the child's chest, saw that everything was all right there, that there was no rickets and told them so— and to step on it. Get him dressed. I got to get out of here.

Him all right? the woman questioned me with her stony

pale green eyes. I stopped to look at them, they were very curious, almost at right angles to each other—in a way of speaking—like the eyes of some female figure I had seen somewhere—Mantegna—Botticelli—I couldn't remember.

Yes, only for God's sake, take him off the breast. Feed him the way I told you to.

No will take bottle.

Fine. I don't give a damn about the bottle. Feed him from a cup, with a spoon, anyway at all. But feed him regularly. That's all.

As I turned to wash my hands, preparatory to leaving the office the man stopped me. Doc, he said, I want you to examine my wife.

He got red in the face as I turned on him. What the hell do you think I am anyhow. You got a hell of a nerve. Don't you know . . .

We waited two hours and ten minutes for you, Doc, he replied smiling. Just look her over and see what the matter with her is.

I could hardly trust myself to speak for a moment but, instead turned to look at her again standing beside the baby which she had finished dressing and which was sitting on the table looking at me. What a creature. What a face. And what a body. I looked her coldly up and down from head to toe. There was a rip in her dress, a triangular tear just above the left knee.

Well— No use getting excited with people such as these— or with anyone, for that matter, I said in despair. No one can do two things at the same time, especially when they're in two different places. I simply gave up and returned to my desk chair.

Go ahead. What's the matter with her?

She gets pains in her legs, especially at night. And she's got a spot near her right knee. It came last week, a big blue looking sort of spot.

Did she ever have rheumatism? You know, go to bed with swollen joints—for six weeks—or like that.

She simply shrugged her shoulders.

Did you have rheumatism? he turned to her.

She don't know, he said, interpreting and turning red in the face again. I particularly noticed it this time and remembered that it had occurred two or three times before while we were talking.

Tell her to open up her dress.

Open up your dress, he said.

Sit down, I told her and let me see your legs.

As she did so I noticed again the triangular rip in the skirt over her left thigh, dirty silk, and that her skin was directly under it. She untied some white rags above her knees and let down her black stockings. The left one first, I said.

Her lower legs were peculiarly bowed, really like Turkish scimitars, flattened and somewhat rotated on themselves in an odd way that could not have come from anything but severe rickets rather late in her childhood. The whole leg while not exactly weak was as ugly and misshapen as a useful leg well could be in so young a woman. Near the knee was a large discolored area where in all probability a varicose vein had ruptured.

That spot, I told her husband, comes from a broken varicose vein.

Yeah, I thought so, she's got them all up both legs.

That's from carrying a child.

No. She had them before that. They've always been that way since I've known her. Is that what makes her have the pains there?

I hardly think so, I said looking over the legs again, one of which I held on the palm of either hand. No, I don't think so.

What is it then? It hurts her bad, especially at night.

She's bow-legged as hell in the first place. That throws the strain where it doesn't belong and look at these shoes—

Yeah, I know.

The woman had on an old pair of fancy high-heeled slippers such as a woman might put on for evening wear. They were all worn and incredibly broken down. I don't see how she can walk in them.

That's what I told her, the man said. I wanted her to get a pair of shoes that fitted her but she wouldn't do it.

Well, she's got to do it, I said. Throw away those shoes, I told her, and get shoes with flat heels. And straight heels. I tried to impress her. What they call Cuban heels, if you must. New shoes, I emphasized. How old is she, I asked the man.

His face colored again for reasons I could not fathom. Twenty-four, he said.

Where was she born?

In Poland.

In Poland! Well. I looked at her, not believing him.

Yeah, why?

Well. Twenty-four years old you say. Let's see. That's different. An unusual type for a Jew, I thought. That's the probable explanation for her legs, I told the husband. She must have been a little girl during the war over there. A kid of maybe five or six years I should imagine. Is that right, I asked her. But she didn't answer me, just looked back into my eyes with that inane look.

What did you get to eat?

She seemed not to have heard me but turned to her husband.

Did she lose any of her people, I asked him.

Any of them? She lost everybody, he said quietly.

How did she come to get over here then?

She came over four years ago. She has a sister over here.

So that's it, I thought to myself looking at her fussing, intensely absorbed with the baby, looking at it, talking to it in an inarticulate sort of way, paying no attention whatever to me. No wonder she's built the way she is, considering what she must have been through in that invaded territory. And this guy here—

What are we going to do about the pains, Doc?

Get her some decent shoes, that's the first thing.

O.K., Doc.

She could be operated on for those veins. But I wouldn't advise it, just yet. I tell you. Get one of those woven elastic bandages for her, they don't cost much. A three inch one. And I told him what to get.

Can't you give her some pills to stop the pain?

Not me, I told him. You might get her teeth looked at though if you want to. All that kind of thing and—well, I will give you something. It's not dope. It just helps if there's any rheumatism connected with it.

Can you swallow a pill, I turned to her attracting her attention.

She looked at me. How big? she said.

She swallows an Aspirin pill when I give it to her sometimes, said her husband, but she usually puts it in a spoonful of water first to dissolve it. His face reddened again and suddenly I understood his half shameful love for the woman and at the same time the extent of her reliance on him.

I was touched.

They're pretty big pills, I said. Look, they're green. That's the coating so they won't dissolve in your stomach and upset your digestion.

Let see, said the woman.

I showed a few of the pills to her in the palm of my hand.

For pains in leg?

Yes, I told her.

She looked at them again. Then for the first time since I had known her a broad smile spread all over her face. Yeah, she said, I swallow him.

To Fall Asleep

THEY HAD GIVEN him the bed of their son, away at school. Tired from the hot September weather, the running about incidental to disembarkation, a big supper and long hours of talk with these dear friends in the suburbs, he had fallen quickly to sleep.

But before turning in, near midnight, he had stood looking out of his bedroom window, a back window, through the mosquito screen, over the neat, small garden. The moon, half gone above the roof-peak of the house next in the rear, its light cut diagonally across the tiny lawn and flower borders, across the pathway of rough, flat stones leaving the garage, at the back, in heavy shadow. *America Suburbia,* he murmured to himself smiling at the necessity for such Latinity, home of the cheap model house (and not so cheap either) run entirely by electricity and the throwing of switches and pressing of buttons. But not this house. I imagine this house must be at least fifty years old!

After Germany today, France—if you must, but especially after Moscow! what the devil kind of people live in places such as this? Fascism, Sovietism seem to have gone colorless here—like those mallows in the moonlight. I've been gone only four months and how strange this place seems.

He didn't know how long he'd been asleep. He opened his eyes and disengaged his head from the pillow to listen better, holding his body motionless with one braced elbow. Not a sound. For a moment he was bewildered and could still feel the long roll of the ship. The stillness was absolute.

Then it sounded again. A very gentle tap tap tap at his

door. He sat up straight in bed. What the devil's that? There was no evidence of a light about the door cracks. Then, in the stillness the knob of the door was turned and the door began slowly to open.

He remained watching.

The door opened quickly now and into the room with the oblong patch of moonlight on the floor came his hostess. She closed the door behind her then leaning back against it stood looking at him.

I can't sleep, Bill, she said, so I thought I'd come in and talk to you. Do you mind? She was in pajamas and barefoot. No, don't light the light. Stay there. I'm terribly sorry. I'll sit here awhile. It's so hot. And lifting his clothes to the table she sank back in the large upholstered chair squatting image like in the center of the room. The moonlight fell across her knees the inner contours showing clearly through the sheer fabric.

The man lay back with both hands under his head, What in hell's happened to Fritz? Or what?

Surprised?

Well, rather.

It's so quiet here. The street lights and the noises from the trucks and cars passing are awful in our room.

He made no reply.

You never married, did you, Bill?

Practically never.

She smiled. Didn't you ever want to?

Now Sally, said the man in the bed—but without moving, What— Where in hell is Fritz?

He went out on a call an hour ago. Didn't you hear the phone?

When's he coming back?

Not for several hours, I'm sure. He does it sometimes.

Does what?

Gets a call during the night—and returns for breakfast. While I stay awake waiting for him. Oh, not always, but sometimes. You're leaving early, aren't you, Bill? You're sure you don't want to rest?

You're sure we hadn't better go downstairs?

The woman answered by half standing and trying to drag the heavy chair behind her toward the bed. It was too heavy for her. The man got up at once to help her. She also stood up and as she did so he took her in his arms. She let herself go. She put her arms around his neck and they kissed.

You lovely thing.

That's enough. Now fix my chair. And you lie down again. You're a charming man, Bill. Any woman would be fortunate to have you love her.

He went to the window and leaning his arms along the top of the lower sash looked out into the dark garden awhile to calm himself. She came and put her arm over his shoulder.

What are we going to do with Fritz, Bill?

Poison him, I suppose.

No, darling. I'm afraid that wouldn't help me.

You're still in love with him?

Chronic case, I suppose. Tell me, Bill, if I divorced him would a man like you marry me, do you think?

In a minute.

Liar, if I know you. But Fritz is so difficult, Bill. I don't know what to do.

Can't you get us a drink?

Surely. But she made no move and he did not insist further.

You go back to your bed, he said. And I'll come in there and sit with you awhile if you want me to—till you can go to sleep.

Will you read to me?

Sure, if you want me to.

Or tell me a story. You'd have to turn the light on to read.

That would be a little difficult, dear.

Oh, but I don't want to go back into that room. I want to sleep. I want to sleep.

Then get in there. I'll sit here and— He stopped short. Poor Bill.

Don't say that. You'll make me sorry for myself. He drew the light covers about her and folded them gently back under her arms. You haven't a crucifix and beads about the house anywhere, have you? Sally, you're very lovely here with me this way and it's not an easy thing for me to—

Darling. I'm so sorry.

Like hell you're sorry. I'm going to get in bed there with you if you don't get out of here, at once. That's all there is to it.

She only smiled. Are you serious? Go on, talk to me, please. I love to hear you talk.

Well, there was once a confounded idiot who went to visit two old friends in the suburbs of New York City—

Not so very old, Bill. Go on. But he made no attempt to continue. Watching him she started to get out of the bed. Really, dear, you ought to be resting. I'll go. Please.

No. He held her strongly by the shoulders.

Bill, you're shaking!

I'll be all right in a moment.

Darling. Get yourself a robe, there in the closet. No. Come in here with me. Come, please. I'm so sorry.

Don't be a fool. Just let me get hold of myself.

He shook so that the heavy chair chattered and joggled. He tried to laugh but it didn't come off as he expected. He got up but it did little good, a heavy chill would come over him so that his knees knocked together. Then he knelt by the bed-stead and put his head down on the covers beside her holding on tightly to steady himself. Neither said a word. She stroked his head slowly, gently and rhythmically.

I'm so sorry, Bill. Is it as bad as that?

Oh, I could call you a bitch, and all that sort of thing—

What do you want me to do?

Nothing. He kissed her eyes and her hair. Then still kneeling there he began. It was lovely in the country about Moscow. Much more beautiful than I thought it was going to be— He shook once more from head to foot, unable to control himself. They've done wonders there.

How many were there of you in the party? All doctors?

And their wives—those that had wives. The shivers were beginning to abate. About twenty in all.

But did you spend most of your time in the hospitals or really look around a bit?

He got up slowly and went to the chair. We didn't see too much aside from the official tours. What's happened between you and Fritz? Break up? I've always thought of you as one of the few happily married couples of my acquaintance.

You haven't visited us for the last eight years, Bill.

What's happened?

Nothing. Nothing new. I'm wondering if the trouble isn't with me, Bill. I'm not up to him in some ways.

Go on.

What was Fritz like when you were in school together, Bill?

He was younger than most of the men in the class. Just a good-looking kid. You know, nothing special. Everybody liked him.

Was he lively? Did he go out much? Did he drink?

Not to my knowledge. If I remember rightly he used to have a pair of binoculars and go out into the cemetery in April looking for song birds. I used to meet him coming back when I was going to breakfast.

Not Fritz! Oh, once, maybe. Yes. But no more than that.

The woman put her arms back of her head and looked up at the dark ceiling. The sleeves of her pajama coat fell back over her elbows. Well—she said. Being a poor boy in college can't have been the best thing for Fritz. You know that man has the devil in him, Bill. He's the most adorable husband a woman could ever ask for—sometimes. Perhaps it's my fault. He loves me, he loves me not. I don't know. I don't think he loves anybody but himself; he's so sweet, so gentle—and such a damnable liar. But I'm not sure. Perhaps I should have told him to go to hell when he asked me to marry him. I was so young. I wish I had—very often.

Isn't it rather late now for him to be—

No. Age doesn't seem to affect him, so far as I can see. Women are such fools. Nothing affects him—except to make him worse. I simply can't trust him, Bill. And that's what drives me mad. You know, his philosophy begins to affect me sometimes so that I find myself defending him— even against myself. Do you know what the fool says?

No. What?

How can a man bring love home if he doesn't go out and find it—like a rabbit.

At fifty, Sally?

You're at least three years older than Fritz, aren't you, Bill?

Oh, well. But I should think when a man's married—to a woman like you—

A silly old fool you are, Bill. You'd be surprised at some of the stories Fritz tells me. But he never tells me anything that's happened any nearer than two or three years back—

Tells you what, Sally? precisely.

No. That's his business. But he doesn't give a damn about me, I'm sure—or he wouldn't act the way he does.

How old are you, Sally?

You know perfectly well how old I am. Look at my hair. I've never been really happy with him, Bill. There are some things I really can't forgive. He played me some dirty tricks when I was first married and most trusted him. I wanted to die. I mean real low down snide tricks—for which there were no excuses. I didn't know anything about men—

Her companion looked down at the floor. The patch of

moonlight had shifted across the floor until it had approached to the right of where they were sitting and begun to climb the side of the bed.

Isn't it silly, at my age. Who gives a damn, really? I suppose—in some ways—I suppose I'm the happiest woman on earth. You know, the man's a genius in his own way. I look at him often and I have to smile to myself, to pity the thing. He does try so hard to be good. And he is good. She laughed. I wish I could sleep.

I'll go downstairs now, if you don't mind. I'd like to read awhile.

No. Stay here and talk to me. You haven't told me a word, really, about Russia. Bill, come here. Put your head down. Now listen, you big fool. I love you. Do you know what that means?

Yes, I know: second best.

No, it doesn't. It means I love you, that's all.

Not a bad teacher that Fritz of yours. I wish he were outside the door, listening.

What the hell, darling. I don't know. Do you? I think I'm just no good.

Well, as I was saying. The hospital in Moscow is just about the most efficient institution you've ever seen. That's the only way to practice medicine. The trouble with medicine here is the money side of it. You can't do what you want to, it costs too much. But there the cost is completely eliminated as far as the physician is concerned.

She had given him her hand which he held lightly between both of his. The moonlight was almost up to her face. He waited a moment, not hearing any word from her, thinking that perhaps she had fallen asleep.

Would you want socialized medicine here? she asked him vaguely after a moment.

No, certainly not. It amounts to the same thing as— Oh, I don't know. Who does?

What were you going to say?

Oh, it's all right for handling the unfortunate in large groups—so long as they exist in large groups. It won't last—in Russia either. The cost is too high. Not in money. But I don't know; I've seen it. It looks different from here—

What do the men there think of it? I mean the surgeons and scientists you met.

After all, they're all Russians, you know. And men as splendid as some of them are will always be in a class by themselves, anywhere. Frankly, what difference does it make where a man is so long as he is working at his trade? He looked to see if her eyes would open. They didn't attempt to propagandize with us. We just talked—medicine —and hospital organization. There was much to see—and to learn.

He placed her hand gently on the bed, unclasping it from his own to do so, and stood up. Going to the window he pulled the shade down very slowly, holding it firmly so that it might not slip away with a bang. When he heard the catch click and hold he let go. Then he tiptoed from the room closing the door silently behind him turning the knob until the latch clicked there also.

Downstairs, in the front room, he switched on a reading light and picked up the first thing at hand, the nearly day-old newspaper lying beside him.

When Fritz returned, through the kitchen, it was still dark. Bill started awake looking at him. The men remained staring at each other for a moment before Fritz could utter,

What the hell?

Oh, said his friend, Sally is in my bed upstairs, asleep. So I thought I'd come down here and wait for you.

Did you have a nice party?

Did you? Get me a drink if you know how to mix one without help, you thickhead.

The Cold World

WHICH IS "the black day"? he asked her.

You can see it there marked on the calendar.

Just two more to go. Then out into the cold world, eh?

You said it's going to be a cold world.

Go on. You're going to look swell in your white uniform.
I bet they'll have you back here on night duty next week.

Why night duty?

You girls always get stuck with night duty at first. You
know that.

I don't care so long as it's not on Male Ward. I've seen
enough of that. Thirty five rough-necks to keep your eye
on, alone there, all night long.

Just thirty five men. That shouldn't bother you.

Trying to kid me, aren't you? Yeah. But if you saw a
man's leg come up over the window sill at two o'clock in
the morning I bet you'd be scared too.

Let's have it.

Naw, I haven't got time.

Whyn't you call somebody?

I couldn't. I just couldn't. I felt my mouth drop open but
absolutely no sound came out of it.

You mean in this hospital?

Boy, was I scared.

What'd they do? What did they want to do, bump
somebody off?

No. They were friends of two of the men in the ward.
One of them was the brother of an old gunman here in the
city. Wild Bill. You must have heard of him. Some rival

185

gang got him three years ago. First they felt me all over. I said, Hey don't get so fresh. I thought they were just trying to be funny. They took away my bandage scissors. Then one of them watched by the window while the other went over to talk to the fellow in bed. I suppose they wanted to tip him off in some way or to tell him what to do or something. I dunno. Tell him what to say in court.

He'd been wounded I suppose in some gang battle.

Yeah.

How long did they stay?

Oh about an hour. And you never saw such a lot of sound sleepers in that ward. The next morning I asked them how they had slept. Wonderful! They didn't know a thing about it.

They knew what was good for them, said the interne.

But the funny part of it was, continued the girl, that I had a cop up there with me all the time supposed to be watching them. He's been in for three nights. So that night he said he thought he'd just lie down a few minutes and he was fast asleep. A lot of help to me.

What did they do then?

That was all. But just as they were going out of the window one of them took out his gun and said, Wha' duh yuh say? Let's bump her off before we go. I don't know what made me do it, it was instinct coming up I suppose, but the window was on a line with the beds and I moved right in between their two friends so they would have to take a chance on hitting them if they shot at me. The last one at the window said to his pal, She's not so dumb. Then they left.

Did you tell the cop?

Not till three days later.

What'd he say?

He told me I'd have to go to court and tell my story in front of a magistrate. Oh yeah? I said to him. And where were you while all this was going on? It wasn't

my duty to chase them, that's why he was there. They
weren't going to get me up into that court, not if I
knew it.

Well, that's a story my dear girl. I'm glad they didn't
shoot you.

Thanks.

What happened to the two patients?

Oh, they went home. I spoke to one of them before he
left the hospital. I told him, Why don't you go straight?
Why don't you go out West somewhere, go on a ranch
or something? But you know how it is. What chance is
there for anybody nowadays, he said. There's nothing for
me out there. No. I'm going to die like my brother. He'd
walk down the street and if he saw somebody he didn't
like he'd plug him, in broad daylight, and get away with it.

How'd he die? asked the interne.

Oh you remember. They caught him and took him out
here in the wilderness somewhere and tortured him to
death. That's what his brother told me anyhow. He said
they tore out his tongue and made him walk back and
forth barefoot over hot coals. I guess maybe he'd talked
too much so they caught him finally.

And this kid wanted to die the same way.

That's what he said. And do you know those men had
the nerve to come back again at visiting hours a week
later—as if nothing had happened. Some nerve.

Where were the boys wounded?

One of them was shot in the legs. Machine gun bullets
I think. The other one had a bullet through his chest. He
died, so I heard, after he left us. Do you know, while he
was here that bullet fell out one night, on the sheet. Some
fight we had for it. He wanted me to give it to him. Nothing doing, I told him. I want that for a souvenir.

How old were they?

Oh in their early twenties, good looking kids both of
them. When they finally left, about a month later, they

wanted to give me something. They told me I'd been awfully good to them. They offered me money. Nothing doing, I told them. I didn't want any of their dirty money. So they gave me a card with an address on it. They said any time I wanted anybody put away to let them know. I have it yet, around the house somewhere.

Better not lose it, said the older man, you might need it sometime.

Gee, when my mother heard about it all she wanted to yank me out of the hospital the next day.

Well, said the man getting up, anything new up here? If not, see you tomorrow. Two more days, huh.

The interne got up also. If you don't mind I won't go down with you, he said. I want to finish my histories while I'm up here.

Suit yourself. And the older man walked to the elevator and pressed the button. As he entered the machine and closed the door after him, he turned to look steadily at the girl through the open grill work as it began to sink below the floor. She too looked steadily at him until he disappeared.

Say, she turned to the interne, what do you mean lying like that. You know you've got no histories to write up up here. Why don't you write up your progress notes if you really want to do something.

Oh yeah.

That's what I said. No, you don't need to look, he's written them up for you. Much more than you deserve. Gee, the girls in this place just love that man.

So I see.

He's been like a father to us—to our class I mean—for the last three years.

Just a father?

Say, wise guy, you never think of anything but the one thing, do you?

Am I wrong?

Why don't you get hep to yourself. Take your hands off me. What do you want up here anyway? I got work to do.

So what?

Well what?

Still feeling the same way, aren't you.

About what?

Why don't you give yourself a break. How about this Saturday night. You'll be through by then. So don't try to tell me you're afraid you'll be caught. That don't go any more.

Say listen to me. I've told you I don't want to go out with you and that goes for today and tomorrow and next week as long as you're around here. What do you think I am anyhow? You can't get away with the stuff you're try- ing to pull with me. I haven't been hanging around this place for three years for nothing. You might get away with it with some of the poor kids just out of high school but I'm too wise for you, big boy.

You mean you'd like to come but you haven't got the nerve. Is that the idea? Afraid?

Of what?

What's the good of your putting on a show that way? Quit your stalling and come on out with me to the movies this Saturday. What the hell. I can't ask you fairer than that, can I?

Say, what I know about you is plenty. You know what you've been up to and don't you kid yourself that I don't know it too. Did you think you could keep them from talking? Go on, get out of here. I'm busy.

What's the matter, don't you think I'm old enough?

What was that crack?

The interne just grinned.

Say, the girl went on, you couldn't be like that man in a million years.

Well, what's it to you? He's married and has a couple of

kids in college. No use breaking your heart over him. Or aren't you breaking your heart?

The young woman looked at him without speaking for a moment, then she asked, Tell me something. Did I say anything out of the way just before he left?

Not that I noticed. You talked sweet as sugar to him as far as I could see. Now listen sweetheart. You're one of the best looking girls in this whole institution and I'd like to give you a good time.

Your idea of a good time and my idea of a good time are something entirely different. Are you sure I didn't say anything I shouldn't have said?

Why?

He looked at me so funny when he was going down in the elevator. Gee, I hope I didn't say anything wrong.

Four Bottles of Beer

HE'S ASLEEP.

Let me look at him before he wakes up. Oh, he looks better, he's got a better color and he's breathing easier; I don't think he has any fever now at all.

You think so? No he's got fever, that's why he looks so good. I wish he would look that way all the time—people always say to me in the street, Why is he so pale? Look, he's waking up, he knows you. Listen to him. He knows you.

Maybe you're right. Let's take his temperature. He looked so pale last night, almost green, he looked as if he was poisoned.

Ha, ha, ha! Look how he stiffens out, he knows what you want to do to him.

That's all right, just hold him a minute. He certainly looks better than he did last night. That's why I came up when you phoned. His breath is all right.

No, it smelled rotten, as if there was something rotten inside him. My mother said it too. That's what worried me. I gave him what you told me to but he kept straining all the time—it took me an hour. The stuff that came out of him was awful.

One hundred and one and a fifth, that's not bad.

But he vomits everything, he hasn't kept a thing down in two days.

Oh well, that's nothing. Do what I tell you and he'll be all right.

It came on yesterday noon. My brother-in-law came home

for lunch and he was out in the yard, he kept poking a stick at him fooling. Then he came in and after a while he got sick.

What's that your mother says?

She says to tell you he won't eat nothing.

What language is that? Russian?

No, Polish.

What did she say? Tadke, what's that?

That's his name. What you call Theodore. Where was you this morning? You told me to call you at eleven o'clock so I did but someone answered—I suppose it was your maid. You wasn't in so I called an hour later and Mrs. W. answered. She said you were a busy man. I suppose the maid puts it down on paper what people say. What does she call you?

Dr. Watson.

And what does she call your wife?

Mrs. Watson.

And the boys?

Bob and Jack.

Oh, neither one of the boys has your name.

Yes, Bob. My name is Robert. His is the same. And my father's was the same.

Oh, then you're a junior and he's a junior.

No, our middle names are different.

Oh, just that.

My father's middle name was George. My people lived in the West Indies so they gave me a Spanish name, Ortiz.

Yes, you have a nice name.

And Bob's grandmother is Danish so we gave him a Danish name, Eric.

You're all mixed up, aren't you? Your wife isn't the same as you, is she?

No, she's Scandinavian and German. Your husband is the same as you, Polish, isn't he?

Yes, he's Polish too—we're both Polish, we go to the

same church and everything. Maybe he comes from a different part of the country than I do—but it's the same country. But what's the difference, mixed up is just as good. Sometimes you get along better that way than if you're the same.

Yes, I suppose you fight sometimes.

And how! . . . How long you had that maid?

Eight years.

Does she cook for you?

Yes.

And you eat it?

Why yes.

I couldn't eat nigger cooking.

You don't know what you're talking about.

Yes, that's what my husband tells me. He says when he was in the navy they were all niggers. He says they cook swell stuff. And he says they don't waste a thing. Every little scrap they save and make something of it.

Why, of course, in the south they do all the cooking. I'll bet you've eaten things they've cooked and didn't know it.

Nope. I've never eaten a meal out of my house in my life.

What! Haven't you been to a restaurant?

Never. I couldn't eat the stuff. I don't know whether the pans they cook in are clean. I wouldn't. When we go to the movies we fill up our stomachs before we leave. Then when we get out we go to an ice cream counter and that's all.

They're worse than restaurants.

Maybe.

What's this, cut up onions?

No. Noodles. I got so hungry I put some in a pan with some butter to cook for myself. But I wanted to scrub the floor before you came and then I didn't feel like eating it.

Everything looks swell here.

Oh well, it's clean anyway.

Look at that kid, he looks all right now.

You laughing at his hair? I can't comb it out. My husband

says his was the same when he was a kid. You can't do a thing with it, it just stays that way, all kinked up.

Why don't you cut it off, except he'd look like a priest.

My people won't let me cut it till May. So I guess I'll have to be European style for once . . . Do you know what my father says? Oh, he makes me tired. He says it's all my fault. He says I'm the one that makes him sick. A couple of days ago he had one of those tops, you know, with a sharp point and he was digging it into my new ice box. I grabbed him and gave him a good licking. Oh, you know I didn't hurt him but I gave him a couple of good slaps. My father came in and raised the devil. He says I was shaking him up side down, and now he says I knocked all his insides out of place and that's why he's sick. He says I don't know how to take care of my kid. He was just in here now before you came. I says to him, Sure, you know how, don't you? That's why you got five sons rotting up there in the grave-yard.

How many?

Five. He makes me tired. Look at that kid. Whenever my brother-in-law comes in he goes over to that drawer and starts to pull it out, he knows he wants a bottle of beer. Listen, I want to show you my new radio. How do you like it? We had a 1929 but this is a 1930. A hundred and sixty nine dollars. I couldn't stand the old one, it had the loud speaker on top, it looked too old fashioned. What do you like, songs or orchestra pieces?

Wow, that's too loud. Turn it down.

Yes, we like it soft, too, we turn it down sometimes so you can hardly hear it. Do you like men singing?

Gee, that's awful.

If you loved me as I love you.

Yes, but it's better than women's voices. But I like or-chestras better. How's that? Do you like something a little jazzy? What you looking at, my monkey picture?

Why, it's you, isn't it?

Sure, in my wedding dress. Look how awful it is.

No, it's not awful, it's pretty.

Say, how would you like to have a glass of beer?

Fine.

We make it ourselves. We always have some. The kid drinks it too, he likes it. Do you think it hurts him?

No.

There you are, how is it?

Darned good.

Why does it always have that yeast in the bottom?

You don't filter it.

Yes, we do.

You need a felt filter, you know, like one of those pointed hats the clown wears in the circus. What's your mother saying?

She wants to give you some to take home. Would you like some?

You bet, this is good.

She'll get you a bag.

No, I can get them in my satchel.

Sure?

Sure. What's she saying now? What, four bottles!

She says she wants the bottles back. My husband will be around to pay you tomorrow.

Oh, that's all right.

No, no. He's going away fishing.

Fishing?

Yes, deep sea fishing—Chipsabay. Is there a place like that?

Sheepshead Bay, you mean.

Yes, with his local union. He'll be up next week and I'll call you on the phone tomorrow at 11:30 to tell you how he is. Look out you don't drop 'em. Good-bye.

At the Front

IF THEY REALLY WANT action let them go to Spain.

I been through one war, he answered, and I'm not going through another. I tell you that little green house on Oak Street looked like a palace to me from over there. I was *so* homesick.

But you never even got to the front, did you?

I didn't and I didn't intend to go.

What were you going to do?

I didn't get there till the end of October. I didn't get a chance more than to take my seat when the bell rang. But I had a good time. If I was sure it was going to be like that again I'd go tomorrow.

What do you mean?

I got taken on as orderly to Col. Martindale. He was one of those southern colonels. And could that boy drink! Him and me. The whisky we put away was something awful. General Pershing will never know how many letters I answered for that baby. All I had to do was shine his shoes and make his bed. But it was vice versa with me. I ate his food, drank his liquor and spent his dough.

How did you come to get the job?

He picked me out of two hundred and fifty others. I told him I was on the road and he took me in. And I haven't seen him to this day. And I don't want to see him. We'd both be having the delirium tremens by this time. Was I fat! All I had to do was take up with those French mademoiselles.

He had told me about them some time ago.

Young ones too. I pretty near married one of them. I still

wanted to marry her when I came home. I wanted to send the money over for her. And she'd have come too. But when the old man heard of it he liked to kill me. Why, he sez, you ain't even got so much as a window to spit out of. And you want to bring a white woman over here—into this house? No sir, he sez. You're just crazy. I guess he was right.

The Colonel took me out of the guard house one day because he wanted me to play ball for them. I'd been away without leave, A.W.O.L., you know. We had a man pitching for us named George Forrest. He could throw a ball from Paris into Germany without trying—and we had to play without gloves. Oooh! They had me on first base. He wound up and shot one at me! I just bowed my head and let it go by. Take him out! Take him out! they yelled. No sir. I'd rather go back to the guard house than catch one of those balls with my bare hands.

But that southern mister treated me fine. We had everything of the best. We were regular hotel spenders wherever we went.

The Right Thing

I KEPT WATCHING the Greek but he didn't look up, his face was like a board the whole time.

You're right, said Alex. If there was a nigger around we didn't have a chance. Or someone with a moustache. A nigger or a moustache, that seemed to be what they liked. I told one of them, Say listen, in America not one in a thousand would look at a guy like that. But it didn't seem to bother them none.

Geez! were you ever in Amiens? Quite a city. Must be a population of 100,000, I guess. The cathedral here and the canal runnin' along through the slum section. Wherever you see a canal, that's where the slums is. We were walking along there one night and we seen a couple of girls. They give us the high sign and we pulled in behind them.

We didn't dare walk with them, the place was patrolled by the British M.P. and that's one thing they wouldn't stand for. You could go into a house any place you wanted to but you couldn't walk with them on the street.

Well, they knew that, so they walked ahead and we come behind them about ten paces in the rear. They started out up one street and down the next, we followin' them, until they come to the cathedral. They went along one side of it, down a narrow alley, across a bridge and then around back of it to another street.

One of the girls lived there and we followed 'em right in.

I'll never forget it. They started upstairs and we right after them. The stairs went up through a door in the back wall, you know, coming in. Right next to the door, on the left, was a stove and the old woman was cooking something. The girls were upstairs already when the old woman let loose.

She started in talkin' loud. I didn't know what the hell she was sayin'. I could understand a lot of what they said but I couldn't understand her, she talked too fast. We was for goin' up anyway, the hell with her. But one of the girls come down and started arguin' with her. It didn't do no good. She started slingin' the pans around and raisin' hell generally.

And what do you think she wanted? She wanted to go up first.

There was no gettin' around her. There was a Frenchman we knew who could talk a little English who told us to do the right thing or we'd get into plenty trouble. So after a while I sez to her, All right, come on. And up we goes. And the old man sittin' right there in the other corner all the time.

After that the place was ours. We just lived there. That was our home. Every time we'd get a couple a days off we'd go there and stay. They fed us and took care of us and we had a swell time. We couldn't of had it better.

There was another fella in the company I used to pal around with. He was from Columbia University, a Frenchman. A swell guy. If there was a piano around you couldn't beat him. But he always got drunk too quick.

I used to tell him, For God's sake, cut it out, Charlie. Take it easy. We want to have some fun. But he'd go right away for the drinks, anything he could lay his hands on. An' he'd be drunk before we could get started.

He had a girl on the same street, just a couple a doors below where we was livin'. A married woman. But her husband was at the front.

One day he was drunk as hell and he wanted me to go down there with him. So I went along more to take care of him than anything else, to keep him from gettin' into trouble.

We come to the door and he started bangin' on it. Nobody came so he started makin' more racket than ever. Pretty soon she sticks her head out of the second floor window and says, After the war, Sharlie! After the war! That was a signal they had, you know, to tell him her husband was home. But he was too drunk. He wouldn't listen to nothin'.

Come on, I says, there may be somebody in there.

The hell there is, he says. She can't get away with that with me. I'm goin' in.

Come on, now, Charlie, I says. Cut it out before you get us into it up to the neck.

What's the matter with you? he says. Yellow?

All right, I says. And in we goes.

Just as we was startin' up the stairs, Froggie comes out of the room upstairs with a bayonet, and starts after us. We lit out into the street and he after us. He chased us four blocks until we come to the boulevard and ducks inside one of those cafés they have there. We slammed the door and put our foot against it on the inside.

One of the British M.P.'s come along after a while to see what the hollerin' was about. What the hell, we says. This guy's gone crazy chasin' us along the boulevard with a bayonet in his hand. We ain't done nothin'. So they puts him in chains and takes him away.

But that guy Charlie was just bound to get into trouble. One time he'd been away three days. We didn't know where the hell he was. Then one day he come in all cut up. He'd been in the hospital. Somebody got to him somewhere.

The Greek hadn't cracked a smile the whole time we were talking.

Second Marriage

BETANZES was a very sentimental man, said my mother to me. And very unhappy all his life.

He lived quite near us in Mayaguez. My brother and he went to Paris together to study to be a doctor.

When he came back to Porto Rico he was a Frenchman. In every way he was French and very revolutionary. Henna and he and some other man, I have forgotten his name— there were three of them—were always talking of the revolution. So much so that at last they all had to leave the country. Henna came to New York and Betanzes went back to Paris.

But when he was a young man just beginning to work at his profession he was engaged to marry a very beautiful girl in San Juan who was taken ill just a few weeks before the wedding. All her trousseau was ready, she had many presents that had been given her before the time and the date had been set. Betanzes decided to take care of her himself, it was typhoid fever I think, something like that and she died.

He had a vault built for her where he buried her. In there he put her wedding dress, her presents that he had given her, the flowers and everything that belonged to her and from that time to his death I never saw him smile. He never smiled.

He was a tall man with a black beard. He would dress all in white, with a black hat and he would ride a big black horse—as they did in those days—when he went to see his patients in the country.

Poor fellow.

But after ten years he did marry. He married a nobody, a girl from the country, very pretty but, men do things like that. I don't know why. It seems so foolish. Her name was Simplicia. A very good name for her.

When he had to leave the island he went to Paris and Simplicia went there after him. He lived in Paris all the rest of his life until he was an old man. But he never enjoyed anything. Simplicia made his life a hell. But a real hell.

She was furiously jealous of every woman that he saw— and that is a bad thing for a doctor's wife. She tormented him, she did everything to him you can imagine. She even spoiled his food or took his clothes away from him, like a child, so that she could make him suffer.

But Betanzes never raised his voice or did anything to bother her. Everything she wanted he gave her, he had plenty of money at one time. She was stingy enough herself but with his things she paid no attention. Everything he had she wasted or gave it away.

His wine though he kept under lock and key; that, he did not let her touch.

How she hated him. She created scenes in his office to drive his patients away, she did everything that was bad. Even when he was dying she went into the room and pulled his beard; when he was dying, mind you, to make him get up.

And it did not stop with that. After he was gone she went into his cellar and sold everything he had there, hundreds of dollars worth of old wines, and old, old brandy I have heard, things that would be worth fifty dollars a bottle maybe— for a few francs. She was stupid and ignorant. She sold the whole thing to anybody for nothing at all—just to be revenged on him for her own stupidity.

A Difficult Man

We've always had queer neighbors, it seems to me.

Oh, I suppose everybody thinks that. It's probably true, too. In fact, everybody's queer more or less when you know them that way, just next door, without ever becoming intimate with them to find out the truth of the matter.

Oh yes, but it's been more than that in this case. Take that English fellow, Hallowel.

He *was* a cuckoo, wasn't he?

Yes, broke in my mother, he was one of the worst. He was always drunk. Oh, he wouldn't walk to the station. That wasn't good enough for him. He had to have a taxi. And he came home in a taxi at night. I think he couldn't walk many times. The man would help him up the steps. And he never paid them anything—I don't know how he could do it. I think he was a public accountant. A very smart man his mother told me.

One of those fellows, added my brother, who sits down at a table with the board of directors of some corporation and says: "Well, gentlemen, what do you want me to show, a profit or a deficit?" He could do anything with figures.

This went completely over my mother's head. She continued: His mother said he was a very bright boy in school, one of the very brightest they had ever had in the school. In England that was. He won all the prizes and finally he won a scholarship to the university.

Then he went to the Boer War, I added, remembering some of the details of those days now so long past when as boys we had watched Mr. Hallowel at his evening arrivals home and heard the racket that prevailed afterward and continued, sometimes, long into the night.

He was a powerfully built man about thirty-five years of age and lived on the first floor of a two family house across the driveway under my own bedroom window.

His wife and mother completed the menage, the latter a lean haggard individual with one of those nervous whiplike bodies which seem never to tire, never to flag even, in any task which the tormented mind sets them to do. Her nose was narrow, her hair black and often disheveled, though on occasion she could appear neatly to advantage. At such times, she talked rapidly, with that distinct English enunciation which Americans often envy, and almost invariably of her son.

This boy, you could see at once, was the center of her universe, and the more she grew conscious of his serious defects, the more she praised him to any who would listen.

Her daughter-in-law was the drudge. She was older than the man and an American, a dry enough specimen who saw, no doubt, in this roaring lion of a husband the very apex of her dreams. To him she also was devoted to the point of total self-abnegation. It was a household of violent extremes; almost, though not quite, of frank insanities.

The wife, Eva, was up before dawn every day slaving for her lord and master who knew how to hold sway over her to a spinster's taste. One could see the lights lighted mornings, and a figure moving behind the drawn shades as she set the table, started the fire. Often she would carry out the ashes, her lean body bending under the load of a heavy bucket while the man arose, dressed in leisurely fashion and, one could imagine after shaving pomaded his hair, twisted his moustache into shape and, finally, breakfast done, issued from the front door to step into a waiting taxi.

It had to be so, explained his mother, he was their sole support, he had to be the gentleman. He had earned excellent money formerly, though times were bad now.

And the wife, no doubt, experienced all manner of satisfaction from her labors. She ate it up, you could see that, it shone in her staring eyes. She jerked herself about the house willingly, with incredible alacrity and without rest. She cannot have weighed more than a hundred pounds. And she, too, looked as did her mother-in-law, like the devil.

But in spite of their sacrifices, the family was always broke. This was the chief reason for our knowing them. Hallowel and my father were even fairly intimate being both Englishmen, but it cost the old man plenty.

Then every once in a while there would be a great to-do next door, a veritable pandemonium. Voices would sound, there would be crashes, curses, yells.

Our first impression was that he was beating up the little wife. We wanted to appeal to the police, to stop such brutality, to see that the woman was protected. But my father would not let us.

Then, next morning, after the gentleman had left for the city, there would come the little drudge as usual, her basket on her arm, hurrying down the street, almost running it seemed but apparently none the worse for recent occurrences.

Mother once spoke to Mrs. Hallowel concerning these happenings.

Yes, I told her, she said, I told her very nicely too, the best I knew how, that if they were going to talk so loud, wouldn't it be better if they pulled down the shades a little.

The advice must have come direct to the man's ears for he seldom looked at mother thereafter.

But one evening during the summer after it had become dark, I had a chance to witness what actually took place in that demented household. I heard the noise as usual and decided if possible this time to have a look. I was in my own room; the window opposite and below me was open and the shade half way up. I put out my own light, crouched down on my knees near the window and prepared to take my time to it.

At first nothing. Then there reeled into the doorway

within the figure of a drunken woman, so drunk she could hardly stand. It was the old lady herself! There she stood protecting herself while her son drunk also in all probability, stood before her cursing her, calling her names of the blackest sort to which she replied not at all save by reeling drunkenly.

Get out of here, he finally said, and, grabbing her by the waist, tried to lift her from the ground. Get out of here, you damned hell cat. The rest was lost in screams and the fighting.

He tried again and again to drag her through the door but she fought wildly, clutching at chairs, at the jamb of the door itself, at the rugs, at his legs, at everything. He could not do it.

I myself felt powerless to act. What could I do? What could anybody do? I thought sooner or later it would quiet down, probably with forgiveness, with tears, maybe. But I did not know the tempers of the combatants.

The old woman was on the floor now. Why didn't she get up and go. Why didn't she do as she was told? She was not wanted there. Perhaps had she kept out of it the man could have made some headway in his affairs, having his devoted wife to slave for him—

I saw the old woman still lying on the floor, half curled up, her hair was loose about her face, she was too hurt, or drunk or frightened to rise. She just lay there while her son leaned over her bidding her to get up.

Finally he kicked her, he kicked her in the behind so hard with his powerful toe that he lifted her whole body off the floor. He did it again and again. Until screaming and holding her hands back to protect herself, she did get to her feet when, this time, he gripped her in such a manner that she could not claw back and, calling to his wife to open the front door, he threw his mother bodily out.

Like a cat the woman landed on her feet. Off balance she ran down the seven steps with lightning agility and away into the dark. I realized then that she was in her stocking feet; her form disappeared under the trees.

I confess I did nothing about it. Coming back from the window, I was flushed, as one might be after witnessing a boxing match, or a football game, but the thing did not impress me as being serious. Why, I do not know. The house next door quieted down immediately and presently I went out for a walk—half expecting to find the old woman somewhere and to help her, maybe. But nothing came of this.

The next day Hallowel went off early to his taxi as usual. The wife followed on foot with her market basket and within a week the old lady could be seen in the back yard puttering around a small bed of ratty flowers which grew there, as was her wont.

No resolution of the situation ever occurred in the family as far as we could tell. Except, of course, the money grew scarcer. They, or I mean the little wife, borrowed desperately from every available source until even my father would lend his British brother no more. They owed all the tradesmen incredible bills, a milk bill, as we heard later, of ninety dollars. How could they do it? How did people let them get away with it?

One day I met Mrs. Hallowel down town, before the ice cream parlor. She was coming out as I was going in. She stopped me and I knew what it was.

I've been trying to borrow a dollar and a half, she said to me, and I can't get it anywhere. Will you let me have it?

No, I said, I'm very sorry but I cannot do it.

I beg you, she pleaded, to let me have it. I'll give you three dollars for it tomorrow. Three dollars tomorrow, she repeated.

I shook my head.

As she turned abruptly and left, I kicked myself for not giving it to her but I did not call after her. Somehow or other they got out of town with their furniture next day.

Danse Pseudomacabre

THAT WHICH IS POSSIBLE is inevitable. I defend the normality of every distortion to which the flesh is susceptible, every disease, every amputation. I challenge anyone who thinks to discomfit my intelligence by limiting the import of what I say to the expounding of a shallow morbidity, to prove that health alone is inevitable. Until he can do that his attack upon me will be imbecilic.

Allons! Commençons la danse.

The telephone is ringing. I have awakened sitting erect in bed, unsurprised, almost uninterested, but with an overwhelming sense of death pressing my chest together as if I had come reluctant from the grave to which a distorted homesickness continued to drag me, a sense as of the end of everything. My wife lies asleep, curled against her pillow. Christ, Christ! how can I ever bear to be separated from this my boon companion, to be annihilated, to have her annihilated? How can a man live in the face of this daily uncertainty? How can a man not go mad with grief, with apprehension?

I wonder what time it is. There is a taxi just leaving the club. Tang, tang, tang. Finality. Three o'clock.

The moon is low, its silent flame almost level among the trees, across the budding rose garden, upon the grass.

The streets are illumined with the moon and the useless flares of the purple and yellow street lamps hanging from the dark each above its little circular garden of flowers.

Hurry, hurry, hurry! Upstairs! He's dying! Oh my God!

my God, what will I do without him? I won't live! I won't
—I won't—

What a face! Erysipelas. Doesn't look so bad—in a few
days the moon will be full.

Quick! Witness this signature— It's his will— A great
blubber of a thirty-year-old male seated, hanging, floating
erect in the center of the sagging double-bed spring, his
long hair in a mild mass, his body wrapped in a downy
brown wool dressing gown, a cord around the belly, a great
pudding face, the whole right side of it a dirty purple,
swollen, covered with watery blebs, the right eye swollen
shut. He is trembling, wildly excited—a paper on his un-
steady knees, a fountain pen in his hand. Witness this signature! Will it be legal? Yes, of course. He signs. I sign after
him. When the Scotch go crazy they are worse than a Latin.
The nose uninvolved. What a small nose.

My God, I'm done for.

Oh my God, what will I do without him?

Kindly be quiet, madam. What sort of way is that to
talk in a sickroom? Do you want to kill him? Give him a
chance, if you please.

Is he going to die, doctor? He's only been sick a few days.
His eye started to close yesterday. He's never been sick in
his life. He has no one but his father and me. Oh, I won't
live without him.

Of course when a man as full-blooded as he is has erysipelas—

Do you think it's erysipelas?

How much does he weigh?

Two hundred and forty pounds.

Temperature 102. That's not bad.

He won't die? Are you kidding me, doctor?

What for? The moon has sunk. Almost no more at all.
Only the Scotch have such small noses. Follow these directions. I have written down what you are to do.

Again the moon. Again. And why not again? It is a

dance. Everything that varies a hair's breadth from another
is an invitation to the dance. Either dance or annihilation.
There can be only the dance or ONE. So, the next night,
I enter another house. And so I repeat the trouble of writing
that which I have already written, and so drag another
human being from oblivion to serve my music.

It is a baby. There is a light at the end of a broken corridor. A man in a pointed beard leads the way. Strong
foreign accent. Holland Dutch. We walk through the corridor to the back of the house. The kitchen. In the kitchen
turn to the right. Someone is sitting back of the bedroom
door. A nose, an eye emerge, sniffing and staring, a wrinkled
nose, a cavernous eye. Turn again to the right through
another door and walk toward the front of the house. We
are in a sickroom. A bed has been backed against the corridor entry making this detour necessary.

Oh, here you are, doctor. British. The nurse I suppose.

The baby is in a smother of sheets and crumpled blankets,
its head on a pillow. The child's left eye closed, its right
partly opened. It emits a soft whining cry continuously at
every breath. It can't be more than a few weeks old.

Do you think it is unconscious, doctor?

Yes.

Will it live? It is the mother. A great tender-eyed blonde.
Great full breasts. A soft gentle-minded woman of no mean
beauty. A blue cotton house wrapper, shoulder to ankle.

If it lives it will be an idiot perhaps. Or it will be para-
lysed—or both. It is better for it to die.

There it goes now! The whining has stopped. The lips
are blue. The mouth puckers as for some diabolic kiss. It
twitches, twitches faster and faster, up and down. The body
slowly grows rigid and begins to fold itself like a flower
folding again. The left eye opens slowly, the eyeball is
turned so the pupil is lost in the angle of the nose. The right
eye remains open and fixed staring forward. Meningitis.
Acute. The arms are slowly raised more and more from the

sides as if in the deliberate attitude before a mad dance, hands clenched, wrists flexed. The arms now lie upon each other crossed at the wrists. The knees are drawn up as if the child were squatting. The body holds this posture, the child's belly rumbling with a huge contortion. Breath has stopped. The body is stiff, blue. Slowly it relaxes, the whimpering cry begins again. The left eye falls closed.

It began with that eye. It was a lovely baby. Normal in every way. Breast fed. I have not taken it anywhere. It is only six weeks old. How can he get it?

The pointed beard approaches. It is infection, is it not, doctor?

Yes.

But I took him nowhere. How could he get it?

He must have gotten it from someone who carries it, maybe from one of you.

Will he die?

Yes, I think so.

Oh, I pray God to take him.

Have you any other children?

One girl five, and this boy.

Well, one must wait.

Again the night. The beard has followed me to the door. He closes the door carefully. We are alone in the night.

It is an infection?

Yes.

My wife is Catholic—not I. She had him for baptism. They pour water from a can on his head, so. It runs down in front of him, there where they baptize all kinds of babies, into his eye perhaps. It is a funny thing.

The Venus

What then is it like, America?

It was Fräulein von J. talking.

They were on their way to take the train to Frascati, the three of them—she, her companion, and Evans.

In reply, he shook his head, laughing—and they hurried on to catch the car.

She could speak English well enough, her companion could not, Dev's German was spasmodic coming in spurts for a moment or two but disappearing as suddenly leaving him tongue-tied. So they spoke English and carried their lunch. A picnic. He was delighted.

This day it was hot. Fräulein von J. seemed very simple, very direct, and to his Roman mood miraculously beautiful. In her unstylish long-sleeved German clothes, her rough stockings and heavy walking-shoes, Evans found her, nevertheless, ethereally graceful. But the clear features, the high forehead, the brilliant perfect lips, the well-shaped nose, and best of all the shining mistlike palegold hair unaffectedly drawn back—frightened him. For himself he did not know where to begin. But she looked at him so steadily for some strange reason, as if she recognized him, that he was forced at last to answer her.

The tram was packed to the doors with passengers. Just before starting three treelike Englishwomen had come rushing up calling out distractedly in English that the tram must not go, that somebody was coming— Do you see her? Oh, what can have happened? She had the correct information, et cetera—until finally Clara arrived just in the moment of the tram's departure and clambered aboard desperately, not a minute too soon. So that now they stood in the aisles, the four of them, sweating and glowering at the Italian men, who oblivious to such violence had long since comfortably settled themselves in their seats.

Fräulein von J. was placed immediately before Evans looking at him absorbedly like a child. Not knowing what else to do or to say, he too looked (as the tram went through some bare vineyards) straight back into her clear blue eyes with his evasive dark ones. She lifted her head a little as if startled, flushed (he thought) just a trifle but did not change her gaze. So they continued, to look fixedly among the backs and across the coats of the Englishwomen in the aisle, who were jabbering away disturbedly about the threatening weather. She did not stir to look away but seemed to rest upon his look with mild curiosity and no nervousness at all. It was, as usual, his look which faltered.

Hearing the talk of the Villa this and the Villa that, about to be visited, Evans felt that he wished he could lose this crowd and was more than pleased when Fräulein von J. suggested that as soon as they should get to Frascati they head for the open country, delighted to find that her mood suited his own so well.

At the market place of Frascati, where a swarm of guides and carriages swooped down upon them, the three pic-nickers moved off at right angles to the direction taken by the rest, up a road that led between two walls around behind the town. They did not know where they were or indeed anything about the place or its beauties—they didn't care. Fräulein wanted to see the Italian springtime, that was the most definite of their spoken desires and Dev, sick of antiquities and architectural beauties, was more than willing to follow. The companion disliked Italian gardens anyway, lacking as they do the green profusion of the northern trees. With this they started, beginning at once to see violets along inside the fences, violets they could not reach. Following a brook which ran beside them, contrariwise down the hill, they trampled on, heading for open country.

What is it like, America? And so Dev began to tell her— Not like this—and all the time somehow he was thinking of his sister. Where is Bess? I wish she were here! till walking and talking, leaving the town behind them, they came quite out into the fields with a hill on the left and a little village off in the distance across the valley before them. They were in a worn dirt gully high hedged on both sides with banks cut into narrow paths by goats' hoofs. Before them four absorbed children gathering violets rushed forward in the path by ones and twos rivalling each other in their efforts to pounce upon the finer groups of flowers.

The children paid no attention whatever to the three hikers, not even by so much as one glance. Running ahead with cries of delight, each racing to exceed the others, they soon disappeared through gaps in the hedge. Evans was over and over startled by the German girl's delicate colouration and hair and eyes. Also, her hands were lovely, her ankles, firm—like the Venus, thicker than the stage or dancehall type, but active too—just suggestive enough of the peasant to be like a god's.

You have not told me yet, what it is like, America.

It is like, Dev began, something muffled—like a badly trained voice. It is a world where no man dare learn anything that concerns him intimately—but sorrow—for should we learn pleasure, it is instantly and violently torn from us as by a pack of hungry wolves so starved for it are we and so jealous of each of us is our world.

I think I know what you mean, she replied, it is that we are all good citizens on top and very much better than that inside. It makes me think of the *Johannesfeuer*. You know Sudermann's play?

America is a pathetic place where something stupefying must always happen for fear we wake up. Yes, I have read the play.

By this time they had come quite around behind Frascati

hill. Here they had lunch in a diminutive, triangular grove of oaks where there was a grassy bank with a few daisies on it, and the tall trees bending overhead. Then climbing through a fence they took the road again up to the right around the hill climbing steeply now on a stony path. It was a hard walk this part of the way and before long they were tired, especially Frau M. who was glad to stop near the top and rest.

But after a few words in German which Dev missed, Fräulein von J. cried, Come on! and they two went on alone about two hundred yards ahead up to the woody summit, to a place from which they could see Frau M. below them lying under an ash-tree. Here there were a few stones of some ancient construction almost gone under the wood soil and rotted chestnut leaves. It was a chestnut grove cut and counter cut by innumerable paths which led north over the brow of the hill—to Frascati, no doubt. But now at this early season, the place was deserted. The random, long, dart-shaped dry leaves covered the ground all about them, two foreigners resting on the old stones. Elsa waved to Frau M. from where she sat, then she turned again to Evans, Tell me what you are. You do not mind? I want to know everything. What is America? It is perhaps you?

No, Dev shook his head.

Is it something to study? What will it do? Shall we go there to learn? she asked in rapid succession.

Dev shook his head.

But you will return to it?

Yes.

Why?

Habit.

No, it is something.

It is that I may the better hide everything that is secretly valuable in myself, or have it defiled. So safety in crowds—

But that is nothing. That is the same as in Europe.

America seems less encumbered with its dead. I can see nothing else there. It gives less than Europe, far less of everything of value save more paper to write upon—nothing else. Why do you look at me so? Dev asked her.

Because I have seen no one like you in my life, few Americans, I have talked to none. I ask myself, are you an American?

And if I am—

Then it is interesting.

He said, To me it is a hard, barren life, where I am "alone" and unmolested (work as I do in the thick of it) though in constant danger lest some slip send me to perdition but which, being covetous not at all, I enjoy for the seclusion and primitive air of it. But that is all—unless I must add an attraction in all the inanimate associations of my youth, shapes, foliage, trees to which I am used—and a love of place and the characteristics of place—good or bad, rich or poor.

No, she continued, it is not that.

Evans felt at that moment, that there was very little in America. He wanted to be facetious but the girl's seriousness was not a thing to be fooled. It made him pensive and serious himself.

He could say—that it was just a place.

But you must not tell me that America is nothing, she anticipated him, for I see it is something, and she looked at him again with her little smile. You seem to me a man like I have not seen before. This is America?

I am a refugee, Dev continued, America is or was a beginning, to clean out the—

Then, she replied, it is as in Germany. I did not think so when I saw you.

And I, Dev answered, did not think so when I saw you.

Why am I in Rome, do you think? she queried next.

He did not know.

To become a nun.

And with a shock he remembered the German youths in their crimson gowns whom he had seen filing down the Quirinal, down the long steps; the Scotch youths playing soccer in the Borghese Gardens Sunday afternoon with their gowns tucked up, or doffed, garters showing and running like college athletes for the ball. He remembered too, the Americans with the blue edge to their gowns, the Spanish, the French.

Yes, she continued, that is it. I am in Rome to feel if the church will not offer me an answer. I was fourteen years old when the war ended. I have seen the two things—to throw myself away or to take hold again. I have seen the women running in the stadiums, I have seen them together. If we were peasants, we could be nearer—but we must lose it all, all that is good. I am a German, an East Prussian. My mother is dead. My father is a general—of course. What shall I do? I do not want anything— Tell me what is America. You must say. Is it just a place to work?

Dev nodded.

You see that I am young—I am young, of course. You come to me carrying a message. I do not know what to do. I believe you will tell me. I am not a fool—and I am not gifted either. There is nothing for me. Is there? I cannot walk about letting my hair loose to surprise men because it is so yellow. You perhaps, yes, if you please—and she smiled —but not those whom I do not want. I cannot marry. It makes me sick to marry. But I want, I want. I do not care that I am a virgin or not. No. No. That is childish. I cannot remain as I am—but I must—until this (and she tapped her forehead) is satisfied. You have said something to me. What do I say to you?

Dev thought "running wild" that if they should do as he wished they would both end that night in the jail at Frascati hungry and very much disturbed—possibly—but no more than that. Fool.

They speak to me of my body. It is beautiful. For what? Of what use to me?

She talked quite coolly.

Within a few years I must lose this. Why not? and I have nothing else unless it is a mind to have, to have and nothing that I want. Not painting, not music, philosophy, tennis—for old men, for young men, for women? No. America, that seems something new.

You would find nothing in America, Evans quickly interposed. The girls there cannot go half a mile out of town for fear a Negro might rape them, or their complexions be spoiled by the weather or the Japanese come too close or they be buried in snow or baked in summer; or they marry their business managers or secretaries and live together two or three in apartments. Their thoughts are like white grass so heavily have they been covered by their skins — and so heavily covered are they to protect them from the weather that when they are uncovered they do not exist. One must snatch another up quickly from the general supply, from a patent container. — Evans was ashamed of this speech of which as a fact Fräulein von J. understood not one word. But the few women he had admired were not pretty and the pretty ones he did not admire. — Never think of America, he concluded. The men are worse than the women.

Are you then one?

Evans had no reply.

When I saw you, I saw something unusual, I am never mistaken. I saw something different from what I see every day, neither throwing away nor taking hold to the old horrible handle, all filthy — Is it America? I asked, but you tell me nothing. It is because you will not do so.

America, he began again haltingly, is hard to know.

Yes, she answered, because she had made him serious so that he must speak his mind or say nothing.

I think it is useful to us, he continued, because it is near savagery. In Europe, you are so far from it that maybe you will have to die first before you will live again. But Dev was not such a fool — Europe, I do not know, he corrected himself. I am seeing a few superficial moments only.

But he had a quick pupil. That is enough, replied Fräulein von J. I see now what I saw at the beginning. You are a savage, not quite civilized — you have America and we have not. You have that, yes it is something.

It is very difficult, said Dev. I am not a typical American. We have a few natives left but they would not know me—

You are holding on to something, she said.

It is very difficult, Dev went on—something very likely to be lost, this is what— So he took out the flint arrowhead he had in his pocket and showed it to her.

She was impressed. She held it hard in her hand as if to keep its impression there, felt the point, the edge, tried it, turned it over.

Yes, she said, I have seen the same thing from our own fields, more finished work—but it is very far, very far. No one believes it is real. But this you carry in your coat? It is very strange. Where did you find it?

In a corn-field in Virginia, there are many of them there.

Are there many Americans who know this that you are saying?

Dev shook his head. I have seen but a few. There are pictures pressed into my mind, which have a great power of argument. Summer pictures mostly, of my part of the country, one of the old pioneer houses fast to the ground. There is nothing like them in Europe. They were not peasants, the people who built them, they were tragic men who wasted their wits on the ground—but made a hard history for me— not for me only, I think; they were like all the earlier peoples but it has been so quick and misplaced in America, this early phase, that it is lost or misinterpreted—its special significance.

You think then it might be useful to—me? Yes, that was what I saw in your eyes. She looked again. Yes, it is so.

She shook her head gently from side to side in marveling realization. Come, she said, I was right. What an America is that! Why then did you not look at me all this week? I was troubled. I wondered what was the matter with me.

Dev said he had been excited studying something he wanted among the antiquities.

But a feeling almost of terror, Dev thought, mixed with compassion perhaps, came now into her eyes as she continued to look at him.

It must be even more lonesome and frightening in America than in Germany, she said. She shook her head. She seemed as if looking off into a new country and to be feeling the lonesomeness of it.

America is marvelous, replied Dev, grossly prosperous—

She shuddered, No. So were we. So will we be soon again. She was frightened. How can you stay where you are? Why do you stay there? You make the church impossible—but you are alone. I will pray for you.

They started to get up quietly from their serious mood and were rather startled to find themselves still in the surroundings of this pagan grove. Not too sure were they that they knew each other as well as they had been feeling they did for the few moments of hard sympathetic understanding just past, projecting themselves out; each feeling, each trying hard, to get at the other's mood. They laughed, and Dev gave her his hand but she did not move away.

It is very difficult, she said, for us to support ourselves after we have passed the semi-consciousness of the peasant, and his instinct. We fall back, do we not? You are brave, she said, to want to find some other way—and one that is American. It seems curious to me.

Moving to rejoin Frau M. they saw that it was getting on into the afternoon and that they must be stepping along if they would be back in Rome by nightfall.

You believe in America like a church, mused Fräulein von J. almost to herself.

Dev did not think so.

Do you believe then that the church is an enemy to your belief?

Yes.

She looked away.

Oh come on, said Dev, let's get out of this.

The Accident

DEATH is difficult for the senses to alight on. There is no
help from familiarity with the location. There is a cold
body to be put away but what is that? The life has gone out
of it and death has come into it. Whither? Whence? The
sense has no footspace.

After twelve days struggling with a girl to keep life in
her, losing, winning, it is not easy to give her up. One has
studied her inch by inch, one has grown used to the life in
her. It is natural.

She lies gasping her last: eyes rolled up till only the
whites show, lids half open, mouth agape, skin a cold bluish
white, pasty, hard to the touch—as the body temperature
drops the tissues congeal. One is definitely beaten.

Shall I call you when it happens or will you come again?
Call me.

It is the end!

It is spring. Sunshine fills the out-of-doors, great basins
of it dumped among factories standing beside open fields,
into back lots, upon a rutted baseball field, into a sewage
ditch running rainwater, down a red dirt path to four goats.

What are you stopping here for! To show him the four
goats. Come on. No? Ah! She blushes and hides her face.
Down the road come three boys in long pants. Good God,
good God! How a man will waste himself. She is no more
than a piece of cake to be eaten by anyone. Her hips beside
me have set me into a fever. I was up half the night last
night, my nerves have the insulation worn off them. But—
Fastened in her seat because three boys may pass near her!

They may even look at her. She knows that they will. She will pick one and play him against the rest. They will try to remain three; she will try to make them one and one and one. And I? Am I mad or starved—or tired out? What is fatigue but an opportunity for illuminating diversions? It is like sickness, a sign of normality. Like death, a sign of life.

The path follows above the gully, red in the flamey green of the new grass. The goats are tied by long cords, one to each of two solitary old trees at the path's end, one to the right, one to the left. The others, a white and a black, are in the rough ground beyond. The white one has its tether fastened to a circular block of turned steel with a hole in the center—the railroad is hard by; the other's is tied to an irregular brown stone.

See the nanny goats! I approach the smallest goat timidly. It is the one fastened to the large tree to the left of the path. It has small but sharp black horns. It draws away beginning to wind its tie rope around the tree. Its hair is long, coarse, fawn colored, fading into white over the face and under the belly where the udder hangs, the two pinkish teats pointing slightly forward. I back the creature around the tree till it can go no further, the cord is all wound up. Gingerly I take it by the ear. It tries to crowd between me and the tree. I put out my right knee to stop it. It lowers its head. I seize a horn. It struggles. I find I can hold it. I call the baby.

He isn't afraid. He lays his face against the goat's hairy cheek. Ah! I warn him away watching the sharp point of the free horn. I think of the child's moist gelatinous eyes. I look at the goat's eyes. They are round, large and grey, with a wide blue-black slit horizontal in the center, the striae of the iris folded into it like threads round a buttonhole.

The child strokes the goat's flanks. The hair is not smooth, there is straw and fragments of dried leaves between the horns, an awkward place for a goat to get at. The nozzle is hairy, the nose narrow; the moist black skin at the tip, slit either side by curled nostrils, vibrates sensitively. A goat.

I push the baby away and drive the goat around the tree again until the rope is entirely unwound. The beast immediately finds new violent green tufts of grass in some black mud half under some old dried water-soaked weedstalks. Thrusting down her slender face she starts to crop away unreflectively at that which a moment before she did not know how to achieve.

To the right of the path the other goat comes forward boldly but stops short and sniffs, stretching out its neck; prop for the nose. It ventures closer. Gan-ha-ha-ha-ha! (as in hat). Very softly. The small goat answers. Also grey eyes but the body is marked in a new fashion. Zebra-like two black stripes down the two jowls between which, tawny and black bands down forehead and muzzle. Ears black fringed. A broad and shaggy black stripe down the backbone to the tail. Starting down from this on either flank a broad white band round and under from side to side. Behind and in front of which the flanks are the same tawny yellow as the face.

The baby goes up to the goat and pats its face before I can get to him to draw him back. The goat is impassive, her eyes fixed on me. I take the baby's hand and draw him away. He strains to touch the goat.

The two other goats look up from time to time from a distance then go on nibbling, pulling at the grass with short jerks of the head.

I grip the child's wrist and hand and drag him back between the fields of green flames and the painted gully along the red dirt path.

As we approach the car the baby stumbles on a flange of the gutter. He falls forward on his hands. For a moment his feet leave the ground and he remains poised with feet and buttocks in the air as if he were about to stand on his hands as a circus performer would. Then his arms give way and his face goes in the dirt.

He cries. His mouth is circled with grit. Fortunately the front of his heavy wool cap has spared his brow from injury.

I sit on the step of the car and taking out my clean hand-kerchief I wipe his face. In the windows of the Franco-American Chemical Co. across the way six women have appeared in two windows, four in one and two in the other. They watch the baby, wondering if he is hurt. They linger to look out. They open the windows. Their faces are bathed with sunlight. They continue to strain out at the window. They laugh and wave their hands.

Over against them in an open field a man and a boy on their hands and knees are planting out slender green slips in the fresh dirt, row after row.

We enter the car. The baby waves his hand. Good-bye!

Under the Greenwood Tree

THE CHIEF CULTURAL INFLUENCE in a community is not always self apparent. If, as Keyserling says: localism alone can lead to culture (and this I give my life willingly to experience and to prove) Jack O'Brien is to me one of the princes of the world that I know.

It has puzzled me for years to solve the dignity of this shabby figure, a steady worker, a silent walker in the worst storms, incredibly resistant, in wide-open shoes, solitary— he would be looking at his feet. Talk to him in summer— and he is old—he'll shift swiftly changing his weight from foot to foot—making a quick half gesture with his elbows —as if boxing. But the solitary snow walker is the more familiar and the more profound sight. He seems to have shed the world and to be standing revealed and revealing—

What is this virtue? Chiefly it is that he is down on it here, now; living—not throwing himself out of a window at a slump in the stock market—a straight impulse, without borrowing, without lie, or complaint.

I had only ten cents in change, my sister-in-law told me, I usually give him a quarter, and that was in pennies and a nickel. I said I was sorry and that I would make it up next time. That's all right, said he, in his slow deep voice, it's more than I get some places and I guess it's more than I *earned*!—he added with rising inflection.

In my eyes his last twenty-five years are the purest. The first forty or fifty must be sketched, but the last are the clear and the fine.

I got a family. I got a brother, he said with some pride.

225

That's Bill O'Brien. He's head yard inspector on the B&M. All he has to do is ride out with an engineer twice a day and look things over. He gets two hundred a month, he's fixed all right. He has a wife and children. I go over and see him sometimes.

That's where he may have been the Thanksgiving in 1929 when I went over to look for him having lost track of him and knowing that he had been in the hospital. The man at the pumping station took me over.

Wait till I get my coat. There was a cold wind coming up. It was about five in the afternoon. The dog came with us. He was an airedale. He kept backing up and scratching the ground around us, expectantly.

Wants me to throw him a stone. I never saw a dog like him. He'll bring it back even at night when I throw it into the woods there. He's got them all picked up around here, said the man failing to find a stone big enough to throw.

Why if I throw it in the river he'll feel around in the mud for it with his fore-feet and bring it out.

In the park one day John had told me something about his younger days.

(The "Influence" is nil, of course, but that is the fault of the witnesses: the schools and the poets.)

His father was a gardener, came over here with his family and settled at Pittsfield, Mass., outside the city. John spoke to me of Hoosic Tunnel and Bridgeport but he seemed to have them confused. Back in the hills, was one of the expressions he used.

He was in the park, that day, toward the beginning of September, Labor Day I guess it was. I told him I had some wood to chop. And I wanted to give him a good leather lined overcoat. He said he'd come down the next day, he still had a couple of lawns to cut. But he never showed up. The wood cutting, as I should have seen, was too much for him and he wouldn't come for the coat without it.

I looked closely at him that day, the creases in his neck

were full of dirt, each pore a small stippling of black. Some-how or other his body didn't smell though. I was rather glad.

He had been sitting there at his ease with spectacles on reading the newspaper. His legs were crossed.

Yes, he continued. I used to drive for a doctor in Pitts-field. I think I must have drove for him very nearly ten years. Dr. Covel was his name. I think he's up there yet, or maybe it's his son.

I understand you were once in the prize ring, John.

Yes, I did a little boxing. He gave me a slow stare as if asking how much else I knew. I can remember you boys, he went on, you and your brother, when you were no higher than up to my knee. How's your mother? She's a fine woman. I still go up to the old house but I don't see her there any more.

She's living with me.

Hm. That's right.

I got a brother living up in Hoosic, he continued, he has varied the place several times. That's Bill O'Brien, he's head yard inspector for the B&M. I see him sometimes. He's living over in the city.

Lady, he would say sometimes to my sister-in-law, I've tended furnaces for the past thirty years. She would rush down when she'd hear him putting on coal because he'd always forget to turn on the draught first.

No, John, she would say, I've told you not to put any coal on. Recently he's been too weak to do much.

She gave him a bowl of fish chowder one Friday. He took it with relish. That's what I call cooking, he said. Sometimes they'd see him looking in the paper bags in the back hall, but he never touched anything.

Now down in "Dublin," he would say, that was a good many years ago. "Dublin" was the street that ran down toward the meadows from the Erie saloon across the track, in those days. It was lined with saloons, and was the tough section of the town— Puck Moriorty and Kack Kane were two of the names that come to me now, as I think back to those times.

Down in "Dublin" you wouldn't dare walk down there if you'd been drinking too much whisky, in them days.

I wouldn't think anything of walking to Paterson, he'd say. I'd walk to Passaic to do my marketing. They'd charge me thirty cents a pound for steak here and I could get it for twenty there—he had the prices down accurately.

The keeper at the pump house told me all he knew. He'd tried to find out from the boys down in Belleville but they didn't know too much or wouldn't tell.

Yes, I know that kind. A friend told me. I read in the papers there was a man, a lawyer he'd been, living in a big three story house all boarded up, living in the cellar. The Board of Health dragged him out and sent him to the hospital to be cleaned up. He was furious.

Well, the pump house keeper said, it seems John had been a hod carrier a good many years ago and he'd gotten in trouble with a saloon keeper's wife down there and had to take to the woods.

I hope he got what he wanted, I broke in.

Yea, but it's a hell of a price to pay for it.

And this is where he used to live! said I stopping short. The dog stopped too and began to smell around.

What! It wasn't a hovel. It wasn't even a shed. It was all fallen apart then but what a place for a human being to have inhabited. You mean to say he lived in that!

That's where he lived for twenty years, said the keeper.

Winter too?

Winter and summer. He used to have it heaped up with twigs, branches and leaves, all kinds of things piled around it on all sides.

The place was not four feet high. It faced southeast, on a little rise of the ground in the middle of the swamp. A stump of an old tree was the foundation. From this pieces of dry branches had been stretched over to an upright—

I suppose he'd crawl in there.

My God!

Twenty five feet farther on was a larger cabin. The door was closed. On it was written in red crayon. *Keep Out.* The door was almost off, an old bolt had been pushed in through an iron staple along with several large nails to close it. There was one hinge.

The pumpman shaded his eyes and tried to look through the little window. He lit a match and looked again.

Haven't seen him for a couple of weeks.

God! he might be dead in there.

Sure, might be.

I think we ought to look in.

I suppose so. So as carefully as we could, without destroying anything, we pried the door open at the top. It caught at the bottom so we pulled it out six inches or more bending it to stare in. The place was empty.

Along the back was a bed with a rumpled and grimy quilt on it. There was a small round bellied stove with a piece of tin chimney up from it through the roof, a big hole that must have let in rain. Beside it was a small metal drum. There was no floor.

That was toward the end of November, the trees were bare, the spot, the most isolated in the neighborhood. Garments in various degrees of colorlessness and decay were hanging to the bushes for fifty feet around. The ground was trampled and black as if from many fires before the entrance to this lair. There was an outdoor table where he must have eaten in summer.

The path back to the pump house was well worn.

I suppose he's worn this down himself.

He's got dozens of them around here.

I stopped again to look at the earlier sleeping place. My God!

Yes, I hope I never get that low, said the pumpman.

I'll bet he was happy though.

Sure he was. Happier than you and me. He must have been a pretty tough bird in his day. It's only in the last couple of years that he's been going down hill. He'd spar around once in a while, like a young fellah.

One thing about him, my sister-in-law said, I never heard him complain.

My brother was even more enthusiastic. He's a character. He's worth the whole town. That made me look at my brother in a different light than for a long time.

I waxed enthusiastic. Do you ever see him in winter?

Do I! take my hat off to him. Slouching along. I don't know how he does it.

I don't feel cold, John told me when I told him that I see him walking around sometimes in winter and wonder how he gets along. A lady gave me a pair of mittens last year, he said. One day she met me on the street. Where are your mittens, John? says she. In my pocket, I says. Aren't your hands cold? says she. Why should they be? says I.

I suppose when he took to the woods, twenty-five years ago, he found this place and some pals must have steadied him out for a while while they were after him. Then he must have liked it, better than a boarding house.

You didn't need much money. You were your own boss. In fact now, he won't take clothes. Or if he did take something, when he was sick, when I asked him: Have you got everything you need over there, John? All he said was—

Well, not *every*thing. I gave him three dollars.

I'll be around to work for this, he told me. And he will.

Well, possibly it was spring, must have been spring or summer, or the woods wouldn't have hid him so well. He liked it. And there he stayed—

It's a price to pay, but it's a price paid. — He's as rich as any man, and he's poor, Bible poor. He's out in the air.

I broke my leg once, down in Dublin, he told my sister-in-law, I'd been drinking too much whisky. But it got well. But I don't drink since prohibition, that stuff'll make you blind.

It's the way he rides evenly over the times. The way he walks unbegging. The way he takes the weather. The way he faces the encumbrance of his condition. Lives uncomplaining. Self respecting, alone.

Did you ever know of any woman he had there?

No, said the pumpman.

I've heard he had an aunt, had a house somewhere around here.

Maybe down in Belleville. I never heard of anybody.

Nevertheless he told my sister-in-law she'd died recently. Last year in fact and he missed her a good deal, an old woman, that used to take care of his clothes for him once in a while, and would take him in, maybe, on the worse nights.

Last fall, when we were banking the roses for the winter my wife told him not to dig too close to the roots. You don't need to tell me lady. You've got no fool working for you today, he said. And he did his job well.

He has tasted rare sweets, enjoyed rare occasions, it is my conviction that his life has enhanced the dignity of the human spirit and that the dirt and debasement of it do not matter but are the effects of causes little to the honor or credit of those who made up his daily surroundings.

World's End

It was getting kinda late. We'd been talking cars. I wanted them to come in on a new model we had just unloaded. He seemed interested but she wouldn't let him buy it. So I kept talking, stalling along hoping for a break.

Pretty soon I hears a car pull up in front of the house and stop. I thought someone was coming in. I waited a while then I ast them if they'd heard it too.

Oh, yes, she says, that's our daughter coming home from the movies.

That was all right but after another half hour and nobody comin' in I spoke up again. I guess you were wrong, I says, about that being your daughter.

No, she says, she usually sits out there with her boy friend for a while before coming in. I suppose she sees the light and knows we're up.

A little after twelve o'clock the car starts up and I could hear it fade out down the street. Then someone comes runnin' up the front steps. The door flings open and in comes the girl. A peach, take it from me. As soon as she sees me she stops and stands there swinging her panties around on the finger of her left hand.

Hello folks, she says then, and lets her underwear go onto a couch. How's everybody?

Evelyn! says her mother, I hope you're not going to bring disgrace and scandal into this house.

Oh don't worry, Mother, she says, we're careful.

Everybody knows about it in school now. But he was worried, let me tell you. But it wasn't the first time for her, take it from me. I don't see how they could be so cool

232

about it if it was—her parents I mean. They didn't want him to pay a nickel. Only her father said if anything happened to her he was going to send him up for it. But they just wanted to keep it quiet. You'd think she'd have told them months before. But they're Christian Scientists and at first the old man said, It'll be all right. God will take care of it. Yeah? I said. But you better go to the midwife first. And she did. Then that damned Polack had the nerve to tell me she'd never been to her. Can you imagine anyone lying like that? I suppose she was scared I'd be a witness against her if anything happened.

After about the second month they wanted to find out if she was that way. He had a young doctor friend in the city who told him about some test with rabbits. If she was, the rabbit would show it when you cut it open. He said if you got some of her urine and injected it into the rabbit's ear you could tell.

That's right, I said.

Well, they tried it and—you know they have to wait forty-eight hours and then kill the rabbit and examine it. Well, the first time the rabbit died next day. Then they tried it three times more and it killed all three of them. When he was telling me this he was so serious about it I got to laughing so they wanted to throw me out of the house. All the rabbits died before the time was up. So they quit trying any more.

Strong stuff, I said.

You said it. Such a lot of excitement about nothing. The Gym teacher in the High School, when she heard of it, told the mother not to worry. She said she'd have taken her to some doctor in New York. She said she'd taken lots of girls there when they needed it.

That's service, I said. One of the teachers, huh?

Yes, he's a good doctor, but I don't like him. They say he's dead now, such a young man. But he didn't do the right things.

She was having pains only five hours. That's nothing. With my babies—in the old country—I was three days sometimes. But she don't know nothing about it. Only five hours—and nothing at all. Just little pains. It was just beginning.

But he said the baby was dead, something like that. He said the baby's heart was getting weaker so he had to take it.

It was New Year's Eve, that was why. He wanted to go out to have a good time. They was waiting for him. I could hear them talking inside.

So he cut her open and he took the baby. There was nothing the matter with it. And half an hour later he was dressed up in his clothes to go out. In half an hour!

She could have gone till next day—easily. But he wanted to make the extra money and to go sporting. That's all he thought of.

In this case the offending woman, or the most offending, was a certain Black Bess. She was a former night club prancer and real dark skinned. The man fell for her strong. He'd been running with her a long time before the wife found it out and continued to do so a long time after she'd forbidden him to see her.

He seemed to struggle hard to keep away from her but sooner or later he'd drive over in his Chevrolet and drop into the old hangout on National Boulevard. Or else it would be she who'd come to see him at his home when the wife was working. He was a fine, big specimen and couldn't seem to resist her.

The two women fought over him time and time again, real knock-down battles whenever they would meet. And that was all he needed to keep him set up. They would roll on the floor, clawing and swinging their fists, kicking, biting till both were exhausted when Black Bess would go home or the wife would leave her where she lay. But that didn't stop the carryings on.

Then one day Carrie, the wife, had an idea. She asked her madam if she could use her typewriter. On it she spelled out a letter, a letter to the Police from "a friend," telling about the house Black Bess lived in and giving full information about her husband's actions. She asked the police if they weren't interested in keeping the town clean and gave them this hint on how to do it.

But they'll know it was you who wrote the letter, said my friend to her. How they going to know that? asked the woman, I didn't sign my name.

An amazing thing is that the police acted. The very next day the husband came home earlier than usual and mad clean through. What kind of a town is this, he said, when a man can't park his car on the street where he wants to?

The police told him that if they found his car parked within two blocks of the house that had been mentioned in the letter they'd run him in. And they told Black Bess to move on. She left town the same day, for how long—I don't know.

That night the wife had it out with her husband once more, beating him up with all her strength. What do you suppose I hit him with? she asked my friend proudly. Why I don't know, said the latter. A baseball bat. I hit him right over the shoulder.

Then there was an Italian girl in Newark the man got to going with, but the wife cut that short quick. She made him drive her right to the house, and in she went. In there she gave that girl a terrific beating, then came out and made the man drive her home. And of course that's just what keeps him where he wants to be. That's a *wife* and he's a *man*, to have the women battling over him in that way.

The place was overrun with cats, we couldn't get rid of them. For a hospital, that was bad. We did everything except poison them. We were afraid of that from there being so many children around.

Those cats would climb the dumb-waiter ropes at night. That was the worst. In search of food I suppose. If it hadn't been such a poor district, they mightn't, perhaps, have been so starved. And what cats! They were the ugliest, most vicious brutes I ever saw. It was no cinch to get your hands on them even after you had them cornered in a room with doors and windows closed. They went wild, ran, sprang, yowled awfully. And then fought to the end when with heavy gloves on we finally did get hold of them.

There was a standing bounty of twenty-five cents a tail on them. Some of us internes, when we had time and they were at their worst, would stage a hunt, late at night when the hall would be deserted. Once in a while we'd catch one of them and carry it into the pharmacy. There we'd soak a wad of cotton with chloroform and shove cat and cotton suddenly under the glass microscope bell. Some job with a fighting cat, that, too.

For a moment the thing would turn slowly around in that narrow space, almost filling it. Then, scenting the chloroform strongly, a sudden convulsion would seize it. Round and round it would spin in that terrible death chamber in an incredible agony of motion. Then die. We were awestruck and fascinated by the scene.

But Olaf, the engineer, the most powerfully muscled piece of old sailor-flesh I have ever encountered, looked at the cats merely as an accessory source of revenue. While we dreaded to hurt the animals and only through an excess of feeling proved so cruel to them, Olaf, when he could catch one of the vermin, would clutch it in his enormous paws— tear him as it might—and avulse its tail (in order to claim the bounty) tossing the rest of the creature into the red hot furnace. He did it with the composure of a man filling and lighting a pipe.

An odd, sluggish creature Olaf. He would come to us and say. I want some alcol to rub on my shoulder. Sometimes we'd give him wood alcohol, just for fun. He drank it just the same and as far as we could tell it never did him any harm. He may have diluted it in some way. I don't know.

From early in the afternoon you could see her sitting there with her back to the window where there was a good light. She looked almost caucasian but her hair was short and had been, I suppose, kinky. We watched the proceeding, as we went back and forth about the hospital, hour after hour.

A man was working over her. He had started at the hairline at the back of the neck and was slowly constructing a head of long, wavy brown hair over the woman's cranium.

It was done by tying wisps of the final coiffure, one at a time, to the stubs of the original wool. Hour after hour the man worked at it with brief periods of rest slowly building up his creation. It was a beautiful thing.

It was an easy going sort of place, the women would come in often during the fifth month—since they had nowhere else to go—and work for their keep. Of course there wasn't enough work for all of them—so a lot would be just hanging around in their loose wrappers. Colored or white, we made no distinctions. Miss Emerald used to say we ought to hang out a sign: Babies fresh every hour, any color desired. And a hundred per cent illegitimate, she would add laughing.

The most paralyzing sight I ever saw—to me as a young man that is—was one night when I was called up to the dormitory floor—to see three of them—well advanced in their pregnancies—lying in a heap on the stone floor of the corridor.

At first I didn't know what to make of it. They were sprawled on top of each other almost motionless and Miss Emerald—who wasn't afraid of anything that wore skirts or pants—crouched over one of them. Help me, she yelled as soon as she saw me come in.

It was a fight. Not a sound. They were locked there, their hands twisted in each others' hair and now and then one would wrench free and try to kick or punch the other in the stomach.

I was afraid of hurting them. So try as I would all I could do was to drag the whole mass of them three feet or so over the polished paving. Until Miss Emerald went for the ether and then they let go. One after the other. Still without a word.

Two of them had set upon a newcomer. All apparently, as I heard, having been impregnated by the same man at that time popular in the quarter.

Everyone was afraid of the little bitch. She couldn't have been more than six, a solidly built little female, who screamed, bit, fought and ran for the exits as soon as the agent deposited her on the main floor corridor. The whole staff was instantly disorganized. They couldn't get rid of her—we had to keep her by law. And we couldn't take her into the ward until she had been quieted. They were afraid she'd crash her brains out against the walls so violently did she fling herself in all directions when the nurses tried to take hold of her. When I arrived the special policeman had her in his lap with both arms around her while she was trying to twist herself around to get her teeth into his face.

I told him to carry her into my office and turn her loose. I followed him, blocked her first rush, and locked the door after him as he went out. Then I sat down at my desk and pretended to read.

She took one look at me then made a rush and sank her teeth into my thigh. I pushed her away, put a blanket over my legs and sat down. She made another rush, we fought over the blanket for a moment then she stood back a few inches and kicked me repeatedly in the shins with all her strength. I found it didn't hurt over much so I let her do it talking to her meanwhile and telling her to be a good girl I wasn't going to hurt her and that she couldn't hurt me.

As I leaned over she made a quick stab at me and aiming at my eyes succeeded in striking me in the face. I wanted to annihilate her for an instant—but stopped short as she turned and dragged practically everything I had on the desk to the floor in a few lightning strokes.

Then she flung herself to the floor screaming at the top of her lungs and proceeded to crash her head against the stone pavement. Good, I said. Harder. See how hard you can hit it. She did it again and again, with all her strength. The thud was unpleasant to hear.

This sort of thing kept on for over an hour or until finally, losing patience, I did pick her up, lay her across my knee, take down her pants and fan her a few times with plenty of steam behind it. Nothing doing. She ran around the room as if she were crazy, knocking into the furniture, falling, getting up—screaming in series of shrieks—until I became a little frightened. I was afraid, it being a public institution, that some damned fool would bring a complaint against me and have me before the Board. She seemed at that moment completely out of her mind.

I couldn't sit there all the afternoon either. I thought I was licked sure. Thought I'd better open the door after all and forget it. And I was getting tired, to say nothing of my sore shins that she kicked until she was leg weary from doing it.

In the drawer were some crackers we kept there for light lunch now and then when we were busy. I took out a few and began to chew them. The child quit her tantrums, came over to me and held out her hand. I gave her a cracker which she ate. Then she stood and looked at me. I reached over and lifted her unresisting into my lap. After eating two more crackers she cuddled down there and in two minutes was asleep. I hugged her to myself with the greatest feeling of contentment—happiness—imaginable. I kissed her hot little head and decided nobody was going to disturb her. I sat there and let her sleep.

The amazing thing was that after another half hour—two hours in all—when I carried her still sleeping to the door, unlocked it and let the others in—she wakened and would let no one else touch her. She clung to me, perfectly docile. To the rest she was the same hell cat as before. But when I spoke severely to her in the end she went with one of the nurses as I commanded.

He had the disturbing figure—when stripped down for inspection—of a man whose skeleton was too big for him—and who had grown fat about the belly on top of it. Pasty, and covered with a macular eruption which was more than likely luetic.

There is hardly a gentler creature among my acquaintances—a lover of cats and plants and one who adored the ground his old mother walked on.

At one time he had a pleasant tenor voice but now a huskiness had ruined it.

No more of this Pollyanna stuff, he told me, on the way to the examiner's. I've taken your advice (my heart sank) and seen life a good bit in the last few years. Oh, I've met some rotters, I'll acknowledge that. But also I've made some beautiful friends.

I've had a terrible itching back there, he told the examiner. It seems worse there than anywhere else. What do you think it is?

But I was sure he knew.

When we were waiting for the laboratory reply on the blood test he wrote nervously telling of various things in the immediate past which might have occasioned the breaking out—the sort of food he'd been eating, the hardness of the water where he lived— Please let me know as soon as you can, he added, for the thing is spreading and today I'm "wearing the red veil."

They say if you want to have a *real* good time you have to go to Sunset Lake at night. I went there once with my boy friend. You had to step over them. And you could see the lights of cigarettes all around in under the trees.

A girl hardly dared go in the water. They'd tear the bathing suit off you. I went in though. I had a battle to get out whole. There's no fun in that sort of thing. I was clawed across my shoulders before I could get back to the shore again.

I used to know two of them in boarding school. I saw them once nursing each other. And one day one of them tried to give me a soul kiss. I spit in her face. And then I had to stand up in General Assembly and solemnly tell the whole school about it. I felt sorry for them. Only I don't see why they had to come bothering me.

He was a great pathologist all right, but listen—
You know how they collect blood for Widal tests? Maybe they don't do it that way any more but what we used to do was to get a few drops from the patient's finger on a glass slide and let it clot there. We'd have a dozen or more loaded slides like that on the table some nights waiting for the "Wrath of God" (that's what we used to call him) to test them up in the morning.

And in the morning!—there wouldn't be a thing there but the slides. Every scrap of the clotted blood would be eaten off them by the cockroaches. That used to make "Krummy" wild.

So one night he got me to come along with him. We sneaked into the lab without lighting the lights. He had a can of ether in his hand with a pin hole in the top and he gave me another like it. When I say, Go! he said, you start to squirt the ether. So we were ready, I by the sink and he where some pipes came up from the steam room.

Go! he yells and flashes on the electric lights. And you ought to have seen those roaches run. Some of them were as big as your finger. We must have knocked out about fifty of them the first time. He was wild.

Five o'clock Sunday morning the office bell rang. I went down and let in a colored boy I didn't know. He was terrified, holding his right ear, almost fainting with pain or emotion—I couldn't tell which.

Anyhow, I examined him and found a bed bug crawling around on his ear drum. You can imagine his feelings. Then he told me he only had fifty cents to his name—which he gave me promising to come back later— Later! Yes, I've heard that often. I'll come back later and pay you . . .

As I came into the elevator to go up, I saw the old fellow who operated it to be in a sullen mood. Behind him, looking at the back of his head was the resident priest, old also. He was angry. Neither paid the least attention to me more than for the opening of the gate to let me in and its closing behind me. The priest resumed, apparently, what he had been saying:

You don't believe it. But it's true. He's out again. Lucifer has escaped and is going about in the world to destroy us. You don't believe it's the end of the world, but I tell you it's true. You can read it in the papers every day—in China, everywhere. He's out, and the world is in danger!

Beer and Cold Cuts

The Burden of Loveliness

As he was screwing the cap onto the tank my friend glanced up at me sidewise with a smile on his swarthy young face.

Wha's a matter, Doc? You look kinda down this morning.

Not especially.

You like the picture? I had taken an advertising leaflet from a box hanging near one of the pumps while he was working.

More legs. They use legs to advertise pretty nearly everything now but I never saw them used this way for gas before.

We get a new set every month.

Come to think of it though it's about the best thing they could use to advertise gas with—and vice versa, if you know what I mean.

Come on, come on, Doc. You talk like an old man. Three dollars is right.

Three dollars! Boy, oh boy. There it goes.

Wha's a matter, somebody been holdin' out on yuh, Doc?

If it did them any good, that's what gets me.

What do you mean?

Perfect suckers for the smooth guys who rock them to a fare-thee-well while they pass up the honest man who is trying to save them money. And if you say anything . . .

Yeah, I had a woman here this morning. Just a little bill, four dollars, and I sent it to her. You act as if you were afraid we're going to leave town, she said. Just because I sent her a bill. Some of them don't like that. Others are entirely different. They like to be reminded.

And still others act sometimes as if their heads had got stepped on while they were being born.

Boy, you got it bad this morning, Doc. How are your tires? Shall I put a little air in them?

Wait a minute! I said, as a swanky open air car pulled into the station on the opposite runway from where I was standing. An expensively dressed young woman was driving it, alone in the front seat.

Not bad, huh? Hey, Jack! to one of the helpers under a car on the hydraulic jack at the far end of the station, take care of the doctor. Pull over there, will you, Doc? I'll be with you in a minute.

Take care of yourself.

O.K., said the boy coming from under the car he was greasing, wiping his hands on a piece of waste. My friend left me to take care of his new client.

Nice day, sir, said the boy in his neat mechanic's uniform, his curly hair neatly parted. He pulled the air hose out and hooked it under a rear wheel.

Yes, a nice day for a murder, I said.

He looked at me. How much pressure do you want? Thirty-five?

Thirty-eight wouldn't do any harm.

Yes, sir. He began putting air into one of the tires.

Dance much, Sonny?

What's that, sir?

Do you take the girls out much to dances these fine October days?

No, *sir*. Not me, and he walked around to the front of the car, flinging the hose after him as he crouched and loosened a valve cap.

Why not?

Costs too much money.

Lots of pretty girls around nowdays would count it a treat to get their fingers in that curly hair of yours.

Yeah, I know. But it's a funny thing. Did you ever look at one of those girls' faces up close? He paused a moment where he was kneeling on the concrete and turned his face at me.

No, not especially. Why?

Well, what the hell's pretty about it? He was serious and for the first time that morning I laughed heartily.

Good boy, I said. You'd make a swell doctor.

No, seriously? he said.

Don't talk to him, Doc, said the older man coming up. He's one of those weak-in-the-head guys you were telling me about a little while ago. He doesn't even know the difference between a G string and a clothesline. We were kidding the shirt off him the other day and he's still worrying about it. Did you get a good look at her?

Who?

That woman that pulled in here just a minute ago. You were the one who first noticed her.

No, to tell you the truth I kind of forget her. She wasn't bad though, at that.

Oh, you should have looked. She's something.

Well, go ahead. We got nothing to do. Let's have it.

Sure you don't know her? 'Cause I wouldn't want to . . .

I don't know who the hell she is.

Say, Doc, look here a minute. He was standing toward the front of the car pointing down at the tires. Not much tread left on that one. We're having a special on them this week.

You mean a sale?

No, the regular price. But we're allowing you something on your old ones. Your tires are an unusual size; they're hard to get. I have a customer could use these right now. Get you a couple of dollars a piece for them.

Nothing doing. I haven't got the money.

It's up to you, only you really owe it to yourself to be careful, you know.

Yeah, I know. Fifty bucks, I suppose.

They'd cost you fifty-two but I can get you four dollars off for the old shoes.

Fifty bucks, eh? Huh! What I could do with fifty bucks. I haven't spent fifty bucks on myself for so long I've forgotten what it feels like. I need a new suit of clothes right now.

Yeah, I know. My wife keeps bothering me for new clothes. But I told her, nothing doing. Not till I get a new suit for myself. She can't see that. Why, the other day I had her down at Bamberger's. I followed her around. She bought some curtains, this and that. I've forgotten it all. Then she started down for the dress-goods department. Where are you going? I sez. I'm going to buy a dress, she told me. She'd been ordering things right an' left and telling them to send them to the house. Things we needed. Do you know how much you've spent already? I asked her. Why no, she says. So I took out my little piece of paper I'd been jotting it down on as I was following her around and I told her: sixty-three dollars and thirty-eight cents. She almost hit the ceiling. What! she says. I'm going right back and cancel those orders. Oh no, you're not, I says. Those are things we gotta have. But no dress for you today. You should have seen her face.

A woman's got to have clothes. If they can't get something new to wear . . .

I know, but I felt sorry for her. They don't have it so easy. How about those tires? Shall I save two for you?

Forty-eight dollars, eh? Say what about that woman who was just in here you were going to tell me about?

She's the wife of one of the big bosses in this town.

So what?

You should have taken a look. A beautiful woman, really. One of these little ones, you know, pocket edition, just perfect.

Well, what about it?

Well, you see I got a friend up here. This was several years ago. He was running a shoe store for one of the big companies and the women used to come in there—you know, looking for bargains. And he'd talk to them . . .

Just at that moment a large flock of blackbirds began passing over us and we both looked up at them. You could hear them crackling the way they do, as they flew by, thousands of them.

Well, you know this town's the place for that sort of thing. Anything goes. So he used to take these women in the back room, any number of them. It was a regular thing with him. They understood it. And what do you think he'd give them for it.

I don't know. A couple of bucks?

No.

Maybe they were looking for something themselves and paid him for it.

He'd give them maybe twenty-five cents off on a pair of shoes or maybe the trimmings they have in the windows sometimes when they have displays, all that sort of junk.

Colored silk I suppose and things like that, I said.

He had 'em by the dozen. But then there was this little girl that used to come in sometimes. Just a kid. But she was beautiful, perfect. Pretty face, nice manners, the most beautiful curly yellow hair you ever saw. And very quiet.

Did he tell you all this?

Yes, we used to pal around a lot together before I was married. Well, after she'd been coming in there for about a month or so he kind of put it up to her. Sure, she was willing. You know he was kinda surprised. She seemed to be different from the others and he didn't feel right about it. I guess he was kind of in awe of her. Something like that.

Talked himself out of it, eh?

Naw, he had her all right, but only a couple of times, once in a while. Maybe three or four times in the course of a year, but most of the time he only wanted to play with her, you know. She was so beautiful.

What do you mean, play with her?

He just wanted to look at her. He said she had the smoothest body he ever imagined. . . .

Oh, so that's it.

Everything about her, you couldn't find a thing wrong with her. He just liked to touch her. Oh, he'd hold her and all that but the best he got out of her was just to sit and look at her. He said he never saw anything like it.

Nice fellow.

Then after a while he kind of missed her. He didn't notice it at first but when he did he just thought nothing more about it. But about a year later he met her on the street one day. She hadn't been in the store for all that time.

She was glad to see him and they stood there talking a while. Then he asked her, Why don't you come to see me anymore? No, she said, I'm going steady now, that's all finished. Why don't you just come around once more for old time's sake? he kind of pleaded with her. No, she said, not any more.

Nothing he could say would make her change her mind. Just once more, he said. There's no harm in it, is there? Then she told him.

What did she tell him?

No, she said. No more. You didn't know how to take care of me when you had me. Now it's too late.

Boy! Was that telling him.

I don't blame her. It must be tough, you know, being that good-looking. A fellow never thinks of it that way. But when you look at it from a woman's side, they don't have it so easy. How about those tires?

All right. Can I pay you ten a week?

The place is yours, Doc. I'll put two of them aside and any time you can leave the car here for a couple of hours we'll fix it right up.

And now she's married.

Yeah, now she's married. He gives her everything she asks for. Awful nice woman to talk to.

Above the River

DID YOU EVER SEE a goosey nigger? You mean you never really saw one? Boy! they're a scream. You come up behind them and . . .

I had to answer the telephone. When I had finished talking he started in again: But the metal-lath men are the tough babies. I tell you, you get to know all kinds of men working on a big job like that. Yes, sir, they're the worst. They stick together though. I happened to notice one of them missing from the regular crew one morning. What happened to Bill? I said. Oh, he spoke out of turn at a meeting last night and we had to throw him out.

What sort of meeting?

The union. He was one of those guys who has to chip in his two cents' worth on everything that's going on. They got sick of it but he kept on insisting until finally they turned on him and threw him out, literally. Right down the stairs. He was a mess. Then they all chipped in and took care of him until he could get back on the job again.

Nise piple.

Would you believe me if I told you the best bridge-construction men we have are all Indians?

Indians? You don't mean Hindus, do you?

No, sir. American Indians. They're all man, too, let me tell you. They come from Canada, most of them. They have a funny legal status, so I'm told. Not like you and me. We're just foreigners. I ain't sure but I don't think they have to have any passports or things like that, and they don't have to pay the regular taxes the way you and I do. They're the original owners of the country. Little divisions like Canada and the United States don't mean a thing to them. They're Americans. And do they know it!

We had one on the Triboro Bridge last winter we used to call Papoose. He was a short, thickset man and very powerful. A sort of secondary chief or leader of some sort. You can never really find out. We had a big chief there once too, a big fellow, six feet tall and more, with a chest on him like a barrel. He was something. But this Papoose was a little fellow. You know.

You mean to say, I broke in, that the construction men on the big bridges that have been put up around New York City in the last few years are American Indians?

Yes, sir, I'm the man that ought to know. I was assistant engineer on the job for two years, I'm telling you.

But I always thought those chaps were all ex-sailors, Scandinavians, most of them.

No, sir, American Indians. You can't beat 'em. They come down from Canada mostly in their Ford cars and stay on till they get some money, then when they get ready they quit and go back again. They ain't afraid of nothin'.

But will they work? I've always been given to understand that the American Indian can't be adapted to the industrial age. That they won't . . .

You ought to see 'em. I suppose the kind of work has a lot to do with it. They're like cats. They go anywhere. Nothin' ever happens to 'em either. You can trust 'em with anything. Fine workers. And they mind their own business and they don't bother anybody else's business.

They're wise too. When these government relief workers come around looking for somebody to fire so's to make room for somebody else they want to put on the job, all they say is, Me Indian. Me stay here. And the Goddamned agent can't do a thing about it. They tried to fire me off the job, too, but I was too wise for them. I'm from Jersey, you know, and they wanted to put a New York man on in my place. You can't fire a supervisor. The law doesn't apply to an engineer. I just thumbed my nose at them.

Well, sir, one day we wanted to finish off a section we were pouring before Friday, so we took all the Indians off construction and put them to carrying lathing down to the metal-lath men so we could use them exclusively on their own work.

What do you mean, metal-lath?

You know, what they use to make reinforced concrete. Concrete alone has no tensile strength, so they put steel through it to strengthen it. The expansion coefficients of concrete and steel are about the same, 1.58 to 1.6, not enough difference to matter, so that when heat and cold hit it they never break apart from each other and . . .

Well, what happened?

What was I saying?

You said you took the Indians off construction and put them to carrying metal-lath. . . .

Oh, yes, that's right. We put them to bringing down loads of the metal-lath by hand. Well, sir, this Papoose I was telling you about was the first one to dump his load. As he straightened up he heard one of the metal-lath men say to another—he had his back turned to them—Here come those God-damned sons of bitches of Indians again.

Papoose went over to the guy and said to him, When you say that to me. Me Indian . . .

He didn't get any farther when the guy he was talking to reached around for his pliers. I saw the whole thing. Uh uh, I said, here we go! That's the first thing you'll see one of those guys do when there's a fight. They carry their pliers in their belts the same as you see the line-men on the telephone crews around town here. They always have them in their belts, and they're a wicked weapon when they come out that way.

But before that guy could move, Papoose grabbed him in the belly. He grabbed him from the front with both hands, took right hold of the flesh of his belly, two handfuls and twisted his hands in toward the center till that man went right down to the ground on his knees. And stayed there!

His pals came running to help him. But you couldn't tell where they came from, the Indians all made a circle around Papoose and the other guy, a circle facing out. That's all they did. Just like you read about with animals. And that's all there was to it. Nobody said a word. It all happened quicker than you could think. Then after a while they all went back to work again and nothing else happened for the rest of the day. That ended it.

Grabbed him right by the belly, huh?

Yes, just like that. How do you like it?

What about the goosey nigger?

Oh, I'll tell you about him some time. You got work to do. I got to get out of here.

No Place for a Woman

WHAT I ENJOYED MOST, having left my family in Geneva, journeying back to the States, was to get up the first in the morning, take my cold tub in sea water and be out on deck before anyone else was about.

I'd not be there long before I noticed a tall, rugged man in heavy clothes and a sort of worn yachting cap who'd be leaning on the rail up forward or elsewhere staring out to sea. I should imagine he must have been a man of sixty or more, to say the least, but as straight as an arrow and well built.

It was inevitable that on the third day we should say a word or two to each other and so drift into a conversation.

Yes, he said, this is the sixth time I've been around the world and the first time it wasn't in my own ship. I couldn't resist one final look at it before quitting. I'm just returning home now.

From the whiff I got of his breath I had the impression that he was taking his day in reverse from mine and would be turning in shortly.

Is your wife with you? I asked him.

No, he said. Never take a sandwich to a banquet. I laughed a little and asked him if he had enjoyed himself.

Oh yes, he said, I always enjoy myself as long as I can get enough good liquor when I want it.

I mean, did you enjoy it as much as if you'd been sailing your own ship?

Oh, yes, much more. I wanted to see some of the places

255

I'd known before from the bridge but never had the time to investigate thoroughly.

Well, did you see them?

Yes, I saw them. I think I saw them all. I never want to go again. But it was something I always had it in my mind to do and now I've done it.

We stood looking out over the water awhile then I turned to him once more. What do you think was the most interesting place you saw on this trip?

They're all interesting if you really have the time to study them. But I've seen some strange places—and some strange people. I was thinking this morning as I stood here of a couple of men I talked with on one of those little islands where they raise sheep in the Southern Pacific.

Some particular island, do you mean?

I don't think it even has a name. There must be hundreds of them, thousands of them maybe, just a few hundred acres apiece without a living soul on them. Plenty of grass—but that's all. Ideal for raising sheep.

Is that so?

Yes, he said. Sometimes they'll put two or three men on them with a flock of sheep and leave them there for years maybe.

You don't say.

Oh, they give them all the supplies they want or need and twice a year or so some ship stops in, takes off the wool, leaves a fresh lot of canned goods, the mail, tobacco, whisky and goes off again for another six months.

Can you imagine such a life? I suppose they've got to have whisky. They'd go crazy without it.

They go crazy anyhow. But they have the best whisky. I'm the one who knows it. It's the only thing that permits them to survive. But they even lose their taste for that. Too weak for them, they say.

You say you talked with those men?

Yes, we were anchored off one of those islands a month

or two ago and the captain let me go in with the first boat-load.

I bet they were glad to see you.

Yes, they were glad. I knew them by name. I'd known them for years but had never had a chance to sit down and talk to them before. It was one of the things I wanted to do. They live in a little shack back from the water. Not a bad little cabin. We sat down to the table where they eat their meals and they got out some of their liquor for me.

For a moment he didn't say a word. I waited.

Well, that was something new to me. I took one drink of it and put my glass down.

Was it good?

Well, they said, Matey. Don't you like it?

Yes, I said, I like it all right. But I got to get a little used to the taste. How do you make it?

Oh, they said. We use the best rye they send out to us. And they get the best, you may believe me. To make a long story short and not keep you waiting here—wasn't that the first call for breakfast we just heard?

Yes, that's right, I said.

Well, sir, what they do is this. They clean out one of those five-gallon petrol cans people use for everything like that in the tropics and put a pound of tobacco in it. Then they fill the thing up with good whisky and bury it in the ground for a while.

Wow!

When they pour off the liquor, they've really got something. They say that's the only thing that gives them any satisfaction. Too strong for me.

In Northern Waters

1 . SCOTCH AND . . .

I CAN REMEMBER the sea so full of pumice it looked like
milk. We sailed through it for days with flames and clouds
of dust to the north of us and we going right into it. That
was when Mt. Katmai exploded, back in 1907. Do you remember? The old *Bear*. That was a boat. Its timbers were
of English white oak, two feet thick. I tell you she could
take it. The old Revenue Cutter *Bear*.

Then in spring sometimes we'd anchor down the coast,
around Vancouver. Sometimes there'd be service ships from
several other nations in the roads alongside us and we'd
have great times visiting each other. You can't imagine what
that meant to us.

There was one British boat we'd always look for. British
Coast Guard Service. The *Vulture* or *Cormorant* or some
such name—I've forgotten now, though I should remember
it. But we were great pals, the men on the two ships, I
mean.

We'd no more than get in when they'd board us or we'd
board them and the fun would begin. Drink, you know.
"Tea" they'd call it. We'd end up next morning stewed to
the gills back in our bunks somehow, we'd never know.
Those were great days. Off duty, glad to see human beings
again. Marvelous.

But there was one British bastard we all had it in for. He'd
be the first on board roaring for it. He wouldn't even wait
to be asked, you might say. That was all right. I think
maybe our supply was more generous than theirs and better
stuff. We were glad to let them have it for the sake of a
little fun.

Only when this Limey would get himself tanked up on our good liquor—and let me tell you our supply wasn't endless—he'd start knocking. Rotten liquor! he'd say. Rotten liquor they give you on these Yankee ships. It isn't fit for a gentleman. Typical British bastard of the worst sort. Mind you, this was when he was drunk, of course. Aside from that he was fair, just fair.

There was nothing we could do about it either. He was our guest. We always gave him all he wanted. International courtesy, you know. So when our turn came we'd go aboard the Britisher and drink all their stuff we could lay our hands on. And I tell you we did pretty well. I don't think they always liked that so much but maybe their allowance wasn't as liberal as ours. We always parted the best of friends. You know. But we never could figure out how to stop that bastard.

What did you drink, I asked him, just raw liquor?

No, no. He was offended. We were officers of Uncle Sam's Revenue Cutter Service. Anything they asked for we had it for them but I must say what they gave us was mostly rum. Scotch and soda was their favorite drink when they visited us. That gave me the idea.

Where did you get the soda? You didn't carry that too, did you, on a small boat like that?

We had the gas in metal cartridges. You know, fill a bottle and charge it yourself.

Oh, yes.

It's a dreary life on a ship of that sort. You know, apart from your work and looking at your wife's photograph on the wall every day you haven't much to think of from one year's end to the other, all winter, north of Point Barrow as we were one year. So your mind naturally drifts quite a bit sometimes. Anything to break the monotony. That's how I got the idea to fix our friend. I thought about it all winter once it came to me.

You mean you planned out how to settle his hash?

Just that. All winter long I laughed to myself how surprised he'd be when I got through with him. It kept me amused through some pretty bad weather. You get that way when you're alone.

What did you do?

There they were, next spring, waiting for us. And let me tell you were we glad to see them. What a party that was! And there he was too, the first up the ladder, roaring for his Scotch and soda. I tell you I chuckled. I thought maybe he'd have been transferred or died or something to fool me. But there he was big as life and I was ready for him.

Everybody started drinking Scotch. I sat next to my friend and drank drink for drink with him, arms around each other's necks, right from the same bottle until we'd finished it. The only difference was he had his soda beside him and I had mine, everything else was the same.

What did you do?

Nothing. I just added twenty-five per cent grain alcohol to his soda bottle before I charged it. He never complained again. He never knew what had happened to him.

2. THE DUCK HUNT

WE HAD a surveying party ashore on one of the large islands near Kodiac and the weather permitting we intended to stay there a week or more mapping the coast line. As Chief Engineer there was nothing for me to do, with the ship at anchor, so I had them drop me on the beach one morning to see if I couldn't bring in a few birds for dinner. I'd seen several ducks the day before so I thought I'd chance it.

Better take your rifle along with you, Chief, one of the men sung out, you never can tell what you might find prowling around these parts. So I slung one over my shoulder on general principles, though I didn't intend to use anything but the shotgun.

I'd noticed a place where a point of rocks cut down across the sand a mile or so below, offering good cover from which you could get a shot at any birds that might be going over. So that's where I headed for.

It was a grand morning as I walked along, a little back from the water, through some low bushes and small trees. But there wasn't a stir of life so I kept on, heading for this spot I'd noticed about a mile or two beyond where the ship lay.

Those are the things you remember. I remember how really peaceful and quiet it was, grass—a coarse kind of grass that seems to just shoot out of the ground up there as soon as the sun comes back, some sort of little yellow flowers—like buttercups but not a bird in sight.

I just wandered along swatting mosquitoes until I came to the spot I'd picked out for myself and sat down to rest a few minutes. It was a beautiful spot. I guess I must have fooled around there for a couple of hours more or less. Nothing doing. Then I saw Mr. Bear come out of the trees a little way below where I was sitting and go down to the water.

Let me tell you, you don't know how lonesome you can feel under those circumstances. He was big as a cow only different! I just sat there and looked at him, not daring to move. I had a moderately heavy rifle and I knew I could hit him where I wanted to if I wanted to. But I didn't want to. Not that Bozo. Why, those beasts will travel two hundred yards with a bullet through their brains if they once get started coming at you. You can't stop 'em with any ordinary rifle—and I wasn't aiming to be a hero, not that day—if I could help it.

What happened?

He started walking away from me down along the shore, close to the water. Then he stopped, raised his head and started sniffing the air. I didn't even breathe. For a minute he sort of hesitated and looked around, then he continued on down the shore until I lost sight of him.

So you didn't want to risk a shot, eh?

I didn't want to risk nothin', not with that baby.

3. A TOAST TO THE CZAR

THAT YEAR we were cruising along the Aleutian Islands watching for Japs. Seal poachers and illegal salmon fishers. The same old thing. It wasn't far from there to the Siberian coast. So one day we sighted a small Russian cruiser, about the same as we were, on patrol. Lonesome work, that. We were glad to see each other. They were a marvelous crowd. Great big chaps and friendly as they make 'em. All our officers were invited to dinner with them.

What a time! They had the best of everything. And what table service! I swear we ate off gold plates. You won't believe it but it's the truth. Maybe they were silver but it seemed like gold to us. They treated us royally.

It was a regular course dinner, things I never even saw before, lavishly served—I don't know where they got it all —and about a dozen glasses beside each plate with the correct wine to go with them. I tell you they did it right.

We didn't know what they said to us—much, but we sure enjoyed the grub. Finally a lot of flunkeys cleared things away and the real fun of the evening began. You know officers in that Navy were like little princes to their men.

It was nothing but champagne from that time on. The Captain, I suppose it was, got up to make a speech and, by God, do you know what it was? It was the Czar's birthday. He gave a long speech. You can imagine what it sounded like.

Everybody was high. Then they all stood up. We stood up too. A toast to the Czar! Down the brook. Then smash! They all whammed their glasses on the floor. We looked at each other, then, wham! we followed suit. You couldn't ever use that glass for any other purpose again. The flunkeys came right in and started to sweep up.

So what did our Captain do but propose a toast to the President of the United States. Then wham! We smashed another lot of glasses on the floor. Boy! what a time we had singing and toasting each other with that beautiful glass-ware. What guys!

Those were great days—when you look back at them and forget the tough spots—the things you had to go without sometimes. One day after we'd had a heavy blow, sleet and the roughest kind of sailing for two weeks on a stretch, we put in at a small harbor on the Siberian coast to get our bearings and trim ship a bit. It was a snug little berth and we were glad to get in there.

In the morning we discovered a little village of some sort, a couple of dozen houses perhaps on the shore about a quarter of a mile south of us below a barren-looking range of low mountains.

It just happened that it was the Fourth of July so, for the hell of it and to kill the monotony, we let go a salvo of thirteen shots, right after sunrise. Anything for an excuse to have a little celebration.

We only used a little one-pounder but you could hear each shot echoing way off into those hills, one shot following the other until it made quite a satisfying sort of a rumpus up there in that desolate silence. Then we went down to breakfast.

About fifteen minutes later there was a yell from the deck and up we went. Couldn't imagine what was going on.

Look! said the first mate. We all looked.

There was a steady stream of people, men, women and children carrying everything they owned going up in a line from the village over the mountain, a steady stream of them.

What the hell do you suppose is up? I said, an exodus?

Our gun. They think we're attacking them.

Sure enough, that's what it was. We got out the gig and put in for shore as fast as we could make it. No good. There wasn't a soul left in the place, not even a dog. I suppose they came back after we pulled out that evening. We never saw hide nor hair of them again.

The Paid Nurse

WHEN I CAME IN, approaching eleven o'clock Sunday evening, there had been a phone call for me. I don't know what it is, Mrs. Corcoran called up, said Floss, about an accident of some sort that happened to George. You know, Andy's friend. What kind of an accident? An explosion, I don't know, something like that, I couldn't make it out. He wants to come up and see you. She'll call back in a minute or two.

As I sat down to finish the morning paper the phone rang again as usual. His girl friend had heard about it and was taking him up to her doctor in Norwood. Swell.

But next day he came to see me anyhow. What in hell's happened to you, George? I said when I saw him. His right arm was bandaged to the shoulder, the crook of his left elbow looked like overdone bacon, his lips were blistered, his nose was shiny with grease and swollen out of shape and his right ear was red and thickened.

They want me to go back to work, he said. They told me if I didn't go back I wouldn't get paid. I want to see you.

What happened?

I work for the General Bearings Company, in Jersey City. You know what that means. They're a hard-boiled outfit. I'm not kidding myself about that, but they can't make me work the way I feel. Do you think I have to work with my arms like this? I want your opinion. That fellow in Norwood said it wasn't anything but I couldn't sleep last night. I was in agony. He gave me two capsules and told me to take one. I took one around three o'clock and that just made me feel worse. I tried to go back this morning but I couldn't do it.

Wait a minute, wait a minute. You haven't told me what happened yet.

Well, they had me cleaning some metal discs. It wasn't my regular job. So I asked the boss, What is this stuff? Benzol, he said. It is inflammable? I said. Not very, he said. We use it here all the time. I didn't believe him right then because I could smell it, it had a kind of smell like gasoline or cleaning fluid of some kind.

What I had to do was to pick those pieces out of a pail of the stuff on this side of me, my left side, and turn and place them in the oven to dry them. Two hundred degrees temperature in there. Then I'd turn and pick up another lot and so on into the dryer and back again. I had on long rubber gauntlets up almost to my elbow.

Well, I hadn't hardly started when, blup! it happened. I didn't know what it was at first. You know you don't realize those things right away—until I smelt burnt hair and cloth and saw my gloves blazing. The front of my shirt was burning too—lucky it wasn't soaked with the stuff. I jumped back into the aisle and put my hands back of me and shook the gloves off on the floor. The pail was blazing too.

Everybody came on the run and rushed me into the emergency room. Everybody was excited, but as soon as they saw that I could see and wasn't going to pass out on them they went back to their jobs and left me there with the nurse to fix me up.

Then I began to feel it. The flames from the shirt must have come up into my face because inside my nostrils was burnt and you can see what it did to my eyebrows and eyelashes. She called the doctor but he didn't come any nearer than six feet from me. That's not very bad, he said. So the nurse put a little dressing, of tannic acid, I think she said it was, on my right arm which got the worst of it. I was just turning away from the oven when it happened, lucky for me, so I got it mostly on my right side.

What do I do now? I asked her. Go home? I was feeling rotten.

No, of course not, she told me. That's not bad. Go on back to work.

What! I said.

Yes, she said. And come back tomorrow morning. If you don't you won't get paid. And, by the way, she said, don't go to any other doctor. You come back here tomorrow morning and go to work as usual. Do you think that was right?

The bastards. Go ahead. Wasn't there someone you could appeal to there? Don't you belong to a union?

No, said George. There's nothing like that there. Only the teamsters and the pressmen have unions, they've had them long enough so that the company can't interfere.

All right. Go ahead.

So I went back to the job. They gave me something else to do but the pain got so bad I couldn't stand it so I told the boss I had to quit. All right, he said, go on home but be back here tomorrow morning. That would be today.

You went back this morning?

I couldn't sleep all night. Look at my arm.

All right. Let's look at it. The worst was the right elbow and forearm, almost to the shoulder in fact. It was cooked to about the color of ham rind with several areas where the Norwood doctor had opened several large blisters the night before. The arm was, besides that, swollen to a size at least a third greater than its normal volume and had begun to turn a deep, purplish red just above the wrist. The ear and nose were not too bad but in all the boy looked sick.

So you went back this morning?

Yes.

Did they dress it?

No, just looked at it and ordered me on the floor. They gave me a job dragging forty-pound cases from the stack to the elevator. I couldn't use my right arm so I tried to do it with my left but I couldn't keep it up. I told 'em I was going home.

Well?

The nurse gave me hell. She called me a baby and told me it wasn't anything. The men work with worse things than that the matter with them every day, she said.

That don't make any difference to me, I told her, I'm going home.

All right, she said, but if you don't show up here tomorrow for work you don't get any pay. That's why I'm here, he continued. I can't work. What do you say?

Well, I said, I'll call up the Senator, which I did at once. And was told, of course, that the man didn't have to go to work if I said he wasn't able to do so. They can be reported to the Commission, if necessary. Or better perhaps, I can write them a letter first. You tell him not to go to work.

You're not to go to work, I told the boy. O.K., that settles it. Want to see me tomorrow? Yeah. And quit those damned capsules he gave you, I told him. No damned good. Here, here's something much simpler that won't at least leave you walking on your ear till noon the next day. Thanks. See you tomorrow.

Then it began to happen. Late in the afternoon the nurse called him up to remind him to report for duty next morning. I told her I'd been to you, he said, and that you wanted the compensation papers. She won't listen to it. She says they're sending the company car for me tomorrow morning to take me in to see their doctor. Do I go?

Not on your life.

But the next day I was making rounds in the hospital at about ten A.M. when the office reached me on one of the floors. Hold the wire. It was George. The car is here and they want me to go back with them. What do I do?

Wait a minute, I said. What's their phone number? And what's that nurse's name? I'll talk to them. You wait till I call you back. So I got the nurse and talked to her. I hear you had an explosion down at your plant, I told her. What do you mean? she said. What are you trying to do, cover it up, I asked her, so the insurance company won't find out about it? We don't do that sort of thing in this company. What are you doing now? I asked her again. She blurted and bubbled till I lost my temper and let her have it. What is that, what is that? she kept saying. You know what I'm talking about, I told her. Our doctors take care of our own cases, she told me. You mean they stand off six feet from a man and tell him he's all right when the skin is half-burned off of him and the insides of his nostrils are all scorched? That isn't true, she said. He had no right to go to an outside doctor. What! I said, when he's in agony in the middle of the night from the pains of his burns, he has no right to get advice and relief? Is that what you mean? He has the privilege of calling our own doctor if he needs one, she says. In the middle of the night? I asked her. I tell you what you do, I said, you send me the compensation papers to sign. You heard me, I said, and make it snappy if you know what's good for you. We want our own doctor to see him, she insisted. All right, I said, your own doctor can see him but he's not to go to work. Get that through your head, I said. And that's what I told him.

He went back to their doctor in the company car.

It was funny. We were at supper that evening when he came to the house door. I didn't have any office hours that night. Floss asked him to come in and join us but he had eaten. He had a strange look on his face, half-amused and half-bewildered.

I don't know, he said. I couldn't believe it. You ought to see the way I was treated. I was all ready to be bawled out but, oh no! The nurse was all smiles. Come right in, George. Do you feel all right, George? You don't look very well. Don't you want to lie down here on the couch? I thought she was kidding me. But she meant it. What a difference! That isn't the way they treated me the first time. Then she says, It's so hot in here I'll turn on the fan so as to cool you a little. And here, here's a nice glass of orange juice. No kiddin'. What a difference!

Floss and I burst out laughing in spite of ourselves. Oh, everything's lovely now, he said. But you're not working? No, I don't have to work. They sent me back home in the company car and they're calling for me tomorrow morning. The only thing is they brought in the man who got me the job. That made me feel like two cents. You shouldn't have acted like that, George, he told me. We'll take care of you. We always take care of our men.

I can take it, sir, I told him. But I simply couldn't go back to work after the burning I got. You didn't have to go back to work, he said. Yes, I did, I said. They had me dragging forty-pound cases around the floor . . . .

Really? he said.

He didn't know that, did he? I interposed. I'm glad you spoke up. And they want you to go back tomorrow?

All right, but don't work till I tell you. But he did. After all, jobs aren't so easy to get nowadays even with a hard-boiled firm like that. I won't get any compensation either, they told me, not even for a scar.

Is that so?

And they said they're not going to pay you, either.

We'll see what the Senator says about that.

He came back two days later to tell me the rest of it. I get it now, he said. It seems after you've been there a year they insure you, but before that you don't get any protection. After a year one of the fellows was telling me—why, they had a man there that just sprained his ankle a little. It wasn't much. But they kept him out on full pay for five months, what do you know about that? They wouldn't let him work when he wanted to.

Good night!

Geez, it was funny today, he went on. They were dressing my arm and a big piece of skin had all worked loose and they were peeling it off. It hurt me a little, oh, you know, not much but I showed I could feel it, I guess. My God! the nurse had me lie down on the couch before I knew what she was doing. And do you know, that was around one-thirty. I didn't know what happened to me. When I woke up it was four o'clock. I'd been sleeping all that time! They had a blanket over me and everything.

Good!

How much do I owe you? Because I want to pay you. No use trying to get it from them. If I make any trouble they'll blackball me all over the country they tell me.

Frankie the Newspaperman

She's one of the funniest women I have ever known. Everything amuses her.

What's her name?

Mrs. Weber. She has a son named Frankie and she's always talking about Frankie. He must be a fairly bright boy at that because he's a senior in high school at seventeen. That's not bad around here. Frankie is always in trouble.

She's your washerwoman, you say?

Yes, just this morning she was down on her knees scrubbing the floor and laughing to herself when I came in from downtown. What is it, Margaret? I said to her. What's so funny now?

My son Frankie, she says. He's in trouble again.

What's so funny about that?

They won't let him graduate from the school this year because he don't have enough algebra.

As a matter of fact Frankie wants to be a newspaperman. That's what he likes but they insist on his taking algebra and he doesn't want to do it.

Well? I said. Is that all?

No. But you know he has an English teacher who has a very flat chest and the children all make fun of her.

That's not nice, I said.

No. But anyhow they do. So yesterday they had some kind of sentences they had to make and she made Frankie stand up for her. They had to give a sentence, they had to make it up. And then when they had given the sentence they had to give an answer to it.

Some sort of exercise, I suppose.

Yes, that's it. So she asked Frankie to make up a sentence and to give an answer to it afterward to tell why he had thought of it. So he says, I think we should ask everybody to chip in a dollar and take up a collection for the teacher.

So then she asks him why. Why should they take up a collection for the teacher? You see he had to give a good answer.

And what did he say?

Well, he says that all the pupils should chip in a dollar each—because she is so flat busted!

What? What? What? I said. No wonder she disciplined him.

But Margaret was laughing fit to kill as she grabbed the brush and started vigorously scrubbing the floor again.

Ancient Gentility

In those days I was about the only doctor they would have on Guinea Hill. Nowadays some of the kids I delivered then may be practising medicine in the neighborhood. But in those days I had them all. I got to love those people, they were all right. Italian peasants from the region just south of Naples, most of them, living in small jerry-built houses—doing whatever they could find to do for a living and getting by, somehow.

Among the others, there was a little frame building, or box, you might almost say, which had always interested me but into which I had never gone. It stood in the center of the usual small garden patch and sometimes there would be an old man at the gate, just standing there, with a big curved and silver-capped pipe in his mouth, puffing away at his leisure.

Sure enough, one day I landed in that house also.

I had been seeing a child at the Petrello's or Albino's or whoever it was when, as often happened, the woman of the house stopped me with a smile at the door just as I was leaving.

Doc, I want you to visit the old people next door. The old lady's sick. She don't want to call nobody, but you go just the same. I'll fix it up with you sometime. Will you do it—for me?

Would I! It was a June morning. I had only to go twenty feet or so up the street—with a view of all New York City spread out before me over the meadows just beginning to turn green—and push back the low gate to the little vegetable garden.

The old man opened the house door for me before I

273

could knock. He smiled and bowed his head several times out of respect for a physician and pointed upstairs. He couldn't speak a word of English and I knew practically no Italian, so he let it go at that.

He was wonderful. A gentle, kindly creature, big as the house itself, almost, with long pure white hair and big white moustache. Every movement he made showed a sort of ancient gentility. Finally he said a few words as if to let me know he was sorry he couldn't talk English and pointed upstairs again.

Where I stood at that moment it was just one room, everything combined: you cooked in one corner, ate close by, and sat yourself down to talk with your friends and relatives over beyond. Everything was immaculately clean and smelt just tinged with that faint odor of garlic, peppers and olive oil which one gets to expect in all these peasant houses.

There was one other room, immediately above. To it there ascended a removable ladder. At this moment the trap was open and the ladder in place. I went up. The old man remained below.

What a thrill I got! There was an enormous bed that almost filled the place, it seemed, perhaps a chair or two besides, but no other furniture, and in the bed sinking into the feather mattress and covered with a great feather quilt was the woman I had been summoned to attend.

Her face was dry and seamed with wrinkles, as old peasant faces will finally become, but it had the same patient smile upon it as shone from that of her old husband. White hair framing her face with silvery abundance, she didn't look at all sick to me.

She said a few words, smiling the while, by which I understood that after all it wasn't much and that she knew she didn't need a doctor and would have been up long since— or words to that effect—if the others hadn't insisted. After listening to her heart and palpating her abdomen I told her she could get up if she wanted to, and as I backed down the ladder after saying good-bye, she had already begun to do so.

The old man was waiting for me as I arrived below.

We walked to the door together, I trying to explain to him what I had found and he bowing and saying a word or two of Italian in reply. I could make out that he was thanking me for my trouble and that he was sorry he had no money, and so forth and so on.

At the gate we paused in one of those embarrassed moments which sometimes arrive during any conversation between relative strangers who wish to make a good impression on each other. Then as we stood there, slightly ill at ease, I saw him reach into his vest pocket and take something into his hand which he held out toward me.

It was a small silver box, about an inch and a quarter along the sides and half an inch thick. On the cover of it was the embossed figure of a woman reclining among flowers. I took it in my hand but couldn't imagine what he wanted me to do with it. He couldn't be giving it to me?

Seeing that I was puzzled, he reached for it, ever so gently, and I returned it to him. As he took it in his hand he opened it. It seemed to contain a sort of brown powder. Then I saw him pick some of it up between the thumb and finger of his right hand, place it at the base of his left thumb and . . .

Why snuff! Of course. I was delighted.

As he whiffed the powder into one generous nostril and then the other, he handed the box back to me—in all, one of the most gracious, kindly proceedings I had ever taken part in.

Imitating him as best I could, I shared his snuff with him, and that was about the end of me for a moment or two. I couldn't stop sneezing. I suppose I had gone at it a little too vigorously. Finally, with tears in my eyes, I felt the old man standing there, smiling, an experience the like of which I shall never, in all probability, have again in my life on this mundane sphere.

The Final Embarrassment

I DON'T KNOW how we came to be talking about such things, said the young gray-eyed woman laying her baby in its crib, but we had been living in her house for over a year, it was right after we were married, you know, and I suppose . . . You know.

Poor soul, I can imagine. Inquisitive, I suppose.

She's really an old maid, though she passes herself off here for a widow. She came into my room one morning while I was dressing and said to me, I don't know a thing about it. What is it like to go to bed with a man?

Did you tell her?

What could I say? What I did say was, Well, why don't you try it if you want to find out? You're not too old.

The old Blarney. And what did she answer to that?

I'd be too embarrassed, she said.

Oh, you'd get used to it, I told her, just like the rest of us. Then the poor thing went on to tell the story of when she had been younger. She said she'd been a matron in a hospital somewhere. That's what she said. And a man got out of bed one day and chased her stark naked down the corridor.

Oh, he didn't catch me, she said. But after that my stomach began to swell. It really did. And I thought I was pregnant. I was sure of it. The poor old soul. And do you know she meant it.

Yes, I thought I was pregnant, she said. But when they came to operate on me—it was only a fatty tumor.

Can you imagine! The poor thing. And my young friend

turned to hang a light blanket over the edge of the baby's crib. I saw her smile.

Come on. Come on. You're holding out on me.

No, I'm not.

Yes, you are. Let's have the rest of it.

Well, if you must. And she laughed. The thing that seemed to impress the poor woman most was that she'd be so embarrassed with a man. What do you do? she said.

Did you tell her?

What do you do? I said to her. Why how can I tell you that?

No. It's not that so much, she answered me. I suppose that part of it would be all right. But suppose you're lying there with him and you want to break wind . . .

That was too much. Can you imagine it?

The Round the World Fliers

Going anywhere near Paterson? he said at the 23rd Street Ferry ticket booth. No, I said looking at him closely—red face, mild blue eyes, long chin and sandy hair. Just a kid, more or less. Why? Looking for a ride?

Yeah. Something in the accent, short and sharp. He was bareheaded and coatless in a short-sleeved and narrow-striped blue-and-white sweater shirt. His face sure was sunburned.

O.K. Get in. I drove the car onto the ferry.

Boy! that's a relief, he said. I just walked down from 116th Street and let me tell you those pavements are hot—and hard.

Where are you headed for?

Scranton. I got relatives there.

Been on the road long?

Five days. Am I glad to get out of that city. What kind of a place is that anyway? He shook his head in retrospect.

What's the matter, don't you like it?

My money gave out last night and I haven't had anything to eat since. Think I could get a drink on this boat?

No, I don't think so, this is just for cars—unless you want to ask one of the hands. There must be some place they get water here.

I can wait, he replied. He looked back at the receding shore line and again shook his head slowly from side to side as if in thought. At this moment it came on to rain in a great burst of heavy drops like marbles pelting the low waves into a thousand pits and a grayish mist of spray.

Think this will last?

No, not more than a few minutes, I said.

It'll cool things off anyway. I hope I never see that place again, he returned to his old theme.

Don't blame you, I said. I don't like it either.

You know, he went on, I stopped in at a restaurant around one o'clock this afternoon thinking maybe I could wash dishes or sweep the place out or something for a sandwich and a cup of coffee. It wasn't a fancy place and not a rough joint either, just ordinary. Boy, what a reception *I* got. I've never done any panhandling but I figured I was willing to work for anything I asked for. I almost got thrown out of the place. The man came out from behind the counter at me, I thought he was going to throw me out bodily. I didn't even stop for a drink.

What'll you have? I asked him when the soda-pop man came by.

Cream soda, he said.

Let me have a straw with it, I told the man.

Yes, sir.

Boy, does that taste good! I tell you you get awfully empty when you can't even get water to drink in a place. You can do an awful lot of walking on just water, you'd be surprised how it picks you up. I've often heard it said an army marches on its stomach. Do I know that now!

Where you from?

Montreal.

Out of a job?

I was only working two and three days a week, then I got laid off entirely—for ten days. They told me I might get steady work after that so I thought I'd look around a bit— while I had the chance. I thought I'd take a look at the city first, then head for Scranton. My relatives will get me home if I can't find anything there.

Have a cigarette?

No, not now.

What are you, a Scotsman? You look Scotch to me.

No, English, Powner, doesn't that sound like an English name? Charlie Powner. My mother and father were both born in England, one in Burton and the other in Broton, just outside London, on the Trent. That's English enough too, isn't it?

I'm half English myself. Have any trouble finding rides?

Not much. The worst was in the city. I hopped on the back of a couple of trucks and when they'd put me off I'd look for another. Say, did you see the fliers come over?

No, I replied. I'm just in on a quick trip. Did you see them?

What a racket! Around two o'clock, I guess it was. I had turned into the park so I could set foot on the grass there for a while to rest my feet after those hot pavements. All of a sudden I heard a tremendous noise all around me, factory whistles, taxi horns, people shouting. What the hell is this? I said. I couldn't make it out. Then I hear the roar of the motors and saw the plane overhead.

Was it flying low?

Not so very, but you could tell it by the color and the two tail fins, the two rudders. What a welcome! It was a regular bedlam in the city for a few minutes. A great flight too. I'm glad they got through. But I was worried during those six silent hours after Fairbanks, Alaska. Boy, those Canadian Northwest wilds are worse than anything they'd find in Siberia. If they came down there, we'd never find them. They'll give them a big parade tomorrow, I guess. It ought to be a sight. Not for me, though. I hope to be in Scranton by that time.

Well, you did what you set out to do anyway. You saw the city. How do you fellows eat when you're on the road that way? That's what always gets me.

Well, when I left Montreal I took a dollar. My wife told me I was crazy but I figured I could make it in five days allowing twenty cents a day for food.

What could you eat for that?

Soup mostly. That fills you up.

Yes, I said, and if you salt it well it makes up for what you sweat out on the road.

Yes, then you drink a lot of water and you feel fine.

Throw it in the river, I told him seeing him sit there with the empty bottle in his hand. He looked at it, it was a tall well-made green bottle.

No, he said, the fellow will want it back or they'll charge him for it. Just then the Syrian returned with his smile to collect the empty.

Getting off the boat I was busy with the controls and we said nothing until he saw the half-completed works at the Jersey end of the 42nd Street tubes.

What in hell's that? he said. Boy! he said after my explanation, you do things right down here in the States, don't you? Wonderful roads too. But we don't have the auto accidents you do and no kidnapping either. But our roads are awful muddy.

As we began crossing the meadows, he said, There don't seem to be many footing it down here.

Why, did you see more of them upstate?

The roads were black with them between Albany and Boston, but they were mostly headed in an opposite direction from the way I was going, out toward Buffalo and Rochester and places like that. I saw two girls day before yesterday; I could see them coming for quite a while and I'll be damned if I could tell they were girls the way they were dressed. They stopped me to bum a couple of cigarettes from me and even when they spoke to me I thought at first they were boys. Only when I looked hard at them did I realize that they were girls. What's the idea, I said, disguising yourselves that way? Oh, they said, we get by without so much trouble in these clothes. They had come from Boston and were headed for Elmira where they lived.

That's interesting.

I slept with two girls night before last. In a box car. I think it must have been a private car for race horses, it was so clean. I was looking around the yards for a place to flop in. There was a colored man there and I asked him if it would be all right if I hopped into that one. Sure, go ahead, he said. And you'll find good, clean straw in there too. So in I got, it was toward evening and did that straw feel good! Boy, I never slept so well in my life, it was like the finest of soft feathers to me. When I woke up in the morning I reached for a cigarette as I always do, first thing, and lit a match. It was getting light anyhow. And there they were, two girls, with skirts on and everything, sleeping in the opposite corner from me. They were snoring away in good style so I got up and left them.

I've read something about that, I said. I understand the railroad men take pretty good care of them through the country.

Yeah, they get the best everywhere. I understand down through the southwest there's nothing but girls. Not for me though. That's one part of the country I'm going to keep out of.

The rain had stopped by now. Steam was rising from the heated roadway. I'm letting you off up here, I said. This is Paterson Avenue. Stay right on it and you'll make Paterson without any trouble. If you have any luck you might even get through to Scranton tonight.

Yeah, I'd like to make it, he said. I don't want to leave my wife up there alone too long. I got a little kid too. You ought to see him. All he wants to do is be outdoors. Put him in a pen and he'll stay there all day playing around. But he don't like to be in the house.

Here, I said, this'll get you some supper and a bunk for the night if you need it.

Thanks a million, he said. Do you mind if I help myself to one of those cigarettes now?

Take the pack.

No, thanks. Just one. And if you're ever in Montreal, stop in and see us. 384 Mount Vernon Avenue. Do it. We'll be delighted to see you. A thousand thanks. So long.

As he was standing there speaking the last words I noticed the material of his trousers, a heavy red-brown woolen stuff of a much better quality than any but the wealthy possess in this country.

The Red Head

THEY WENT round and round the block. Yes, I thought, hearing her tell it, Under the stars and the trees. Round and round, the two girls in front and the two boys a few paces back of them.

They're so cute. How can people say the things they do about such children? Not that they aren't up to mischief. But twelve and thirteen years old, we ought to be more generous. Where can they turn for advice if we cut them off?

Anyway, they just kept on walking.

You see, I had a little girl living with me whom I had thought of adopting. A friend of hers lived down the street from us. One of the sweetest children you ever saw. She still lives there. You'd think she was one of the most demure children in town. We'll call her Mary.

One night after supper last May the front doorbell rang and my Helen went to see who it was. She didn't come back. I could hear whispering. Then I thought I heard someone sob. Then the door closed and there was silence.

I ran out at once and saw the two girls starting up the street together with two boys I knew walking back of them. Where are you going? I called to them. Oh, just for a walk. All right. What could I say? Though I had already sensed that things weren't just as they ought to be.

The poor kids. I got the story later. They walked round and round the block. Can you imagine it? Mary in front, hysterical, the others trying to comfort her.

I'm going to have a baby! she said. I'm going to have a baby!

One of the boys kept insisting he wanted to marry her, that he'd do it in a minute and make it all right if she'd have him. But Mary could not be consoled. I'm going to have a baby! is all she would say. And then she'd sob and blow her nose and they'd walk on and on, round and round the block, hushing when they had to pass anyone and starting again as soon as they were by themselves again.

It was terrible! Helen said afterward. We tried our best to hush her crying. We told her that if she didn't stop it her mother would find it out and then she *would* be in trouble.

John kept telling her that he'd marry her and there was nothing to worry about. Finally I got mad, said Helen. I told her if she was going to make a fool of herself nobody could help her. If you're going to have a baby, you're going to have a baby. So what? We've got to do something about it. John said he'd marry you, didn't he? What more can we do?

I'm going to have a baby! I'm going to have a baby!

Finally I told her, if she wouldn't listen to me or to John or to anybody, I, for one, couldn't do any more about it. Why don't you marry John and that will fix everything!

But suppose it has red hair, like Donald!

Oh, boy! said Helen, that finished *me*.

What happened finally, I said.

Nothing. One of the nicest kids in town.

Verbal Transcription—6 A. M.

THE WIFE:

ABOUT AN HOUR AGO. He woke up and it was as if a knife was sticking in his side. I tried the old reliable, I gave him a good drink of whisky but this time it did no good. I thought it might be his heart so I . . . Yes. In between his pains he was trying to get dressed. He could hardly stand up but through it all he was trying to get himself ready to go to work. Can you imagine that?

Rags! Leave the man alone. The minute you're good to him he . . . Look at him sitting up and begging! Rags! Come here! Do you want to look out of the window? Oh, yes. That's his favorite amusement—like the rest of the family. And we're not willing just to look out. We have to lean out as if we were living on Third Avenue.

Two dogs killed our old cat last week. He was thirteen years old. That's unusual for a cat, I think. We never let him come upstairs. You know he was stiff and funny looking. But we fed him and let him sleep in the cellar. He was deaf and I suppose he couldn't fight for himself and so they killed him.

Yes. We have quite a menagerie. Have you seen our bluejay? He had a broken wing. We've had him two years now. He whistles and answers us when we call him. He doesn't look so good but he likes it here. We let him out of the cage sometimes with the window open. He goes to the sill and looks out. Then he turns and runs for his cage as if he was scared. Sometimes he sits on the little dog's head and they are great friends. If he went out I'm afraid he wouldn't understand and they would kill him too.

285

And a canary. Yes. You know I was afraid it was his heart. Shall I dress him now? This is the time he usually takes the train to be there at seven o'clock. Pajamas are so cold. Here put on this old shirt—this old horse blanket, I always call it. I'm sorry to be such a fool but those needles give me a funny feeling all over. I can't watch you give them. Thank you so much for coming so quickly. I have a cup of coffee for you all ready in the kitchen.

The Insane

WHAT ARE they teaching you now, son? said the old Doc brushing the crumbs from his vest.

Have one, Dad? Yeah. Throw it to me. I got matches.

I wish you wouldn't do that, said his wife trying hard to scowl. It was the usual Saturday evening dinner, the young man, a senior in medical school, out for his regular weekend siesta in the suburbs.

I'm curious, said the old Doc glancing at his wife. Then to his son, Anything new? She placed an ash tray at his elbow.

I go on Medicine Monday, said the boy. We finished Pediatrics and Psychiatry today.

Psychiatry, eh? That's one you won't regret, said his father. Or do you like it, maybe?

Not particularly. But what can we learn in a few weeks? The cases we get are so advanced, just poor dumb clucks, there's nothing to do for them anyway. I can see though that there must be a lot to it.

What are you two talking about? said his mother.

Insanity, Ma.

Oh.

Any new theories as to causes? said the older man. I mean, not the degenerative cases, with a somatic background, but the schizophrenics especially. Have they learned anything new about that in recent years?

Oh, Dad, there are all sorts of theories. It starts with birth in most cases, they tell us. Even before birth sometimes.

That's what we're taught. Unwanted children, conflicts of one sort or another. You know.

No. I'm curious. What do they tell you about Freud?

Sex as the basis for everything? The boy's mother looked up at him a moment and then down again.

It's largely a reflection of his own personality, most likely. I mean it's all right to look to sex as a cause, but that's just the surface aspect of the thing. Not the thing itself. Don't you think?

That's what I'm asking you.

But everybody has a different theory. One thing I can understand though, even from my little experience, and that is why insanity is increasing so rapidly here today.

Really? said his mother.

I mean from my Pediatric work. He paused. Of the twenty-five children I saw in the clinic this week only two can be said to be really free from psychoneurotic symptoms. Two! Out of twenty-five. And maybe a more careful history would have found something even in those two.

Do you mean that those children all showed signs of beginning insanity? said his mother.

Potentially, yes.

Not a very reassuring comment on modern life, is it?

Go ahead, son, said his father.

Take a funny-faced little nine-year-old guy with big glasses I saw in the clinic this afternoon. His mother brought him in for stealing money.

How old a child, did you say?

Nine years. The history was he'd take money from her purse. Or if she sent him to the store to buy something, he'd come back without it and use the money for something he wanted himself.

Do you have to treat those cases too? asked his mother.

Anything that comes in. We have to get the history, do a physical, a complete physical—you know what that means, Dad—make a diagnosis and prescribe treatment.

What did you find?

The story is this. The lad's father was a drunk who died two years ago when the boy was just seven. A typical drunk. The usual bust up. They took him to the hospital and he died.

But before that—to go back, this boy had been a caesarian birth. He has a brother, three years younger, an accident. After that the woman was sterilized. But I'll tell you about him later.

Anyhow, when she came home, on the ninth day after her caesarian, she found her husband under the influence, dead drunk as usual and he started to take her over—that's the story.

What's that?

Oh, you know, Mother. Naturally she put up a fight and as a result he knocked her downstairs.

What! Nine days after her confinement?

Yes, nine days after the section. She had to return to the hospital for a check up. And naturally when she came out again she hated her husband and the baby too because it was his child.

Terrible.

And the little chap had to grow up in that atmosphere. They were always battling. The old man beat up his wife regularly and the child had to witness it for his entire existence up to two years ago.

As I say, she had a second child—three years old now, which, though she hated it, came between the older boy and his mother forcing them apart still further. That one has tuberculosis which doesn't make things any easier.

Imagine such people!

They're all around you, Mother, if you only knew it. Oh, I forgot to tell you the older kid was the dead spit of his dad who had always showered all kinds of attentions on him. His favorite. All the love the kid ever knew came from his old man.

So when the father died the only person the boy could look to for continued affection was his mother—who hated him.

Oh, no!

As a result the child doesn't eat, has lost weight, doesn't sleep, constipation and all the rest of it. And in school, whereas his marks had always been good—because he's fairly bright—after his father died they went steadily down, down and down to complete failure.

Poor baby.

And then he began to steal—from his mother—because he couldn't get the love he demanded of her. He began to steal from her to compensate for what he could not get otherwise, and which his father had given him formerly.

Interesting. Isn't it, dear?

So young!

The child substitutes his own solution for the reality which he needs and cannot obtain. Unreality and reality become confused in him. Finally he loses track. He doesn't know one from the other and we call him insane.

What will become of him in this case? asked the mother.

In this case, said her son, the outcome is supposed to be quite favorable. We'll explain the mechanism to the woman —who by the way isn't in such good condition herself— and if she follows up what she's told to do the boy is likely to be cured.

Strange, isn't it? said the old Doc.

But what gets me, said his son. Of course we're checked up on all these cases; they're all gone over by a member of the staff. And when we give a history like that, they say, Oh those are just the psychiatric findings. That gripes me. Why, it's the child's life.

Good boy, said his father. You're all right. Stick to it.

The Good Old Days

In 1910 I was one of a number of passengers going along the Grand Canal in a gondola toward the Venice railway terminal. We had only a minute or two in which to catch the train as suitcase in hand, I tore up the steps, swung through the waiting room, bought my ticket and made for the gate. As I went through, hot under the collar and breathing fast, a guard stopped me.

Piano! Piano! he said in a quiet voice. *E sempre tempo in Italia!* That may not be Italian but that's the way I remember it. Easy! Easy! There's always time in Italy! He was right. I had plenty of time in which to make that train.

It was a lovely country. Yes, and when my brother went over during the first war to take up his duties with the Red Cross it was much the same.

He tells how, when the Americans arrived and the Italian units were turning over their offices and equipment to us, there was a big, formal to-do. It wasn't so big perhaps as it was formal and, in a sense, not too formal at that. Anyhow they made an affair of it, in true Italian style.

The Americans, naturally, had the cash and all that. There was plenty of work to do too so they started in under Colonel Davidson in true big-business style. Everything in the old offices was cleaned out. Modern equipment was moved in—it had all been brought along from New York.

There were half a dozen typewriters, all sparkling new, desks, chairs, filing cabinets, cards, stationery, boxes of ribbons, carbon paper by the bale, everything. And assistants and girls to go with them. It was impressive and the old

Italian force was impressed. They thought it was wonderful.

No wonder Americans go places. You can see it right away. A great people, a great nation! Business geniuses. The American staff was rather proud of it themselves.

Well sir, when everything was set up they had this little affair that I mentioned. Colonel Davidson spoke in English and my brother translated for him. A few messages and telegrams were read and transmitted then, last of all, the old boy who had been at the head of the Italian office before the Americans moved in stood up to make a final gesture. In his hands he held a heavy, round stone.

As he talked all eyes were on the stone.

After a few preliminary remarks he turned to Colonel Davidson and said, I have been greatly impressed by your American efficiency. But there is one thing I should like to present to you, one reminder of the old Italian spirit, part of our own past equipment, which I beg you to keep and to use for what it is worth.

Everybody wondered what the hell he was going to say next.

You see this stone. This is for your correspondence. When letters come into the office you will place them in a neat pile and lay this stone upon them. You do not disturb them then for two weeks. At the end of that time you will begin to take away the letters, one at a time, from the bottom of the pile, five or six letters every day. And you will find, if you do this, that most of them have answered themselves when they are opened. It is a very efficient system and saves much labor.

A Good-Natured Slob

IT WASN'T that the kid was so sick, just that they couldn't hold him without a doctor's say so. That's the only reason they called me in. He was sitting on the bed laughing when I arrived. I told him that with a throat such as he had they wouldn't let him inside the school door no matter how he felt. So he said, O.K., and let it go at that.

It seemed ridiculous to call me just for that, I told the mother. That's just throwing your money away, I told her.

Well, I wanted to be sure. I'll send you the money on Saturday.

What's that? said the burly-looking father coming tousle-headed into the room. Pay him now if you called him. How much, Doc?

Let her send it up.

Here. Take it out of that, and he handed me a five-dollar bill.

Go back to bed, said his wife. Then, turning to me, He didn't get home till ten o'clock this morning, she said, and he's got to go back at one. The fellow stood there in his vest, pants and slippers rubbing his hand over his unshaven chin, his hair all mussed up. What's the matter with him, Doc?

The doctor says it's nothing replied his wife. Then, turning to me, she continued, Once a month he's got to work twelve hours right on through. And such a place. Right under Times Square.

Forty-five feet down, he added for exactness sake. The only thing that bothers us is the dust. Steel dust, from the

293

trains. It gets into everything. Aside from that I don't mind it.

You say he got home at ten this morning and has to go back at one?

Go on back to bed, said his wife by way of reply.

I should think it would be dangerous, he'd fall asleep on the job.

No, not when I've got five telephones round my head ringing all the time.

Wha' da yuh mean?

I get thirty-five hundred calls in half an hour sometimes.

What!?

Sometimes they ring all at once and you got to know which one to pick up first. Sometimes I have as many as fifteen men on the same wire. But I answer them! Give 'em a number or switch 'em where they want to go. But when you get a "block" on top of that, that's what holds you up.

What's a block?

Oh, when everything gets tied up.

2. THE KID BROTHER

IF YOU'D ONLY stayed there another eight months, till September, I told him, you'd have had your Mate's papers. No, he had to come here now—in this weather and bring her with him. You'll kill her, I told him. But he says he can take his examinations any time. Or the Eastern Steamship Company'll sign him on. Only he wants to stay around New York here and he wanted to have her with him. You know.

What'd he do, quit? Or did they fire him?

No, he's got some kind of leave of absence or something. But she's likely to die of pneumonia before that. He's nuts. They haven't got here yet, have they?

No, I said. But, you're right. Take a kid out of a place like Havana where she's lived all her life especially at this

time of year—and she's not well either after what they did
to her. It's dangerous. She's a swell little kid though.

You said it. He's another. Two years ago he come to me,
as soon as he got a job with the fruit company and wanted
to hand me over his pay. Nothing doing. Then he tried to
give it to my wife. She wouldn't take it either. What the
hell, he said, all I'll do is spend it. So I told him, Take it to
the Post Office and deposit it there. Then you give me the
receipt. That way you'll have the money and neither one
of us can touch it.

Good idea. Who is he anyway, your son?

No, he's my kid brother.

How long have they been married?

Just four months. He come up here last September and
told me he wanted to get married. Well, I told him, go
ahead. Take the money out of the bank and go to it. He's
saved up seven or eight hundred dollars by that time. So he
did. But hell, he shouldn't have brought her up here now.
He could have waited till June.

Yeah, I said, she told me she nearly froze to death the
first night she got here.

That's right. The kids wake me up about six o'clock every
morning and get me a cup of coffee before I clear out. When
I was putting my clothes on I heard someone talking downstairs. Who the hell is that downstairs? I said. That sounds
like Joe.

It is Joe, they told me, all excited, and his new wife. She's
just a kid, they says, but she's beautiful. Well, I went down
and that damn fool had got into Newark this morning. He
brought her up on the bus from Miami and she was so cold
he had to get a cab to bring her the rest of the way home in.
She was damn near frozen.

Poor kid. I don't suppose she has the right clothes either.

I'll say she hasn't. So I put her over on top of the radiator
and put some blankets around her and gave her a couple of
shots of hot rum but still she was shivering. So I told him to

put her to bed. She can't talk a word of English and he don't know a damn thing about Spanish. Just nuts. So finally, I says, take her up to my friend. Take her up to Doc, he'll take care of her.

He was sitting in my inner office all this time with his overcoat on, smoking the last half of his cigar. They must be out there waiting now, I said. Yes, here they are.

Hello, sweetheart, said the big chap holding his cigar in one hand and embracing the girl with the other. How are you?

She suffered his attempted smack good-naturedly.

The husband, wearing strong glasses, not any taller than she but a smart-enough-looking man for all that, wanted to know if I was ready. She just looked at the floor, in her little flimsy sport coat—glancing up only when I told her in broken Spanish to walk into the inner office. The men remained outside.

Is this the first time you have seen snow? I asked her in my best—God awful!—suburban hodge podge of the language of Cervantes.

Yes, this was the first time she had seen snow.

And do you think it is beautiful?

No, she didn't think it was beautiful. Rather she thought it was too damned cold to be anything. So she lifted up her skirt, I gave her the shot in the buttock, to guard her against a possible hangover after the operation she had gone through and that was that. A frail, childlike youngster, pure Cuba, with big brown eyes. She had lost five pounds since leaving Havana and couldn't eat a thing, she said.

Here, get this tonic for her—though it's not a damn bit of good, I told the young man. She says she wants to go back to Havana.

Yeah, I know, he said. But I want her up here with me now.

A Lucky Break

Come in, she said opening the door to my ring. Congratulate me. Sure, I said. What for? I've got me a butler. A butler? Uh hum. I got me two at once, a butler and a maid. Well, I said taking off my coat. That's somep'n, isn't it?

I don't know whether or not John is gonna let me keep 'em, but there they are.

Her lovely mother was knitting in her corner of the couch. She began to put her work aside when she saw me and to take off her glasses. It's true, she said. We got ourselves a butler. What do you think of that? And the recommendations he had from Richmond are of the best. They say he's a good gardener and you know there's work enough here for a man all summer long.

And he can drive a car, said the lady of the house. Shall I bring you a drink?

After that, yes, said I, as her mother and I sat down.

What's happened?

We're dead. Bernice just didn't come back this week so we've been doing all the work between us and Helen isn't used to it.

Look at me, said her daughter coming back with the tray of Scotch, water and glasses. I've lost five pounds.

But you know you couldn't stand it, said the older woman. She just isn't used to doing the cooking, the cleaning, taking care of the baby at night and then taking a whole washing and ironing on herself like she did this week.

I just had to do something, said the younger woman, so I called every agency within any distance of here and just told them they had to get me someone. I had a woman coming here yesterday for forty-five dollars a week then that little Jewish agency in Passaic called me up and asked me if I would be interested in a couple.

How much did they want?

Forty dollars. Apiece? I said. No, both of them. Wow. Are they elderly? No, just about in their thirties. How come?

Well, it seems they got themselves stranded here. Some agency sent them up from Richmond and when they got here there was no job for them.

Wasn't somebody responsible?

Yes, this Levy in Passaic. He didn't know what to do with them, that's why he spoke to me about it. They were in the Police Station when I heard about them. They didn't have any money and the police were going to force the agency to put up the money to send them back to Virginia. But they didn't wanna go.

Hum, I said. Maybe it's somebody else's wife.

We're not responsible for their morals, said the older lady. I never bothered about that when we used to have servants in the old days.

That's strange, I said. I wonder who sent for them.

Oh, it's just a racket, said the younger woman. The poor nigs get told that if they'll raise ten dollars the agent will get them a good job up north—where they pay high wages. So they save fifty cents here and a dollar there until they get themselves the ten dollars. They give it to the agent and he puts them on the train or the bus—or somebody takes a load of them in a big old car and brings them up here. There's no job for them. He pockets the ten dollars.

But will they stay?

Oh, yes. They been talking big for months down there about how they're going north to work for serious money and all that. They don't want to go back broke. Anyway, I told them. I don't want you staying here just a week or so and then as soon as you get your first money, running out on me. Oh, no, ma'am, they said. We'll give you a guarantee for a year.

And you've got just the house for it. Just perfect for you. There probably isn't another person in town that is used to handling them like you and with a big house like this—it's just perfect.

And the baby loves them.

How long have they been here?

Just an hour. Listen to them out there. He thinks they're wonderful and he's choosey, too, let me tell you. She's from Virginia. She said her mother had nine children. He's from South Carolina. He said his mother had fifteen. So they're used to children.

I could hear him singing to himself in a resonant baritone voice as he worked in the kitchen. I think I got the original singin' parson, said the lady. I had a big pot of stew I'd made yesterday so I told them as soon as they got here that they could fix themselves something to eat. He looked at me and he said, Lady, you don't know how good that sounds to us. We haven't had anything to eat since yesterday morning.

So what are you going to do now? I said.

You haven't got any old white intern's coats left around the house? she said. I got me a butler, I tell you.

Well, said the old lady, I know what I'll have to do. I'll have to go upstairs and put in my false teeth. That is, if John lets us keep them.

Three weeks later they were gone. His son or their son, perhaps, had been killed by a car and they had to go back for the funeral. No one ever heard from them again.

The Pace that Kills

No, THANKS, I said, as he offered me a cigarette. That's right, he said, you're not smoking. He told you that yesterday, interposed his wife.

Well, sir, he continued glancing sidewise at her, you don't mind if I . . .? Not at all. Have you got a match? Yes, right here. I enjoy it. And it doesn't seem to hurt me. You ought to have seen this place last night. We didn't get to bed till after one this morning. The air was blue with it.

You old fellows are tougher than we modern weaklings. I can't take it any more.

Yes, I'm getting along I guess, he went on. Why, one of the girls last night was looking at a few daguerreotypes we have here. She didn't know whether they were tintypes or what they were. And I told her, you young people take everything for granted, automobiles, airplanes, telephones, even electric lights. You act as if they've always been here. You don't mean to tell me, she said, that you remember when there were no electric lights? She didn't want to believe me.

So I told her I remembered when they had the first electric lights at the Centennial Exhibition in Philadelphia in '76. We were little children, of course, but I remember it. It was just a toy then. Nobody thought it would ever amount to anything.

Yes, I said, even I can remember when Pop swore he wouldn't have a telephone in the house. Why, he used to say, your privacy will be gone forever after that. How right he was.

Sit down—my old friend really had got hold of something this time—sit down if you have a minute, said he, and I'll tell you something you'll hardly believe. His wife in her easy chair smiled but didn't open her mouth, she the easy, stable one, he the voluble, active one of the pair.

J. G. Geoghan, of East Orange. I don't know what he is now, President of some big corporation in New York. He was the first manager for the Newark Telephone Co. Yes, sir, the first manager. And he's still alive and active.

Just a few years ago he had facsimiles made of the first subscriber list, the year the exchange opened. He distributed them around among some of his acquaintances. I had one—but it's gone now. It may be around somewhere but anyhow it's gone.

It was a card, maybe eight by ten inches or so and it had on it two columns of names, maybe fifty names. Just the names, mind you, that's all, no numbers. That was the Newark Telephone Directory. So that when you wanted to call up somebody in Newark you asked for Mr. So and So. What do you think of that? Just a few years ago. And look at the size of it today.

Yes, sir. Time moves, I said. But our lives become shorter and shorter.

In one short lifetime all those chances, and that's only one thing.

Yes, it adds up but it doesn't multiply. No wonder we've gone nuts, huh?

Lena

You got good fish here, said Pete.

Yeah, said the man back of the bar. Best in the States. He was leaning forward, facing his two customers, his hands busy behind the counter, so that when he spoke he had to look up at them with his big, watery eyes.

It's the butter, said Lena. Don's inquiring stare shifted from the one who had first spoken to the gray-haired woman erect at his left. He made no reply.

I see you have to keep your windows screened though, said Lena. Then, to the hulk of a man sitting next to her, Funny to see lemons growing on a tree; can't get used to it. Smells nice, too. Just like the medahs in the early spring.

You like it? said the man in the dirty white coat back of the bar.

No, she don't like it, said Pete.

Any better up in Jersey this time of year?

The two on the high chairs looked down at him. How did you know we come from Jersey?

Look, Pop. People from all over the United States come into this place and nobody ever says medahs the way she said it just now. I come from Rutherford myself. You know where that is? I thought so. How long you been here?

Two days and she wants to go already back. You own this business?

No, I just work here. First time you been down?

First and last, said Lena. There was no one else in the place at that time of morning and the two on the high chairs seemed disinclined to move. Heinselman's my name, said the

302

big guy. Pigs. Secaucus. This is my wife, Lena. What's your name?

Don. Just Don. So she don't like it, huh? Stick around. It'll grow on you.

I like it all right, but I don't want it. She turned sidewise and looked across the courtyard with its palm trees and oleanders, toward the arcades of the big dining room opposite. Twenty bucks, that's what we had to pay when we eat in there last night.

Hell, Lena, said her husband. We're down here on a vacation—the first we had together. That was expensive food, that's right . . .

But you gotta admit it's good, said the man behind the counter, and if we didn't make 'em pay they wouldn't like it. But I'll tell you, you get the same food right here in this bar. What d'yuh say? The coconut cream pie's good today.

No, just a cup of coffee.

You act as if you were homesick. What are you, bride and groom?

The big man laughed. Bride and groom! That's good. What you say, Lena, are we bride and groom?

Seeing there was no answer forthcoming from the woman, Don spoke up again. Looking hard at her, his lower lip hanging down in the way he had, There's something familiar about you, he said. Were you ever over in Richfield?

Sure, I guess so.

Did you ever stop at Don's Clam Bar?

Why not?

That was my place. Then, turning to the big fellow, Look, he said. I'm getting out of here at two o'clock. Stick around. Lemme show you some of the high spots. O.K., Lena?

Fresh guy. But something in the way he said it made her smile. Sure, why not? Anything from up home.

Take it away! cried Don. I knew you the first time I saw you. We'll get along fine.

They were sitting on one of the park benches facing the water where far across the bay you could see the flashing lights of the outer city. Lena was in the middle, flanked by the two men.

I had a chance to make a pile of dough one time. And I did too. Sand-pit up near Haverstraw. A woman gummed it up on me.

And drink, maybe, said Lena.

But the thing that really finished me was that oldest boy of mine. He didn't even get into the war, just a training flight. He flew out from somewhere near New Orleans—that's a place you ought to see—and never came back. Ran out of gas, as simple as that. They got his body for me.

That must have been some time ago, said Lena shifting her position.

Yeah, kind of stiffens you up sitting here on these benches. What do you say we go over to my place for a little game of pinochle?

Come on, Lena, said her husband. And some beer, huh?

Sure, the place is lousy with food. And I'll show you the model I got for a machine to clean shrimp.

You make it?

No, I invented it. Come on, just a half a block down the street here. O.K., Lena? It's only nine o'clock, kid. Come on.

By eleven o'clock Lena wanted to go back to the hotel. We leave tomorrow morning.

Can't get you to change your mind?

Na, Lena. A couple of weeks. Here it's warm and pretty. What can we do home?

Work.

I ask you, Don, what a woman! said the big man shaking his head.

You're lucky you got her. What do you say, Lena? I don't meet many people I can pal up with down here. I'll give you a good time.

Where's your wife and the other two kids you was telling

us about? Lena countered. I don't trust you. You just like
to talk and hit the booze. I know your kind.

Don laughed. Look Lena, stick around and we'll take old
Peter here for a hayride. I mean it. You ain't seen nothing
yet.

What you want to do this for me for? I'm no young
chicken. You trying to make a fool out of me? I don't get
you.

Tomorrow morning. I can't go with you, I'll be working,
but there's a swell trip you can take around the lagoon
and . . .

On what? We haven't got that kind of money.

It's on me. I got a 1948 Cadillac. It's a honey. And a kid
to drive it for you. Anything you like.

What'n the hell's the matter with you? said Lena. You
don't know us.

Look, you're from up where I came from. Look. You
think I'm putting up a game on you?

Lena, said her big husband. Don is a good guy. He wants
to be nice to us. He wants you to stay here, I want you to
stay here—for a couple of weeks. We got the cash.

Yes, but not to throw away on a dump like this. Well
O.K. I'll stay till Sunday if that'll satisfy you.

Atta girl! Ever see a cock-fight, Pete? And we can take
in the ponies Sat'day afternoon.

Betting too, no less, said Lena.

Ten bucks! What can you lose? I'll treat you right.

He's getting drunk, she said sidewise to her husband.

No, said Don at the little metal table under an awning
where they'd been sitting since the last race on the card.
He'd cleaned up thirty bucks. She'd lost. Pete had come out
about even, more or less. I'm not drunk, only a little sticky.
I never get drunk.

Well then, stop drinking, said Lena.

's all right by me. Stop drinking, she says, so I stop drinking. And he took the half-full bottle of Old Grand-dad by the neck and threw it out onto the grass under the palm trees where it rolled crazily about, spilling whisky, until it landed against the concrete wall of the neighboring pavilion and stopped there, without breaking. She's right. Stop drinking, Don. For you I stop drinking. Because it's you. You got a heart, But that bitch I married . . . Sorry. Sorry I said that. She's got no heart. She's got the two girls. What the hell more does she want? What have I got? And that ain't the half of it.

Lena looked as though she were about to push the table into his lap and go. She glowered at him and bit her lip. Her husband, a little sunken about the eyes, was watching her, waiting for what she would do next. She was staring at Don who was leaning forward, mouth open, his arms hanging between his knees, fascinated.

Let's have another round of beer, said Lena. Then we'll go home.

Where is she? said Don next morning at the bar. Sleeping it off?

I wasn't sure you'd be open this morning.

What's she up to?

Packing up our suitcases to go home. Thanks for the use of the car. I had a good time.

She can't do that to me, said Don. Tell her to come down here. I wanna talk to her.

She's a funny girl. You know how I made my money, huh? Pigs.

Yeah, said Don. She told me.

It smells bad. So I buy her a little house out in the country.

Yeah, yeah, said Don. She told me.

A fine little farm, just like she said she wanted. The finest farm country in the state. Pine trees, grass. It smells good. We got a few chickens, everything she wants. Everything convenient. I just put in the latest combination dishwasher, laundry and sink, just the way she wanted it. And what do you think she says?

Hell knows, said Don, what a woman wants.

She wants to sell the whole damn place. She wants to go back down where I got my business, in the medahs. That's why I married her, to get her out of that place.

Don looked down at the glass he was polishing.

So I said to her, Come on down to Miami for a couple of weeks, maybe you'll change your mind.

Take it easy, said Don, without raising his eyes. She's coming up behind you. Then looking up and pretending suddenly to have seen her, Hi there, Lena, old muskrat. What'll it be?

She smiled. How I'd like to see a mus'rat again. Just a cup of coffee. Plain. I feel like a new woman, I do. We're flying back this afternoon.

Flying, no less!

Yep, it's the quickest way. She was in high spirits. Do you know what I was thinking about last night? You know, Pete?

I never know what you thinking.

I was thinking, lying there with the planes going over my head the way they do down here. I was thinking of a story one of the boys told me once, one of my two young brothers I brought up after my father and mother died. They used to go hunting in the medahs, when they was big enough. You know once they brought me home three, what they call Canada geese they shot. But they was pretty fishy.

The way you give it to us you'd think it was an estate you had up in Westchester. I knew the medahs too when I was a kid, don't think I didn't.

Yeah, but you never loved it the way I do, said Lena.

She lived in a little shack down there with the boys when she was young, said Pete. It was all she had.

Come on, give it to us—about the dream.

She supped her coffee, fiery hot and looked at Don reproachfully over the far edge of the cup.

Look out you don't burn your tongue, said her husband.

Well, I was thinking, said Lena of what one of my boys told me. I remember that day, I thought he'd never come home. I thought maybe he shot himself—it was so late. The thing is he wanted to see how the blackbirds come in at night so he hid himself early in the cattails and caneys for hours. For hours he had to wait for them.

To shoot 'em, huh?

But mostly to see. He hid himself good. Because to fool things like that you really got to know how. He was lying on his back almost asleep when he began to hear like firecrackers goin' off all around him. At first he didn't know what it was. He was scared. And what do you think it was?

I don't know. Jesse James and his brothers?

The birds. They're pretty heavy, you know, those blackbirds. And when they come down, hundreds of them, maybe thousands and when they light on those long, dried reeds they break off like pistol shots, he said. That's what he heard —all around him and the birds coming down to roost on those reeds. I never forgot it.

There was a long pause.

You know, Don? Last night thinking about you I taught myself something. I'm a wife now. I forgot that. I guess I got to give up all those things.

Country Rain

IF THIS were Switzerland, I thought, we'd call it lovely: wisps of low cloud rising slowly among the heavily wooded hills. But since it's America we call it simply wet. Wet and someone at another of the tables asks if it's going to stop raining or keep it up all day.

It's what they need for the crops, said one of the elderly school teachers.

The young man sitting opposite her at her table replied, It ain't enough, that's what the farmers always say. We got to have more, this ain't half enough. Everybody laughed.

Then Ruth came in with the toast. Fairly short, a big mouth, fine teeth, and dancing blue eyes that missed nothing. You could just catch a glimpse of Helen back of her, leaning over a table in the kitchen, pouring coffee.

Where you been, Ruth? someone asked her.

I tried to quit you, she replied, but I couldn't get away with it. And she laughed. Everyone laughed immediately after he or she had said anything loud enough for all to hear, that was the custom.

Someone said, Good morning, Ruth.

Oh, good morning! she replied. I always forget to say it. Good morning! And she gave everyone her smile as she moved from one of the three tables to another.

We missed you this morning.

Ruth looked at them. Who do you think was making the pancakes?

Soon breakfast was over and all ten of us filed out into the front room and the wide, covered porch to see if the rain were stopping or to read the mail Ruth had brought from the village on her early trip to the Post Office.

Walk? said the young man who had spoken earlier, refer-

ring to his wife, Geesses, she'll walk the feet off you. I like
to walk but not that much. I think it's going to clear.

The three men of us among all the women—George, that
was his name, the old man and myself, stood watching a
Diesel engine immediately below us in the valley shunting
an empty freight into the siding. That's my job, said
George, Diesel engineer. No, they're not clean, you can't
say that—but they got a big future. It was something, here
on vacation from the big city, which he could talk about
with authority.

Last night, Helen's father, the old man, from Basle,
watching a heavy freight approaching the tunnel, had said,
Not like in Europe. He had the gentle face, the round, blunt
nose, receding but good chin of a circus clown with the
paint off. And always wore a peaked cloth cap, indoors and
out. He sat about the rooms most of the time in his shirt-
sleeves, white collar and black tie, cuffs kept under control
by efficient sleeve-garters. He had been an expert weaver in
the old days.

In Europe they don't make so much noise, he said now.
And not so much smoke . . . When they leave the station
they don't blow that horn. Just a little bell and they leave.
Here iss too much noise.

But the trains are heavier here, I replied. All the equipment is heavier. They carry heavier loads.

Yes, he acknowledged, last week I counted hundred
thirty-five wagons. That's a lot of work. To pull hundred
thirty-five wagons. He tried to continue the conversation
but his words failed him. Iss fine here, he ended. After I
been here one week I feel good.

Yes, the air is good, I said, glancing back at the big front
window of the living room where the deep-green leaves of
a luxuriant begonia were pressed flat against the pane.
Everything is clean here and grows well. At home if you
go into the garden and wipe your fingers across a leaf they
came away black with grease.

View Crest the girls had called the place, because it over-

looked, without obstruction, the quiet valley, its swift shallow stream, and the road climbing south beyond it to East
Halsy out of sight beyond the opposing ridge. But as a
matter of fact the large white house they had taken over for
business purposes occupied not the crest, rather a forehead
of the land's contour, the hill fully outlined, up and up to
the Tilford place in the distance, and again up to the high
ground beyond that where his sugar woods lay. It was an
idyllic spot, no doubt of that.

Still raining! It'll lift by noon, I think.

As we returned to the front room where the women were
whipping themselves into an intense heat over a complicated
jig-saw puzzle, I noticed the obverse of the begonia leaves I
had seen from the outside, glossy green against the glass.
From here they were hairy, veined and a deep maroon-red,
translucent as if they had been hands pressing to the light.

I pointed to an African violet plant in bloom on a small
table. How long has that been here? I asked the old man.

Two years, he said.

I thought they had bought it recently; it looks as though
it had just come from the florist.

No, just there, he said.

Wonderful water! Flossie commented enthusiastically
coming from her bath that morning. I drank two glasses of
it. There are so many things lovely about this place, and the
charming atmosphere of it!

That's the girls—and the others.

The vegetables taste so sweet.

That's because they're fresh.

That squash last night was particularly good. Really delicious. We buy it here in the village, Ruth had told her, it's
grown here. We'll have our own next week.

Why don't you write a story about the place while it's
raining, Floss said, now you've got your typewriter set up.

Country Rain, said I, looking out of our bedroom window
over the ploughed field. Or, *The Dark Helen*, huh?

Ruth had found me a little table from the kitchen for my machine. Do you mind my typing? I asked her; my room was just above where they worked.

Oh no, said Ruth. Sometimes we think we hear thunder.

I thought it might remind you of the old days at the office and make you want to return to them.

Never! she said. If it weren't that my sisters and their children live there I'd never go back, not even for a visit. When I do I'm so happy to return here I can't tell you!

Yes, agreed Flossie, she said the same to me. Isn't it nice, too, the way they have fitted in the old man? He isn't made to feel at all in the way. He cleans vegetables. That belongs to him.

And have you seen the cellar? said one of the other women.

Ruth's mother turned on the light at the top of the steps and took us down.

Oh, how beautiful! For the first thing that met our gaze in the electric glare as we descended was the variegated rows of canned fruit and vegetables in glass jars, red and green and yellow ranged regularly on shelves almost to the ceiling.

We're low at the present moment. But I noticed yesterday the tomatoes are just beginning to ripen. We'll be up to our ears in it again next week. I get pretty tired, added Mrs. B.

I can imagine! sympathized Floss. Oil heat, I suppose? Of course. But why the two tanks?

That was Mr. Tilford's idea, said our guide. Two hundred fifty gallons each. You see, in winter it's pretty hard for the trucks to get up here through the snow; we have twenty feet of it sometimes. So we have to give them plenty of warning. By never using more than one tank at a time and keeping the other always in reserve we're never out of oil.

And your water supply? I was wondering about your water supply.

There, surrounded by a low cement collar about a foot from the floor level was a square cistern four to six feet deep into which was flowing a constant stream of clear, ice-cold water. We both tasted it from a tin dipper, catching it below the inlet and not dipping into the pool.

But look at this! It was a large paper bag up under the rafters marked, Ruth's Boots. We all laughed.

Could you tell me what that white flower is that comes on a vine among the squashes? A beautiful thing, said Floss. I've never seen it before; it's like a large white morning-glory. But sweet. It's unbelievable.

Oh yes, that must be the gourd flower. We always let a few of them grow there. Ruth likes the gourds—just for ornament, in the fall.

Good for her, said Floss.

That evening Ruth offered to show us their pictures. A few of you have already seen them, she apologized, but maybe you won't mind sitting through them once more.

Four reels of film, in color, together with dozens of stills, winter, spring, summer and fall—showing the inauguration and development of the place. Excellent work. Without photographic aid, you could sense the girl's enthusiasm but, especially for the city provincial, the graphic record well brought out their ability and courage.

Isn't she lovely! sighed the women as Ruth in dungarees looked up from planting her tomato plot to brush the sweat from her streaked face.

Helen is all for the movies; Ruth takes the still shots and does all her own developing and printing.

Helen and her sister do the cooking and Ruth does all the baking, said one of the women in a low voice. Her mother takes care of the rooms.

Oh, there's Mr. Tilford! whispered one of the women in the dark. His wife's in England for the summer. Can't get a plane to fly back in.

That's our standby! said Ruth from the front of the room as a middle-aged man following a farm cart appeared on the screen. That's his house you can see up the hill. The sturdy figure continued striding after the cart over the freshly ploughed field as his collie dog romped beside him. That was last fall, said Ruth.

He's a fine man, volunteered the Diesel engineer to me privately. A live wire around here; he runs the town. His house burned to the ground a few years ago, they tell me. In February. All they could do was stand around and let it burn. They couldn't do nothin', just watch it burn—to the ground. They didn't save nothin'. No furniture or nothin'.

I'll bet they had some pretty fine old things in there too. What a shame to lose them that way, I said.

That's the way it is, he replied. The town staked him to another house. Built it all up again for him. He's Deputy Sheriff in the place; owns the whole side of the valley here. Was born there on the hill, I hear. Quite a man. That's his cat. Look at that cat! Trying to get into the house on us. Look at him, Pop. He's smart, huh? Get out of here, District, you can't go in there. There was some boys camped here during the war, men from the third district, give him that name. District, they called him.

The mail wasn't yet sorted at the Post Office next morning when Floss and I called for it to save Ruth the trip, so to spend the time we decided to drive up a side road we'd spotted earlier at the edge of town—the rain was very gentle—to see what was there.

It sloped up steep and slippery but leveled off almost at once above the floor of the valley. Here we came to a stop before the weathered boards of an old covered bridge, not a spectacular specimen but an authentic reminder for all that of other days, with a neon light though fastened up under the gable facing us. Bridge closed, said a sign standing in the roadway a little to one side. But a car had preceded me; I could see its tracks in the wet. He also crossed—gingerly.

Her mother told me, Floss was saying, that she had plenty of admirers. But when she came up here she didn't tell any of them where she was going. I was disappointed, she confessed, but Ruth wanted to do it. So here we are.

And why not? said Floss to me. Be done with men and all that sort of thing if she likes it; that's her business. But she's too pretty and smart to have it last, I think.

No, I commented. Women can get along all right together without a man, unless they want an alligator in the bathtub or something of that sort.

Of course, said Floss, ignoring me, they could use a man and occasionally need one, like a farmer needs a horse. But if they have ability and aren't particularly amused by sexual diversions they can get along all right; even save time and energy for more productive things.

I wonder even if they couldn't adopt a child if they wanted that.

She has a cousin, continued Floss, thinking vaguely of Ruth, who is in the State Department at Washington. Some Swedish name. She told me but I've forgot.

That gives her national connections, I said. She looks it.

I stopped the car in a dark, heavily wooded portion of the road dripping with the rain from the overhanging spruces. Floss looked at me. There was a sharp drop to the left beyond the half-rotten section of a crude guard rail where in the intense silence a small stream could be heard talking to itself among the stones.

What are you stopping here for?

I want to look at a rock. As I spoke I backed the car about twenty feet, drew in toward the embankment and shut off the engine.

The rock lay at about eye level close to my side of the road, the upper surface of it sloping slightly toward me with the hillside. Not a very big rock. What had stopped me was the shaggy covering which completely inundated it. The ferns, a cropped-short, dark-green fern, was the outstanding feature, growing thickly over an underlying cover of dense moss. But there was also a broad-leafed vine running lightly among the ferns, weaving the pattern together.

That wasn't all. The back portion of the rock, which wasn't much larger than the top of an ordinary dining-room table slightly raised at one side and a little tilted, supported both the rotten stump of a tree long since decayed but, also, a brother to that tree—coming in fact from the same root and very much alive, as big as a man's arm, a good solid arm—a ten-foot tree about whose base a small thicket of brambles clustered. Ferns of three sorts closed in from the sides completing the picture. A most ungrammatical rock.

Isn't this magnificent! Let's bring the two school teachers out here for a ride tomorrow, said Floss. They'd love it. Have you ever talked to them? she added. They're sweet.

No, I said, observing the woods ascending the hillside in the rain, but their situation among the dones, the aints and the seens amuses me. I've been wondering what they are thinking.

Don't worry, said Floss. They know what it's all about.

Look, I said, after we had rolled forward another half mile or so, do you see what I see?

Oh, said Floss, raspberries!

We stopped again, it was still raining, so I told her to stay where she was while I got down to pick some of the fruit, the remainder of what I could see had been an abundant crop recently growing at the side of the road sloping toward the stream.

Oh, taste them! said Flossie when I had brought them to her in my hand. They're dripping with juice. Anyone who would put sugar on such berries, well, would be just a barbarian. Perhaps we could stop again here tomorrow and pick enough for everybody.

A steady, heavy rain, she added. The farmers will like that. And then as an afterthought: Do you think Ruth will ever marry?

Why? I answered her.

Inquest

IT WAS a cold day. A woman waiting for a bus, her hands in a small muff, was rocking back and forth, knocking the sole of one shoe against the heel of the other.

What we save, what we have, what we do. No matter. That which we most dearly cherish, *that* we shall lose, the one thing we most desire. What remains?

To be and remain interesting—with reservations—perhaps. The sweatshop worker, I suppose. But she isn't a woman, she's just a thing. An important thing to whom justice should be done but surely not a woman. What about a woman who works in the fields. In America?

Sexually interesting? Is that what you mean? Mama? What has mama to do with that? Not me.

And to be tough, like a man. Men, generally. Tough-minded. Tough. To be able to take it. What a joke! Nobody can take it except in the funny papers. That's what the funny papers mean: nobody can take it. That's what the atom bomb means. Nobody. I can take it—if I am soft enough, yielding enough. Anybody can take it, especially a woman. They live longer and worse, worse than men.

Let them fertilize us and then cut off their heads, that would stop wars. Wouldn't it?

There are two kinds of love, blond and brunette. The white, tinted by fair hair, is good, sacred. It has the blue eyes of the angels. And the Renaissance painters. So that men feel a little closer to the angels when they possess it. The dark skin and black eyes go with evil. A very dark skin is always evil. There is always something evil about a man whose body is covered with black hair. So easily are we deceived. Blocks of false thought—in an idle brain and we think we can dislodge them with our toothpicks of learned devices. But a woman can do a job. She can. A man's job. And do it well. I can. And must—now.

Without a home. No home to go to any more or ever. Only a number at which to alight from the bus—never having possessed more than the thought of a home. What is that? It has at least no further existence. It was because it exists no more. But now it is gone.

I'm not going to sentimentalize over it. I have my job, I have my instruction. I even have my country. My murderous country. I have my murderous country as second best. I have it as substitute—substitution. I will not love the poor. I detest the poor. I'll keep what little money I have to use for myself.

And that's what may happen to an instructor of philosophy who lost her almost-husband at Okinawa. If she shows up at her classes a little—tight.

If she were or is an instructor of philosophy at a learned institution—she wouldn't do it. Being a woman.

Finis.

Oh, wouldn't she? With the existentiality of the dissolute what it is. Investigate "Mr. Anthony" as a thesis and end by—marrying him, after showing him up. That's a woman.

Behind her was the softly lighted window of an expensive flower shop. The light generally from it was green—with emphasis on prismatic yellows, reds and blues. A pail partly hidden by artificial moss, gave up a practical bushful of forsythia branches in full flower filling the whole corner of the window. Forsythia for insanity. In the center of the window was an apple tree, you might say, of pink and white blossoms hacked off at the shoulders. A smoky porcelain jar of pussywillows—for virtue, perhaps, who knows? Little pudenda, whole branches of them. And evil—or just monkey-like—what are they called? Tropical spathes, calla-lily-like brilliant carmine with something coming out of the center, yellow, partly twisted and long. A pot of just plain daisies, white-weed, Mother used to call them. And a big pale-green fern in a green tub. Greek anemones. Even pansies. African violets. Why violets, which they're not?

One thing sure, modern dancing calls for less of the "lovely"—if it requires any of it—than the Degas ballet. His women were ugly enough, God knows, from the American viewpoint, with their almost deformed legs. Dumpy little things. But businesslike. You can see it by their faces. And you see they're French by their faces. Petit bourgeois. He thought they were lovely. No. He thought they made good paintings. Perhaps he saw very well that they were, individually, anything but lovely. Horrible little beasts.

Gyrating together in a ballet-intermezzo they fitted his purposes—and the thoughts of the times. Fit.

Until the Russians with their big peasant women—made into dancing dolls—displaced them. And the leg muscles of Nijinsky made the men slobber. Very wonderful, though.

Now they fight against Martha Graham. But what else is there to do with the ballet except what she does? It can't keep repeating that saccharine putridity, "Brie"—but that's not saccharine even if it is a sort of putridity.

It makes every part of you ache. You are standing on a street corner and every muscle is conscious, as conscious as you are of what is going on. Even your fingers have a separate existence. And your belly. And your back. Each muscle has a personality.

Each muscle is a thought—quite apart. Quite different from the conventional ballet. Martha doesn't grow old. And it doesn't make any difference. All that training.

Every muscle a thought and every thought a muscle. To the eyelids. What has that to do with the movies? And what, Darwin, has that to do with my—very athletic chest. My pectoralis major is tuned like a fiddle. Poor old movies. I wonder if they'll ever become an art. Martha knows.

Martha knows everything—except how my legs ache. But her feet. Pavlova's feet too, if I remember. Anybody's feet.

The only thing that unites the old and the new: feet. The brass sandals of the furies that got Aeschylus thrown out of the city. Can't you hear them on the stones!

Oh, my feet!

Peasant stuff. The brainless classic ballet, the whole thing. The shiver of a horse, she reminds me of at times. But there's sense to that. The mind shivers before death—it doesn't do a Dying Swan. Asinine. Cliché. Peasant stuff. The mind shivers like a horse and—dies. I don't care how you drill them and school them from infancy: peasant stuff.

You take a woman's body and make it do what it was never meant to do and it's the dance. It really is. Sexless.

Only when you make it sexless can it properly express sex. Because it isn't sex any longer. It's the dance. See.

She turned her back to the wind and faced the window. It was blowing colder as the street lights went on—though still light. A man with his collar turned up but without an overcoat stood beside her a moment then went to the shelter of the florist doorway. He was thin and middle-aged with a grotesquely hollowed-out face, the cheeks absent, a small lopsided chin and clear blue eyes that flashed at her and hit the pavement all in one glance.

Who knows what attracts us and why? I wish I knew. I wonder if they can tell. Maybe an odor. Probably an odor. Not in this wind. Why not? They always seem to know.

Why can't I behave myself? Why should I? I remember what he told me. Take my advice and quit it. Do you think that's the thing to do? I said. And he said, No. Good old Doc. I suppose he felt sorry for me or wanted to protect me.

To be careful around the middle of the month, he said. At least that, he said.

It wouldn't have been so bad to have a baby. At first

maybe—for a while. I would have gone to California. I think it would have been fun.

I told him ever since I'd been twelve years old. Well, that's about right, somewhere around there. Just anybody? he said. Anybody that's right. Just like that? he said. Sure.

Let me see.

Then he said, Do you consider yourself a typical American girl? And I said, I suppose so. Why not?

Then he asked me about Sis. And I told him she was an artist. At fifteen? he said, didn't he say that. Well, she has something all to herself.

I'm no abortionist, he said. But I'll try you out and see if you're pregnant. So I had to go three days. Each day he gave me a poke with a needle in the shoulder. Hard. It hurt.

Serves you right, he said. Good for you. I made a snoot at him. And he said it was lucky he was an old man.

Then after three shots I was all right. I was all right. I was just getting ready to go on the roller coaster at Palisades Park. God, how I hate those things. It was all I could do to go on it. They scare the life out of me. And as I stood there looking at it and trying to make up my mind—I knew I was all right.

So I said to the boy friend, Let's go home.

My God, he said. You bring me all the way down to this dump to give you a ride on the roller coaster and when you get here you say you want to go home. What the hell's the matter with you?

Good old Doc, he certainly was sweet.

But why do I do it? It's a certain kind of man, I just can't explain it. Not necessarily good looking. A sort of weakness I suppose. That's what does it, a sort of weakness. I suppose everything comes from weakness. And now again.

Comedy Entombed: 1930

Yᴇᴀʜ, I know, I said. But I can't go three places first.

When can you come then? he answered.

I told you I've already promised two people to see them as soon as I've had breakfast. Why don't you get somebody nearer if you're in such a hurry?

Because I want you. You know where it is, don't you?

I'll find it.

There's a little wooden house behind the shoe shop between Fourth and Fifth. I'll be looking for you. You sure you'll come.

Oh, Lord! I said, hanging up the receiver. What next?

Did you get the name? said Floss.

No. Porphyrio, Principio—something like that.

Well, she answered me, shrugging her shoulders.

There he was, at ten sharp, waiting on the street, coatless, with a narrow face and his hair standing up long and straight at the top to make it seem still narrower.

I felt a little self-conscious as I got out of the car in my light-gray broadcloth suit and gray topcoat and went to follow him. The old car seemed large and costly in those poor surroundings, especially so before that diminutive wooden house. The place as if it had been abandoned long since and later reclaimed it was so tumble-down and yet attractive.

That old familiar smell—of greasy dirt—greeted me as we stepped inside the door. It was a pleasant October day and the stove wasn't on full so there was no emphasis, but there wasn't a clean place to lay my coat. I chose a green painted kitchen chair, folding the coat up into a little pudding so it wouldn't spread over too much of the surface.

Watch your head on these stairs, said the man ahead of me.

Hello Doc, said a boy of about ten coming to my side at the moment. What you here for?

Well, Sonny, why aren't you in school?

I got to stay home and take care of my mother.

Isn't your father here?

Yeah, he's here now. He kept woggling his head, looking down at the floor then up at me with a silly sly expression to his face, swinging his arms around the while as if it might be a clown imitating a monkey. I took up my satchel and leaving him started to climb the stairs, remembering just in time to bow my head so as not to hit the back of the opening above. All short people in this house, I could see that.

At the top of the steep stairway, which merely went up from a corner of the kitchen through the ceiling and landed you in the middle of the bedroom above—I came out between two large iron double beds standing there as if they had been two boats floating in a small docking space, no carpet, no other furniture. Seeing no one I went through the only door to the other room, at the back. These two rooms comprised the whole upstairs.

Here y'are, Doc.

There she lay, in another double iron bed backed against a window. She seemed quite comfortable and rather amused at that. You could see her form, not unattractive, under the old quilt and above it on the pillow a blonde head with a somewhat scarred pointed face. A young woman, Polish in appearance, looking at me, half-smiling.

Well, what's going on?

She's having a lot of pain, Doc. She was five months along and scalded herself on Sunday pretty bad. The pains started yesterday morning.

Here it comes again! she said as we men stood like a

couple of goofs watching her while her face got red and she gritted her teeth and closed her eyes tight for a moment or two.

How often do they come? I asked her after she had relaxed again.

Oh, every few minutes. They're not so bad. But he, indicating her husband, thought he'd better get somebody. We don't know what it is.

You know what it is, I said.

Yeah, I suppose so. But what's this I got here? She put her hand to her lower abdomen. I thought it might be a tumor or something.

Let's see. Why, that's just the womb. You know, I said.

I don't know nothin', she came back at me. Anyhow I wanted you to see it. Then she looked at me with a half smile on her face. You don't recognize me, do you?

No.

You brought one of the children, the first one, ten years ago when we were living down at the Hill.

You don't mean it.

Sure. Don't you remember? Naw, you don't remember. When do you think it'll come, this one, I mean?

I didn't want to bother you, Doc, broke in the man. I'm used to these things but it began to look pretty bad.

How many children you got?

Four. All boys.

This one was supposed to be a girl, said the woman smiling broadly.

Then she began to have another pain and everything stopped for a moment. We watched her until her features gradually relaxed again. It didn't last long but I could see now that she really meant business.

Say, these are coming pretty fast, I said to them. Before we get stuck here let's take a look at that burn.

All right. She threw the covers carelessly down again exposing her thin, well-formed body almost to the knees.

There was an oblong piece of folded cotton rag covering the length of the left thigh, held loosely in place by narrow adhesive strips above and below. I loosened one side of the lower strip and saw the burned area. It must have been a foot long with a big, half-shriveled blister in the center as big as the palm of your hand. I replaced the bandage. We'll leave that alone. Does it hurt much?

Nothing to it. She seemed completely at ease lying there, with none of the deformity apparent that you'd find in a maternity case at term, like a well woman who might be feigning—in all her soiled sheets. Her color was good. She didn't seem greatly concerned about anything—and she was not unattractive! I remarked it again. It was odd to see that rather amused expression on her face. Whom did she remind me of? Oh yes, the woggle-headed kid downstairs. Clowns, the two of them.

I guess it's a good thing, she said. We got enough already.

How much are you getting? said the man to me at that moment.

Are you working?

Yeah, I get eighteen dollars a week but I haven't had more than three days recently.

What do you do?

I work for a house-wrecking company.

Is that so! Well, that's interesting. I thought of what Floss had said. I want to hear more about that later.

I can tell you anything you want to know. How much is it gonna be, Doc?

Well, I said, I don't know. Infection, hemorrhage. That sort of thing; she'll need a little watching. How about ten dollars?

O.K. I'll get you some money. What else do you need?

Nothing I won't have with me.

Don't you want to examine her, Doc?

I don't think so.

But suppose it's coming.

All right, I said. Let's see where we're at. I made a quick examination. The outlet was still contracted; it didn't take me long. The man looked at me as I turned away in mild astonishment.

Is that all?

That's enough for now. She's all right. She's going to have it. It's too bad but it can't be helped. Leave this basin just as it is. I'll be back in about half an hour, just as soon as I can make it.

All right, he answered. I got to walk down to the plant and get some money, it'll take me about that time to get back here too. I'll get the other things. But you'll be back sure, Doc, won't you? You won't not come back, will you? I'll have the money. I won't have it all but I'll have a couple of dollars.

Yeah. And if anything happens while we're gone, I turned to the woman, you just stay where you are, don't get up, don't touch anything. Just stay put. You understand.

I know. All right.

In half an hour I was back at the house again, as agreed. There was an old black-and-white cat lying in the sunny doorway who literally had to be lifted and pushed away before I could enter. As I shoved him off with my foot and kicked open the door—the boy came out from a sort of cubbyhole closet behind the stove, staring.

Oh! he said with wide eyes. You here again? and he looked down at the two bags I was now carrying, one in either hand. You scared me! I thought it was some man pushed open the door to let the cat in. I noticed then that he was wearing a cowboy belt with a large-size snapper pistol in it. One can imagine what he must have been thinking.

Two bags! he said with amazed emphasis. How many times you coming here?

How's your mother?

Oh, she's all right.

Get that cat out. It had followed me into the room.

Get out! he yelled and closed the door behind the slinking beast.

I took my time to look around a bit as I stood there wondering. The whole place had a curious excitement about it for me, resembling in that the woman herself, I couldn't precisely tell why. There was nothing properly recognizable, nothing straight, nothing in what ordinarily might have been called its predictable relationships. Complete disorder. Tables, chairs, worn-out shoes piled in one corner. A range that didn't seem to be lighted. Every angle of the room jammed with something or other ill-assorted and of the rarest sort.

I have seldom seen such disorder and brokenness—such a mass of unrelated parts of things lying about. That's it! I concluded to myself. An unrecognizable order! Actually— the new! And so good-natured and calm. So definitely the thing! And so compact. Excellent. And with such patina of use. Everything definitely "painty." Even the table, that way, pushed off from the center of the room.

What you gonna do to my mother? the boy asked.

Your father come back yet?

No. What you gonna do?

Just fix her up a bit, I said. I understand you got four boys in the family. No girls at all?

No girls except my mother.

That's right.

Upstairs again, through the bare bedroom. She looked just the same.

Anything happen?

Not yet. The pains seem to be getting worse, that's all.

I sat on the edge of the bed to wait. You haven't had any chills have you?

So quiet, so lovely, so peaceful in that room. So strangely comforting. I couldn't make it out. Now the woman had another pain. I watched her.

They been coming that way right along?

About like that.

I sat at the foot of the bed while we talked and waited.

What's all that fluffy stuff on the screen? I said turning to the window.

Yeah, I was wondering about that too, said the woman.

Oh, I see, it's from the meadows, cat-tail down. That wind we had the other day must have blown it up here, quite a distance, isn't it?

When the husband came in with his supplies I removed my coat and took out my light rubber apron.

Now the butcher work begins! she smiled.

There wasn't much change in the situation. So the husband gave me the four dollars he had for me and we fell to talking of the house-wrecking job.

Can't you give her something to ease the pain a little, Doc? said the man.

Sure, if she wants it. These aren't very strong but they may give her a little relief. Just leave everything else the same. I got to get some lunch now, then I have office hours. After that I'll be back, around three o'clock, if you don't call me sooner.

How's it going? said Floss a half hour later.

Just a five months' miss. She's all right.

What sort of people are they?

You can imagine.

Are they going to pay you.

Yes, he gave me four dollars. Said he'd bring me some more when he had it. By the way, here's something interesting, he's a house-wrecker. What do you know about that?

Well?

It's an idea, isn't it?

Didn't I tell you something would come of it? What did he say?

Oh, I didn't get much chance to talk to him but he said they do go out of the state if it's worth their while.

Did you tell him about the stone construction?

He said that don't make no difference. They'll level that off and even fill in the cellar if you have to have it that way. I'll ask him more about it when I get back.

When's it coming off?

I dunno.

What a day! There was the old cat, as before, obstructing the doorway. I felt as though I lived in the place and had lived there always. Inside, the boy was lying on the floor playing with a half-busted mechanical engine and cars. He didn't stir this time or even look up at me. I had to walk over his legs to get to the chair with my coat. Not a sound. Where's your father?

He's upstairs.

I ducked my head instinctively this time. As it came above the flooring into the bedroom above the man got up suddenly from where he had been sleeping on one of the children's beds, rubbing his eyes to open them. He was half-dazed as I walked past him into the woman's labor room. She too had been asleep, opened her eyes and smiled. Marvelous!

I must have been asleep, she said stretching and smiling pleasantly at me.

What's happened to the pains? I said.

It must have been those pills. I had to take them twice but after that the pains left me.

I heard a commotion downstairs, then a grand stampede and clambering on the wooden stairway. Get out of here! I heard the father say loudly. Go on, the whole bunch of youse. Go downstairs. I had to go to look. There they were, all four of them, the three youngest fresh from school, standing around the stairhead like so many pegs, in amazement. I'm hungry, one of them said. Go on, get downstairs. I'll get you something later. But he had to take them bodily, one at a time, and push them ahead of him before he could get them below.

What do you say, Doc? She all right?

Sure, leave her alone.

Am I sleepy, he said. Up all night and doing the cooking and taking care of her. I'm dead. I sat down beside the woman and felt her pulse.

Are you gonna examine me again? she said. No. That's good. I'll come back when it gets ready.

Sure everything's all right, Doc? Those must be good pills you gave her.

Looks like it. Even put you to sleep without taking them, huh? Have you bled any? to the woman.

No, nothing much. I feel good.

All right. I guess then I'd better move on. I got work to do. Call me when you need me—and don't make it four-thirty A.M.

We don't want to bother you, Doc. I'll watch her and let you know when it's coming.

Say, about that wrecking business: How much does it cost to take a house down like I told you.

They'll give you a hundred dollars maybe or if somebody else is bidding maybe they'll make it a hundred and a quarter. It won't cost you nothin'. Have you got a card with you? I'll have the boss see you in your office.

We've got a house eating up seven hundred dollars a year taxes, and nothing coming in. Belongs to my mother-in-law.

Yeah, you can't keep that up.

The kids were waiting for me with open mouths at the foot of the stairs. I rumpled the heavy blond head of hair of one of them and all smiled delightedly following me with their eyes as I said so-long to the father and disappeared from them through the door.

It was four-thirty the next morning when the phone finally rang. Four-thirty! Of course. Aw right, aw right.

It's here, came the voice back at me. Take your time. She can wait till you come.

These are the great neglected hours of the day, the only time when the world is relatively perfect and at peace. But terror guards them. Once I am up, however, and out it's rather a delight, no matter what the weather, to be abroad in the thoughtful dawn.

He was waiting for me in the semi-dark, in his shirt-sleeves, at the curb, and we went in together.

Upstairs the four kids were asleep in the big beds. Two were lying across the one at the right, their heads all but hanging over the edge nearest me, side by side. The older boys were on the other bed, the head of one near the feet of the other. There was no cover on any of them and all were only partially undressed, as if sleep had overtaken them in the act of removing their clothes.

Good for you, I said to the woman. Did you have strong pains?

Yeah, all night but as long as I knew it was all right I could stand it.

It's still in the sack, he said. It all came together.

He was right, the whole mass was intact. Through the thin walls of the membranes the fetus could be plainly made out. About five months.

Is it alive? he asked me.

No.

It was alive when it was born though, she said. I looked and I could see it open its mouth like it wanted to breathe. What is it, Doc, she continued, a boy or a girl?

Oh, boy! said the husband, have I got a bellyache tonight. She laughed. Guess he's having a baby. He's worse than I am.

I feel like it, he said.

Maybe you are, I told him as we started to work over the woman to make her comfortable.

You'd be more famous than the Dionne quintuplets, she smiled. You'd get your pictures in the papers and talk over the radio and everything. Say, Doc, she continued, you haven't told me. What was it?

What do you want to know for?

I want to know if it's a girl.

I looked. Yes, it would have been a girl.

There, she said, you see! Now you've got your girl. I hope you're satisfied.

I haven't got any girl, he answered her quietly.

I'm hungry, yelled a sleepy voice from the other room.

Shut up! said the father.

The Zoo

Go THAT WAY, the Missus said, pointing or rather waving with her whole hand downtown. It isn't very far, ten or twelve blocks, on this—she motioned again—side of the park. You can walk.

Yes, I can walk, said the stocky new Finnish girl, Elsa, and looking at the Missus with her big blue eyes, she smiled brightly.

Um, said the Missus. Well, then walk. And come back by five o'clock. Five o'clock! She held up her hand with the five fingers spread wide. Five. You understand?

Elsa was hurt. Yes, I understand good. One, two, three, four, five. Five o'clock.

All right then, said the Missus. Out with you. And she held open the door of the apartment for the new maid to wheel the little go-cart through it. No, take that down first, right to the street. Then come back for the baby. I strong! Yes, I know, said the Missus, but be careful.

Saturday afternoon, cool air, but not too cool, the trio came at last to the high wire enclosure of the zoo and began following a group of children running ahead and calling back to a heavy-set man and woman to hurry. They were in before they knew it. And before they knew it they were standing in front of a rather narrow outdoor cage, containing an ape with a banana in his hand. He was sitting there peeling and eating it, darting looks about right and left from time to time though he was quite alone in the cage.

Elsa's mouth fell open in amazement. Lottie looked up at her and then at the animal. The beast finished the banana,

333

threw down the skin and came to the front of the cage as though looking for more. Elsa turned to the people around her. There were six or eight of them watching. They seemed to think it very funny.

Flossie apparently didn't see anything.

Squirrels were running about over the grass. The maid with her two small charges went up and down among the outdoor enclosures. She saw wolves like dogs with fierce eyes, narrow-snouted foxes, and deer with astonishing, many branching horns, elk and bears in big strong cages against some rocks. But many of the cages were empty due to the beginning chill that was in the air and she did not quite dare venture as yet into the various houses here and there about her on either hand.

She looked through the window of one low building half-covered with ivy where a peacock, all white, at large on the premises, was sitting quietly. Not two feet beyond it through the glass Elsa saw an enormous snake! She could only see part of it. She shuddered from head to foot. Not there, at any rate and hurried on dragging the children with her.

Why not go in? The Missus hadn't told her not to. Anyhow it was beginning to get cold walking around, and though the baby was happy and contented, maybe it would be warm in there. She would go. Here was one with cages outside and places for the birds to go inside, too. She would go in there to see the birds. She went to wheel her carriage through the door but a guard stopped her.

Can't go in there with baby carriages. There, he said, pointing. So Elsa was practically forced to do what the others were doing. She stood the carriage aside, carefully took the baby into her arms, told Lottie to come on and went through the door. She stopped short. The smell was appalling. Dead fish, dead something, anyhow foul, it gripped you in the throat, you could taste it. She made a face, looked right and left at others about her, but after a long moment, seeing many lively fowl before her, went ahead.

Once you got a little used to the fetid odor of the place, the din hit you. Shrieks and catcalls on all sides. The baby clung to the girl's neck. In a big central cage were ducks, and terns and gulls, some huddled on the sandy cage bottom, incredibly colored, others with their beaks open laughed loudly, so it seemed, with piercing volleys of calls about the cage, moving aside carefully as a big gray bird with a pouch under his chin took off from the pool and landed heavily among them wobbling forward a few additional steps before he could come to a stop. Some birds were brooding on barkless pieces of dead branches hung from above, two by two, all letting their droppings go when they would. Immediately in front of Elsa and the children a white, long-legged bird was feeding, sloshing his bill, spoon-shaped at the end, right and left sidewise through a pail of half-liquid stuff before him.

The little servant circled the cage. About it were other birds in cages along the wall. She couldn't believe it. Long red and green legs that slowly moved about the narrow confines of the enclosure flexing and straightening—so long and thin you'd think they'd snap. Eyes and pointed bills . . . No! she turned uneasily, holding her breath—without appearing to hurry. Come, Lottie, she said. Let us go.

It was better in the air again. There was a water creature lying on its back or its belly, she couldn't tell which, on the rocks near a cold-looking pool. She went on, looking up at the sky quickly to see how much of the afternoon remained to her. As she passed along the edge of the pool there was a swirl of the water and a sharp pointed snout arose and barked once then the thing turned and with the speed of a serpent plunged under and was gone again.

Well, maybe that was enough. Perhaps she'd better go home. It was a long walk and the sun was already beginning to fade from its midday position in the sky. Still—maybe so, why not?

You want to go? she asked Lottie and the baby.

Go, go! the baby said earnestly.

You want to sit in the carriage? the little maid asked Lottie. Yes, that was what she wanted, Lottie assured her. So Lottie was seated at the foot of the little go-cart and, reassured, Elsa decided to continue her investigations a little further.

Going quietly along now, the flaxen-haired girl steered away from the crowd.

The house of the pachyderms admitted carriages; Elsa saw a woman working one up the three steps to the entrance and followed eagerly. Warm in here and high, and there were sparrows chattering up under the roof beam. And there was an elephant! Alone behind its bars one hind foot chained to an iron ring in the floor. There was a crowd before his cage.

Elsa saw what was going on. There was a man at the back tossing in hay with a fork and the enormous beast seemed to want to be loosened. But the man bowed his head and backed out through a small door at the rear and the elephant quieted down again. He didn't seem to want the hay but took a wisp of it in his trunk, rolled it up into a little bundle, raised it swingingly to his mouth and then as gracefully lowered his trunk again with the hay still in it, two or three times, before he ate it.

Elsa watched every move, looked at the eye and the ears of the beast without stirring. Still swinging its stocky trunk as it rocked from foot to foot, the enormous beast suddenly uncurled it forward, through the bars toward the people standing there, opening the tip of it like a small hand begging. Elsa strained forward to see beyond the backs of the people before her as a child placed a peanut in the opening. The elephant, without a movement, still held the trunk there waiting.

The little blue-eyed maid woke as if from a dream when she heard Lottie say, I want to get down, and felt her struggling on her arm. She hadn't realized that she was holding her. Sighing as if she had forgotten to breathe for the last five minutes, Elsa suddenly recollected her duty toward her charges and turned away from the crowd once more.

But what astonished the little maid more than anything else was the head of the hippopotamus. Unlike the birds and many of the other beasts, here was something, alert as it seemed, that did not move. There was no more than a faint turning of the eye from time to time and a slow shift of the head hardly to be perceived. This was something beyond the imagination! The skin of an eel, the ears of a pig, but the mouth! The bulk of the head and the breadth of it! Incredible! The thing didn't yawn, it didn't rise or move. . . . Elsa looked into the faces of the people about her and discovered no wonder. She looked at the children and moved on.

These things lived naturally in all their deformity in the same world as she. What are they for? She did not know. The less than pig eyes of the rhinoceros and his broken horns! It made her shudder. And she was startled by their stillness, too. They hardly moved. Yet with that leathery bulk of insensitivity before her, she heard a distant rhythmic . . .! Was it a cat had got into the place? She looked about. Again, an almost imperceptible small sound. No, it was the beast itself! It was the rhinoceros, mewing like a kitten.

The elephant, to the admiration of the crowd which grew silent at this point, let go its bladder—as though someone had dumped a barrel of stale cider down a drain.

Come, Lottie! said the girl.

It was an exciting game. In one house there was a very small dainty-footed deer, no bigger than a terrier, walking quickly up and down inside the bars while another, the same, was lying curled up, its head upon it flanks asleep in the straw. Kangaroos, red and gray, powerful and delicate, one of them sitting upright upon its fat tail, the forefeet with their narrow wrists dangling idly.

Zigzag went the little maid about the room, the wild swine with coarse black hair, curling tusks and knobs of crusted filth, she thought, between them where he couldn't scratch. Was it from that or—in the next cage again beyond belief—that there came such an overpowering stench!

Elsa wanted to go but could not resist the desire to see this other thing. No head at all, just a slithering body tipped with a snout a yard long, armed with filthy eyes, tapering from a shaggy neck, the head no more than a slight bulge in the snout itself—on the body of, almost a bear! she thought.

Whew! that's terrible! she said aloud.

Lottie was already moving away.

Coated with long dangling wiry hair that swept the floor as the beast paced up and down, filthy with dust and straws, the tail a bulky hanging mass of long, spiny hairs dragging on the bottom of the cage—and powerful forelegs armed by one fierce long claw—whew! Terrible.

I'm tired, said Lottie. So Elsa loaded her once more into the foot of the carriage and started for home. But first—it was still so early—passing another building the little maid thought, Why not?

No, no, no! said Lottie.

Yes, said Elsa. So she parked the carriage. It was getting to be an old thing now, took the baby in her arms, Lottie by the hand in spite of her hanging back, and went in behind some others. It was just before three o'clock; she saw it by her big watch which she always carried by a chain in her pocket.

Timid but responsible at the same time, Elsa saw at once that she was among the lions. She got just inside the door and there she stood. On the right were the cages, while along the other side of the room, up three steps, was a row of benches all occupied.

Most of the people were at the other end of the room whither several newcomers hurried, leaving the little blonde maid and the two children almost alone. The people on the benches were looking at her. She didn't understand.

But near her in the first, no, the second, cage, next to two big black cats with green eyes, was an enormous shaggy-maned lion pacing alone up and down inside bars. Now he would come toward the young girl with the two children then turn away again to the far corner of his cage, stop, press his heavy head forward into the bars, trying to look around the corner, up beyond, then drop his head, turn and come down the face of the bars again. Back he would go once more. Look and return. Elsa didn't move.

Then the beast stopped. Cocked his ears. Stared. Opened his jaws. And split the air with a terrifying voice of thunder.

The baby clung to the maid's neck and began to whimper. Lottie clung to her skirts. Elsa herself was spellbound—standing almost alone, not knowing whether to retreat or go farther.

I want to go home! said Lottie whimpering. The baby, loosening the little maid's neck a moment, turned her head around a little way timidly to see what had happened. Several ladies were laughing. Elsa flushed crimson.

This was no place for a child, said one of the women on the benches to her companion. Can you imagine a mother sending two small children out with a maid like that—in this crowd?

Pretty little thing, said the other. As much of a child as they are. This is going to be fun.

Then a commotion began at the other end of the room. There, they're going to feed them.

There was a scurry and a hubbub followed by fierce guttural roars. An attendant was going down the aisle between the spectators and the cages poking something in under the bars. Growls and roars, half-muffled, savage and repeated, menaced the ear. And then the big lion let go once more.

Lottie, bewildered, put her hands up to her ears and ran—forward into the room as Elsa clutched the baby which suddenly had again clutched her. The two ladies were pointing and laughing as Elsa went to grab Lottie and missed, caught her and tried to get hold of her hand. . . .

Another deafening roar.

In terror the little maid and the children escaped through the door nearest them.

She must really go home now. She must. But to prove to Lottie that she mustn't be afraid . . . You want to see the monkeys? Then we go home. All right we see the monkeys.

Monkeys are funny in all languages—she'd try here—on her way to the exit—the last place and then go.

As she had hoped, they were funny, very funny. Even more than that, shocking. So that you felt the blood come into your face watching them. Never mind. Nobody else seemed to.

You could hardly follow them, quick as birds. So surprised they always looked. Frightened. Fear is written in all their faces. And their faces never change. Hands and feet and tails made for getting away.

She didn't hurry this time, she had learned what to do—but there were already too many people inside. Nevertheless, nothing ventured nothing won; she'd go ahead.

Monkeys on all sides! Little ones blinking and clinging to the bars, calling, looking furtively at their fellows, eating, scratching or walking slowly about. After all, Elsa was doing no more than the others about her. There were a number of men and women with children of all ages.

Monkeys! Oh, look, monkeys! Wouldn't you get lost in the cage with the monkeys?

This is the monkey house, what else do you expect to find here?

Look at the old man up there thinking!

Elsa didn't know what they were saying exactly. But as she followed the direction of the pointing fingers, sure enough . . . ! She stared with her mouth open where, on a perch, at the very top of a cage which she had thought empty, was the dark and huddled figure of a man-like ape. He was black-haired and looking down at the crowd below him had, his hand supporting the lower part of his face, half-covering his mouth, the appearance of thinking.

Monkeys are interesting people, said a tall woman to a man beside her. But Elsa could not get over her astonishment. No ungainly bird's legs, the colors of the rainbow, here, nor hippopotamus and rhinoceros heads of misshapen bone and blubber, hides like armor, not even the grace of a deer—but a sort of people in contour and motion.

The black, thoughtful creature rubbed his hand over his eyes while what seemed to be his wife along the same shelf, a little smaller, held a piece of paper in her hand putting it to her mouth now and then nibbling, then puffing out her lips and blowing her breath through them with a soft high-pitched clatter. She moved about more than her mate, but neither one was particularly active.

In this house the crowd was getting to be almost impassable. It was entrancing, the most exciting place in the whole gardens. Baboons, walking stiffly on all fours, whose behinds when they turned from the astonished Elsa were blue and crimson. A shriek of laughter went up from several young girls whenever the beast would turn away from them.

And opposite them long-armed gibbons swinging from the cage wall, to the trapeze, to the iron upright in the cage's middle in prodigious leaps, never failing, up and down and around with lightning agility.

Suddenly a great roar of laughter went up from the far end of the building. Then it quieted and as suddenly burst out again in gales of merriment. The call was irresistible. Elsa was drawn inevitably that way along with the rest.

As she came up, the thing was clapping its hands, excitedly, wildly. Then it leaped directly at the crowd! Elsa involuntarily shrank back, bumping into a fat woman who gave her a hard shove with her elbow. And the crowd let out another spasm of roars. The thing inside had disappeared into the back of its cage. Then it leaped again! It hit the bars with the whole weight of its body and clung there snarling and shaking from side to side.

What if it should get loose? Everybody was laughing, but Elsa could see that the beast was furious. He hated the crowd. He wanted to kill them. She could see that. Where was Lottie? Lottie! Lottie! Lottie! The child had disappeared from her hand. Lottie!

The beast was waving its arms and now it spit. It spit into the crowd which laughed and gave way suddenly. And there was Lottie all alone. Elsa ran forward and grabbed her by the hand. Come. And this time she was through.

An attendant came and drove the beast toward the back of the cage. Go on, he said to the people. Go on. Keep moving. Don't stand in front of the cages.

Elsa was tired when she got back to the apartment. So were the children. Well, did you like it? the Missus said.

No, schtinks! said the little maid. I see elephant and many things. Well, some day you can go again, said the Missus. No, said Elsa. Schtinks! I see once, I see too much.

The Farmers' Daughters

The Farmers' Daughters

WHAT DID they feed you Margaret when you were a kid?
asked the doctor.

Oh—chick peas and fatback, I guess.

That ought to have put more flesh on those skinnybones
of yours.

I hated it, used to throw it under my chair.

Her friend Helen was of much the same temper: It was
bad enough before—but when my brother was killed . . .

What happened?

That old man. He told him if he caught him hunting in
his woods again he'd kill him and he did. I hate the place.

Did they do anything to him?

Huh! I see you don't know anything about the South
where I come from. But that's nothing. I love *you* . . .
(with a laugh).

When a chance guy asked: What about the kids? Margaret said: Agh, they'll be all right. If they yell, the
woman next door will hear them.

Where a' we going?

Same place. Wait a minute! She ran back into the house
and returned with a small blanket.

What the hell? It isn't cold.

It may be by the time we get back.

There's something to that.

So he started the car. Hey! as she threw her arms about
his neck, pulled his head around and kissed him. I'm driving
the *car*! You wanna wreck us?

You can drive with one hand.

Yeah, but not without my head.

Am I glad to get out of that place tonight.

Have you heard from your husband?

Yes, that son-of-a-bitch; and I mean just that. I wanna
get drunk. I gotta get drunk tonight.

O.K., if you do it on beer.

We'll see about that. That li'l hunchback will give it to
me on tick if I don't pay.

What's your favorite flower, Margaret?

Why?

I just want to know.

What's yours?

No. Come on—don't be so quick on the trigger so early
in the evening. I think I can guess.

Petunias! (emphasizing the second syllable.) God knows
I've seen enough of them. No. Red roses. Those are really
what I love.

It is Helen's turn now: Talk, just keep talking, the doctor
said to her.

Both hands. I had to hold the glass with both hands to
drink from it—so I could drink from it. I drank just gallons of water. It was last Tuesday I made up my mind.
Let's see. Yes, it was last Tuesday. I said to myself, I was
lying on the bed before breakfast, I said, just as if it was
two people talking: What's the matter with you? I didn't
answer. Don't you know what is happening to you? Yes,
I said, I know. You're a goner if you go on in this way.
Yes, I said, I know. Well, are you going to stop it? I
didn't answer. Because if you don't, you're finished. If you
give in now you'll never . . . You know where you're
headed? For a nervous breakdown—of the worst sort.
Do you know what that is? You've seen enough of it, you
ought to. Yes, I said, I know. And are you so stupid, so
weak, that you can't stop taking a drink? Are you? I
didn't answer. Tell me. You haven't the guts to do what

you know you've got to do. No answer. Then stop it.
Yes, I said, I'll stop it. Right now, I said. Right now. Not
another drop of wine. Not another drop. But it's been hell
I tell you. When I made out my grocery list—this is cute
—I always put down at the bottom—*Wine!* They know
what to bring me. I held the pen in my hand and said a
regular merry-go-round: I won't do it, I won't do it, I
won't do it, I won't do it. Isn't that cute?

Marvelous! He kissed her on the cheek, under the ear.
I'm proud of you.

Oh, I could have gone to the phone any time and they
would have sent it up. Then that old merry-go-round
would start again: I won't do it, I won't do it, I won't
do it. I kept it up until I tired myself out. That was Tuesday. Wednesday I was so weak I stayed in bed almost all
day. I drank gallons of water to sweat it out. I was dripping. But I wouldn't give in. I wanted to call you up but
I was afraid you'd be mad at me. I took some of those pills.

A simple antispasmodic, they won't hurt you.

Can I take them? Then on Thursday I went out in the
yard—and just for a minute it would flash across my mind:
Order the wine! and the merry-go-round would start
again: I won't do it, I won't do it . . . I just kept saying
that so I couldn't get in another word. And finally tired
myself out again, saying that every time I thought of
the wine. But today, almost a week later, I woke up and
knew I was over it. I'll never touch another drop. Never.

I believe you.

But just today I began to wonder: What comes next? I
don't know.

.   .   .

Why are you so good to me? Margaret said to her friend,
the doctor.

I admire your guts.

Just that? Um . . . (poking her little chin out aggres-
sively). She pouted: Don't you love me . . . just a little
teeny bit?

What the hell did you come here for tonight? Just to talk? Because . . .

Why shouldn't I? You told me I could come any time I wanted to. Didn't you?

Yes, I mean anything special?

You want me to go? Because if you do just say the word.

Now *look*! dumbbell, don't be miffed. I love you. I'm crazy about you—and your pretty little face, like a pansy. Your beautiful black hair . . .

It's getting grey.

—even white teeth and . . .

My eyebrows are much too heavy.

Listen! You've got a complexion and as fine a pair of black eyes as I have ever seen. Not vicious, like a horse . . . but can't you see that I'm *busy*!

Do you want me to start kissing you?

No! for God's sake.

Then tell me some more about myself, how pretty I am.

Then look at your little ears, like pink sea-shells. Your nose, perfectly made. Cupid's mouth . . .

Now you're poking fun at me. That's not what I came for. Can you give me something to develop my *breasts*? Look at them. I used to have nice little breasts. Why, we were playing strip poker the other night—with our husbands—and Helen had to take off her brassiere—right to the skin. She was beautiful. Pink and round. And me . . .

She hasn't had two kids the way you have.

I know, but lots of women have had children and still have pretty breasts.

Not many.

Can't I *do* anything?

Wear one of those brassieres.

No, but I mean seriously, isn't there something I can really do to develop my breasts?

I heard of a woman answered an ad: they sent her a picture of . . .

I've heard that one before: a picture of a man's hand.

I'll try. I told you I'd try. But you got to get a little *weight* on you first.

When Helen first met Margaret, a neglected and lonely woman from the South among all these strangers, her heart began at once to beat violently.

When she learned that Margaret too had been a farmer's daughter, was about to have a child, was small, pretty, apparently defenseless, there was nothing else for it but that she must be taken at once under the other's protecting wing. More than that, she loved her, loved her at first sight. Besides, Margaret really needed her badly.

How far did you get with your schooling?

Middle of my second year at the university.

You did better than me.

But you're a trained nurse.

All the good that did me.

In the first burst of confidence Margaret and Helen had learned all they needed to know of each other to make up their minds and hearts.

What did *you* do?

Practically ran away. Lied about my age and entered a nurses' training school in Florida. What happened to you?

I got married.

Local boy?

Boy from military school I met at a dance. Don't ask about him. Anyway he's away on construction jobs most of the time when he isn't looking for another wife.

Any children?

One—a boy. And this . . . (placing her hand on her belly).

Good!

They became friends for life. They both had come recently into small inheritances which they similarly spent for small new houses. Helen's was, like herself, charming in every detail, within and without. Her husband's family, an old one in those parts, possessed some old furniture, silverware, some quaint knick-knacks and pieces of jewelry and signed letters and documents from the early 1800's of which they were justifiably proud.

I'm going to bundle them all up into a heap some day —I'm sick of them—and throw them into the fire.

She was much more concerned with her canary, a beautiful rich yellow specimen who would come to the edge of the cage and kiss her each morning as she talked to it in endearing terms.

All the birds of the neighborhood knew her, winter and summer, and came to her for their sunflower seeds, pecked diligently at the device her husband had made for the suet which she would make ready for them whenever the supply ran low.

Her house was painted white, the rooms were sunny and papered in attractive colors. She would meet the doctor at the door in what he took to be lounging pajamas —and sometimes change her clothes during his visit for no reason that he could ever determine.

The garden was Helen's special pet. Once he was looking at a picture on her wall, an 8 x 10 snapshot that had been given her by the photographer. It was a winter scene, taken within the suburb itself a few years back, a stubble field covered by new fallen snow.

In the background was a young elm, on a sky of loose clouds. To the right, nearer the camera, an oak tree of about the same age cut off by the edge of the frame. The trees were leafless, as would be natural at that time of year. But the remarkable thing about them, that could not be seen except in a good light, was the branches and the bushes near them, covered by a coating of thin ice!

Caught by the camera-eye it sparkled as he had seen it, often, in the many ice storms he had witnessed in the past. This filled him with nostalgia.

Helen, when she saw how he was affected, took the picture from the wall and, handing it to him, insisted that he take it home and keep it as his own.

He had never seen such gaiety, celebration, depicted in a picture—not an entire countryside filled with apple blossoms. Helen, as soon as she had it pointed out to her, kept pace with his appreciation. The trees blossoming with ice seemed to them both a triumphant thing; it made their hearts sing, therefore he was grateful to her for the picture, wanted to keep it where he could see it when he was depressed.

The doctor gave her the shot of vitamin.

My patients used to say I have wonderful hands, she said. You never have been loved as I could love you, my sweet. Come in when you are passing sometime and have tea with me. There's nothing wrong with that, is there? Sometimes you look *so* tired.

A lot of boloney.

What I liked about you, she said to him, is that you told me it was killing me—I knew that—but you never told me to stop it. And the stupid thing about it, that's what made me so mad, is that I didn't want to drink.

I've never seen anybody deliberately kill himself with drink. Didn't you really take anything but wine?

I hate the taste of whisky!

You must have drunk a hell of a lot of cheap wine in your day.

Yesterday, Helen went on, I thought what I needed was a little exercise so I thought to break up some ground in the backyard—to plant me a mess of turnip greens. You always like them. But the ground was too hard, so I used a pick. I like to kill myself. I really needed that shot.

Anytime you like.

I don't believe that last lot *was* turnip greens. Down home we scattered it broadcast—with the oats. It came up anywhere. Then you just mow the oats and there it is.

Can't you get a job these war years at your own profession? You were a top flight nurse you know.

Not in this town. I read a good joke in the papers today. Two girls who lived together. Somebody asked one of them what kind of liquor her friend drank. I don't know, she replied. What do you mean you don't know —hasn't she given you even a taste of it? She got it for Christmas, the label was off, she was afraid to drink it so she uses it for perfume.

She went on: We were never allowed to call them "niggers" at home, my father wouldn't stand for that. He'd whip 'em or lynch 'em but we never could use that word.

In her new house Margaret would lie by the back fence in her abbreviated bathing suit and let down the front of it, as much as she dared, to get herself sun-tanned—as if it were down home. Her neighbors laughed among themselves and were mildly shocked at the "indecent exposure." Their kids came around her and stared. She was unconscious of making a spectacle of herself.

Margaret was a demon house cleaner from way back. It drove her crazy but you could feel her saying to herself, it has to be done, so she'd do it. Besides it quieted her nerves when her husband would be away—would put her mind to sleep.

At first the doctor didn't mind it so much. She would exhaust herself, he would remember, her head done up in a cloth, until he had to warn her: You'll have a miscarriage if you keep that up.

She had a mania for scrubbing floors and woodwork until he thought she'd scrub the paint off the walls, so desperate did she seem.

You can't keep a good gal down.

That's what keeps you so thin. Take it easy. You'll wear yourself out.

Go on! I'll never wear myself out that way. What am I going to do with myself? I can't read *all* the time.

The next day she'd be laid up with a sick headache. He never caught her at it but he knew she'd take a slug of whisky sometimes—to calm herself.

What's a girl to do?

As Helen phrased it: Yuh hear? That's too much for any woman, leastwise fuh a woman like Margaret who was never built for it. She can't stand it much longer, the poh child.

Her older boy drove her crazy: What can I do with him? I'm going to beat him some day . . . I'm really afraid of myself.

She would scream at him when he was out playing, until you could hear her round the block—a voice high-pitched and shrill that used to bring her father and brother in from the far field. Enough to set her neighbors' teeth on edge. No wonder the boy looked shamefaced and abashed at her and took pleasure in thwarting her in small ways. He didn't trust her.

When she offered the doctor a glass of wine as sometimes happened, he'd hear the boy perhaps say: Mother, stop drinking! This would infuriate her. She'd leap from her chair, seize him by the shoulder and in spite of his resistance push him out the back door: Go on and play.

Aside from each other the girls didn't seem to have a friend in the world, anyone they could let their hair down for, except the doctor. He would say: I'm no good for them. But he was fascinated.

Margaret's face was undoubtedly the thing which first led him on, and the suppressed excitement of her manner. Until in a flash she would turn vulgar, empty her mouth of some expression that would make a mechanic green with envy.

Blushing crimson: That just slipped out, she'd say with a laugh, Pardon me!

Only her emaciated body kept her from being picked up by any but the rough guys who didn't give a damn for details—if they looked close enough. She was sitting perpetually on a powder keg without knowing it. If she'd only had a *body*! She looked more like a boy than a girl.

He had seen her, many times, as her doctor, naked. She

was painfully thin, really starved in appearance, with skin
unhealthy, dark and dry, with prominent veins over the
chest and belly that made her anything but attractive.
Nothing about her to excite passionate approaches except
the savage fistful of black hairs sticking out prominently
at the bottom of her belly, heavily matted and, due to her
thinness, plainly to be observed under a thin dress—as she
well knew.

All her energy of whatever sort, due to her loneliness
as she grew more desperate, seemed to center finally, there.
Gradually her life withdrew its more tender advances and
fell back on something she could more count on for success. Her mind, such as it was, was thwarted. She talked
sometimes of the past but she was still too young for that.
She occasionally would visit the farm—she was trying un-
consciously to find a way. Christmas, or one of her mother's
increasing illnesses were occasions, as time advanced. She
thrashed about as her life funneled on.

She had Helen, yes, but Helen wasn't a man.

.   .   .

Thanksgiving was always a big day.

Margaret would go down to the farm for that day dragging the children along. They would have a meal, cooked
by her mother, of Maryland turkey, the best turkey in
the world, with cranberry sauce and oyster filling. And
Margaret would always see that some of it would be set
aside for the doctor, her devoted friend—slices of white
meat, a leg or whatever could be had for their annual
banquet—a rite of unacknowledged significance which she
meticulously counted on come hell or high water.

This would be a Saturday, let's say, to allow time for
traveling. He'd go to her house about noon. The children
would already have been fed and sent outside or into the
cellar to play. She'd be in her best bib and tucker. A table
would have been set, usually in the kitchen, for two, with
all formality, and they prepared to eat.

Cocktails—they invariably began with cocktails!—soup,
the turkey with stuffing, and whatever vegetables there

were in the market to be had at the time. Then would come cake, one of her mother's famous cakes, or pie. Coffee and, this was *de rigueur*, a small glass of Hennessy Three Star brandy.

The whole affair was a poetic occasion, a love feast, a feast dedicated to the heart and to the mind, a despairing avowal and celebration.

This went on for several years.

Once in a while he'd hear indirectly from Helen how she and her husband had been on a little party with Margaret and Mac, the new boy friend. But he always put the guy down, although he had never seen him, as being rather sappy. As a matter of fact, as we all learned later from Helen (who else could have told us?), Margaret had been intimate with her new friend for a long time. He appealed to her in a way she could not resist. He was sensitive, more refined than she, the college atmosphere, knew Paris and Rome and being unmarried with a good bed at his sister's couldn't see why he of all the deserving loafers there are in the world should look for a job. He didn't. That the boys around his home town took him for somewhat of a fairy didn't bother him in the slightest.

Margaret used to lend him money surreptitiously until she ended up by practically supporting him. She was always a sucker that way. She sympathized with him, mothered him until finally when he came to her with tears in his eyes she took him in, "broke down" and made him her lover.

One day all hell broke out. The fracas started, if the doctor had been correctly informed, very innocently as serious events in love or war have always started, the evening before.

Helen being away, or it might not have happened, Margaret had gone out with Helen's husband and the boy friend to drink a little beer. But that evening, for no reason as the boresome hours wore on, Margaret found herself with two protectors at her side growing low down drunk. Nobody could stop her or even noticed the condition she was in until they all started to get to their feet about one in the morning.

About that time the men had decided that it was time to get the lady home to her children, asleep as usual in their beds. They set out but with the fresh air in their faces Miss Margaret decided that she'd have none of it. She began to put up a fight and when they got to the front door of her house refused to go in.

At the racket she raised all her neighbors were awakened. She started to curse and yell at the top of her voice. Lights began to go on all about them.

The men, embarrassed, decided she'd have to go in whether she wanted to or not! They opened the door which was not locked, pushed her through and left, driving off into the night—thinking no doubt that she'd quiet down and behave as soon as she realized that her situation was hopeless.

Not Miss Margaret.

She broke out of the door and down the street after the car screaming: Come back you sons of bitches! But being quickly outdistanced, she changed her tune, calling out for Bill, Bill the milkman, to come to her aid.

There was a terrific scandal—the police were called. The children wakened and cried. Finally, with the assistance of the women in the neighborhood Margaret was undressed and put to bed.

When she realized next morning what had happened she decided to end her life. She took her children into the garage with her under pretext of driving down to the farm—but they were big now, beyond her calculations, too big for her to handle. She put them into the back seat of the car, got in herself and started the engine without opening the garage doors.

Her whole life, the life of the community at large as it existed for her, threatened at that moment to tumble about her head. She must have felt a certain despairing exhilaration. There was the church, the civic order, the man and woman of it, every artistry the spirit could propose, by her own act to be broken into pieces—broken to pieces everything that even the Board of Health might stand for, the beams and shingles of every private residence of the community no matter how pretentious or humble they might be shattered beyond repair.

But the boys, particularly the older one, realized they had been trapped and would be suffocated if they remained longer in that place. They broke from the car. She fought them but they got away screaming and ran off.

At this turn of events Miss Margaret reopened the garage doors, backed the car out and took off, ignoring the kids, to find her companion Mac of the night before. He was not at home. She caught up with him at an ice-cream parlor, picked him up, drew three hundred dollars—all she had—from the local bank. Following which the two of them fled, onto the roads of the state.

It was all as anyone could easily have foreseen: drink, immorality—but to have dragged poor harmless Mac along with her, member of such a really decent family, was just too much. What a bitch a woman can prove herself in the end to be. A man is at least courageous about it! Even tried to kill her own children to boot. My God, a potential murderess!

The family came and collected the children who, when it was over, found no doubt that they had enjoyed all the excitement and attention. Everyone felt relieved, that was that, let her go, who gives a damn?

Helen got a postcard from her after weeks of agonized waiting; she and Mac were spending the night at a roadhouse somewhere in Pennsylvania before moving on.

Then a brief letter, posted along the road. They had what remained of the $300. When that was spent, they planned to blow their brains out.

Good-bye, darling, I love you. Don't think bad things about me, I had to do it . . .

It was left unsigned.

Helen was alarmed and heartbroken.

．　　．　　．

They never liked me down there, said Helen to the doctor.

I can see that.

What can you see?

That they never liked you down there.

I was too fussy. When I was in the operating room it had to go just so. I was suture-nurse for some of the best in the city . . . Two little colored boys took care of my sister and me when we were small children, George Mills and Norris Rance. Joe Scott danced. Oh I wish some day I could write a story, a true story about people.

That's what everyone wishes.

They're just like us. When I was a child, me and my sister, my mother had a raft of children and she didn't have time for us. So she had a little colored boy to take care of us—when I was about five or six years old, about like that. His name was Neil. He lived in the house and watched us so we didn't get into trouble. There was another little colored boy—he didn't live very far away. And my sister and I would get up on the hill in the woods and scream our lungs out for them. They both would come running and we'd play there all morning. We'd have a wonderful time together. Years later, after we were all grown up and he'd gone away—when he came back to see us all once more—we were the only ones he wanted to talk to. And the other one named Scott. My sister and I would wait for him in the evening sometimes before my father would come in—oh, around five o'clock or like that. We'd put up a game on him: Scott, dance for us! Won't you? We were just little children and he'd dance, tell us a story with his dancing and we'd love it. He'd been ploughing in the fields all day and yet he'd dance for us any time we'd ask him. It was wonderful. It would be a young man calling on a girl. He'd go to the door and knock. Her mother would come, he'd talk to her. Then she'd tell her daughter to pick up some chips and he'd dance that. Then she'd tell her to dig potatoes. Everything like that—all danced out before my father could come home and catch us at it. He was wonderful.

(Telephone. She answers it.)

Who was that?

Oh, just the telephone company tracing those calls that were bothering me last week.

Who was it?

Just some little boys across the street. I don't mind but I was a little jittery then . . . and when I'd go to the phone and hear: Oh go drop dead! I almost jumped out of my skin. It made me mad so I thought I'd try to find out who it was. I knew it was them . . .

I was only nine years old when I was baptized, Helen said. In a creek—I was ducked. I had on my best pink dress and I didn't want to get it wet. In the name of the Father and the Son and the Holy Ghost! Splam! My father didn't want it done, he said I was too young. But when he was looking over the fields or something like that my mother had made me get dressed and out of the house, in a minute—and I was baptized. I was always a sickly child and she probably thought I might die unblessed in the night. When you've been baptized you can take communion. Everybody drank out of the same cup. Blackberry wine, everybody was drinking blackberry wine. My aunt used to make it. That's how I acquired a taste for wine. My mother used to make it too. Not very much but we always had some around the kitchen if anybody had diarrhea or a belly ache. I don't know if it did any good but we always got it anyway. If you didn't make it just right it turned to vinegar. One day I just got some poured into a teacup when I heard my mother coming! So I drank it down quick. It was vinegar! But I wouldn't let on. Vinegar!

Do you want to hear something funny? It'll make you laugh.

He laughed.

I'll tell you. You know the woman, a friend of mine, you've met her here but no matter. She told me to use acetone to take the lacquer off those brass andirons that I was polishing. You've seen 'em. So I called up the drug store. You're used to my southern accent so you know what I'm saying but some people don't understand me. What? he said, and I could see he didn't know what I was talking about. Then it flashed on me what he probably thought I said: some acetone to take the lacquer off my *ass*! I got laughing so I could hardly talk to him. Don't you think that's funny? I'm glad you like it. It tickled me slap silly. Jeepers Creepers! Will you excuse me, I have to go to the bathroom again.

While she was out of the room his eyes began playing about, out the window to the garden and came to rest after a moment above the fireplace on the mantel where a small china doll occupied a place apart.

When she came in he saw that she had changed her dress, her Dresden china blue eyes blinking at him above a house-coat of mixed colors and faded blue slacks.

That? he queried, pointing. Yes, that little doll.

That's Pauline. I've had her all my life.

He took in the lace boudoir cap over yellow curls, bound up with pink ribbons and smiled; Well?

She cost fifteen cents. She was given to me when I was two years old and went all the way through training school with me. She's full of sawdust, you know, all but the head and hands and feet. I used to play with her, mostly when I went to visit my grandmother. Once she got lost and I spent almost a whole day looking for her. Do you know what? When I washed her her head came off. I took her to a doll hospital and what do you think they did? Sent her all the way back to Jacksonville. Just

where she came from. She's never been away from me
. . . No, I'm not beautiful. There's nothing beautiful
about me.

You're not the one to judge: when you talk about that
doll you're beautiful.

Anyhow, if there's anything that's beautiful about me,
it's you; you know *that*, darling. Do you hear those church
bells ringing? I can stand it now but a month ago they
drove me nuts.

I hear them.

They have a new minister who used to be a Presby-
terian and so, naturally, he has to be High Church. The
old one was pretty deaf—he was a dear. This one has
those bells ringing at all hours—whether there's a service
or not. I think he just likes to hear 'em. First it was just
one old bell but now it's chimes—worked from the street-
current. I hate 'em. But the worst is, those damned chimes
sound exactly like my front door. I used to get up early,
put on my bathrobe, give my husband his coffee and go
back to bed again—to sleep till noon or any time.

With your bottle beside you?

Naturally. Until I'd hear the front door bell ring, get
up bleary eyed, struggling to put on my bathrobe, and
stumble to the front door thinking it might be a special
delivery letter from a friend or anything at all. Nobody
there. I couldn't make it out. Until one day when I knew
nobody was at the door I heard that damned bell. I listened
until after a while I was sure of it. It wasn't my own
chimes I'd been hearing but two blocks away those church
bells dragging me out of bed at all hours.

(Finally she appealed to her doctor.)

A lot of people are in your position, he told her. They
don't like it either but what can you do to stop it?

You tell me and I'll do it.

Well, you might go to the dominie, tell him it disturbs
you, ask him to cut it out.

Is that what you want me to do?

I don't want you to do anything, but if you are annoyed that's the first thing to do. Go up to his door, ring the bell and tell him what you want. Are you an Episcopalian?

No, but I'll do it.

.   .   .

He invited me into the parsonage. I went in. The first thing he said to me was: You've been drinking.

That's none of your business. I've come to complain about the constant ringing of your church bells.

You shouldn't drink. Do you know what it leads to?

Are you going to answer me? If not please let me go.

What's your objection to the chimes?

They annoy me when I want to rest. I don't like them and I think I have a right to my privacy and rest.

But many people like them.

I don't know anything about that. They annoy *me* and I wish you'd stop ringing them at all hours of the day.

I'm afraid I can't do that but I'll be glad to call on you some time and talk it over again. You really ought to stop drinking. It isn't good for you.

With that, I left.

He did call one evening when my husband was home, looked around the house, maybe he thought he could talk to him but he wouldn't have anything to do with it. He just referred him back to me.

You're living in a romantic dream, like a child, and that is why you drink, he said. You're trying to escape reality and it's ruining your health. You'll have to face reality sometime. Look at that little doll you have on your mantel there. That's what you're trying to be again, a romantic child.

That's not just a doll, I said. That's Pauline.

He started to laugh. I stopped him.

You don't understand. That doll's got much more personality than you could ever think of having. Don't speak to me that way. If you can't stop those bells from annoying people who have no reason to want to think the way you do, you'd better go. I mean it.

And he went.

Never let that man come in this house again, said my husband. Why did you let him come in the first place?

Well, after all, I said, he wanted to come. Let him see for himself.

I'm mean as a snake today and moody as the devil. How was the last specimen I sent you? she said to him.

Normal in every way.

I thought so. Stop in and see me, any time at all. I'm working like a fool, putting in time on the lawn today.

Don't work too hard.

I've got to work. It's the only way I can sleep. Have you got a minute? Talk to me, I need to hear your voice . . . I just stand behind a wall. I'm two persons. I watch everybody moving around me and I can't mix with them. It makes others want to do the hula but not me, it leaves me cold as a stone.

That's your Dutch ancestry coming out. (She had told him once that she was a direct descendant of Henry Hudson. From no more than the blondness of her hair he had believed it—the generations her forbears had spent among the savages of North America.) All you can do with the most beautiful woman in the world is to go to bed with her—thoroughly. Sounds awful, doesn't it? And you can do that with any woman . . . except . . .

Except what, she said.

Except for her beauty. And what can you do with that, even if it has not beat you before you begin—as it will certainly beat you after. That's why all the great dramas with love as their theme are tragedies.

Sweetheart, you never fail me. That's the reason I love you.

There it is, ungettable. We can't possess it . . .

At least I can't, she said.

. . . and if we don't succeed in that, it will destroy itself, give it only a little time.

Come on out in the kitchen. I'm really proud of my biscuits. It's one of the few things I can do well. But this arm! I've been ironing too much with it. Sometimes I don't know what I'm talking about . . . do you know the meaning of roses?

No.

Love. And do you know the meaning of jonquils: I desire affection. I never had any interest in sex as a child. We were a big family and used to play and all that. We had a lot of fun but I never thought of anything else. It never occurred to me.

Well, it occurs to some women.

I know it. As far as my mother was concerned, said Helen, it's as much her fault as his. Why, he slept with every woman on the place. She knew it. He had a little house, as far as from here to the garage, with two rooms in it, where one of the women lived who worked on the farm. Now you know why he kept her there? If my mother wanted to leave him, she should have left him then. Now it's too late.

Margaret and Mac, her boy friend, didn't of course, commit suicide. Instead, when they got their breath, she got a job in a Miami restaurant, and for a while in a flower shop.

The shop where she landed was delighted to find her. The woman who owned it had been hard pressed. Cash again. Nothing to do but take care of flowers! She proved herself as deft, after a few days, as any professional and almost as speedy at making up bouquets for weddings and funeral wreaths. She was a success, making a moderate salary and for a month or two happy as a lark.

But, Mac had his bike stolen one night and as befit a gentleman had taken a taxi, at three in the morning, at considerable expense. That made Margaret mad.

Do you think I'm made of money? Bad enough for me to have to buy you a new bike, but why you have to ride around in a taxicab after midnight . . .

When Helen arrived four months later, preceded by a telegram, Margaret almost ate her up for joy.

Amid tears and embraces, during those few days they had together, the two women spent the hours day and night in an almost continuous exchange of confidences. Mac was entirely forgotten.

They had really only one room. They saw him once peering at them through the woodwork of the closet in which he lived and later observed him in a most undignified position at which they laughed fit to kill, calling each other to the crack to witness one after the other.

They giggled together in wonder at the shocking sight.

After a few days Helen had to go north again vowing, in a shower of kisses, to return at the proper time for the wedding which Margaret was still determined to go through with.

She had cut her finger in her work about the shop and had it wrapped up in a dirty bandage. There was no one else in the church but the minister's wife. She and Helen stood beside each other and cried. Buckets of tears came from their eyes all through the ceremony.

The doctor had a climbing rose in his garden named Jacquot which his wife and he both very much admired. It was a peach-pink rambler, the petals fading to a delicate lavender after the first flowering. More than that, the rose throve in their garden against odds thought by the man who sold them the plant to be overwhelming: It winter kills in this climate, it'll be gone after the first two or three years.

In spite of that its vigor was phenomenal, you couldn't kill it. It covered the trellis with a profusion of blossoms that in early June were a wonder to see. In addition it was delicately scented so that their whole yard smelled of it when it was in bloom. He had never encountered it in any other garden.

Once he spoke of it to Helen and invited her to come over and see it and whiff its odor during the flowering season.

They gave her a layered shoot; she planted it and it took hold at once. It throve phenomenally in ground specially prepared by her husband and when she unexpectedly sold her new house and moved farther into the country, Jacquot went with her.

When Margaret came north again, after Mac had had his teeth fixed and been inducted into the army, she had been completely sobered as far as could be seen.

When she appeared at last at the doctor's office she almost fell into his waiting arms for gratitude.

Mac was shipped off to his camp in the Great Lakes region. She had found employment at the Bendix factory manning an electroplating set-up.

It was rough. At the plant she wore dungarees from morning to night, kept her hair covered, and was treated as well as her lack of bulk would permit, as a man. She heard profanity and other foul talk and dished it up, some of it addressed to her own person, with the best of them. She didn't like it but the pay was tops. She could handle herself; no one was kidding her. She was the only woman in the department.

A few grey hairs were beginning to show. He saw her rather regularly now, when she'd come to show him her deposit book at the local building and loan. She'd hold up her hands pathetically for him to see how stained they were, the fingers permanently blackened, the knuckles cracked to the very wrists from the acid they were using.

Gloves are impossible. Nobody can do fast work with gloves on his hands. I'm out for the money!

Why don't you ask them to shift you? There must be a softer job they could offer you.

Oh, I could do better if I wanted to but I make more *money* this way and I don't have to go out to supper with anybody.

Mac kept begging for money—to buy cigarettes, kept yowling that he couldn't get along on a soldier's pay.

He's no man! I'm through with him.

But she yielded as she always had—sent him what he'd ask for—up to a good slice of her weekly check.

You know I got a husband in the service, I got to look out for him.

One of the most affecting things she did, as far as the doctor was concerned, was to bring him her bank-book once a month to show him how much she had deposited during the time. It crept up steadily, that deposit.

That cigarette money! Mind you he has his pay, all of it. He never sends me a cent.

Sometimes he'd come right out with it and ask her for fifty dollars. She'd send it to him. Sometimes she spoke of other men and women she'd entertained in her apartment. She asked him more than once to visit her himself there.

Come on over and see me. You don't even know how nice I've fixed it up.

He went, finally, and found it very clean and attractive. She didn't tell him that her landlord had just borrowed forty dollars from her to pay his oil bill—or she might have been cold over the weekend. She certainly was a sucker for a hard-luck story.

Helen told of a brawl they'd all been in at a nearby tavern: Margaret was drunk as a coot. Her cousin, from down home, along with her boy friend of the moment, from the plant, had been at it all evening. He was jealous of the guy in uniform—and with good reason perhaps

God damn you, said Margaret, stop pickin' on my cousin.

I'm not pickin' on anybody.

You've been doin' it all evening and I'm tired of it.

He's not only my cousin but my friend, been my friend, my intimate frien' for a long time.

You said it!

What do you mean by that crack?

You heard me the first time.

You contemptible little son-of-a-bitch . . . But she didn't have time to finish the sentence when he cuffed her alongside the head, as it happened, fracturing her eardrum so that she had to be taken to a doctor because of the pain of it.

That finished Helen. She told Margaret that she was through with her and that if ever she came into her house again with that man her husband would throw him into the street.

Armistice Day! The war over, Margaret told her doctor of another man who during those years so rapidly fading into the past had attracted her interest, her maternal interest in this case. He was a frail creature she had encountered among the other workers in the shop, the other men would have nothing to do with him; a frightened kid, whom, as a consequence, she had taken under her wing.

He told her his story, how, after many minor adventures he had met an Episcopal bishop in New York who proposed that the boy should be a woman to him; that if he would consent to it, all his financial worries would be over for life.

Margaret listened, sympathetically, though she was tremendously amused and put up a fight for her sex against the bishop's blandishments. Apparently she must have taken the boy on among her other conquests; he was about her own size, had had no success with women up to that time. It was a mere idle gesture of friendship on her part to fill in the time for other game to appear.

Afterward he wrote her a letter, when the plant had been closed at the end of the war, telling Margaret how grateful he had been to her for her sympathetic understanding of his "case," adding that he was going with a nice girl now and expected shortly to marry her.

Money was the thing now. Margaret had saved close to $2,000 by her industry. The war over, Mac would be coming home soon—and she didn't want to see him. She was afraid she'd weaken and take him back and she didn't want to do that. Soon she'd be heading back south to Florida for her new divorce. Nothing would be permitted to interfere with that.

Don't tell anyone! I'm going to find a new job somewhere and settle down permanently.

You'll never do that—if I know you.

Wise guy, huh?

I know you too well. Some sharp-shooter will get around you and some morning when you wake up your $2,000 will be gone.

You think so?

I'll bet a quarter on it.

So you take me for a nut?

I take you for what you are. We all love you and you don't make it easy for any of us to say that.

She pouted—like a child.

You'll do it all over again and nobody can stop you. You've done things to *us* which are inexcusable. And yet . . . I don't blame you. That's a trait that people like you exhibit—to our envy—and despair—a sort of power that you have over us. I still believe in you, that you are not guilty.

She was looking straight into his eyes now with her mouth slightly open.

He continued: Not only that, but in many ways you are the best of us, the most direct, the most honest—yes, and in the end, the most virtuous.

Suddenly she wrapped her arms around his neck, curled up on his knees and sobbed quietly. He held her a moment then gently put her down.

Listen kid, someone trying to get your money away from you right now?

She gave no direct answer: My father died last year, you know, and he left us the farm. My share, when my brother gets around to it, will be $3,000. If you think I'm going to let any man bamboozle me out of that you're mistaken. I've made my will.

Have you?

. . . and it's in my safe deposit box. When I die everything is going to the children.

Good! But listen to me. If ever you get into a jam, if someone gets you cornered, just make out a check for the whole amount, if you have time, stick it in an envelope, address it to me and drop it in the first mail chute you find handy. It will be safe.

Helen told me the same thing.

In New Orleans, after her divorce, the next thing we heard was that she was starting a new life. She had been offered employment as an assistant in the dental office of two brothers; took one look at them and decided to seek elsewhere.

It turned out to be an assistant again, to a department store photographer. He offered her $25 a week and an opportunity to learn the business. She was still pretty and quick-witted and as she knew now from her experience in the war plant, able with her hands. She got on fine with her employer, in fact made a hit with him.

Both the doctor and Helen, who long since had forgiven her completely, heard from her by letter—with snapshots enclosed. Everything was working out fine. The weather was just her dish, New Orleans was beautiful, so much better than New York to live in . . .

I'll bet the little so-and-so is married! Helen said. In fact I know it. She would have written me more often if it weren't so! And I know who it is. It's that bastard she had a brawl with in the tavern, the man who hit her in the ear. She always said she was going to get even with him for that . . . that time her cousin was up here from the South . . . and if it *is*! . . . I don't trust him. I hate him, and she knows it. She's a fool.

Then came a letter. She *was* married, and to that very man.

I knew it. I knew it! He's ten years younger than she is. That's all she wanted.

> *—we've been married four months. Perhaps this is the biggest mistake I ever made in my life. But you wouldn't know him. He's so kind and helpful in everything. He never goes out with the boys but brings me all his pay every Saturday night regularly. I built me a house . . .*

I knew it, said Helen.

> *—it's the cutest little thing you ever saw. It's on an irregular plot of ground like this . . .*

There was a pencil-sketch of a plot narrow at the front and broader at the back, on which was placed the floor plan of a small bungalow.

> *—we've done practically all the inside ourselves. I've got me a raise at the store and we're buying furniture. I never want to live again as I did those years up north . . .*

So the letter went on.

The very day after Helen had shown the doctor the letter, her husband came home with a clipping from the New York paper. Helen called the doctor up at once: Come down here just as quick as you can! She's dead. I can't talk now.

The story ran like this. There had been prowlers in the neighborhood on several nights prior to the shooting. To protect themselves and their property Margaret's husband had kept a loaded .22-caliber rifle lying on the floor at his bedside. It was a dog barking, so the man testified, that had wakened him and his wife at about the same moment. Margaret's bed lay between him and the window.

Shoot out of the window! she said.

The figures were vague. He became excited and bewildered. He fired and his wife cried out: I'm hit! and collapsed on the floor. He rushed into the yard, fired four more shots to arouse the neighbors.

He deliberately murdered her. I know just how it happened. It didn't happen at one A.M. like the first clipping said. It was six A.M.—that makes all the difference in the world. It was Monday morning when she'd be getting dressed to get ready to go to the office. I know her well, sitting in front of her dressing table fixing her hair—she had such pretty hair. I'm sure they had been fighting. She probably made him furious over something she'd said— you know she could be insulting and say the most maddening things. He said he'd shoot her and she dared him to do it. Then she leaned over, this way, down to the left to pick up a bobby-pin she'd dropped—I've seen her do it a thousand times—with her back to him. So he shot her, through the back, as she was leaning over. I'm sure of it. No one came to the funeral but her family and me. They didn't open the casket. There were no flowers beside the bunch of red roses I'd sent her, her favorite flower. —How are you, my sweet? Take good care of yourself 'cause I can't afford to lose you. When she died, I died too, you're the only one I have left.

At the inquest, the bullet, a .22 long, was found to have entered the body by a small hole, at first unobserved, low on the right side, at the back just above the waistline. It traveled diagonally upward through the chest toward the heart, from the inside, passing through that organ, flattening itself against the left collar bone, killing her instantly.